My Travels with a Dead Man

STEVE SEARLS

Black Rose Writing | Texas

©2020 by Steve Searls
All rights reserved. No part of this book may be reproduced, stored in a retrieval system or transmitted in any form or by any means without the prior written permission of the publishers, except by a reviewer who may quote brief passages in a review to be printed in a newspaper, magazine or journal.

The author grants the final approval for this literary material.

First printing

This is a work of fiction. Names, characters, businesses, places, events, and incidents are either the products of the author's imagination or used in a fictitious manner. Any resemblance to actual persons, living or dead, or actual events is purely coincidental.

ISBN: 978-1-68433-512-1
PUBLISHED BY BLACK ROSE WRITING
www.blackrosewriting.com

Printed in the United States of America
Suggested Retail Price (SRP) $19.95

My Travels with A Dead Man is printed in Calluna

*As a planet-friendly publisher, Black Rose Writing does its best to eliminate unnecessary waste to reduce paper usage and energy costs, while never compromising the reading experience. As a result, the final word count vs. page count may not meet common expectations.

To my life partner, Clara, the most courageous person I know, who inspires me every day to be better.

To my two children, Daniel and Rachel, the unexpected loves of my life.

To Shari, my first and best editor, who told me I was a writer, despite all evidence to the contrary.

And lastly, to my parents, who always believed in me, even when I did not.

I am forgotten as a dead man out of mind: I am like a broken vessel.
Psalm 31:12 KJV

My
Travels
with a
Dead Man

BOOK I

CHAPTER 1

I lay on a metal surface, unable to move, in a dark room except for a single light bulb swinging in a far corner. But it put out enough light for me to see a shadowy figure nearby, swaying around me, like smoke from a pipe or cigarette. Breathing was difficult, for the air was heavy and dank. *What is this place? How did I get here?* Then I heard a voice behind me, and I panicked.

"Are you sure she's the one?" a male voice asked. I tried very hard to see him, but all efforts to move were stymied, as if a great force pressed down on me, holding me rigid as a corpse. The same voice spoke again.

"I understand, but you've been wrong before. What's different this time?"

No one answered, but the voice resumed talking. "I know that. But you yourself said she's never done it. What makes you so certain she can?"

The unknown speaker paused, as if it listening to someone or something I couldn't hear. *Is he talking to that shadow?* I wondered. I still struggled to free myself, but without success. Then the temperature in the room dropped. Afraid, my heart raced faster and faster.

"Yes, I trust you."

His words now reverberated off unseen walls, in a basso profondo tone so low, it vibrated the metal slab that held my body in its grip, vibrations that passed into my bones until I felt like a living tuning fork.

"I would never suggest that. But you must understand, after the last time..."

But I never heard the rest, for my eyes flooded with lights of every color, and with the light came tremendous pain, like a bomb exploding in my brain. My lungs stopped taking in air.

I can't breathe! I can't breathe! Oh God, don't let me-

• • • • •

A stinging sensation on my cheek woke me from my nightmare. Hovering above, I saw a large male face with a rough beard. For uncounted seconds, I stared at him, disoriented. My head ached something fierce. I tasted bile in my mouth. The man talked, but it took forever before I understood he was speaking to me, and more time to grasp I lay slumped over a park bench. The left side of my face felt numb.

"I'm sorry," he said, "I saw you having convulsions. They told me to wake you." He held up a bottle of Poland Spring, the one from my purse. *Why is there a bottle of water in my purse?* I asked myself. Then I remembered. I planned to meet some friends at the park before going to the Summer Jazz festival. The day was hot, so I brought water to drink while waiting. I got tired, so tired and a little dizzy. The bench was there, and I sat down. I didn't remember falling asleep, though. And the man was a complete stranger. Still, I let him dribble a few drops into my open mouth. "I called 911 with your phone," he added, appearing sheepish. "An ambulance is on its way. Don't worry."

His clothes were shabby; washed-out, ripped jeans and a plaid shirt several sizes too big for him. He kept speaking, but I couldn't follow a word he said. I think he intended to reassure me, but the urgent tone in his voice, and the rapid way he spoke, made me anxious. I tried to sit up, but found it hard to move, and that scared me more than anything.

Two paramedics, a man and a woman, appeared and began to do things to my body. They acted in a hurried, but practiced manner. One stuck an IV needle into a large vein in my left arm, while the other placed a pressure cuff around my right, and shone a light in my eyes. "What's your name?" he said.

"*Watashi wa jēn desu.*"

The paramedic looked at his partner. "Do you know what language that was?

"Chinese, maybe?"

"Damn. We need a translator."

The bearded man interrupted them. "No, she speaks English. I heard her talking on her phone before she sat on the bench and fell asleep. I think her ID's in here." He handed them my purse. The EMT dug around until he found my wallet with my driver's license.

"Jane Takako Wolfsheim," he read aloud. He kept glancing at me and then back at the license, a bemused look in his eyes. "Jane. Is that your name?"

"*Hai*," I said. Only then did I realize I was speaking Japanese. I coughed, and tried again, but speaking English proved difficult. "Ye-esss. I'm Jane. Jane Wolfsheim."

"Okay, Jane," he said, while the female EMT opened my blouse and placed a cold stethoscope between my breasts. "I need to ask you some questions. Answer them the best you can. What day it is?"

"The weekend? Saturday?" It was strange I wasn't sure.

He asked a few more, simple things like the date and the year, my birthday, but I didn't know the answers to any of them. Then he took out a pen-shaped implement and, pushing it into the skin of my forearm, ran it down to my hand, where he used the point to prick at my palm and fingertips. "Do you feel that?

"A little," I said. "I felt some pressure."

"Any pain? A sting or a scratch, maybe?"

I shook my head.

"BP's dropping," said the other EMT.

"Okay, call it in," he said to her, his tone more urgent than before. "Jane, we're taking you to the hospital. From what your friend told us, you need to see a doctor to determine what's going on. You had a seizure. Do you understand?"

Seizure? I tried to sit up again, but flailed about like a fish out of water. A weird noise came out of me, eerie and unintelligible, which reminded me of the time I startled a screech owl on a camping trip as a girl.

"Jane, stay with me! You'll be fine. Take it easy."

But I couldn't. I panicked, afraid of dying. As the two paramedics wrestled my body onto a stretcher, I gasped for air, unable to take in a breath. A bright light burned from inside my head, straight into my eyes, blinding me. Then, I felt a cool hand touch my forehead.

"Breathe, Jane Takako. Just breathe. You will not die." My vision cleared. The bearded man was kneeling by my head, his hand gently stroking my hair. "These people know what to do. Let them help you." Then he got up and started to amble away.

"Wait," I shouted after him, fearful for reasons I could not discern, convinced his presence was necessary, though why I thought that was a mystery. "Make him wait!" I shouted at the paramedics as they strapped me to the wheeled stretcher. As if by miracle, his face reappeared, and my anxiety lessened. He walked by my side, and I grasped his hand with as much strength as I could muster. He said nothing until they lifted the stretcher to place me into the ambulance. Then, with an odd, but graceful motion, he bent down and kissed my hand before releasing my fingers. I shot him a look of desperation. "Stay," I pleaded.

"I'm sorry, but I can't go with you. I'm not a relative." He stood and watched as the paramedics secured me in the back of the ambulance, stuffed to the gills with an assortment of medical gear I did not recognize. The female EMT was about to close the door when I shouted at him, my unknown savior.

"Who are you?"

"Jorge Luis Borges," he replied. Then the ambulance doors slammed shut, and the siren erupted.

• • • • •

I awoke to a loud beeping noise. Eyes heavy, I wanted to drift back to sleep, but the damn beeping wouldn't let me. My eyelids fluttered as I tried to open them. Then I heard a voice I didn't expect.

"So, doctor, you're telling me you don't know why this happened?" It was my father.

"As I said, Mr. Wolfsheim, your daughter had a grand mal seizure in the ambulance. She also had one at the park, according to the paramedics. They administered a sedative, and we gave her another dose upon her arrival. At present, we're still pushing IV fluids as she was dehydrated when admitted."

"That's not an answer, doctor," my father said.

"Sir, I explained that we need more information before we can give a proper diagnosis. Her medical records show no prior history of any neurological disorders, other than a concussion at age sixteen."

"She was unconscious for eight hours. It was terrible." *Oh god!* I thought. *Mom's here, too?*

"I understand your concern," replied the doctor, "but I doubt that had anything to do with this incident. I spoke to Dr. Geronosky, head of Neurology. He ordered a number of tests to help us determine what caused these episodes. Until then…"

"Until then," I interrupted her, "could someone please turn off that damn noise."

"You're awake!" my mom shouted, which was so out of character for my proper Japanese mother. "Jane, you gave us such a fright." I felt her breath on my face.

"Give her some air, dear," my father said, pulling her away. "How are you feeling, daughter?" Dad sounded calm, but he called me daughter only when upset.

"My head hurts," I said. "It would help if the noise would stop. Why is it so loud, anyway? Where am I?"

"Is that normal, her head hurting?" Mom said.

"It's not uncommon after a seizure," responded the doctor, a brown-skinned woman wearing a lab coat. A black scarf covered her entire head. I knew it had a name, but I couldn't remember it. "Excuse me, but now that she's awake, I need to examine her." She moved closer to my bed. "Jane," she said, "My name is Dr. Ajmal Choudhury." Reaching over my bed, she pushed a button on a machine with many colored lights, and the noise stopped. "There, is that better? Now let me look at you." She flashed a penlight at my eyes. "Do you know where you are?"

"A hospital?"

"Yes. Do you remember why you came here?"

"There was an ambulance."

"Is there anything else you can tell us?"

"I was at a park. And there was this man. He woke me up."

"Yes, Jane, a man found you on a park bench. Do you remember what you were doing there?"

"I was dreaming, I think. Then I woke up. My face hurt. He talked to me."

"What's wrong with her?" Mother, again. "She's never like this!"

"There's no cause for alarm, Mrs. Wolfsheim. Confusion and memory loss are not unusual after a seizure. It should resolve over the next day or so. Long term ill effects are rare."

"Define rare."

"Please, Hanako," my father said. "Let Dr. Choudhury do what she needs to do."

"Choudhury?" I said. "That's an Indian name, right? Are you from India?"

"Close," she said, with a tight-lipped smile. "I'm from Bangladesh. But, Jane, you were telling us what you remembered before the ambulance brought you here."

"I was?"

"Yes, Jane. You said you were at a park. That you were having a dream, and a man woke you..."

"Oh! Oh! I remember now!"

"What, Jane?"

"The man who saved me," I said, "was Jorge Luis Borges. Jorge Luis Borges saved my life! Isn't that amazing?"

All three of them – Dr. Chaudhury, Dad and Mom – looked at me like I was a crazy lady.

CHAPTER 2

Twenty months after my "accident," I sat outside the office of my father's former protégé, Martin Schneider the III, to interview for a job as his executive assistant. It was the last place I wanted to be, but I was unemployed and desperate.

I first met Martin Schneider when I was six, at a Christmas party for the staff's children put on by my father's law firm. Schneider spent the whole afternoon plastered to my father's side, helping to hand out presents. He acted like he was thrilled to be there. I remember how he bounced the little ones on his knee, making them laugh. He told all the kids to call him Uncle Marty, but I sensed something was off about him. When my father left to deal with something or other, Marty dropped the act. His eyes narrowed, and an ugly expression of unspoken anger emerged as he watched my father leave. It lasted for only a moment, but in that moment, he revealed his true feelings towards my father. I didn't understand the source of his enmity, but despite my age, I knew it was real, and it frightened me.

I never told my father, because to him, Marty Schneider was the perfect associate. Dad often called him the best young lawyer he worked with, so it didn't feel right to blurt out my less flattering opinion of the man. But every Christmas, when I ran into 'Uncle Marty' again, I did my best to avoid him. He even attended my high school graduation, pretending to love Dad, but I still sensed great anger seething beneath his façade. After my father retired, and Schneider became the firm's managing partner, my contact with him ended, which made me happy. Yet here I was, begging him for a job, the last thing I ever expected.

"He's ready for you now, Ms. Wolfshiem," said his secretary, a young woman named Samantha Harris. "Go right in."

With trepidation, I opened his door. Before I could introduce myself, he spoke.

"Well," Marty Schneider said from behind his black mahogany desk, "speak of the devil. You haven't changed a bit since I saw you last, have you, Janey-girl? How long has it been? Ten years? Never thought I'd see your face again. Just goes to show how unpredictable the future is, don't you agree?" He laughed, as if this struck him as particularly amusing. I smiled, ill at ease, not sure what to say. Then the laughter stopped.

"You were supposed to submit a resume. Where is it? I don't have it."

"I brought it with me," I said. "Just a moment." I reached into my purse and handed over the folder with my resume, which he snatched from my hand.

"This should have been on my desk yesterday. I gave strict instructions to your father."

"My apologies. I didn't know. He said I should bring it with me."

"Oh, so now you're blaming your old man for your screw-up, is that it?"

"No, not at all," I replied. "I must have misunderstood."

"So, you're either not very bright, or your lying. Which is it?"

I had no reply to that, so I just stood there, like a complete idiot.

A nasty look crossed his face. "Well, since you're here, we might as well go through the motions. Sit down." He pointed to a chair opposite him. Smoothing my dress, I did as he asked. Then I saw a blackbird flash outside the large window in his corner office that overlooked downtown Minneapolis. It startled me, but Schneider, already scanning my resume, didn't notice. I took a deep breath to quiet my nerves. Other than his desk, on which rested a personal computer, a phone and a few stacks of paper, his office was quite austere. No shelves, no paintings or personal items, nothing but blank walls painted slate gray. Other than the view outside the windows, the room felt barren, like it belonged in a prison. The longer I sat there, the more anxious I became.

Schneider flipped through the pages of my resume, emitting an occasional short, caustic snicker. After reading the last page, he tossed it across his desk at me. It landed near my chair. I reached down and picked it off the carpet.

"So," he said, with a grin I found unnerving, "I see you have no legal background whatsoever. In fact, you haven't worked in almost two years. Why is that?"

"My father told you about my illness, didn't he?"

"I want to hear it from you. I'm interviewing you, after all, not him."

So, I told him about my long stay in the hospital, where I suffered daily seizures. About all the specialists that examined me like vultures fighting over a rotting corpse. The gamut of medical tests I endured, including a lumbar puncture and positron emission tomography scan, the results of which always came back inconclusive. How I lost my job, and my healthcare insurance, which led me to file bankruptcy for unpaid medical bills. And the humiliation of returning to live with my parents.

I left out my depression, and my frequent suicidal thoughts. Nor did I mention the anger I felt toward the man named Jorge Luis Borges for bothering to save my life. There was no reason Schneider needed to hear about that. He listened to my story, his face expressionless, but I sensed enjoyment in him at my expense. Maybe it was the gleam in his eyes, which seemed to feed on my suffering. Before I finished, he interrupted me.

"And yet here you are, all better. How is that possible for someone with such a severe ailment? Magic?"

"I don't know," I said truthfully. "Three months ago, I woke up one morning with no more seizures. My dad took me to a respected neurologist who agreed to see me for free, and he found no evidence of anything wrong. He said I was a medical anomaly."

"So," Schneider said, "you're living proof miracles still occur, is that it?"

"I wouldn't say that. It just happened. No one knows why."

"How amazing. Quite the story, isn't it?" Schneider smirked.

"If you don't believe me, you have my permission to review my medical records."

"My dear Jane, who said anything about not believing you? But you must admit it's not something one comes across every day."

"I suppose not," I replied, wary of saying more.

"Why not return to your career in engineering? It would pay more than what I can offer."

"I tried, but it seems no one is hiring." I didn't feel the need mention that I applied for hundreds of jobs, including ones not in my field. The process was humbling. Many interviewers said I was overqualified. A few said my bankruptcy was an issue. Others expressed concern that my medical condition might recur. Most of the jobs for which I applied didn't bother granting me an interview. Looking for work during the recession that followed the 2008 crash didn't help, either, but I knew mentioning any of this to Schneider would look like me making excuses for my own failures.

"How awful for you." Then Schneider's tone turned sarcastic. "And now you come to me, hoping to trade on my relationship with your father. Is that it?"

"I came because I need a job," I said, steely-eyed, "and yes, Dad said you had one I could interview for."

"Can you type?" Schneider asked out of the blue.

"Well, yes. I prepared memos and progress reports for my work at -"

"No, that's not what I meant. Have you ever held a job as a typist? That is, can you type a letter or a brief or anything at all for me while listening to a dictation recorder?"

I hesitated. "I'm sure I could learn," I said at last.

"So, the answer is no." He continued to smile at me, as if this was all terribly amusing to him. "Ever made coffee? Answered the phone? Filed legal documents with a court or at the County Clerk's office?"

"Well..."

"I'm sure you could learn," he replied, mocking me.

"Yes, I'm sure I can. If you hire me, Mr. Schneider."

"I'm sure you would try," he said. "But why would I want someone like you, with no experience and no training? Why should I consider you for any position?"

"I'm sorry to have wasted your time," I said. "Please forgive the intrusion. I'll let myself out."

I started to get up, but Schneider slapped his hand on his desktop so hard, I fell back into the chair. "Did I give you permission to leave?" he snarled.

"Uh..."

"Uh? Uh? Does that mean yes or no?"

"No," I said.

"No what?"

I thought of walking out on him right then and there, but stopped myself. My father would feel so hurt if he heard that I walked out of my interview with Schneider, since he went to such trouble to set it up. And I could imagine what my mother would say. "You have dishonored your father and our family name. How could you?" So, I did what I had to do. I humbled myself because I needed a job, any job, even one working for Martin Schneider.

"No, sir," I said, "You did not. Forgive me."

He smiled again. "That's right. No, sir is the correct answer. And you better not forget it. I can't stand insubordination from my employees, no matter who their father once was."

"I have the job?" Then added, "Sir?"

Martin Schneider placed his hands on his desk and leaned forward. "You had the job when your daddy called me, begging to find something for you. Don't pretend you didn't know. But that doesn't mean I have to put up with a whiny little brat who goofs off, thinking just because her father was the founding partner of this firm, she can do whatever she wants. Do I make myself clear?"

I said nothing. Not at first anyway. After a moment's hesitation, I said, "I won't be a whiny brat, sir. Whatever you want, I'll do."

"Damn right you will, or you'll be out of here so fast, you won't be able to sit down for a week because of the rug burns on your fucking ass." He glared at me for a solid thirty seconds, but then the smile returned, as if nothing was amiss. Picking up his phone, he punched in a number.

"Miss Harris, can you come to my office and fetch Miss Wolfsheim for me? She has some paperwork to fill out. Yes. That's right. Thank you." Then he turned his gaze back to me. "Welcome to the firm, Miss Wolfsheim. No, let me rephrase that. Welcome home, Janey. You don't mind if I call you Janey, do you?"

"No, not at all. Sir."

"Oh, let's not be so formal, shall we? You can call me Mr. Schneider." He was still chuckling to himself when Miss Harris arrived to escort me out.

CHAPTER 3

Sitting in my car, I looked at the card Marty Schneider gave me thirty minutes earlier. It read, "Phoenix, Ltd.–Resurrecting the Souls of Fine Antiques since 1899." The name matched the sign on the brick façade of the building across the street from where I parked. The neighborhood looked run down and dodgy to me, but I got out and hurried across the street to the store's entrance, hoping it was still open.

This was my third week working as Schneider's personal assistant, and my experience to date had been far from pleasant. I was nothing more than a glorified gopher, tasked with doing anything he wanted done, no matter how odious, from cleaning the Men's room, to bringing him coffee every morning from Starbucks. Now, on a late Friday afternoon, he'd decided I was the perfect choice to pick out an anniversary present for his wife.

"My wife is fond of antiques, early to mid-20th century Americana," he told me thirty minutes earlier as I was packing up to leave. "I'd be forever in your debt, if you would take time this evening to pick out something appropriate for her."

"But I know nothing about antiques!" I sputtered. "Or what your wife might consider appropriate for the occasion." A lame response and he knew it.

"Lucky for you this doesn't require any special expertise." That's when he handed me Phoenix's business card. "If you hurry, I think you can just make it before they close. And tell them I want it delivered to my house no later than noon tomorrow. Now go." As I ran for the elevator, I could hear his all too familiar cackle.

When I reached the storefront, the sign in the store's window read, "Closed," but the door was open just a hair. I entered, shutting it behind me. The store's dim interior, filled with weary-looking tables, desks, ottomans, lamps, rugs and fixtures, looked like the prop room for a film adaptation of a Jane Austen novel.

"Hello," I called out, only to hear my voice echo weakly back at me. "Is anyone there? Mr. Schneider sent me to pick up his wife's anniversary gift." After no response, I made my way to the rear of the showroom toward the only source of light, no easy task. I wandered through a maze constructed of old furniture and bric-à-brac. Without the light as a guide, I would have soon become lost. After a bit, I squeezed between two old dressers and arrived at a gray metal door marked "Main Office," over which a naked light bulb hung. With trepidation, I knocked.

"Enter, please," came a muffled response in a deep male voice. Upon turning the doorknob, I entered a cramped little backroom office. In one corner stood a gray metal desk, like those seen in old factory buildings. A dark-haired man sat behind it on a metal folding chair, his head bent over some paperwork. When he looked up at me, exposing his long neck for my inspection, I gasped. There sat my Jorge Luis Borges, the man who saved my life in the flesh. Younger than I remembered and clean shaven, but the same man.

"You!" It was all I could get out in my shock at seeing him.

"Ah, the young lady from the park. Sooner or later I knew you would find me." I hope you've recovered from your illness.

"How?" I said, unable to utter more than one monosyllabic word at a time.

He shrugged, as if it was not a matter of great import to him. "It always happens like this," he said, "for me, at least."

Upon hearing those words, the room spun about and I lost consciousness.

• • • • •

When I came to, a damp cool cloth lay over my eyes, but below my neck, my body felt warm and comfortable. Music played in the background, a piano concerto, and then some classical guitar. After a while, I heard humming. My limbs felt like lead and it was difficult to move. I wondered if I suffered another seizure and became anxious. Then a voice spoke.

"Hello there," said the man I knew only as Borges. "Returned from the dead, I see. There was no seizure, you just fainted. I was quick enough to catch you before your head struck my desk." Hearing that, my panic went away. No seizure. What a relief. I never stopped to consider how he knew I worried about that, or why the sound of his voice calmed me so. I just accepted it.

Instead, I muttered something indistinguishable even to myself.

Whatever I said, he replied, "You've been out for three hours. Sorry about your clothes. They're being washed now. In the meantime, there's a robe on the bed when you feel strong enough to get up. Would you like some tea? Or I can make a fresh pot of coffee, if you prefer."

That's when I realized I was naked under the covers. Oddly, I felt no shame. Nor any anger toward him, which surprised me. *Why wasn't I angry?* Somehow my rage toward him no longer existed, almost as if it was erased from my mind. But I did have other concerns. "What happened? Where am I? And can you take this–washcloth?–off my face?" I heard him chuckle, but not in a mean-spirited way.

"So many questions. Let me consider what to answer first. The last, I think. I'll remove the cloth, but first, let me dim the lamp." After a clicking noise, he whisked away the cloth from my forehead. I opened my eyelids a sliver. A great brightness appeared everywhere, except where blocked by his shadow, which loomed over me like a storm cloud. I blinked several times until the brightness dissipated like dye dispersed in water. Once my eyes adjusted to the light, I saw a man with a smile even the Mona Lisa might envy.

"As for where you are," he continued, "you're in my bed. I live in a loft over the store. You remember coming to my store, don't you?"

"Yes," I said, trying to recall what kind of store this might be. Then the memory of why I came here returned. "Oh, no! The gift for Mr. Schneider's wife! I must ..."

"I've already arranged the delivery of a vintage 1962 Broyhill Brasilia credenza for her," he said. "Trust me, she'll love it. She adores mid-twentieth century early modern Danish designs, though it's a passing fad in my opinion. But to each her own."

"Thank you," I sighed.

"To answer your first question, you passed out right after entering my office. I spilled coffee on your dress in my haste to prevent you from hurting yourself. My apologies." It was odd I had no recollection of him holding a cup of coffee, much less undressing me. Yet I was certain he took no advantage of me while I was unconscious. He gave off the air of a man you could trust without question, and though his name still bothered me, I felt safe.

"I'd like that coffee, if the offer is still open – and perhaps something to eat?"

"No problem. Do you like shortbread? I have a tin of the very best from Scotland." I nodded and with a quick wave of his hand, he left, shutting the door behind him.

Twenty minutes later, swaddled in a white terrycloth robe many sizes too large for me, I sat on a blue couch, stuffing myself with a variety of cold meats and cheeses while he stood watching me, sipping a cup of coffee. The loft's floor, constructed from blonde-colored wood, shined brilliantly. In the farthest corner, I saw a kitchen which included cabinets stained a dark-reddish color, a small dining table and a large island with a polished granite countertop. He poured me a second cup of coffee after I finished my first. His eyes never left me.

The moment I finished this impromptu dinner, he cleared away the remaining food. When he returned, he stared right at me, and for the first time all evening, a measure of discomfort crept into my heart, and I turned away from his gaze.

"I imagine you have many questions," he said after an uncomfortable pause. "Please, ask me anything."

Determined not to be shy, I plunged right in."What did you mean when you said you knew I'd find you? How is that possible?"

"Ah," he said, "but that is two questions, and neither is the one you want me to answer." His face wrinkled, displaying deep creases I failed to notice before, as if contemplating what to say next. "Well," he said after about a moment of silence, "it's complicated. How did I know we would meet again? It's because you're not the first person who reappeared in my life like this. There's a pattern to it, you see. I don't believe in fate, only chance and choice. Still, one cannot deny the obvious."

I must have appeared dazed, for he added, "What I mean is that people may have freedom to decide many things–what to eat, what clothes to wear–but still, the universe has its purposes. I've crossed paths with many people in my time, as we all do. We forget most of them and we never meet them again. Yet, whenever I help someone in crisis–such as when I saw you having that seizure–each person I choose to I help finds their way back into my life. Sometimes it takes a few weeks, sometimes several months. Sometimes longer. But they always do. I have no explanation for it, but things happen every day which we can't explain. Don't you agree?"

"I suppose," I replied, my voice quieter than I planned. "So, because we met when I was sick, you knew you'd see me again?"

"Not because we met, but because I chose to act. That choice meant I would see you again. It was mere chance you fell ill, but my action sealed our fate. Well, not fate. I have issues with that word. By using your phone to call 911, I made a choice. Do you see? And whatever actions you took since that day, they also played a role in bringing you here. This meeting was inevitable."

I thought about what he said for a while, before speaking. "How many times has this happened, this choosing thing? Before me, I mean?"

"You're number eight." He sounded irritated. "Now ask the question you most want me to answer."

"Who are you? You're not Jorge Luis Borges. He's been dead for decades."

He laughed. "You speak of the Latin American writer known for his absurdist short fiction? Well, while I may not be him, a man burdened with the mental disorder of hypergraphia, I assure you but I am Jorge Luis Borges."

"That's not possible," I sputtered.

"Would you like to see a copy of my birth certificate?" He glared at me with an uncompromising look of disdain. I watched him clenching his fists until the veins stood out on the back of his hands. Then, the muscles around his mouth relaxed, and his tense expression vanished, like smoke in a drafty room. "My mother gave me my name." He turned his head to the side, in profile, and I saw the man I met at the park, older, weary with life, even helpless.

"Why that name?"

"She said she named me after my father, who I never met. But I have no reason to doubt her. She was the most honest person I ever knew."

"Who? When?" I was back to speaking in monosyllables.

"She was Norwegian," he responded. "Blonde hair, color of gold. A real Nordic beauty." He turned back to face me. "She met my father in Texas and seduced him. He was not very assertive in matters of the opposite sex, so she took the initiative. That was just like her. When she wanted something, nothing could stop her. She left the next day and never saw him again. Nine months later, I was born." An indefinable sadness passed over his face.

I knew then that she must have died. "I'm sorry. But, can I ask, are you sure your father was the author 'Borges?'"

"Ha!" he snorted. "Who knows? I never learned I shared a name with a writer until I was twenty. He's not as famous as you think. No one reads anymore, you know. They watch television or movies. I prefer movies to most books these days."

"But have you ever read him? Your namesake, I mean?"

"In college; the class was an elective. His work is overrated. Give me Cortazor or Bolaño any day over Jorge Luis Borges."

I thought about that for a bit. "But don't you want to verify if he's your father?"

"No!"

"But why not? Aren't you the least bit curious?"

"It would be unlucky for me," he said, as if that answered everything. "We should move on. There's so much we have to do together."

Do? I thought. What could we possibly have to do with one another? "We have a future?" I asked him instead.

"Haven't you been listening? Yes, we do."

"So what's next?" I said, half in jest.

"We become lovers." He got up off the couch, and, leaning over me, placed his fingers underneath the tie to the robe I wore. "Let me help you out of this," he said, before kissing me full on the lips.

CHAPTER 4

Three weeks later, on a hot summer's day when the shop's air conditioning unit broke down, sweat pooled in the hollows of my collarbones and drizzled down between my breasts, staining my blouse. That's when Borges informed me he was closing the shop for a month. "It's time for a trip," he told me. "Have you ever been to Kyoto?"

By this time, nothing about him surprised me. The night he kissed me, we made love, and I fell head over heels for him. It caught me by surprise, yet I never questioned why. Why this man, or why now. Everything about my love for him felt natural and inevitable. I informed my parents, gave notice to Martin Schneider, and moved into Borges' loft the next day. When I told them, both adamantly opposed me living with him, but after Borges took us all out to dinner at Mom's favorite sushi place, they were both so charmed they dropped all their objections. As we left the restaurant, my mother hugged me and whispered, "I'm so happy for you, Ojōsan." Her delight shocked me, because she never approved of anyone I dated, but with Borges, it was different.

Soon, I was busy helping Borges at the store, managing his schedule, making appointments and doing his books. His business was in awful shape. The red ink in the ledger far outweighed the black. Yet when I questioned him about it, he seemed disinterested. "Money isn't that important to me," he said one night over dinner. "Like the tides, it comes and goes."

Yet now, he was suggesting we shut down and take an expensive trip. "We're not breaking even," I reminded him. "How can we afford to travel to Japan? What about our clients? If we close, won't they go elsewhere?"

"Ah," he said. "You don't understand." He raised his hands over his head in a distracted manner." Mea culpa." He sighed. "This business of mine you seem to believe is so important means nothing. I bought it as my mother lay dying, to make her happy. But I don't rely on its earnings in the least."

"What do you rely on then?" I asked.

"Two days after our first encounter, a dapper, silver-haired man in a pin-striped blue suit approached and handed me ten lottery tickets. He must have been paying off a bet, or perhaps he acted out of a perverse sense of humor. Whatever the reason, he stuffed them into my hands as I sat on the same park bench where I found you. He grinned at me, said, "Lotsa luck, chump," and then walked off with several other suits, colleagues of his, I presume. I could hear their laughter from half a block away as they slapped him on the back.

"Yet, I knew that this absurd, even surreal gesture would radically alter my fortunes. Two days later, I walked into a grocery store and scanned each of them, one by one. The last ticket contained the winning numbers. I received ninety-six million dollars after taxes. It came too late to save my mother, though." He paused then, looking abashed. "You know, I never told her. She died, believing I'd found work as a back-up musician for a famous singer."

And that's how I learned Borges was rich. It nagged me he took so long to reveal the truth about his finances. The old, dust-ridden antique shop with its sluggish sales and non-existent profits was only a sop to appease the dying wish of an old woman, to whom, for reasons he never explained, he could not bear to tell the truth. He lied to the woman who loved him, who raised him without a father, as she lay dying. What that signified, I did not yet comprehend, other than it appeared he preferred to live in the shadows rather than expose too much of himself to the world. But the thrill of discovering we had more than enough money to do whatever we wished overrode my misgivings.

"So, we have all we need to go to Kyoto," he continued. "Though first, a stop in Tokyo is in order, I think. What do you say?"

"Japan?" I said, trying to contain my excitement. "I'd love to, but why?" I knew he had never been outside the continental United States before, or at least that was what he told me during our nights together when, after our love-making ended, he spoke of his past. I heard all the stories about his youth, his mother, his college days (before dropping out), his sundry affairs with both men and women, and his work as a session musician for a well-known music producer, until I drifted off to sleep in his arms. Not once did he ever mention Japan.

"Why? Oh, many reasons, I suppose. I'm a big fan of Ozu and Kurosawa, Japan's two greatest film directors. I've always wanted to see Mount Fuji. Also, I'm fascinated by Japan's ancient Buddhist temples, some of the finest in the world. Kyoto has a great number of them. It survived the war unscathed, you know."

That I knew. My mother met my father when he served as a sailor with the U.S. Navy on an aircraft carrier stationed there, long before law school was even a blip on his radar screen. My Oba-chan, my Japanese grandmother, lived through the firebombing of Tokyo, and had horrific memories of the day the bombs and incendiaries dropped by General LeMay's B-29s rained down from the sky. She regaled me with stories of the war the one time she visited America.

While the rest of her family lived with cousins in the countryside, she, the oldest daughter, stayed behind in the city to assist her father, a doctor, take care of his patients. She never forgot the sight of those silver B-29 bombers, just visible against the blue sky. Soon afterwards, the concussive rumble of high explosives shook the streets, followed by a second wave of bombers that dropped white phosphorus and jellied gasoline bombs. In the air, they looked like so many sticks of wood. Deafened by the initial explosions, the flash of the incendiaries blinded her. She crawled over rubble to get away from the firestorm that raged a mile north of her father's clinic. She never saw my great-grandfather again. They became separated in the chaos of smoke, wind and flames. She could not recall the moment his hand let go of hers. Perhaps that was a mercy.

"We lost so much," she said, "but at least the kami protected To-ji, Ginkaku-ji, so many other temples in Kyoto, and the Todai-ji temple in Nara where the Birushana Nyorai rests. But the one I love most is the Amida Buddha, the Great Daibutsu of Kamakura. It has no temple to protect it but the open sky, and that is why it is best. One day, you must promise me to go there and see it yourself." Hearing that, I pledged to visit the Daibutsu. I wanted to see a smile on my grandmother's face and receive her kisses. How little I understood the power of promises.

Borges' decision to take us to Japan brought up the memory of that long ago vow to my Oba-chan. I knew it might be my only opportunity to fulfill that promise. "Can we visit the Great Buddha in Kamakura?" I asked in a weak voice. Borges looked at me with his characteristic nonchalance, displaying a close-mouthed grin. He knew I was half-Japanese, but I never told him the obligation I owed my grandmother. "The Daibutsu?" he said. "Sure, no problem. It's appeared often in Ozu's films. I've always wanted to see it in person. I've heard it makes you believe you're in the presence of the living Buddha."

"When do we leave?"

"Tomorrow morning. I've already booked the flights."

• • • • •

We were at the temple of the Great Buddha in Kamakura, and I felt hypnotized. No, that's not the right word, but how can I sum up in just one verb what I felt that day seeing the Daibutsu, that massive cast bronze statue of the Amida Buddha, above us on his stone dais?

The sun was often absent. Rain clouds passed over every few minutes, threatening showers, but failed to deliver on their promises. Yet had a thunderstorm broken out, I wouldn't have noticed. One would think the shadows, cast by those clouds, would have darkened the glow emanating from its cracked, green tarnished metal skin. Instead, they enhanced the feeling that a living–spirit?–lurked behind the two slits that represented the Great Buddha's eyes. As I stood there in that plaza, rimmed by the surrounding hills and uncounted trees waving in the swirling breeze, those eyes pierced me to my core. A fearsome intelligence lay behind them that held me rapt by its gentle manner and calm omniscience.

Borges rambled on, lecturing me, as was his wont. He described the many scenes in which the Daibutsu appeared in Ozu's films. In addition, he couldn't help speaking to me of the history of the Kamakura period, when the Emperor lost his power to a famous samurai warlord who established his capitol at the base of this small peninsula below modern day Yokohama.

My Borges loved to lecture, and most of the time I humored him. Displaying polite, if not obsequious, respect for men was drilled into me at an early age by my Japanese mother. But under the gaze of the Daibutsu, the Great Buddha, I could not endure his prattle. Over the course of my life, my parents took me to see many famous statues and monuments, including

Michelangelo's David and Christ the Redeemer, which towers over Rio de Janeiro, but none ever affected me as deeply as the Great Buddha of Kamakura. It was more alive than any living being I ever encountered. Its élan vital immersed me in its embrace. I was awestruck.

"Erected in 1255," Borges droned on, "to promote the sect of Pure Land Buddhism and create a shrine to attract pilgrims and other devotees, at almost 45 feet in height, it is the second largest Buddha in all of Japan, and the largest bronze cast Buddha in the world outside of China. A great tsunami destroyed the outer temple in the year–say, are you paying attention to me?"

"Oh shut up!" I said. "Just let me enjoy this." At that moment, I only wished to stay by the Great Buddha forever and bask in its meditative gaze, entranced by the indescribable emotions it evoked. Borges' interruption broke the spell. He walked away in a bad mood, sulking, refusing to speak to me for a good half-hour, though he would have said he left out of respect for my privacy. My Borges could be such an ass, but then, what man isn't?

I sat on a bench near the Daibutsu while he stalked about, taking photographs with his digital camera. At one point, a group of Japanese middle school girls, all decked out in their traditional apparel–white blouses, knee length navy blue skirts and red scarves or neckties (the one fashion accessory allowed them)–descended upon the plaza en masse. They didn't give the Daibutsu a second look, more interested in talking among themselves, while their teacher went off to purchase tickets for a tour of the Daibutsu's hollow interior. More restrained than American children of the same age, their conversations never rose above the level of high-pitched humming, like the sound of honey bees near a hive.

That changed when a couple appeared with their three-year old toddler in tow. The father, a slender, classic-looking WASP, taller than Borges, carried the boy on his shoulders, while the mother, who appeared Japanese and stood a foot shorter than her husband, described the scene to him. They spoke English with a Midwestern American accent.

At once, the schoolgirls, like flies drawn to an open can of Coke, surrounded them, chatting and pointing at the child, who seemed to take their interest in him as his rightful due. The mother spoke Japanese to them. After a while, she said something to the father. With a great sigh of relief, he raised the boy over his head and set him down among the mass of young girls. Delighted, they erupted in excited outbursts, passing the little boy among themselves as he whirled around and shouted with glee like a miniature dervish. They kept repeating over and over a single word while they giggled, placing hands over their mouths as they did so: "kawaii," meaning "cute," though the true definition's far more nuanced.

The little boy cavorted about the square, surrounded by his admirers. The girls' movements resembled a flock of birds twisting through the sky on a summer day. As for the boy's parents, the woman slumped against the man, who endured her weight like a true stoic. She kept her eyes trained on her son, but the man looked at the Great Buddha, transfixed, the only other person there as enchanted with it as I.

Suddenly, I noticed Borges' absence, and for a moment, feared he deserted me. I almost went in search of him, until I noticed Borges weaving his way through the schoolgirls, his upraised hands holding two cups of macha, a tea flavored ice cream I cherished. He smiled as he approached, handing me one as a peace offering. We sat on the steps and ate our treats, watching the children. When the teacher arrived with the tickets, the boy's parents reclaimed him from his temporary guardians. The father picked up his son, now much less energetic, and put him back on his shoulders. The boy rested his head atop his father's, using his chubby arms to reach around and grab the man's neck. With a little sigh, he closed his eyes.

"Would you like to take the tour?" Borges asked, but I declined. Seeing the hollow space inside the Daibutsu did not appeal to me. I didn't want my memories spoiled by the reality that it was a man-made metal construct, nothing more. Like the young boy, I needed nothing further. "Then we should go," said Borges, and I did not object.

We walked to a nearby cemetery, which Borges kept referring to as a Shinto shrine, and then ate lunch at a local noodle shop. Later that night, back in our room at the Sheraton Grande Tokyo Bay, after dinner at a high-end sushi place, Borges begged off making love. "I'm tired," he said, and when I let my disappointment show, he added, "You must remember I am an older man."

"Take a Viagra then," I retorted, and he erupted with a great resounding laugh that continued for some time. By the end, he had me laughing along with him. Not long thereafter, he fell dead asleep, snoring away, Still awake, I tried to read a Mary Karr memoir, but I couldn't concentrate. My mind kept going over the events of the day–the train ride to Kamakura, the impact of the Daibutsu made on me, and the little boy who so captivated the schoolgirls like some mischievous incarnation of Krishna. I kept re-reading the same sentence of Karr's memoir, before I switched off the light and fell into a light sleep.

My dreams filled with the usual oddities, none of which I could later recall, until everything changed. A dark man without a face was thrusting himself inside me, and though I resisted, I could not help feeling aroused. Yet, I also felt shamed by my arousal and afraid of the actions of this dark, featureless figure, who said nothing even as I struggled against him, even as I could feel the sexual tension mounting inside my body, until I awoke screaming.

"Shhhh," whispered Borges, his mouth tickling my ear. He was inside me, having entered from behind while I slept. He kept pushing into me, until with a shudder, he finished. This was a first for us, his taking me in my sleep without asking permission, like an animal.

"Why?" I asked, my eyes tearing up, shocked and humiliated at what happened.

"I changed my mind," he said with a shrug as he pulled out. I reached for him then, but he was already off the bed. A light from the bathroom of our suite flicked on and I heard water running. He was taking a shower. I found a small towel, dried myself, and lay on my side, waiting for his return. What he did disturbed me in ways I couldn't define, but our relationship changed that night. I still loved him, still needed him, but that love, that need, no longer felt so innocent, so magical.

I kept imagining-the implacable eyes of the Daibutsu looking at me. I wanted the Great Buddha to provide me with comfort, even grace perhaps, but did such things even exist in my world? I was lost. The realization that the man I loved had treated me as an object for his sole gratification, devastated me. As I drifted back asleep, I thought how like a waterfall the shower sounded as it splashed upon the naked body of my lover, once more a stranger to me.

CHAPTER 5

The tall, bronze Buddha, wreathed in lights of every color, bent down, holding a lotus blossom. I lifted my arm to him, but the sun was hot, and sweat, like melted butter, drained from my pores. My hand could not quite reach the proffered flower, though I continued to extend my fingers toward it. Blood roared in my head, and my world wobbled like a child's top that spins just as it is about to succumb to gravity. The Lotus' scent suffused the air. I feared that, if I failed to grasp it, my spirit would be lost forever. The halo of colors blinded me, and the thick miasmal air made it difficult to breathe. Only the Daibutsu's image remained constant, his visage full of compassion, but I found no comfort in it.

"Please," I gasped, "help me." And then I cried out, "Borges! Where is my Borges?" I struggled against myself, caught in an invisible web. Was it one of desire or suffering? I couldn't tell.

"Borges is a dream," said the Daibutsu. "He has always been a dream, a dream with no beginning and no end." His gleaming metal hand, which held the lotus, inched ever nearer, but the pain in my forearm became excruciating as its muscles began to cramp and spasm. My hand retreated from the beautiful white flower, despite all efforts to stop it.

"How can he be a dream? I've seen him, tasted him, touched his lips, felt his warm breath on the back of my neck. Borges is real. He must be." Yet even as I spoke, doubt crept in, an infant's doubt, slow to appear and full of ignorance.

The lotus was very near now, almost near enough to touch, though the closer it came to my outstretched fingers, the more clouded my vision became. "Please," I begged, staring into the abyss of the Daibutsu's lidless eyes, black as the deepest caves under the earth, an image both endless and terrifying. "Please find my Borges and return him to me." Then my hand shrank from the beautiful flower, defeated.

"As you wish," spoke the Daibutsu, "so shall it be, but not by my doing. I claim no power over others. I only teach my dharma to those who will listen. You may follow it or not." The lotus vanished, and when it did, I felt hollowed out.

The Daibutsu's face retreated in a white fog. As it vanished, my arm exploded in agony. I awoke screaming in a room I did not recognize, on a damp bed under sheets soaked in sweat. Sore and battered, I forced myself over onto my side and used my left hand to massage away the spasms in my immobilized right arm.

When the pain receded to a dull ache, I looked around me. The bed was smaller than the one at the Tokyo Sheraton, its mattress thin and full of lumps. A great mesh net hung from posts at the four corners of the bed, surrounding me on all sides. Overhead, a ceiling fan whopped-whopped away, its blades chopping the warm air into discrete chunks. The breeze it created passed right through the wet camisole I wore, giving me chills. Thousands of unknown insects creaked, along with the chirping of birds, and other strange noises. Nothing was familiar, nothing spoke to me of home.

Where was I? Where was Borges? A large moth struck the net at that moment, and my mind shattered into a million shards of glass. In terror, I huddled under the sheets. Then I heard a scuffling noise, and my heartbeat soared. It was the sound of a chair leg being scraped across a well-polished wood floor. I arose, parted the mesh net, and slipped off the bed. The tile floor felt cool. Then the acrid odor of a lit cigar reached my nose. I crept to the open French doors and walked out onto a wooden deck. Stars peered at me from the sky's vast dome, which ended at a horizon marked by silhouettes of trees, tall palms, but many others of varying heights, I could not identify by shape alone. Beneath the trees, darkness spread from a thick layer of undergrowth. I walked on.

Turning a corner, I found my Borges in an old wicker chair, one leg crossed over the other. With a delicate grace, he inhaled his cigar. Its red tip glowed as if it had a life all its own. Then he blew an enormous plume of smoke that dispersed as it drifted toward the forest.

"You are up early this morning, my dear, just in time to catch the dawn. Come, sit beside me." He rubbed out the cigar in a copper ashtray atop a small oval side table. Across from him was a second wicker chair. As I sat down, a thin flame of coral highlighted the treetops. Amazed by the spectacle, I didn't speak for several minutes. I shot glances Borges' way, but not once in all that time did he look in my direction.

"Where have you taken me?" I said." What is this place?"

"Ah, you've been dreaming of Japan again." The calm tone of his voice disturbed me far more than what he said.

"Yes," I answered. "I dreamed of the Daibutsu. But we were in Japan just yesterday in our room at the Tokyo Sheraton." Then I stopped. It must have taken more than a day to travel from Japan to wherever we were. How much time had I lost?

"I know you believe that," he said, "but we never went to Tokyo." He sighed the sigh of a sad and weary man.

"You still haven't answered me," I said. "What is this place? Why are we here?" A sense of vertigo returned, but I held it at bay. The dawn's colors, which back-lit the forest canopy, grew wider, revealing shades that spanned the spectrum from rose to the pinkish-orange of salmon.

"We are where you asked me to take you after–" He paused for a moment, but then resumed. "We are in Costa Rica, near the town of Samara, about five miles from the beach. You asked me to take you someplace far away where you could, though you never said it in so many words, forget your grief. We have been living in this villa," he waved his arm in a grand sweeping gesture, "for the last six months."

My mouth opened in disbelief.

"You grew tired of San Jose and all the wealthy tourists there," he continued, "so we moved here. It provides solitude and a place to for you to read and work on your painting, or so you tell me when you're in the mood to talk."

This obvious falsehood outraged me. I stopped painting years ago after high school. I only took Art class to provide company for a shy and lonely friend, a true prodigy, talented far beyond my meager abilities.

"Stop lying! We visited Kamakura, saw the Daibutsu and then returned to our hotel. That was yesterday–well, a few days at most. And I don't paint! Not anymore!" My voice must have carried farther than I realized, for the forest erupted in a raucous cacophony of sounds from birds of all kinds, parrots, cockatoos, and others, too. Their unfamiliar calls startled me.

"You don't paint?" Borges replied. "What's that then?" He pointed to the far end of the deck at an easel and canvas, along with several paintbrushes, a color palette and a variety of oil paints arranged on a small table. " That must be my painting of the Buddha." A bitter little laugh escaped his lips.

I scrambled out of my chair, stumbling in my haste, and hurried over to the canvas. I could not deny my eyes. It was a portrait of the Daibutsu, not clothed in green tones of tarnished bronze, but gleaming with rays that emanated from him like a pinwheel of many colors, just as in my dream. My signature was in the lower left-hand corner. But I couldn't have painted it. It was too beautiful, too well composed to be my work.

"This can't be mine," I said, challenging Borges. " And we did travel to Japan, the two of us. We visited Kamakura where the Daibutsu sits in the open air at the Kōtoku-in Temple. Remember the Japanese schoolgirls, and the couple with their little boy? You bought me ice cream!" I was near hysterics, but Borges didn't react to my outburst. He looked away, and the lack of his gaze on me was like a blast of winter air so cold it freezes your breath.

"Time is not what you think," Borges muttered, almost as if he were talking to himself. "Time doesn't exist. Not the way we perceive. It's not linear, not the arrow that only goes forward. It twists and turns back on itself, like the spirals of a conch shell. Like the earth, it spins and revolves, passing through the vacuum of space, never repeating its course, though it appears to repeat. Time may branch off in any direction, either at random or as part of some larger pattern we cannot discern. Maybe some part of your mind has been in Tokyo all this time, even while I've watched you here, painting, living with your silence. Anything is possible." During this odd soliloquy, I didn't move, frozen to the spot, but Borges must have noticed how close I was to the precipice that divides sanity from madness.

"It was early in the morning," he said. "We were waiting to board our plane for Tokyo, when we heard your name called over the loudspeakers." He spoke as if delivering a well-rehearsed speech given many times." The airline rep told us it was a family emergency, nothing more. Then a police officer came by and we learned that your father died in his sleep the night before. He was at the morgue, awaiting an autopsy. A police escort took us there so you could identify the body, because they couldn't locate your mother."

I became unsteady on my feet, and my Borges reached out with his large hands, holding me until he could sit me down in a chair. Kneeling, his face level with my own, the concern in his eyes was unbearable. I closed mine and received a vision, which seemed like a true memory; whether real or false, I couldn't tell.

• • • • •

I sat in the front seat of my mother's 1979 Buick Riviera, which rattled in the cold morning air, rolling down a street I knew well, for it passed by my old high school on the way to Lakewood cemetery, where my father's casket would be lowered into a six-foot hole, prayed over by a rabbi and then covered with dirt. The noise came from the car's muffler. Part of its manifold was detached. The same issue had been going on for over a year. Each time she took it to the shop, her mechanic soldered it back together. Within a month or two, however, another crack would open and she would live with the noise until gasoline fumes infiltrated the car's interior, requiring her to drive with her windows down to keep from gagging. Mom believed the car cursed. She acknowledged these thoughts were silly and irrational, but then she'd laugh and add, "Fairy tales never really leave you."

Yet she refused to buy a new car, though my father and I begged her to get rid of her junker. "No," she would tell us, "it would be like abandoning an old friend, just because she came down with an incurable disease." After the funeral service, the funeral home offered to drive is to Dad's gravesite in its limousine, but she insisted on driving herself, despite everyone begging her to reconsider. "I'll be fine," she said, and that ended the discussion. I went with her, afraid of what she might do if left alone. Borges wasn't with us. In my vision, I never saw him at the funeral, which I found strange. Where else would he have been?

My mother left the church ahead of the official police escort. She drove with the recklessness of a teenager, full of youthful omnipotence. Her eyes flitted all over the place, often away from the road in front of us, as if she didn't mind if we ran off it. A mile or so from the cemetery, she drifted across the centerline. Loud honks from a car in the opposite lane brought her back, and she hit the brakes hard. I fell forward, with enough force that my seat belt left a band of bruises across my chest. They hurt, but I I ignored them out of fear for what might have been. Through luck, those following behind us slowed down in time. I turned to see the rear of the car that she just missed hitting head on growing smaller as it flew away from us, dead leaves rustling in its wake.

A motorcycle cop's knuckles rapped on her window. He asked if we were all right, and I nodded after Mom failed to say anything. "Not so fast," he told us. "Keep your speed under thirty from now on." Another cop came by. The two of them conferred for a minute while shooting the occasional glance at my mother. When we started again, one of them led the way, making sure he kept his motorcycle with its flashing lights in front of her car.

Driving again, in my mind, I looked at her and saw not a sixty-something woman, but the petite young Japanese woman my father met when she worked as clerk for his commanding officer at the U.S. naval base in Tokyo. He could never take his eyes off her, she once said, though he was too frightened to ask her out for a date. So, she forced the issue after four months of waiting. Then that young woman dissolved, and the older one took her place, driving slower now, consumed by grief.

• • • • •

The vision ended. Of the burial itself, I recalled nothing. Opening my eyes, Borges still knelt beside me on the deck, maintaining that calm intensity I found so unique. "Help me up," I said, and he did. The world was a blur. Only Borges remained in sharp relief, only he had my complete attention. He took me to the kitchen, and he made breakfast, my favorite: Eggs Benedict and dark roast coffee, black, no cream, no sugar. Where he came by the Canadian bacon and English muffins, I didn't know. When finished, he removed my plates and washed them.

"My mother, how is she?" Those were the first words I spoke since being led back inside.

"She took her own life two weeks after the funeral," he said. "We're both orphans now."

CHAPTER 6

Borges made no objection to my immediate demand we return to Minneapolis, the city of my birth. I needed to visit the gravesite of my parents. He speculated aloud that perhaps my grief over losing them affected my memory, creating temporary amnesia. We each of us, for different reasons, I suspect, did not discuss the subject of Japan or the Daibutsu. The important thing was to get me home.

I recall only bits and pieces of my time before we left. Staring at the ceiling fan in a trance as its blades wobbled above me, for example, which must have occurred more than once because those memories were so distinct. One afternoon a violent thunderstorm caught me outside over a mile from the villa, wandering aimlessly in a grove of orange trees. Panicked, I ran until I found a large Guanacaste tree to shelter under, getting drenched. I don't remember why I went there, nor how I made it back to the villa, where I shivered on the tile floor of the kitchen, under a blanket Borges draped over me.

My worst recollection? The morning I took a large kitchen knife and slashed my painting to shreds, the image of the Great Buddha unrecognizable and I stood over it as I shouted angry curses into the wind. And there were so many days like that, days forever lost to me now. Time ground to a halt amid the crushing weight of guilt that ate away my spirit. I could not stop crying, racked by obsessive thoughts about my parents. I tried dredging up memories of my last conversations with them without success. Had I ever told them how much they meant to me, how much I loved them? A veil of hopelessness enveloped me. I considered ending my life. One night, as I kneeled on the rug in the living room floor, surrounded by my luggage while Borges smoked his evening cigar on the deck, I started to wail. It began as a low, almost imperceptible moan, but it grew louder and higher-pitched.

By the time Borges reached me, my body rocked back and forth, my arms folded over my belly, in pain from convulsions. My ability to speak in coherent sentences disappeared, and I didn't understand a single word Borges said. He held me close, looking helpless because nothing he did made a difference. My emotions were too overwhelming. Only my tears existed for me.

We stayed at a hotel room near the Juan Santamaria Airport in Alajuela the evening before our scheduled departure. While asleep, I had a most unusual dream. Recalling anything but fragmentary images from dreams is rare for me, but this time, I recalled every vivid detail. The dream world felt far more real to me than my waking one. Colors were brighter and sharper, odors more intense. A cool breeze tickled my bare skin with such clarity that I could feel goosebumps forming on my arms. My senses were on high alert.

I walked down on a dirt path through a garden of flowering trees full of pink and white blossoms. The wind was at my back, and a bright sun above revealed a cloudless sky. Petals fell like snowflakes, and some, as they swirled to the ground, struck my cheeks, their touch soft like silk. I spun around in great circles, arms extended, my skirt billowing up to my waist, giddy as a young child, not knowing where I was, but not worried. No fear, no sadness, no anger, no emotion, nothing but unadulterated joy. It was glorious.

"Beautiful, is it not?" a voice spoke, and I stopped dancing. An old man with Asian features stood beside me, wearing a floppy, well-worn hat of faded green held on his head by a drawstring pulled tight to his chin. He gave me a closemouthed smile before dipping his body in a low bow. I bowed in return.

"This is a special place," he said. "I am happy you discovered it. We have so few visitors these days, and the flowers love to show off when one comes along. Stay as long as you need. I suspect we shall meet again." He then showed me his back and departed, a stooped figure using a cane. I watched him until I could no longer make out his silhouette against the horizon. A carpet of lush grass spread between evenly spaced trees beckoned, and I lay down upon it. Dappled sunlight flitted through the branches. What did the old man mean about meeting him again? On reflection, his words seemed ominous, but my concern faded as I breathed in the oxygen rich air. *It doesn't matter*, I thought. After closing my eyes, red and white spots dotted the inside of my eyelids. The sound of my alarm ended my slumber. It was 6:30 in the morning. The flight home was scheduled to depart at 11:00 a.m.

• • • • •

I left Costa Rica in a fog of dread and confusion. Climbing into a taxi at the hotel was my last memory. My next lucid moment did not occur until I awoke slumped down in a first class window seat on board a jet airliner. Borges sat next to me, holding my hands. He stared at me with such a fierce expression that my initial reaction was to pull away from him. The shock of emerging into consciousness and seeing those dark eyes frightened me. Upon recognizing the situation, I asked Borges where we were.

"About 30,000 feet in the air somewhere over the Carolinas," he said. "Flight 665 out of Miami."

A simple, laconic answer, but it soothed me. Vague memories of boarding our first plane at Juan Santamaria Airport, our arrival in Miami, passing through U.S. customs, and the three-hour layover we endured before boarding our next flight, returned, bringing me relief that was indescribable. I smiled for what must have been the first time in forever. Borges smiled, too.

"You are back," he said. "My Jane is back, are you not?"

"Yes. I am." Then a sudden anxious moment. "You're still my Borges?"

"Always," he replied. "I will always be your Borges."

Nothing else needed to be said. The days of madness I suffered in Costa Rica were not memories I wanted to relive, and Borges never alluded to them thereafter. Then again, why would he? He was consistent that way. *Nunquam retro respicere.* "Never look back" was his motto. Not that he was averse to speaking of the past if I brought it up, but he saw little value in it as a guide for the future, or so he often intimated, anyway. A nameless flight attendant appeared, and I ordered a vodka and tonic from her, downing it in one gulp and ordering another.

"How much longer until we land?" I asked when she came back.

"We're a little over two hours out of Minneapolis," she said.

I nodded, then looked to Borges. "I'll take a nap."

"Sleep well, my dearest," was his reply.

• • • • •

The next morning, after spending the night at Borges' loft, I drove to my parents' last resting place for the first time, at least as far as I could recall. Spring was early that year. The dogwood, cherry, plum, apple and pear trees that lined both sides of the roadway were in full bloom. The air rushing into my car through the open window, thick with their blossoms' competing scents, was intoxicating. Under other circumstances, I would have welcomed them, but not on that day. Their colors and fragrances felt oppressive, a cruel mockery of my melancholy. Halfway there, I almost turned around, but didn't. At breakfast, I told Borges that before anything else, I must go to them. When he asked to accompany me, I declined. How would it look if I returned after saying I needed to mourn them by myself?

I drove down the narrow asphalt lane through the cemetery grounds until I reached a red-topped post marked with the number 33. I parked and got out. The rest of the way required a quarter mile or more of walking, according to the gatekeeper. The mid-morning sun was warmer than expected. Beads of sweat broke out on my forehead as I strode past row upon row of tombstones. Unbuttoning my light sweater, I tied it around my waist, leaving shoulders and arms bare. My black spaghetti strap tank top soaked up the sun. Distracted by the wet patch dampening the seat of my yoga pants, I almost missed my parents. They were near a tall oak whose old branches reached over their graves as if to comfort them.

Their plot, larger than most, surrounded by an ornate wrought-iron fence about three feet high, had a gate I opened to visit them. A wide, striated gray and white marble stone rose from the ground to my left. Its polished surface contained my father's name and the dates of his birth and death, nothing more. So like him, just the facts, with no superfluous platitudes. He used to say that living life to the fullest was the only legacy anyone needed.

A few feet to the right, in stark contrast to my father's stone, I saw an embedded granite plaque, marking the spot where my mother rested. No name was etched on its surface, only the kanji for "chrysanthemum," her favorite flower. A symbol of Japan's Emperor, the chrysanthemum also represents lamentation for one's beloved dead. My eyes formed tears as I ran my fingers over the engraving. How apropos and how like her. Even in death, she lay in my father's shadow, the dutiful Japanese wife. Did she choose this marker before or after he died? I had no recollection of burying either of them. What an awful daughter I was not to remember. My tears fell on my mother's stone, landing without a sound. In silence, I rubbed them into the crevices of the kanji with my fingers until they evaporated with the morning breeze.

"A daughter's tears fall, a gentle rain embracing the chrysanthemums."

Startled, I turned and looked for the voice that intruded upon my sorrow. Behind me, hunched over, with one hand holding a rough walking stick, was a grizzled, elderly Japanese man, a monk perhaps, dressed in a shabby green cotton robe, which fell to just below his knees. Baggy pants, also cotton, covered his legs, but left his ankles bare. On his feet, a pair of simple Zori sandals made of straw. On his head, a soft cloth cap, its design not unlike a fez, covered all but a few strands of salt and pepper hair that peeked out around his ears.

"*Sumimasen deshita*," he said, bowing his head. "Forgive my impudence. It's just that whenever I feel a hokku forming, I must allow it to be born."

"Hokku?"

"A short verse form. You are American, yes?" His question seemed rhetorical, but I nodded anyway. "Here it is known by another name: haiku."

"A poet? From Japan?" A stupid question, but I couldn't stop myself.

"Hmmm. Poet." Silent for a moment, he stared past me into the unfathomable distance, as if rolling the word around his tongue, savoring its flavor. "Yes, that name will suffice."

"Who are you?" He evoked no fear in me, but as a stranger accosting me at my parents' graves, at the least, he should introduce himself.

"I am a traveler, like you." A smile exposed deep creases in his face and around his eyes. "My family name is Matsuo, and my birth name is Munefusa. But the name I chose for myself is Bashō. It means banana tree."

"Bashō?" I said, "The Bashō?"

"Yes."

I felt the blood drain out of my face. This couldn't be happening. Not again.

"But you're dead," I protested.

"Yes," he said, "I am."

CHAPTER 7

I didn't believe him. You don't look dead, I said, and how can a man who died in 1694 still be walking around over 300 years later? He noted his death occurred in Year 6 of the *Genroku Nengō*, but he understood my attachment to the Christian calendar. When I demanded proof of identity, he shrugged, as if to say, 'What proof could I offer?' Out of frustration, I asked if he thought me foolish enough to believe he could be a ghost, yet even that left him nonplussed.

"Now that is an interesting question, one I have long pondered. In my country, the word that corresponds to 'ghost' is *yūrei*. A *yūrei* is a spirit that remains behind after a person dies from violence, or one who was not at peace when they died, who still struggles with powerful emotions, attachments that keep them bound to this world. *Yūrei* haunt the living, in particular those they once loved or hated."

"That sounds like a ghost to me."

"*So desu ne*," he replied. "It does. And what is the nature of such a being?"

"What do you mean?"

"Does a ghost appear as a living person, or as a pallid reflection of life, an apparition, and never in the full light of day, but as a shade, at night?" When I hesitated, he continued. "Do not ghosts inspire fear and panic when they appear?"

"Well..." He caught me off guard.

"Here," he said, extending his arm, "touch my hand." When I did, he said, "Do I feel like a shadow or do I feel real?"

"Real," I admitted.

"So I experience myself as well."

"The dead do not walk among the living," I said, not without a note of anger. "They don't surprise people visiting the graves of loved ones and make ridiculous claims, either, like you. You're not Bashō. You're just a liar." My tone was more strident than intended. The absurd twists and turns my life took since meeting my Borges left me unbalanced and vulnerable. No matter. The old man did not mind my bad temper. His rich, brown eyes, which displayed no frustration or anger, watched me until my breathing slowed. His unearthly equanimity was unsettling.

"The grass grows thick and the spring flowers bloom despite ill-favored dreams," he said. "Another hokku you inspired." Then he began a series of slow, choreographed steps, turning around in a circle. I waited for him to complete his curious movements.

"Where are you?" he asked when he stopped.

"Where am I?" What the hell kind of question was that? "This," and here, I pointed to my father's tombstone, "is where my dead parents bodies lie buried, and this," and here, I swept my hand through the air in a wide arc, "is Lakewood Cemetery in Minneapolis, Minnesota. But you already know that." Once more, I was furious.

"You traveled to Japan, have you not?"

"I don't know," then, "No, I haven't." What other answer was there? The past few months called my sanity into question. My memories of the Daibutsu, and of Tokyo, no longer felt real to me. It was as if they happened to someone else. They resulted from a delusional state into which I descended after my parents' deaths. A belief my Borges encouraged.

"Not true," said Bashō. "I know you visited Kamakura."

"How? I've never seen you before."

He responded to me with a non sequitur. "Let me show you where I am today."

How to describe what happened next? Nothing changed, *and yet* the sky became bluer, the grass greener, and the quality of light itself clearer. My eyes watered. After wiping them with the back of my hand, I saw a tree, not the oak by my parents' graves, but one I couldn't identify. Below its tight bundle of branches and thick, bush-like leaves, several narrow, moss-covered stones inscribed with kanji characters emerged from the earth.

"That's a Gingko tree," Bashō said, "and these are samurai grave markers. There are many such graves in Kamakura."

Astonished, I took in the view, one much like the Kamakura I remembered, memories my Borges kept insisting were delusions. "Were you here the day I came to see the Daibutsu?"

"The Daibutsu is over there," he said, pointing to my left. Then he shifted to my right. "In that direction is Tsurugaoka Hachimangu, the most renowned temple of Kamakura, just north of the train station. You arrived by train from Tokyo the day you visited the Great Buddha, did you not?"

My knees weak, I nodded. "How do you know these things?"

"Call it my fate, if you like."

"Fate?"

"Fate is a Western concept, but since my death, I've met many *gaijin* and learned much from them." I detected a note of irony in his voice, but said nothing. Disoriented, it felt safer to keep quiet, rather than challenge this old man who I now feared might be who he claimed to be. "Since I died, my spirit has roamed across my country. Though my body feels substantial, most people do not see me, or if they do, they take no notice of my presence. Yet, there are times I can interact with the living. But only with people who visited the places I visited during my life. *Wakarimasu ka?*"

"*Hai*," I said, slipping into the Japanese learned from my mother. "*Wakarimasu.* I understand." If anything seemed real to me, it was that I had lost my mind. Then Bashō did the unexpected, laughing with a deep, resonant sound like that of a bassoon. This went on for a long time, or so it seemed. When able to gather himself, he bowed, until his stiff back paralleled the ground.

"*Moushiwake gozaimasen deshita.*" Then, as if recognizing he spoke to a *gaijin*, and an American at that, despite my mixed racial heritage, he repeated his apology in English. "Forgive me. That was rude to an excessive degree. I am ashamed." He lifted himself back up, and the subtle old man, possessing a tranquility to which I could only aspire, reappeared. He then waved his arm, and all traces of Kamakura disappeared. I found myself, once more, beside my parents' graves. Bashō smiled, but I could muster only a wan grimace, while my heart hammered beneath my ribs.

"Please, sit." He motioned to a spot under the oak where sunlight dappled through the leaves. How could I refuse? We arranged ourselves on the lawn, facing one another, I with my legs curled to one side and Bashō in the classic Lotus position. The cool grass comforted me. "Though you showed great compassion not to condemn my inappropriate behavior, allow me to explain why I reacted so. I saw in your eyes what I once felt, many years ago at a *tsuya*."

"*Tsuya?*"

"The Japanese equivalent of an Irish wake," he replied. "I remember falling asleep the night before I died, sick and worn down by my journey to view the ruins of Osaka Castle. Friends expressed concern for my health, but I refused a physician, despite stomach pain. Death and I, we had an arrangement. I wouldn't worry about Death, and Death would do me the courtesy of not inflicting undue suffering when my time came. Death kept its part of our bargain.

"The next day, I attended a *tsuya* for someone unknown to me. Incense and the odor of warm sake filled the air. I sat with friends and students around a long table, all dressed in black, as was customary. Only I, in contrast, wore a white silk kimono, which confused me, as I did not own such an expensive garment. Everything about that tsuya was strange, to be honest. Tears flowed openly from many eyes, but no one spoke in memory of the deceased. It was as if they had no tongues.

"Though it shamed me, I asked the man next to me who died. He did not answer, not even after I raised my voice. No one else answered, either. Irritated with their silence, I stood and, bowing to all, went to pay my respects to the deceased at his shrine, a small table covered in white paper, with several books and flowered wreaths placed upon it. I intended to light a stick of incense, pray and offer a gift, one only a poor poet could give, a hokku in his memory. Kneeling, it shocked me to see my name on fine silk laid with reverence over one of my books. This was my tsuya. My first thought was that it was all a bad dream. My second, that I was mad."

He stopped and looked at me a long time. "That is why I understood your emotions when we stood together in Kamakura. Once I also believed reality abandoned me, and I was insane. But neither of us is mad. The universe is just very *fushigi*."

"What?" I asked.

"It has no direct translation into English. *Beyond comprehension*. That is the closest I can come. But, Jane-san, I'm sure you need no explanation, now that your life has become entangled with the man named Jorge Luis Borges."

My jaw dropped. The day was going swimmingly, and not in a good way. In order to salvage the situation, I pulled a bottle of generic Xanax from my purse and dry swallowed three one mg tablets. Because, why not?

"*Moushiwakegozaimasen ga*, Jane-san, please forgive my rudeness, but western medicine will not solve your problems."

"With all due respect," I replied, "shut the fuck up." When in doubt, I've always found vulgarity to be an effective means of communication. It's surprising how often it works. And it did this time, for Bashō nodded and said not another word.

Closing my eyes, I leaned backward. A lukewarm breeze blew my hair. I imagined myself on an ocean liner late at night, the stars overhead my only companions. A handsome young man and a beautiful, somewhat zaftig young woman walked by, holding hands, and I found their unspoken love for one another soothing. When they kissed, my anxiety washed away.

I forced my eyes open. Above my head, hidden from view by the tangle of leaves and branches of the oak, a solitary bird cooed; its slow repetitive call one of the saddest sounds I ever heard. I wanted to cry. Maybe I did.

"Ah," said Bashō, "the song of the mourning dove, so lovely and so lonely."

Damn, I thought. I pushed myself upright. He still sat next to me with that same equanimity I found so unnerving.

"Please, no hokku," I said.

"Some moments are poems in and of themselves. But, Jane-san, you are, if I may say so, avoiding the elephant in the room. Your Borges."

Like a slap to the face, he refocused my attention. "How do you know him?"

"Excellent question. *Yoku kiitekuremashita*, Jane-san." His head dropped. "How do I know of your Borges? Because I met his father, the writer Jorge Luis Borges, in 1979, when he visited Japan near the end of his life. He was a most unhappy man."

"You–you met him?" That Borges, not my Borges, but the author Borges, ever visited Japan was news to me.

"Oh yes," the old man said, "several times." He sighed. "Ever since the Meiji restoration, more and more gaijin have visited our shores. The obligation I owe is to help not just my own people, but anyone who sets foot in my country."

"Obligation?"

"Duty, if you prefer. Since my death, I must appear to anyone who suffers from great pain, but of the mind, not the body. In America, you would say they have nervous breakdowns or perhaps have lost their minds. At first, I did not understand why I must do this for them. Was it a punishment from the gods? The Buddha? But not every question has an answer worth pursuing. Do you know the five remembrances the Buddha taught in the Upajjhatthana Sutra?"

"I'm not sure." Eastern religion and philosophy was not my strong point. "Are they related to the four noble truths?"

Bashō smiled at my naïveté. "The five remembrances are five facts one should contemplate daily. The practice of remembering them guides all who seek the path that leads away from dukkha and toward true freedom. We contemplate them to help us overcome what underlies our willful ignorance. The last is the one I find most useful. When I contemplate the fifth remembrance, these are the words upon which I reflect.

"I am my actions, for they are all that I am and all I will ever be. Whatever I do, whether good or not good, I carry with me in this life and all that flows from them."

"What's it mean?" Then I remembered that he didn't answer my original question about how he knew my Borges. "Anyway, why's it important? I want to know about my Borges, not Buddhist meditations."

Bashō's eyes closed, as if deep in thought. Then they opened, and he tilted his head in such a way that his eyes twinkled, though it may have been just a trick of the light flitting through the leaves.

"Forgive me," he replied, "but before I can answer, I must tell a story about myself. When I was young, younger than you are now, I suffered from the boundless enthusiasms and monumental despairs to which young people are subject. As I aged, the only thing I found helpful, and for which I possessed some talent, was poetry. Renga, hokku, haibun–these were where I found solace for my suffering. Despair, I confess, was a frequent companion. I turned to the practice of Zen to find a path out of my–morass? Yes, morass will serve.

"In later years, I chose to make a radical change to my life. I abandoned the comforts of home and the daily routine of teaching. It came to me that only through traveling as a beggar who relied upon–and forgive me, but I have grown to love this phrase–the kindness of strangers, could I find enlightenment. So, I undertook many journeys. Writing down my experiences became my path to live in the present moment, without a care for the many attachments formed in life."

"That's interesting," I said, concerned our conversation was going off the rails, "but—"

"But," he said, with a wistful look in his eyes, "I forgot the one attachment that never left me: my desire to compose poetry. I engaged in renga contests almost every day. My desire to transcend the world through writing, to practice *fuga-no-michi*, the Way of Elegance, bound me ever more tightly to the material world."

I didn't know what to say. I thought of my father's favorite adage from Lincoln: "*Better to remain silent and be thought a fool than to speak out and remove all doubt.*"

"Lincoln, eh," Bashō responded, laughing.

"You read my mind!" I gasped.

"Yes," he admitted. "My condition comes with few benefits, but one is an ability to understand the thoughts of those I seek to help. Do not concern yourself. It's rare that I use it. But now I am the one ignoring the elephant. Let me do my best going forward not to forget him."

At last, he'll tell me about my Borges, I thought, but I couldn't have been more wrong.

"I was speaking," Bashō continued, "of my failure to recognize that one cannot escape the self by the simple act of stepping outside the door of one's home. For me, travel and writing poetry were a means to achieve *satori*, the flash of awareness that opens one up to the true nature of the illusion we call the world. But it was a grave error to think they would lead me to the Way."

"So all you did was for nothing?" That he thought so little of his life's work surprised me.

"No," he said. "Those who value my hokku, or my haibun, where one combines poetic prose with hokku, do me honor. But my passion for my art was the anchor that held me to this world. We are what we do in life, nothing more, nothing less. That is the fifth remembrance meaning, and why I still serve others, long after my spirit should have departed this world."

"Is that why you met Borges–the writer, that is–when he visited Japan?"

"Yes. Despite his talent, his formidable intelligence and his charm, he was a man who lost his way. He feared his approaching end. To deny his fear, he poured himself into his essays, parables, poems and stories. He crafted imaginary worlds from words with such care, that he forgot his fictional labyrinths, filled with such meticulous detail, were only a pale shadow of the labyrinth he spent his life constructing to hide himself from himself."

"Were you able to help him?"

"No. I failed."

"Why didn't you–I mean, what happened?"

"He sought what I cannot offer: to live forever."

"But you're immortal."

"Me?" He smiled. "The air you breathe, I cannot. Delicious meals you savor are denied me. Rest, sleep and dreams, I lack. The man who named himself after the banana tree in his garden does not exist. Whatever I am, it is but a pale shadow of you, Jane, who are alive to all the richness of the world. I tried to make Señor Borges understand, but his fear of losing that great mind of his, with its wealth of knowledge, and all the beautiful cathedrals he created from nothing but thoughts and memories–that fortress was beyond my ability to breach.

"He himself wrote of the futility of his desire. His stories showed he understood the world; that it changes, and, thus, that immortality is a curse, not a blessing. These things he knew, I reminded him. But he would not listen. Just as his diseased eyes blinded him to the beauty you see all around you, Jane, so his dukkha blinded him to the one great truth of this world. But writers are like that. They lie, even to themselves. So, yes, I failed. I often fail."

He said no more, and I didn't ask. I forgot all about my Borges, so lost was I in what Bashō said about his failures to help those in his care. Instead, we sat together for a while, listening to the cry of the mourning dove, sad, lonely and beautiful.

CHAPTER 8

Under the rising sun, now shining directly down on us, the day grew warmer. By the gravesite, all traces of the cool morning breeze ceased, and the oak leaves hanging over us were motionless, as if they existed on canvas, a painted landscape forever frozen in time. And Bashō and I were a part of that canvas. We sat so still and quiet I could hear my heart beating. My mind might as well have been a whiteboard wiped clean. What put me in a state beyond feeling, like the monuments to my dead parents?

"Come, Jane," Bashō said, breaking the silence as he reached his hand to mine. With little or no effort, he stood, bringing me up with him. I stretched my back and shoulders, for they were stiff, while Bashō leaned upon his walking stick, holding it with both hands, one atop the other, watching me.

"You could not help the Borges you knew," I said. "What makes you think you can help me?"

"I do not know if I can, for I have no special insight into what path you will choose," he responded. "I only know it is my duty to try. But I must go now."

"What?" My voice squeaked in protest like a child whose older brother just snatched candy from her hands. "You can't. Not yet. We haven't spoken about my Borges, the son of the man you failed! You said I'd become entangled with him. What the hell was that about?"

"This has been a good beginning, Jane-san," Bashō replied, unperturbed. "But there are other people who wish to talk to you." He pointed behind me. When I glanced over my shoulder, there they were, two large men wearing light blue shirts and dark blue pants with something resembling Batman's utility belt strapped around their waists, carrying all the accouterments of their trade: a long, heavy-looking flashlight, some orange gun-like object, likely a taser, and a holster with the requisite handgun. They were policemen. One was bald and fat, with a face that screamed wife-beater. The other, a good six inches taller and twenty years younger, with muscles ready to burst through his uniform, looked like a refugee from a Mr. Universe pageant.

"Bashō, please," I begged. "Let's go back to Kamakura and finish what we started. I don't want to talk to these men."

"That is not possible, Jane-san."

As the cops approached, the bald one spoke into a microphone attached to his right shoulder. Neither of them seemed to be in any great hurry, even as they made a beeline straight toward Bashō and I. Why were the police coming for me? What had I done?

I felt the urge to run away, but before I could move, the cops arrived, halting ten feet in front of me. The bald guy looked bored, but Steroid Boy assumed a fighting stance, his weight on the balls of his feet, one a bit forward of the other. His right hand firmly gripping the taser on his hip, he stared me down, daring me to give him the chance to make his day.

"Bashō," I whispered, but there was no response. I turned to look for him, screaming, "Bashō!" But he wasn't there. And me with no more Xanax. Life can be so cruel.

"Whoa, Missy!" Bald cop was talking now, hands raised to show me his meaty, grease-stained palms. "No one said nothing about bashing anyone. We just want to talk. That's all. You're Jane Tak-KAY-ko Wolf-Skeem, right?"

"Takako," I said. "And it's Wolfsheim." I hate when people mispronounce my name. Not that it ever helps to correct them.

"Okay then, Miss Wolfsheim. Jane. I'm Officer Gutman, of the Minneapolis Police Department, and this is my partner, Officer Gunderson. We need you to come with us to the precinct for a little chat."

"What about?"

"Well, Jane–you don't mind if I call you Jane, right?–I'm not at liberty to say. It's above my pay grade, if you understand me. But a couple of detectives there want to go over a few things with you. That's all there is to it, I swear to god. So, if you'll come with us, we'll take you right to them, and I'm sure things will get cleared up in no time."

"What if I don't want to talk? Am I under arrest?"

That's when Steroid Boy pulled out his taser and pointed it at me. "We can do this the easy way or the hard way," he growled, and I shrunk in on myself.

"Larry," bald cop said, "shut your pie hole and put that damned thing away!"

"But, Sarge, she's resisting." He sounded whiny.

"Shut the fuck up and do what you're told," said bald cop a/k/a Sarge a/k/a Officer Gutman, "or you'll be pulling night shifts for the rest of your miserable fucking life, you dumbass." Then he smiled at me as sweet as any psychopath you've ever seen Robert DeNiro play in the movies. I wondered if he practiced that smile in the mirror. "I'm sorry, ma'am. You gotta excuse Larry. He's a little new at this. And to answer your question, no, you're not under arrest. Not technically. But we gotta detain you. Protective custody, let's call it. But only until the detectives finish asking their questions."

"Protective custody?"

"Yeah. Hold on a second." He pulled out a piece of crinkled-up paper from his pants pocket and handed it to me. My name was on it. Then it got worse.

"This is a warrant for my arrest as a suspect in the murder of my parents. There's nothing here about protective custody."

"Oh, that," said Gutman. "Probably a mix-up. The boys at the station must've used the wrong form. I'm sure the detectives will clear up any misunderstanding. Now, if you don't mind, we're parked this way. Oh, and I'm afraid you'll have to give me your purse. And, purely as a matter of protocol, you understand, we need to cuff you. What can I say? Rules are rules."

I handed my purse over, and then Larry spun me around, pulling my arms tight behind my back until they hurt, as he placed a set of plastic handcuffs around my wrists. Then Sergeant Gutman took hold of my upper arm, and said, "Let's go."

I noticed he wasn't smiling anymore.

"Again."

I lifted my head off the cold table so I could see. Through blurred eyes, the walls of Interrogation Room No. 2 looked the same as when I first entered hours ago. Except for one wall covered by a shiny, black piece of glass, the room was a dull shade of split-pea green. I wanted to puke.

"Where's my Coke?" I said. "You promised me a Coke."

"We got Pepsi, not Coke. I already done told you that," replied the one female officer in attendance. Her bulky frame blocked the door, and with thick arms crossed over a broad chest, legs spread wide apart, she appeared indifferent to my plight. The very stance she took hours ago, just after two older men, Detectives White and Black (I swear those were the names they gave), sat down across the table from me to ask a few questions, as they put it.

"Where's my Pepsi, then?"

"I done told you, we ran out of Pepsi." *Was that true?* Somewhere in the back of my brain, the fact I didn't know bothered me, as bile churned inside my stomach.

"Jane," said Detective White, the one who removed his blazer and draped it over the back of his chair, "let's go over your story one more time. That's all we want. Just to clarify a few details. And then I promise we'll get you your soda. You like ginger ale? We got ginger ale, don't we, Shaniya?"

"All's that's left is Sprite and Code Red. And coffee."

"How 'bout a Sprite, Jane? Everybody loves Sprite." He pointed at Shaniya, who might have been a solid block of black marble in another life. "Officer Burkstead will be only too happy to get you one as soon as we've run through your story one final time."

I hated Sprite, and the bastard knew that. I told him so the last time we went through this little charade, of that, I was certain. And then my gut joined the conversation. "I'm going to throw up." I told White. My belly cramped, preparing for the eruption about to come. That's when the other detective, Mr. Black, the one still wearing his jacket, kicked a small trashcan my way. It rattled to a stop after sliding into the legs of my chair. My luck it was lined with a thin film-like plastic bag tied off around the rim.

"Feel free," he said. "Just don't miss." Black played the bad cop.

"Now, Jane," continued White, "let's take it from the top. You said you traveled to Japan with your boyfriend, Mr. Porkies–"

"Borges!" I spat the name back at him. "And I never said we went to Japan, I said I thought we did, and–"

That's when I bent over the trash can and a torrent of a yellow, sour-smelling liquid came spewing out of my mouth. Understandable, considering I'd had two eggs over easy for breakfast. And then it happened again, and again, and again, until there was nothing left but the bitter, acidic taste of bile left on my tongue, and pain in every single one of my abdominal muscles.

"Jesus fucking Christ!" squealed Black, as I spit the last of my breakfast into the receptacle he so generously provided. I didn't know what his problem was. Not one drop hit their precious linoleum floor. White, meanwhile, handed me a box of tissues, and I used a couple to wipe off the leftover drool clinging to my lips.

"Thank you." White, his face now the same shade as his last name, nodded. Black, in contrast, gave me the evil eye, his face full of disgust. Only Officer Shaniya Burkstead acted as if nothing happened. I admired her sangfroid.

That's the moment someone knocked on the door. An imperious voice shouted, "White. Black. Get your asses out here. Now!" Mystified, I watched the two of them scramble to their feet, knocking their chairs over in their panic, as they stumbled to the door. I thought they'd run right over Shaniya, but that woman must have been part cat, for she deftly sidestepped them both. They collided with one another before White could unbolt the lock on the door.

Just outside stood a rather stern, silver-haired man who I assumed was their superior, and next to him, the person I least expected. My old boss, Martin P. Schneider, III, attorney at law. I took one look at his familiar smirk and promptly threw up again.

• • • • •

Goosebumps rose on my forearms despite the cardigan draped over my shoulders, but I refused to ask "Marty" to turn off the AC in his BMW 328i Gran Turismo. Not out of stubbornness, but because, if history was any guide, my request would be met with outright dismissal. There was a better chance he'd lower the temperature instead. We headed west, the glare from the setting sun shining mercilessly into my eyes. Dizzy and still nauseated, the events of the past twelve hours pinballed around the inside of my head, refusing my best attempts to make sense of them. The sadness my parents' gravesite evoked. Meeting Bashō, and our surreal trip to Kamakura. Bashō's cryptic comments about my Borges. My arrest for murder. Hours of interrogation in that ugly room, repeating the same answers to the same questions over and over until my stomach revolted. And the topper? Marty Schneider obtaining my release, the last person I expected as my knight in shining armor.

"I can't believe you spoke to those detectives," he interjected. "I thought your father taught you better than that."

I blushed. It was true, I should have remained silent. But I was sure I could convince them they'd made a mistake. Instead, I replied with as much disdain in my voice as I could muster, "I can't believe you're my attorney. When did I retain you?"

Schneider snorted, and I saw snot flying out of his beaky nose. "You didn't," he said. Eyes still on the road, his right hand unclasped an expensive, soft brown leather litigator bag, reached inside and pulled out a piece of paper, which he tossed in my general direction like a Frisbee. My hands flailed about, unable to catch it before it landed right in my lap.

"What's this?"

"You can read, can't you?"

Annoyed, but unwilling to reveal my irritation, I gave it the once-over. It was a court order. It didn't take long for me to realize what happened. "You had me declared incompetent!" I said, more in shock than anger. "You can't do that. I have rights."

"Actually, that's not accurate," Schneider responded. "You gave a power of attorney to your boyfriend, Joseph Borgeson, to handle your affairs in the event of mental or physical incapacity."

"That's not–my boyfriend's name is Jorge Luis Borges. And I never signed any power of attorney."

Schneider cackled. "That's the spirit."

"But that's not his name!"

Schneider only laughed harder. "Can't remember her boyfriend's name. That'll play well."

Confused, I wondered if my Borges changed his name. "I don't know any Borgeson," I said, now with less conviction.

"Is that so? The antique dealer you shacked up with for months here and in Costa Rica? Oh, Janey, you're making my job easier each time you open your mouth." He then reached back into his bag and took out another document. Before he could throw it at me, I snatched it out of his hands. It was a power of attorney granted to Joseph L. Borgeson, with what looked like my signature on the last page.

"That's forged," I said. "I would never agree to this."

"It's signed by three witnesses, and notarized by Jeff Webber, of Webber & Webber, LLP. I believe you know Jeff. He sure remembers you, when he testified before Judge Wilkerson this afternoon. So did several others who gave testimony about your erratic behavior and delusional statements."

"Jeff?" Jeff Webber had been another of Dad's associates until he left to join his father's firm. We dated briefly when I was a senior at Northwestern and he a third year law student. I looked again at the last page. Schneider was right. The power of attorney, printed on Webber & Webber letterhead, included Jeff's signature as the notary. I even recognized one witness, Jeff's secretary, Barbara DeVries. I scanned it again, searching for evidence that this was all some elaborate hoax. And then I found it.

"Aha!" I said, more than a little giddy. "The date says this was signed September 23rd, 2015. That's almost four years off. It's only 2012."

To my surprise, this set off a monumental laughing fit by Marty Schneider. After a good minute, when it became obvious he couldn't stop himself, he pulled over to the side of the road. "Keep it up," Marty finally got out.

"I don't see what's so funny," I said icily. "Even if it's a typo, all you have is an ex parte order from the court." I refused to be bullied. "This," I said, waving the order in front of his face, "is good for only 72 hours before I'm entitled to a hearing before a judge, and won't you be sorry then." For some reason, that caused Schneider to erupt once more in paroxysms of laughter. With tears in his eyes, he pulled a copy of the Minneapolis Star Tribune from his bag and let me grab it from him.

I unfolded the paper. The main headline was the first thing to jump out at me: "Trump Wins Indiana–Sews Up GOP Nomination." The date in the upper left-hand corner was Wednesday, May 4, 2016. *This can't be*, I thought. *Romney's the Republican challenger. Trump? Donald Trump?*

"This is a fake," I said at last. "Donald Trump could never win the Republican nomination. The man's a reality TV show host, for gawdssake!"

Schneider's face took on a sober mien for once. "Cross my heart and hope to die, it's all perfectly true." Then he broke out giggling like a schoolgirl.

"But it can't be," I said, more to myself than to him. "How could four years of my life just vanish?"

"How, indeed," said Schneider, with his familiar smirk. "Guess Crazy Janey has some 'splaining to do." As he pulled back onto the road, those words echoed in my brain. And the trouble was that Crazy Janey couldn't explain anything to anyone anymore, least of all to herself.

CHAPTER 9

Schneider's BMW accelerated as silent tears ran in parallel streams down my cheeks before hitting the newspaper on my lap. I wanted to wail like a banshee, but there was no way I would give Marty Schneider the satisfaction of knowing how upset I was. Besides, for all I knew, he was secretly recording me. There was no need to give him further evidence to use against me in court. Not that a bit of primal screaming wasn't justified after learning that, not only were my parents killed, but I was the primary murder suspect.

My lawyer, legally-appointed guardian and temporary chauffer, couldn't help gloating. "You know, in my haste, I neglected to answer your question in full. Allow me to make amends. As to why I'm your counsel of record, that's easy. I'm executor of your parents' estate. Since you're the sole remaining beneficiary of the various trusts your dear papa created in his will, it was only natural I should take an interest in your welfare. Can't have the heiress of my beloved mentor lose her inheritance over a murder conviction, now can we?" The relish with which he reveled in my misery made me want to slap him.

"You're fired," I said nastily.

"Ah, yes, well, about that," he replied, chuckling to himself, "since the court appointed me your legal guardian–at the request of your boyfriend, the one with the power of attorney–it appears you're stuck with me for the time being."

That barb stung. Why did my Borges, or whatever the hell he was calling himself now, betray me? That's when I lost it. Any semblance of composure just floated away. I sobbed, screamed, and thrashed about, like a dumb animal caught in a trap from which there appeared no escape. Exhausted, I leaned against the passenger door window. Beset by hiccups, my stomach twisted in painful spasms.

"Are we done now?" asked Marty. A rhetorical question.

"Why," I said, between hiccups, "do you care? My father's dead. What more can you do to him? It's not like he left me much. Just an old house and some memories." I wanted to cry again, just thinking of him.

"You really don't know, do you?" he said, real surprise in his voice. Our eyes caught hold of one another, and he looked confused, but only for a moment. "What a sly old bastard," he said. "Didn't tell Daddy's little girl of his fortune. I thought was devious."

"What fortune?"

"Oh, don't worry your pretty little head over it, princess. Uncle Marty will take good care of you. You'll get the best treatment a psychopath could ever need and all the psychoactive meds a girl could ever want. It'll be much nicer than a maximum security cell in the Shakopee Correctional Facility for Women. That's your other option."

"I didn't kill my parents!"

"Well, not while you were sane, Janey, and that's all that matters, isn't it?"

I considered spitting at him, but then the car exited the highway. Well out of the city now, I saw an occasional copse of trees, and farms with dairy cows grazing lazily on lush green grass. During my tantrum, I didn't pay much attention to where he was taking me.

"Where are we going, Marty?" I spoke with a false sense of bravado, scared out of my wits.

"Not to worry, Janey. You'll be in good hands, safe, sound, and most of all, secure. Very secure."

His snigger of contempt caused my heart to jump. We passed several farmhouses with paint peeling off them, and then a long stretch of what might once have been an apple orchard, before Marty turned onto a muddy gravel-pocked path too narrow to call a lane, bordered on both sides by birches and tall spruces that shut out the fading sunlight. The car crawled along now to avoid the many potholes and dips along the way. I assumed Marty probably worried about wrecking his precious Beemer's suspension.

After a half-mile, we headed up a steep slope, which forced Schneider to downshift to maintain traction. Then, as if by divine intervention, we crested a round-topped hill. A big valley opened before us, with a fair-sized lake below. The sun's rays glinted off its surface, transforming the water into golden fragments. Down by the lakeshore were a series of nondescript gray buildings, and two vehicles, one larger than the other, a white van of some sort, the other a dark-colored sedan. "Home again, home again." Schneider's sing-song manner disturbed me.

"What's that?" I asked with a catch in my throat. I thought he was taking me to a psychiatric hospital, but now I didn't know what to think. It looked ominous and Marty breaking out in laughter, again, didn't help.

"A deserted chicken farm, sweetie, where we can have a nice little chat with two new friends, and your boyfriend, too. Like me, they all have your best interests at heart." I shivered at the way he emphasized the word *new*. As the car zigzagged down the hill, my skin crawled; a physical manifestation of terror. And to think the best part of my day had been visiting my parents' graves.

The road ended in a patch of dirt and dead grass that served as a parking lot for the chicken farm where my *friends* waited. It took less than five minutes to reach it, but that seemed like an eternity. I tried to calm myself by gazing at the wildflowers in bloom, growing in fields that stretched to the lakeshore; blueberry bushes and black-eyed susans, interspersed with purple and red flowers, whose names I did not know. I choked up, thinking those flowers might be the last things I would ever see.

The BMW stopped, tires groaning, beside the white van. And there he was, my Borges, not ten feet from its hood. He wore a black suit with a black collared shirt, unbuttoned at the neck. No emotion showed on his face. A step behind him stood two large men, at least three times my weight and a good half-foot taller than Borges himself. With their white shoes, white pants, white mock turtleneck shirts, and white lab coats, they resembled orderlies at an insane asylum. Their ramrod straight posture and steely-eyed looks made it clear they were the hired muscle.

Marty opened his door and made to get out, but Borges raised a hand to stop him. "Get the girl first," I heard him say. One of the white coats opened my door, unlatched my seatbelt, and pulled me into the cool night air. He took me to Borges, never letting go of my wrist.

"Hello, Jane." The glare of the sun at his back shielded Borges eyes from me. "We'll talk as soon as I finish up some business with your lawyer." After a quick nod to the white coats, he beckoned Marty Schneider to come forward.

"Martin," Borges said by way of greeting, "I see you had no problem finding the place. You're punctual as always. How did it go with the police?"

"Good to see you, too, Joe. No trouble at all. Chief Ellison performed as expected, just like Judge Collier. Amazing how little it took to buy them both." The smirk he gave Borges was horrific. *Oh my God!* I thought. What little hope I still clung to leaked away.

"Did she tell them anything? I mean anything..." Borges' voice trailed off, leaving the rest unstated, but Schneider didn't seem put-off by the question's ambiguity.

"Nothing she hasn't told you a thousand times already," he replied, "at least according to the detectives who interrogated her. The Japan trip she never went on, and some vague recollections regarding her father's funeral, which didn't match the truth. She came across as appropriately unhinged, by all accounts."

"Anything else I should know?"

"Just one amusing fact, that ought to come in handy at our next court appearance. Believe it or not, she believed it was still 2012. When she learned it's 2015, that was priceless."

Borges smiled and reached out to shake Schneider's hand. "Thanks for all you've done, Martin," he said, pulling the man closer to him. That's when I saw the dagger. A second later, Borges plunged the blade straight into Marty's chest, an upward thrust, so strong, it lifted him off the ground. I gasped as a spit bubble of blood emerged from the lawyer's mouth. Marty's lips formed a single, unspoken word. *Why?*

"When a man has an appointment with death," Borges said in an unhurried voice, "God finds a way to see he doesn't miss it." Then Borges released him, leaving the knife sticking out of Marty where his sternum ended. A strangled cry died in my throat. In disbelief, I watched Martin P. Schneider III, eyes wide with horror, crumple to the ground. There, his head jerked once, never to move again.

Borges turned toward me. I tried backing away, but couldn't go far, not with my arms held by Mr. big ugly, his grip as tight as shackles on a dungeon wall. But Borges nodded, and the man released me. "Go dispose of the garbage," he said, and the goons left to do his bidding. For the time being, we were alone. I fought the urge to run, knowing it was useless.

"You have nothing to fear, Jane," Borges said in a sad voice. "I wish there had been another way, but–"

"But what?" I said, my voice quivering. "I don't even know who you are anymore, or what to call you. Are you Borges, Borgeson, or someone else?"

"The lawyer knew me as Borgeson, an alias. I haven't used my real name in years." That didn't reassure me. That and the fact he just killed a man.

"Look," I said, "I didn't much like Marty, but not enough to want him dead. And I sure as hell don't understand why you killed him."

"Then let me explain. I promise when I'm done, if you're not satisfied, you can leave and never see me again. Deal?"

What could I say? "Sure." As good an answer as any.

• • • • •

"How much?"

"Fifty to seventy-five million," said Borges, "and that's a conservative estimate."

My legs turned to rubber, and I swayed a little until Borges grabbed my upper arms to steady me. Borges walked me over to the nearest building, where he set me down on a rough-hewn wooden bench, its back abutting a rusting corrugated steel wall. My nose caught the distinct odor of rotten eggs.

"My father never said a word." I knew my father made a good living, but hearing the estimated value of his estate floored me. Then another thought came to me. "Did my mother know?"

Borges shook his head. "Your father was a very secretive man. His accountant knew, I imagine, but as far as I can tell, no one else was privy to all the details of his investments."

"But how? My father was a lawyer, not an investment banker."

Borges shrugged. "It seems he was good with numbers."

How little I understood the one man in my life I truly adored unconditionally. I wasn't angry, just numb. Why didn't he tell me?

Not telling my mother, I understood. Mom never changed much during the three decades she lived in America, always the dutiful Japanese wife whose world revolved around taking care of her husband. Oh, she picked up the language and could mimic a typical American wife of her generation when required to do so, but her inner core never changed. The only rebellious act in her life was when she went against her family's wishes and married my father, her 'great white male barbarian,' as she joked about him.

It was a love match, much frowned upon by her conservative family, but I think my grandfather might have come around to seeing things her way if my father had been Japanese, and came from a suitable background. But to marry an American GI with no money and no prospects, and then move to America with him? Completely unacceptable. Her father disowned her. Only my grandmother stayed in touch, visiting us in America once when I was thirteen. When she died in a tragic train accident, no one notified my mom. She only learned what happened a month later after a friend of my grandmother called her. Aged fifteen, that was the only time my mother cried in my presence, the phone receiver still cradled to her ear long after the call ended.

Despite her estrangement from her family, she never regretted marrying my father, and he gave her no reason to doubt him. He always brought home gifts for the two of us when he returned from business trips. No one could fake the joy he took in seeing her smile. Each month, he wrote her a check for household expenses and all the other bills that needed paying. Growing up, I recall him saying, "Better your mother handle the bills. I'd just go blow it all on something stupid."

"Like a pony, Daddy?" I'd respond, and the two of us would laugh ourselves silly, because everyone knew little girls loved ponies. But horses terrified me, with their big teeth and long heads, which jerked about unpredictably. I preferred the stuffed animal version.

The upshot being that we lived comfortably in a beautiful brick home just south of Lake Calhoun, among all the other beautiful homes there, but I never thought we were rich. Unlike many of my friends, we employed no servants, not even a cleaning lady. I worked alongside my mother from an early age. Both my parents were big believers that chores were essential to build character, and by that measure, I developed character to spare. My father didn't spare himself either. He often worked in the yard and even did all his own car repairs. He used to say, "Why throw away good money on some mechanic when I can screw things up just as well at half the price."

During my undergraduate years, he also insisted I work at least twenty hours a week to help pay for my tuition. "It'll keep you out of trouble, kitten," he told me when I complained, and though he was not entirely right about that, he wasn't entirely wrong either. So, to learn now, after his death, that he'd been sitting on a pile of cash, was a stunner.

"No wonder Marty didn't want me facing criminal charges," I said. "So long as I'm incompetent to stand trial, he could milk the estate for all it's worth. That would have generated huge fees for him."

"That was the idea," said Borges, "He offered to pay me a generous sum to testify against you. He even tipped off the police as to your whereabouts this morning. All part of the plan."

"Did you take his money?" I asked, more than a little bitter at this confession, but my Borges just smiled.

"I don't think I'm in any position to collect from him now. Besides, I have more than enough. Another $100,000 was nothing to me, though he didn't know that." I forgot my Borges was wealthy. But then, my memory was full of so many gaps of late.

"Did I kill my parents?" There, at last, I said it. I trembled, because in truth, I doubted everything I thought I knew about myself. Maybe I had done it, and then out of guilt, repressed the memory.

"No," Borges said at once. "Don't even think it. I know who ordered your parents' murder, and it wasn't you."

"Who then?"

Borges pointed back toward the BMW, where the men in white were placing Marty's body into the trunk. "Your former lawyer. Once he learned of your father's fortune, he couldn't help himself." Borges sighed. "Your father's fatal flaw was his inability to see the bad in people. Though he helped Schneider become a partner, your father was profoundly ignorant of the depths of Martin's resentment."

"When did he learn Dad was rich?"

"I'm not sure. My best guess is when your father appointed him executor. All I know is Martin's plan to kill your parents and pin the blame on you was in place by last year, sometime around the end of June."

"How did you learn that?" I said.

"They told me," Borges replied, pointing at the two men dressed in white over by Schneider's BMW.

"They're the killers?"

"They prefer the term cleaners," Borges replied drily. When they finished slamming the trunk on Marty's body, Borges left to speak to them. I heard something about whether they had a match for "the girl" and an admonition to make certain that when they torched the car, there would be no possibility of identification. Then Borges reached into his jacket and pulled out a thick envelope, containing, I assumed, freshly pressed hundred-dollar bills. They nodded, took the envelope, then drove off, one behind the wheel of the van, and the other driving the BMW.

"Where are they going?" I asked Borges. "And what's all this talk of bodies and burning? And why in hell are they working for you if they killed my parents?"

Borges sighed. "It's a long story."

• • • • •

In 2015–I still couldn't accept that I'd lost four years of my life–Schneider began plotting to murder my parents. The big uglies in white were his clients, and Marty was well aware of their profession. He offered each of them $50,000 to "clean" both my father and mother in such a way that the police would view me as the prime suspect.

One evening, while my mother attended a concert, the cleaners broke into our home. My father, as was his habit, had taken an Ambien and gone to bed early, around nine-thirty. While asleep, they injected a concentrated dose of potassium chloride into a vein in his thigh. It's the same chemical used in states where lethal injection is the preferred method of execution. It works by cutting off all electrical activity to the heart, leading to death by cardiac arrest. It induces a heart attack.

Normally, Borges informed me, potassium chloride rapidly breaks down into potassium and chlorine, present in all human bodies. An autopsy would reveal elevated levels of potassium in the victim's blood, but not enough to lead a forensic pathologist to suspect the person died from anything other than a heart attack. However, the cleaners dosed my father with enough to kill an elephant, which left much higher traces of potassium in his system. That led police to suspect homicide. All this happened while I was in Kamakura, visiting the Daibutsu, assuming I visited Japan as Bashō claimed.

Borges continued to act as if my memories of visiting Japan were all in my head.

The day after my father's funeral, Minneapolis police received an anonymous tip that led them to a hypodermic needle hidden in the bushes of our neighbor's yard. Lab tests confirmed it contained traces of my father's DNA. Within a week, an informant who worked at a hospital pharmacy, prompted by news reports, told the MPD that prior to my father's death, he witnessed a woman with "Asian features," remove a box of single-dose vials of potassium chloride from the pharmacy's stockroom. When confronted, she bolted. He reported the theft to his superiors, but thought nothing further of it. When the homicide detectives found out, they first suspected my mother. Then, a day after being questioned by the police, the police found her body at our home, dead from an overdose of vodka, Vicodin and Diazepam. Borges said we left for Costa Rica the day after her funeral.

"At first, police investigators believed she killed herself out of guilt," Borges said, "because a suicide note on her bedside table admitted responsibility for your father's murder."

"That's not possible. My mother couldn't even squash a bug. She was a devout Buddhist."

"True," Borges continued. "Schneider hired a private investigator who obtained a copy of the note. When shown to her friends, they denied it was hers. The handwriting was all wrong, and its word usage not typical for her, a person who learned English as a second language. A second autopsy of her body discovered abrasions in her esophagus, the kind caused from force-feeding using plastic tubing."

"Oh my god!" I felt sick. I imagined my mother struggling against those two monsters as they forced the tube down her throat, then choking and gagging the whole time they poured the mixture of pills and vodka into her, all the while trying to vomit it back up, until she slipped into unconsciousness. What an awful way to die.

"And these are your men now?" My voice rose, anger getting the better of me.

"Trust me, they were my only option." He lowered his head and turned away from me. "If there had been any other way..."

I watched as, for the first time, my Borges' vaunted composure crumbled. He used the sleeve of his coat to wipe his face. Was it possible I drove him to tears?

"When Schneider emailed my business account, I learned the police were looking for you. He knew we were a couple. He expressed concern for your safety. Somehow, he knew we were out of the country. The next day, I hired someone to watch you at the villa, and flew back here. It was only a guess, but I knew he must be responsible. Martin used to vent to me about your father whenever I sold him antiques. Upon arriving at his office, he asked if I knew where to find you. So, I let him know that, for a price, I'd deliver you right into his hands." Borges laughed bitterly. "Betrayal he understood very well."

Hearing his words, I felt faint. It sounded so cold-blooded, this talk of selling me out. "But didn't he run a great risk bringing me home, knowing the police planned to arrest me for murder?"

"Not that great. The evidence against you is far from airtight. True, you're the obvious suspect as the only surviving family member and heir, which gives you a motive. You also fit the general description of the 'Asian-looking' woman who stole the potassium chloride vials. And then there's the fact that you fled the country." I started to object, but Borges raised his hand to cut me off.

"I know you don't remember any of that, but try to understand how the police look at it. Even so, no one at the hospital identified you as the thief of those drugs. The police have gaps in their case. That was why the lead detectives brought you in for questioning. They planned to wear you down and get a confession. But Martin prepared for that contingency.

"He counted on having you declared unfit to stand trial. As long as you were deemed unfit to stand trial because of mental incapacity, no prosecution could take place. As guardian and executor, he could hire his own firm to represent you. He could place you in a psychiatric facility that he and his friends controlled through a limited partnership, another means of draining the estate's funds into his own coffers. It was all very well thought out. He was a clever man. Just not clever enough to understand that not everyone's motivated by the same things that drove him: a desire for riches, but also revenge."

"Revenge?" I asked. "For what?"

"Oh, a thousand little slights, that he kept locked away in a little grievance box inside his blackened soul," Borges replied. "Your father correcting the legal briefs Schneider prepared, even after he made partner, for one."

My eyes began to tear up again. Why kill over anything so trivial? My father always spoke of Marty Schneider in glowing terms. And now he and my mother were gone forever. They died still young in my eyes, still in love, still happy together. And because Marty Schneider held a grudge against my father, now they were dead. I broke down sobbing, snot running out of my nose and all over my face, until it dripped onto my blouse. Well, what was one more meltdown after a day like that?

CHAPTER 10

"Ouch!" I cried. "I thought you said you knew how to cut hair."

"Stop moving your head so much," Borges replied. "That would be a big help."

I wanted to use a few choice expletives, but decided pissing off the man holding scissors close to my scalp might not be wise. Standing in front of the bathroom mirror in a Motel 6 outside Buffalo, New York, I struggled to make sense of the past 48 hours. I should have asked Borges questions about why we were on the run instead of exposing Martin's murder of my parents, but it seemed each time one came to me, it flitted away like the butterflies I chased as a child. In the end, I stopped trying.

We left Minneapolis in a hurry, with just the clothes on our backs. Borges drove. Emotionally and physically worn down, I slept in the back seat of his car. While asleep, I dreamed of Marty Schneider. He would appear out of nowhere, blood pouring out of his chest where Borges knifed him. After each nightmare, I awoke in a cold sweat, terrified, as we passed through dead end town after dead end town, stopping only for gas, or to go to the bathroom. Now we were at the Motel 6. I watched Borges' reflection in the mirror, chopping off my lovely long hair. With each snip of the scissors, I felt a piece of my former life falling away.

Borges wanted to make me a blonde. I objected, but he was not a man to gainsay once his mind was set. I hoped he knew what he was doing, though his overall plan to evade capture remained vague. The only details I knew for certain were the changes to my appearance. When I asked why, he simply said that the MPD's crime lab investigators might discover that any teeth left by the other Jane wouldn't match my dental records.

"Other Jane?"

"The other Jane the cleaners placed in Martin's BMW before they torched it."

A curt response to a foolish question, but I was in bad shape. Processing all the horrible things that happened since I went to the cemetery was impossible. My brain had a hard enough time just avoiding a lapse into catatonia, or worse, hysteria. Yes, the other *Jane* the cleaners found god knows where must do her best to convince the police Jane Wolfsheim died in a fiery crash along with Marty, her lawyer, guardian, and old family friend.

The MPD considered me the prime suspect in my parents' murder. That was obvious after my interrogation, but I couldn't quite recall what evidence implicated me. In the middle of the night, before we reached the motel, I asked Borges what would happen to my father's estate if they declared me deceased. He told me not to worry, that everything would, in his words, "be taken care of." My take away? Best not to ask too many questions. When the last of my hair hit the floor, I placed my head over the edge of the tub so he could wash my hair with the detachable shower head. The warm water felt so nice that I dozed off. Ammonia from the dye Borges worked into my scalp rudely awakened me when I started gagging. But despite my vigorous objections, he soldiered on with his makeover effort.

Around 2:00 p.m., he finished, and I crawled into bed, and fell fast asleep, this time without dreaming of Marty Schneider. The smell of coffee roused me, and pizza. Borges stroked my hair as my eyes struggled to open. His caresses felt so damn good, I almost I drifted off again, but my stomach, once aware food was available, demanded I eat.

This was my first meal since coffee and eggs for breakfast before I headed to the cemetery and my fateful meeting with Bashō. I guzzled down a bottle of water Borges gave me in the car, but nothing else. I devoured four slices of pizza in less than ten minutes, while draining a full glass of Coke. When done, I let out the largest belch in my life, and didn't feel the least bit ashamed. Slumping into the pillows on the bed, I was a contented woman.

"We need to talk," said Borges. His timing was impeccable. I would have preferred to watch Animal Planet or even re-runs of the Kardashians on TV, but no, it was time to talk. Now, on his schedule, because he said so.

"What about? Why we're here? Where we're going next? Your plan to keep me out of jail?" The answer was none of the above.

"Have you ever heard the term 'Elsewhere?'" he said.

"Elsewhere?"

"Forgive me," Borges said. "I should provide some context. Let's see. How best to go about this?" Elsewhere? What the hell did that mean? And what did it have to do with my parents' deaths or killing Marty Schneider or why I was a fugitive from justice?

"You have my full attention." And he did, if only out of a perverse sense of curiosity. But then Borges wasted the next thirty minutes of my life with a detailed and utterly confounding story about the Jejune Institute, and what he variously referred to as a social experiment, a cult and an Alternative Reality Game.

The Jejune Institute supposedly developed high-tech solutions to world problems. Beginning in 2008, its television ads in the San Francisco area recruited volunteers, and assigned them to pursue bizarre scavenger hunts. Volunteers then were approached by a resistance movement known as the Elsewhere Public Works Agency or EPWA for short, which warned them the Jejune Institute was an evil, manipulative scam run by a sociopath that needed to be overthrown.

"Fascinating," I said, interrupting him, "but I'm not seeing any connection to my situation."

"I was just coming to that," Borges said, not miffed. "The most interesting part regarded the alleged disappearance of a young woman named Eva, daughter of one of the Jejune Institute's first employees. Participants learned, through fragments from Eva's video diary, that she vanished on the night of October 17, 1988, twenty years before the game started. Her videos portrayed Eva as a teenage punk rocker who possessed a charismatic, savant-like nature with the unheard of ability to go to places other people could not, places she called 'Elsewhere.'"

"So?" I said. "Eva never existed. Or am I wrong?"

"No, you're right. Eva was fictional, but also critical to the game. Her disappearance and rumors of her return intrigued enough people to continue taking part in this crazy alternative reality project."

"Again, what's this have to do with me?"

"Do you know Shakespeare's play about ancient Rome, Coriolanus?" Borges said, ignoring my question. Exasperated, I shook my head. "In the play, the common people of Rome deposed a haughty aristocratic consul, Coriolanus, who made no bones about how much he despised them. They banished him, the worst punishment possible for members of the nobility.

Without Rome, in their eyes, he was nothing, a nonentity. Do you know what he said as he left?"

"No idea."

"Coriolanus said, 'There is another world elsewhere.' He's saying Rome is not the world. Other places exist for him, places to which they cannot go, because they do not have his dignitas, the power of his personality, if you like. Exiling him is futile because he can create an alternative world for himself. Casting him out of Rome did not erase his essential nature."

"You're losing me."

"Think back to Eva, Jane. In the game, she has this ability to create alternative worlds, to go 'Elsewhere.' Eva was a fiction, but you, Jane, are very real. You have the power to create alternative worlds, the real power to go Elsewhere."

My first thought upon hearing him say I possessed a magical power was that it was another mind fuck. I didn't know what to make of his ridiculous assertion. He must have seen the doubt in my eyes, because he crouched down beside the bed, took my hands in his, and petted them, as if I were a puppy.

"I know you met Bashō yesterday," he said.

"I don't know what you're talking about." My cheeks flushed. I could only hope my olive complexion hid them, but how could it? Like my father, he noticed everything.

"Please, Jane," he said, "don't lie."

"I'm not," I said, trying to brazen it out.

Borges' head leaned to one side. His lips puckered, which was a habit of his whenever he considered what to do next. I shuddered, thinking back on how only yesterday, about this time, he plunged his knife into Marty Schneider's chest with brutal efficiency. Until that moment, I never thought him capable of murder. Now, I knew otherwise. Then, in an instant, his head snapped back, no longer a bird on its perch, constantly on guard, examining its immediate surroundings. "Bashō talked about meeting the author, Jorge Luis Borges. But he also referred to our relationship. I believe he used the phrase 'now that your life has become entangled with the man who calls himself Jorge Luis Borges,' am I right? And he uttered a vague warning to you about me."

"How do you know this?" I said, my façade falling away. "I told no one, not even those detectives."

Borges displayed a thin-lipped smile. "When we first met, I said when I choose to help someone, that person becomes a part of my life. I should have told you all that entails. It means I know things. Things that just pop into my head. On the morning you visited the cemetery, I knew the moment that meddlesome pest first spoke to you."

"Meddlesome?"

"For me, that's a euphemism. I could use stronger language. This Bashō, who calls himself a spirit guide or whatever, is a known liar. His greatest work, the haibun, *Oku no Hosomichi*, alleged to be an accurate account of a 1,400 mile trek through the northern interior of Japan. Yet did you know he spent five years revising it, taking artistic liberties to make it a more literary work? All writers lie."

I spoke to the real Bashō? Borges implied as much. "Okay, he wrote fiction. So what?"

"He mentioned his funeral and spouted some pseudo-religious gibberish about his obligation to help troubled people if they visit Japan. But that's not the reason I am bringing him up. He gave you the impression that he took you to Kamakura. Don't deny it."

"But he did! I was there. It looked just like I remembered."

"I don't doubt you, but he didn't take you there. You did that. This ability of yours, the power to go 'Elsewhere,' that's how you went to Kamakura. Think back. Did Bashō ever say he transported you there himself?"

"Nnhh–no. But he waved his hand and–"

"And you believed he did it. But that's a magician's trick, if you will. The wave of his hand activated your ability at an unconscious level. You took yourself to Kamakura that morning, even if you were unaware of doing so."

I didn't know what to make of all this "Elsewhere" stuff Borges kept going on about. It sounded as weird as what Bashō told me. Sinking deeper into the bed pillows, I had a brief episode of vertigo, as the room spun around me. I closed my eyes, and when they reopened, the spinning stopped. "This is a lot to take in," I said, "So many things to consider." I didn't mention that one of them was the fact I was sharing a bed with a killer.

"I understand, Jane, and I wish I didn't have to bring it up now, but it's critical you know this about yourself. Not just that you have this ability, but because we may need you to use it."

"Can I ask you a question?" I said. "What made you decide I've got this Elsewhere thing after all those denials you made about our trip to Japan to see the Daibutsu of Kamakura? Why now do you believe me?"

"Do you want the truth?"

"Of course," I said, though why he gave such an answer troubled me. Is he admitting he lied?

"I suspected this ability of yours when we were in Costa Rica. Your intense dreams and recollections of Japan unnerved me. All the time you spent painting the Daibutsu, too. But after our arrival there, you couldn't remember anything about your parents' deaths…" He trailed off for a moment, then said, "At that point, I began to think I finally found the one I'd been searching for all my life. No, let me explain. I owe you that much.

"As a toddler, I was different from other children. I could read minds and predict future events. My mother knew. Perhaps, she suspected even before I was born. She first told me about my unnatural talents when I was two or three, though in a way that a child could comprehend. As the years passed, she filled in more details. She explained my father was responsible, though she made a point that my special abilities came from her. My father had been looking for someone, someone like you, Jane. Or hoping to find her might be the better way to put it."

"What do you mean?"

"My father was a weak man, but a genius. Her words. Yet she didn't identify him. I learned who he was when a high school language arts teacher mentioned I shared the name of the great South American man of letters, Jorge Luis Borges, and asked if my mother was related to him. It hit me then that this man was my father. That caused quite the fight when I came home from school, as I shouted obscenities at Mother for hiding his identity, while she, in a rage, threw expensive chinaware about the kitchen, which created quite a mess. It ended when she collapsed in a heap, sobbing on the floor amid all the broken porcelain. We didn't speak to one another for a week after that."

He turned his back on me, hands clasped behind him, thinking god knows what. Until now, my Borges denied any connection to the 'Great

Man,' and yet, for the longest time, I suspected he was the son of the famous Borges. It wasn't rational, more based on intuition. Now that I knew, I had a million questions, but I asked only one. "Why do you need someone like me?"

"Why? Because my mother told me that the things I could do, things no one else could, would destroy me unless I found a woman who could go Elsewhere like her, though she never used that word for her gift, as she called it. She always said when she chose my father it was the biggest mistake in her life. Only my choice of the right person could repair the damage. And you are the one, Jane, the key to my destiny."

He turned to face me, but his hands remained behind his back. The muscles in his arms grew taut, and rippled, as if fighting with one another. "Her desire to bear the child of a great man was a mistake. She acted with an incomplete understanding of the consequences for her and for me. When she chose my father, she ignored his motives for wanting to be with her, or she assumed the usual motives, let's say. Only after I was born did she discover the truth, but by then it was too late."

Motives? Mistake? "What difference could it make what his motives were?"

"Because she chose him," he said, as if that explained it all.

Confused, I said, "So?"

"She should have seen into his heart, for she is like me in that regard. But it's not so simple. This knowing, it's not as easy as I made it seem earlier. With you, it took months. My mother never told me how long she was with my father, when their relationship began, when she chose him. I suspect he disappeared from her life before she knew him for what he was."

"And what was that?" I asked. When he hesitated, I added, "And what does any of this have to do with you needing someone who can do this crazy Elsewhere stuff? I'm sorry, but this makes no sense, even if I can do this Elsewhere thing. Why do you need me? You have your own abilities. Aren't they enough?"

Borges gave me a look that bordered on deranged. "You can't imagine how difficult my life has been," he said through clenched teeth. "So many things you don't understand. My entire existence depends on what you can do. Please, just have faith I'm doing what's best for us both."

"You're right. I don't understand."

Borges tried to respond, but emitted only a strangled guttural noise. I saw desperation in his eyes and panic written on his face. His chest thrust forward even as his lower body held him back. In that moment, he struck me as the opposite of Bashō, lacking serenity, a man on the brink of some great explosion, capable of anything. Then, just when it seemed he was about to strike me or worse, the room darkened. Fast moving rain clouds blotted out the sun. Thunder shook the walls. Sheets of rain fell from the skies, forming a waterfall that poured off the motel's slanted roof onto the tiny balcony outside. Both Borges and I stopped and watched the storm together, yet very much apart.

To me, the storm acted as an enchantment. Flashes of lightning pierced the downpour. Despite its fury, I felt calm, and something else no words can describe. I envisioned a vibrant green world, a magical place with thousands upon thousands of ferns, bushes, tall trees, vines and other plants of all kinds. A place where verdant mountains rose straight out of the ocean, and unimaginable creatures gamboled about, playful, happy, unafraid. Somewhere else, the storm still raged, and in that place stood a man I adored and yet who frightened me. A man I no longer trusted, but who I still loved, strange as that seemed. However, the reality where he existed was a pale shadow compared to the green world I gazed upon. It was my Borges' voice that brought me back. I heard my name, like a whisper on the wind, but then louder, spoken with more force each time I heard it. *Jane. Jane! JANE!*

My green world vanished. In our room, Borges grasped my shoulders, his hands shaking me as a baby shakes a rattle. The rain still fell and the thunder still rumbled, but only as a faraway rumor. When I looked up, only then did he release me, stepping away, visibly distressed. "You were leaving me," he said, not so much to me as to himself.

"I'm back," I replied, though from where, I didn't know. Yet I wanted nothing but to return there, so beautiful, so peaceful, a paradise.

"You were about to go Elsewhere," he muttered, his voice quaking. I didn't argue the point.

CHAPTER 11

Borges decided we needed to leave the country as a precaution. He even let me pick where to go, and I chose New Zealand, but we never made it there out of concern the forged passports Borges got through some shady connection wouldn't hold up. So I chose another place. "How about British Columbia? We could be newlyweds on our honeymoon."

I loved camping as a child. With its gorgeous mountain parks, where we could hike, see amazing vistas, and cook over a campfire the occasional trout he might catch from its pristine lakes, British Columbia seemed perfect for us. Now, over a week after leaving Minneapolis, we headed up a steep trail on a bright beautiful morning through one of the greenest places in the world. After three days, however, my legs burned, protesting their abuse. I was in far worse shape than expected.

Around noon, I shouted at Borges, thirty yards ahead, I needed a break. He came back to me, leaned against a tall ponderosa pine and said nothing. Rubbing my cramping legs, I sat on a lichen-encrusted boulder surrounded by aspen saplings. Borges shook a cigarette out of its pack, lighting it with a single match. Smoke covered his face as he exhaled, like a gray beard. As I massaged my legs, the roar of rushing water nearby filled the air. It sounded like ocean surf flowing up upon the coastline, a low, murmurous sound that served as an accompaniment to birds singing overhead. Borges finished his cigarette, crushing it out on the bark of the pine.

Cold and sore, I wondered if I should have picked some place warmer; one that included a hot sun, the drowsiness of *piña coladas* and *mai tais*, and afternoon sex on some private beach. British Columbia no longer held much appeal for me. Borges' love-making was not the issue, for our first two nights in our tent reminded me of our first days together, when passion and desire burned so hot that we spent hours in bed, thinking about nothing but each other's body. Borges was so tender once the sun went down. His entire manner in the nighttime, wind buffeting the tent, a lone owl hooting in the distance, was like a dream I didn't want to end. Yet, come sunrise, his mood changed, and he became a demanding and surly taskmaster. Our nights, lovely as they were, provided no relief from my growing uneasiness. Nor did they eliminate the despair that hung over me since I learned of my parents' murders. The difference between daytime and nighttime Borges gnawed at me.

Walking up this stupid trail, with its well-placed rocks and tree roots I kept stumbling over, didn't help. The urge to abandon these mountains and find a hotel—any hotel—where we could simply fuck and drink champagne and fuck again was strong, but Borges' capricious nature scared me. The day he knifed Marty Schneider, I lost faith in him. Even when he was on his best behavior, I couldn't forget what he did. Perhaps I should have ditched him in Vancouver, but, when I had the chance, I chose not to. It was as if my will no longer had any say in the matter. Why that was so, I didn't know, but having chosen to stay, I could only let things play out and hope for the best.

I felt trapped. Though I still loved him, knowing he could kill, in swift and unexpected ways at any time, made all the difference. I wanted to ask if we could return to Vancouver, but I feared his squinty-eyed, accusatory stare, and couldn't bear the thought of seeing, reflected in his eyes, his disappointment in me.

Out of pride, I refused to let him diminish me that way. That's what it came down to. *This is a test*, I told myself, *and I do not fail tests.* It was stubbornness, the kind that comes when you feel you have to prove yourself all the time, the kind when you do not know who you are or who you might become. A paralysis fueled by a fear of failure.

After ten minutes of rest, Borges said, "Ready, babe?"

It wasn't a question. That part of him I understood well, his demands framed as questions. But these sexist nicknames were new, and they bothered me. Yet when I complained, he recited his 'little endearments' all the more. So, I gritted my teeth and said nothing. *It's a phase*, I thought. He'll stop calling me "babe" and "honey" and "kid" once I stop rewarding his bad behavior with attention. One always hopes for change in those we love.

I slipped my pack back on my shoulders. The entire time I massaged my legs, Borges did not remove his own pack. It was far heavier than mine, but I saw no sign of fatigue in him. Not a drop of sweat appeared anywhere on his forehead or his neck, nor seeped through his shirt. Wishing I could say the same for myself, I held out my hand. "Help me up."

With a quick yank, he pulled me to my feet. The pack shifted up as I moved forward and then thumped down hard on the base of my spine. I muttered, "You bastard!" But he just flashed a mischievous smile. How I hated him in that moment.

"Come on," he said. "We're almost there. It's less than a mile. The hard part is almost over. Soon, it'll be all downhill. You can manage that, surely?"

"Oh yes," I replied. "Surely."

He laughed then, like an older boy taunting a younger one. Soon, we reached the spot where the trail began its descent between the pines and firs that blocked our view. The path ahead was narrow and steeper than the section we just climbed. *Good thing I didn't have to walk up that*, I thought.

The previous night's rain made the footing slippery and treacherous. I proceeded with caution. The sound of rushing water grew louder. My blistered toes and heels burned, insisting with each step I stop, but I knew the pain would continue, regardless. The night before, I treated them with ointments, gauze pads and medical tape from our first aid kit, but found little relief. My feet were unlikely to get better until our trek ended. My main concern was they not become infected.

Borges was immune to such things. He skipped down that slick clay path like a nimble mountain goat. Everything I found a torment delighted him. My bangs dripped from sweat streaming off my forehead, stinging my eyes. Watching my feet, so as not to slip, when Borges abruptly grabbed my arm, I almost fell.

"We're here," he said. "Isn't it amazing?"

It was. We reached Devil's Falls, the grandest vista in the Park. The tree canopy opened up, exposing a clearing that ended in a dramatic drop off. I looked out upon a series of three waterfalls, separated by pools that formed in the bend of a small river as it roared down the mountainside. We stood at a spot that overlooked the middle one. Right below my feet, a great streaming mass of water rushing past appeared close enough to touch. Next, I turned my gaze to the upper and lower falls. Each waterfall dropped a hundred feet or more, a truly fantastic sight.

This high up, the river was little more than a fifty yards wide. After each successive drop, the violent waters foamed and churned. A cool mist that rose up and caressed my face obscured the pools below. The temperature dropped by ten degrees or more, despite a cloudless summer sky, but I ignored the chill, awestruck.

Borges took my hand, and together, we walked close to the edge where an ancient pinewood fence a meter high provided a barrier. A weathered post stood sentinel there, with a metal plaque attached. I read the information etched into it: the name of the first man to discover the falls (the first European, that is); how they acquired their name–because of a legend that young women either fell or threw themselves over the edge, plummeting to their deaths–and other stuff regarding the geology of the area describing the rock formations over which the torrents of water flowed. Borges took off his pack and let it fall to the ground. Then he waved his hand in front of my face to get my attention.

"Get your camera! I want pictures! You take some of me, first. Okay?"

I nodded and then took off my pack. The relief in my shoulder and back muscles was instantaneous, a lightness which I did not expect, so inured was I to its weight. Loosening its tie string, I unzipped the main compartment, and removed my camera–a Nikon my father gave me when I turned fourteen–from a tangle of fleece pullovers. A real beauty, much larger and heavier than newer digital models. My Borges posed by the fence, making silly faces at me as I adjusted the f-stop so the film wouldn't get overexposed. The sun, almost right overhead, provided a benefit. Still, I was taking too much time for his liking.

"Hurry up," he shouted.

"I'm almost ready," I replied as I fiddled with my camera. "Just give me a second to set the shutter speed."

"What?" Borges roared. "I can't hear you!"

"I have to adjust my camera!"

He lifted his hands from the fence rail against which he leaned. Palms up, he shrugged, indicating he still couldn't hear. I pointed to the sky and then my camera lens, trying to make him understand. He looked upwards in apparent confusion, and, as he did so, the fence rail broke and he toppled over backwards toward the rushing water below.

"No!" In terror, I scrambled to where the fence gave way, almost losing my balance. At first, I didn't see him through the mist, but when I lowered myself to the ground, he came into view. The drop to the river was not sheer.

His body spread itself across a ledge of uneven, cragged rocks, perhaps fifteen feet below me. He must have twisted in the air, for he laid on his left side, holding his leg with both hands, a painful grimace on his face.

"Borges! Can you hear me? Borges!"

It took him a moment to find me. His pale face had a bluish tint, though I couldn't tell whether that was from the rising spray or from shock.

"Jane?"

"Yes! I'm here! Are you all right?" He didn't answer right away, so I continued. "What should I do?" That was when I remembered the corded nylon rope attached to his pack, a good fifty feet of it, rope intended for rock climbing. Why he brought rope with us, I never understood, since I was no rock climber, but now I was happy he had. "Wait," I yelled down to him, "I'll get the rope! You can tie it around your waist and I'll pull you up! Be back in a minute."

"No!" His voice sounded strained and harsh to my ear. "I broke a leg!"

"What?" I couldn't believe what I heard.

"My femur, the thighbone, broke through the skin when I landed. It's bleeding bad. Plus my ribs hurt like hell. Might have broken some of them, too. There's no way you can pull me up without my help, but I can't! I'm just dead weight! You're not strong enough!"

"My god! Please, don't die on me!"

"Listen," he screamed back. "I'm not going to! I promise! But you have to get help! Understand?"

I wiped my eyes clear of the tears that began to form and nodded. I had no idea how to do that, but I couldn't let him see me panic. "I'll try."

"Just listen! This may be my one chance to say this. Don't know how long my voice will last." I nodded. He was right. The sound from the falls was thunderous. My throat felt scratchy and rough from yelling. "Empty my pack," he continued. "Find the first aid kit, a water bottle and my spare belt! I need it as a tourniquet to stop my leg bleeding! Put those back in the pack and lower it on the rope down to me! Got that?"

"Yes!" I dumped everything in his pack on the ground. The first aid kit, the rope and his water bottle hung on his pack's metal frame, attached with carabineers. That was the easy part. But I didn't see the belt he wanted, not at first. Frantic, I dug through the pile until at last it showed up. Placing the items he wanted into his pack, I tied it to the rope with a simple sailor's knot my father taught me." Borges," I screamed, "I have everything! You ready?"

He nodded, conserving energy. Already, he looked much weaker. I let the rope down and he untied my knot easily enough. He used the knife he carried to cut a slit up his pant leg. Even from a distance, it looked ghastly. Dark blood oozed from the bone fragment sticking out of his thigh. A wave of nausea hit and I wanted to vomit. He took the belt and looped it around his leg, then with a sudden jerk, pulled it as tight as he could. His scream was otherworldly. His eyes rolled back and his head slumped to one side. For a second, I thought he fainted, but then he recovered. Opening the first aid kit, he grabbed every gauze pad inside, slapping them over the wound. Next, he wrapped an Ace bandage around the pads and then wound medical tape over everything until the roll ran out. Only then did he take a drink of water. Sweat poured off him now and his whole body trembled.

"Jane," he called, "you there?"

"Yes!" He was looking right at me. How could he not see?

"Raise my empty pack with the rope. Take the cover off my sleeping bag, unroll it up and stuff it back inside. Grab my fleeces and two blankets. Put them in, too."

" Anything else?"

"No." I started to carry out his orders, but he called me back. "No, wait! First, find the trail book. It's in a zippered pouch. You'll need it."

"Why?"

"So you don't get lost when you go to find help."

"I can't leave you."

"You must."

"Someone else is sure to come along. I—I just can't."

"Yes, you can. You must, you hear me? We've seen no one for the last two days. There's no way to know when the next group will come by. We can't take that chance. By the time they show up, it might be too late. Just do what I say!"

You don't understand, I thought. *I'm not you.* "I'll get lost," I said. "I'll be too slow or something will happen and–I'll end up killing you because I don't know what I'm doing!"

"Jane! Look at me!" His fierce voice jolted me upright. "This isn't a damn test. This is real. You can do this. You're the only one who can. I'll walk you through it. Trust me."

I shook my head, sobbing now, but did what he demanded. He was right. This wasn't a mere test. It was life or death. I found the trail book. Then I put everything inside the empty pack he wanted: blankets, fleeces, and his unzipped sleeping bag. Using the same knot as before, I tied the rope around the shoulder straps. "Coming down!" I called out.

"Wait! Did you find the trail book?"

"Yes!"

"Get it!"

I went back and grabbed what resembled a large pamphlet—thirty pages of maps and photographs of scenic vistas.

"Good," he said upon my return. "Find the page in the Table of Contents that lists all the maps. There should be one that labeled Devil's Falls to West Pine Lodge. Found it?"

"Yes."

"Good. It shows the trail from here to a lodge where there are rangers. They'll be able to come for me. Look at it. The trail follows the river until it comes to a bridge where you can cross to the other side. See?"

Bridge? I remembered nothing about a bridge. "I thought we ended up back where we started, that Visitor Center? That's what you told me."

"That was the plan, but you'll never make it there in time. There's a ranger station across the river that's much closer, but you have to cross the bridge to West Pine Lodge to get there. Now do you see a bridge on the map?"

"Queen's Bridge?"

"Yes, that's the one. How far is it from here?"

Using the scale provided, I measured the distance out with my fingers. "Thirteen kilometers. How far is that?"

"About eight miles."

Eight miles? We hadn't done a hike that long the entire trip. "That's a long way," I said, trembling. A hike over treacherous ground.

"Don't worry. It's downhill and you won't be taking your full pack. Just the map, a water bottle and a fleece in case you need it. Now tell me how far it is to the lodge from the bridge."

"Six and a half kilometers."

"That's four miles. Call it twelve altogether. What's the time?"

I checked my watch. "It's 11:30."

"Okay. You've got sunlight for another nine hours. You should get there in plenty of time for them to send a rescue team. Now, tie the rope to the post with the plaque and lower my pack to me. Leave the rope tied to the post. With luck, if anyone comes by, they'll see it and find me here."

I did as he asked. He grabbed his fleece and pulled it on over his head. It took longer than normal. Next, he removed the blankets and covered himself with them as best he could. Then he pulled out the sleeping bag and spread it over himself. Last, he wadded up the now empty pack and stuffed it under his broken leg, crying out again in pain as he did so. Then he laid his head down on the rocks, exhausted.

"Borges?"

"Yes?"

"I think I should stay–"

"No! Get going. There's plenty of time. Don't waste it. You were a jock once, right? Suck it up."

"I'll go, but I don't want to." My tears resumed, worse than before.

"I know you don't," he said, "but it's the only way I'm getting off this ledge!"

"I love you. Don't forget!"

"Never, Jane. Never! Now go! Sooner you start, sooner I get help, okay? And Jane—"

"Yes."

"We'll be together again before you know it."

"Goodbye," I said. He waved his hand, a feeble reply. I started walking down the trail and left him, the water's roar my only companion.

CHAPTER 12

How I made it to the bridge I'll never know. I recall bending back into the forest and the muffled sound of the river as I half-ran, half-stumbled down the trail. The sun's rays shone through tall pines, birches, alders, cedars, their narrow beams of light intercut with shadows. My hands were clammy, and my throat raw. My fleece became damp with sweat. I should have taken it off, but I didn't think about anything but hurrying as fast as I could. Gasping for air, I stopped for a drink. That was when I discovered I left my water bottle and the trail book with its maps back at Devil's Falls.

This is insane! I thought. I could hear the thrum of my heart in my ears and feel the pulsing arteries in my neck twitching. It was the adrenaline, I suppose, causing me to freak out, fogging my brain.

"Fuck!" I screamed. "Fuck! Fuck! Fuck! Fuck!"

That needed to get that out. There on the trail, the river gurgling not far away, angry at my stupidity, I cursed myself, Borges, and God himself. A flock of birds shot into the sky, spooked my outburst. After swooping over my head, they settled back down on different trees, different branches, for there were hawks flying high above. Borges pointed them out to me the day before, circling, riding the air currents, their wings pushed outward from their bodies, stiff as kites.

• • • • •

"Look, a red-tailed hawk," he said. "And over there—a peregrine falcon." I watched for a while, but lost sight of them after he gave me his binoculars.

"Where are the eagles? Didn't you say there were eagles up here?"

"We may see some closer to the river, tomorrow. They prey on large fish when they can find them or dead animals. Eagles are scavengers, you know. They're so big they scare away just about anything but a wolf or bear."

"So what do the hawks and falcons eat?"

"Other birds," he said with a grin on his face. "Eagles are too slow to catch most birds in flight, but a falcon, well it's something to see a falcon chasing a jay or a crow, even a small bird like a wren or sparrow." Excitement crept into his voice, but I felt a little sick to my stomach.

"I'd rather just watch them flying around in circles," I said, pointing to the sky.

"Don't worry." He laughed. "You aren't likely to see them catch anything. It happens so fast that it's rare that you see a kill. They snatch their prey right out of the sky. They go after the odd rodent on the ground too. Chipmunks, mice, squirrels."

"Okay," I told him, "I get the picture."

"Am I making you queasy?" That superior smile of his was back.

"No," I lied. "Just don't give me all the gory details, if you don't mind. I'm not that interested."

"As you wish," he said. That's when I hit him on his arm with my fist. He didn't have time to prepare for it and I was glad to see him wince.

"Ow! What was that for?"

"For being a smartass, Farm Boy."

He laughed so loud then, I heard echoes from the surrounding rocks.

"Whatever you say—Princess Buttercup."

I took another swing at him, but this time, he was ready for me, grabbing my arm and dragging me toward him so quick that before I could escape, he pulled me into his arms, my hands held fast, and he was kissing me. Surprised, I let him, before pulling my face away, but he kept kissing my neck and nibbling at my earlobes. A few minutes later, my shorts were down around my ankles and he had me up against a tree, thrusting inside fast from behind and then faster. I cried out when he came. He cradled me against the rough bark and kept pushing into me until his penis softened and slid out. He turned me around and began kissing me again until I pulled away.

"Don't do that again," I said.

"I thought you liked it. You didn't complain. I would have stopped if you'd said anything."

"I know," I said. "It's just a girl likes to be asked. Anyone could have seen us out here."

"Unlikely," he replied, "but point taken. Next time, I'll have my lawyer send a consent letter first." He often teased me like this, but I wasn't sure of anything anymore. Though he was right about one thing; I hadn't complained. What gave him so much power over me, even after I watched him kill a man in cold blood?

"There may not be any next time," I said, pulling up my panties and shorts. When I felt semen dripping out of me, I grabbed a small towel from my pack and wiped down my legs.

"Oh, you never know," he replied. "Funny things happen when you take a trip to where the wild things are."

I tossed the towel at him then, but he ducked in time. He came up smiling, but not in a mean way.

"Come over here, you. Let's kiss and make up. Please."

So I did. We kissed again, and I nuzzled his neck, even though his stubble scratched my cheeks.

"You're a real SOB, you know?"

"I know."

• • • • •

That happened only two days before, but it felt like ancient history. Standing alone among the trees, knowing he was lying in pain on a cold, rocky outcropping, just out of reach of those damn falls, I wanted more than anything to have never suggested this trip, but it was too late now. I looked at my watch. One in the afternoon. I needed to move.

The shadows prevented the sun from drying out the trail. It remained slick, a thin layer of mud over hard clay underneath. Here and there, puddles of water lingered. I fell at least five times, but avoided tumbling head first. Still, long before reaching the bridge, I'd bruised my hips, thighs and tailbone pretty bad. Mud stains covered my clothes, both legs and the right side of my face. That occurred when I fell sideways after my right ankle gave way. It hurt something fierce, but I could still walk on it.

Despite jogging through the hottest part of the afternoon, I was cold. The humid air was thick with the scents of pine and cedar. I was exhausted by the time the path leveled out. The valley's floor ran parallel to the river, which was much wider than up above. Without shade, the bright sun glinted off its surface, hurting my eyes. I looked away to avoid the glare and shielded my eyes with my hands. Now, my watch showed ten after four in the afternoon. My sprained ankle throbbed, causing me to limp.

Queen's Bridge came into view around five o'clock, after the trail rounded a tight bend in the river. A narrow slatted pedestrian footbridge, it comprised one concrete pillar at the river's midpoint, and two anchored on each shore, that split it into two sections. Each formed a downward arc as they extended from their respective pillars on land to the central pillar standing in the river. It reminded me a little of the Capilano Suspension Bridge in Vancouver, which we walked across during the second day of our pretend honeymoon.

The pillars nearest the river bank rose about forty feet, with a metal staircase that one climbed to reach the bridge proper. As I came closer, I saw something that made my heart drop. A metal fence, ten feet high or more, ringed with barbed wire, surrounded the stairs to the bridge on my side of the river. Attached to a chain locked gate were several large diamond-shaped yellow signs. When I drew close enough, I read the following in bold red lettering accented by a thin black border:

WARNING
Bridge Under Repair Due to Hazardous Conditions
Do Not Use Under Any Circumstances
Parks Canada

AVERTISSEMENT
Pont en réparation en raison des conditions dangereuses
Ne pas utiliser en toutes circonstances
Parcs Canada

Beneath the warning was the image of a suspension bridge inside a circle drawn with a red line across it. A second, smaller sign, with black lettering on a white background, stated bridge reconstruction was slated for completion in June the following year.

I lost it again. At some point, I tried to throw my pack over the fence, but without success. Next, I tried to climb the fence, but the barbed wire at the top angled outward, and all I accomplished before falling back down was to rip my fleece open and gash my hands on its barbs, leaving puncture wounds on my palms a quarter inch deep. The worst dug a ragged line about an inch long near the base of my right thumb. It bled badly. Both hands hurt like hell.

The pain helped me focus. Climbing the fence was now out, which was just as well. Looking at the bridge, I saw big gaps where slats had either fallen into the river or been removed by construction workers. The largest gap measured a good twenty feet. If I'd made it over the fence, I would not have been able to cross. Down by the riverbank, I placed my hands in the cold water, first to numb them, and then to cup them together to drink the water. Crystal clear and cold, it tasted sweet, a surprise. Sitting on the gritty wet clay of the riverbank, dotted with small pebbles, I considered my options.

If I kept to the trail on this side of the river it would eventually lead back to the Visitors' Center where we started, but without the trail map, I couldn't tell how far away it was, nor how long it might take. Borges and I hiked four days to reach Devil's Falls, and I suspected the distance back was greater. Worse, it would be uphill most of the way. With no sleeping bag, no blankets and bloody hands, I'd need luck to make it there myself, but even if I did, Borges would bleed to death long before help could arrive.

My second option was a return to Borges in the hope someone would come along in time to save us, but the more I considered that, the more I realized it was as bad as continuing along the trail past the bridge. First, I would have to climb back up the way I came, a near impossible task. Going down had been bad enough.

And if I did, what would that accomplish? Nothing. I might save myself (my sleeping bag was there and our tent), but in all likelihood, that choice would seal his fate. Besides, I couldn't bear to see the look on his face when he realized I gave up. He believed I was the only one who could save him. What would that say about me if I quit now?

There was one other option. Wade the river. I looked across all that water to the spot where the bridge ended on the other side. Though hard to judge the distance with the sun in my eyes, it looked to be 200 yards, give or take, a great deal wider than where the falls tumbled down the mountainside. Whitecaps out by the river's midpoint showed that large rocks lay hidden there, a sign the current was strong enough to complain about the obstruction they posed. Still, distance wasn't the main concern.

The river's depth and the speed of its current worried me far more, and neither could be judged from the bank.

Never a strong swimmer, I figured I could wade across, if the water level didn't reach above my shoulders. My upper body musculature was weak, but years of running and jumping during high school and in college playing soccer and volleyball strengthened my leg muscles. Near the bank, the water level appeared shallow for a good hundred feet, maybe more, but beyond that point, I couldn't tell. The river bed might drop precipitously the farther out I went, and that's where the current appeared faster. The risk of drowning was real. As a rule, water levels dropped in late summer, but a safe crossing to the other side was no certainty. Like it or not, I might have to swim, and that risked being swept downstream. Any number of things could go wrong.

Worse, even though this was August, the river was freezing cold, because it was fed by glacial runoff. Wading takes longer than swimming, and I expected to be immersed in it a half hour, and perhaps longer, even if the distance was less than estimated and the speed of the river's current less than anticipated. Once I entered it, the danger of hypothermia would increase the longer it took to reach the other side.

How long did I sit there, thinking this over? Who knows? Drinking more water, I allowed the sun to warm me, and dry my clothes. My hands still bled, but not as much as before. Once more, I checked my watch, but its digital display was gone. Dipping my hands into the river must have been too much for its circuits to bear. Looking at the sun, I noticed how close it was to the horizon, a mountain range to the west. Was it six o'clock already? Later? There was no more time to wait.

I stripped off my fleece and tied it around my neck, then loosened my shorts to make it easier to remove them if I found myself in deep water. With misgivings, I took off my boots and socks and left them on the bank. If I sank, there would be no chance to swim to shallower water wearing them. I shivered thinking about it. Heart pounding and mind racing, full of anxious thoughts, I forced myself to walk into the river.

The cold water washing over my bare feet shocked me, despite being prepared for it. Gritting my teeth, I forced one foot to follow the other. *Just keep moving.* That thought dominated my thinking. My feet sank into a soft, sandy muck at first, but after about thirty yards, I stepped on larger pebbles and smooth stones, which made footing perilous. More than once, I slipped and almost fell. I slowed my pace, searching with numbed toes for anything that might take me down. The level of the water rose sooner than expected. By the time I reached a quarter of the way across, it swirled over my waist. Up ahead, bubbling whitecaps clustered near the central pillar of the bridge that I hoped to use as a guide. Not what I wanted to see.

In my sophomore year of college, on vacation with friends in Colorado, we took a rafting trip down the Arkansas. My raft flipped over as we crossed a rough patch of foaming whitewater, and I still remembered the terror I felt when I found myself underwater. That time, wearing a life preserver, I soon bobbed to the surface, swam to the river's edge and pulled myself ashore, avoiding the worst of the rapids.

This time, I lacked that protection. I saw no other option but to head up river against the current, now running faster as I approached the middle third of the river. My goal was to avoid spots where the churning white foam looked the worst. Leaning forward, I formed my arms into a tight v-shaped wedge, hoping to create a slipstream around myself that would make my passage easier. Still, I made slow progress, zigzagging toward the far shore with every step I took. The water covered my shoulders now, and the cold force of it sapped energy from my muscles. *God*, I prayed, *please help me*. My first prayer in years.

Then, with no warning, the fleece tied around my neck ripped away. Foolishly, I reached for it and lost my balance. The full might of the river took me down then, throwing my head underwater, tossing me this way and that as it carried me along. When I breached the surface, gasping for air, my worst fears were confirmed. The river carried me straight toward the central bridge pillar and its churning mass of white foam. There was no time to avoid a collision. Seconds later, my left side slammed into it.

Wracked by sharp pains in my ribs, I couldn't breathe, the wind knocked out of me. As I struggled to take a breath, the foamy water battered me, keeping me pinned to that mass of steel and cement. I was trapped, like a fly on flypaper. Twice, the current pulled me under, only to push me back up again through no effort of my own. Each time, my back rubbed up against the concrete pillar, scraping off skin.

Time altered, speeding up and slowing down at random. *I'll die here*, I thought, and in my mind's eye, I watched as an ebony casket was lowered into my grave. Desperate, I forced a small amount of air into my lungs, enough to hold at bay an oncoming blackout, though my vision remained grainy and blurred, a million snowy particles dancing everywhere I looked. Suddenly, as if an angry river god grabbed my legs, the river sucked me down again, beneath the roiling surface into the murk below.

I lost all sense of direction, and, in that darkness, I knew not how to find my way back to air and life. Arms flailing, panic overcame me. A hand–not sure which one–hit a hard object with a curved exterior, not once, but several times. *Grab hold of it!* a voice inside my head implored me. Somehow, I wrapped my fingers around it and held on, as the current rag-dolled my body back and forth. It was a metal cable, perhaps one severed during the reconstruction work.

Through luck, my other hand also found the cable and grasped it. Together they worked to provide me a modicum of stability, making me less subject to the whims of the river. Yet I wondered what good was it to continue to hold on, for the cable also swung back and forth, dragging my knuckles through the silt and muck of the river bottom, over which it twisted and turned.

Pull yourself to shore! The same voice again, not my own, but familiar, if unrecognizable. Perhaps it was a hallucination or the last gasp of my brain as it shut down. Still, what else could I do? With all the energy left me, I pulled myself hand over hand along the cable's unknown length. The outside world no longer existed. The only sound heard, the pounding of my heart, and the only heat felt, my burning muscles and lungs and arms. Each moment was an eternity unto itself as I scuttled in the mud like some primeval creature. After an eternity, small rays of light filtered through the murk. Somehow, I reached the river's west bank and threw myself onto solid ground.

I can picture only vague fragments of my journey through those pathless woods as day turned to night. The orange and rose sunset slipped away at the exact moment I fell onto a bed of pine needles. Numb to all pain, my awareness of my surroundings sank below the horizon as well. But before exhaustion took me, I heard the voice one last time. *Child, I warned you*, it said. *Yet this day chrysanthemums shall not bloom, nor will candles float to the sea.*

Bashō? Then I blacked out.

• • • • •

In a white room, the man in black pinned me to the wall by my wrists, pressing his indistinguishable body against mine. He made no sound as he thrust something–a hand? a knee?–between my clenched legs, worked inexorably to force them apart. I screamed for him to stop, but no sound came out of the tangled pathways of my lungs. I struggled against him in that bright and terrible space, in which nothing was present other than my naked body and his dark, ambiguous form. A hard, cold erection pressed into my belly, and a shapeless mask where a face should be, glared at me. Twisting and turning to no avail, I begged God to save me from him, but in vain. A rough growl reverberated inside my head. At last, I recognized it. Someone was calling my name.

"Jane!" The same voice as before. "Jane!" It repeated, louder and louder, and each time my body slammed into the wall and a stab of pain shot through me. I couldn't breathe, I couldn't–

"Jane." A man stood over me, his gentle hand resting on my shoulder. "Wake up."

"Borges?"

"No, Borges is not here." The man removed his hand. "At least, I cannot detect his presence." A voice I could not put a name to it.

"What...?" My parched mouth struggled to get that question out.

"You were having a nightmare, Jane," he responded, "but it's over now."

"Where am I? Where is my Borges?"

"Look around."

I did as he asked. I was on a bed covered in white blankets in a dull, off white room. My head lay upon a sterile white pillow. Plastic tubing ran from a vein in my arm to an IV bag on a metal stand. A monitor with a screen beeped.

"How long?" I asked.

"Three days. You were near death after fighting the river. You remember the river?"

"Yes." How could I forget that?

"You broke half your ribs and one of your lungs collapsed."

"Are you a doctor?"

He held up a clipboard attached to the frame of my bed with a metal chain. "I read your medical chart, but I already knew how much harm you incurred. The river spirits were angry with you for defying them. You are most fortunate." Those words struck me with a flash of recognition.

"I know you, don't I?" I said. "We've met before. Who are you?"

In response, he stepped back and stood erect. As my eyes came into focus, I saw him: the same old ragged robes, the odd hat, the wrinkled visage.

"Bashō?"

"Is that a question?" he said.

"No. "It was the same person I met at the cemetery by my parents' tombstones not so long ago. Why did I not recognize him?

"A cuckoo cries from inside the bamboo thicket under a moonless sky." I sat up as he spoke his hokku until the pain in my ribs pulled me back down onto the bed.

"What are you saying? You meant that for me, didn't you?"

Bashō answered me with a question of his own. "When you went to Kamakura and saw the Daibatsu at the temple of Kōtoku-in, was that a dream?"

"I thought it was," I said, "because Borges told me so. But now I don't know. You said I went to Japan. And Borges admitted he might have been wrong." I didn't bother to add Borges confessed his doubts to me about our trip to Kamakura after killing Marty. Nor did I tell him that, according to Borges, my ability to go Elsewhere transported us to Kamakura the day we met. I assumed he already knew.

"Borges was right to call it a dream," said Bashō.

"But at the cemetery you said I went to Kamakura," I spoke through gritted teeth. "You said your obligation to help others only applied to those who visited Japan. Are you lying now or were you lying then?"

"I told the truth. Then and now."

"That's crazy. It's either one or the other. Stop fucking with me! I've been fucked with enough!" That generated a coughing fit, and for a while, all I could think about was how bad my chest hurt, and my throat hurt, and damn near everything else hurt. He remained by the bed with a serene, if sad expression on his face. Angry, I glared back at him until the fit subsided. The pain, not so much.

"Do you know the expression 'tell it slant?'" Bashō said. At that moment, I wanted to grab his skinny little neck and choke him. I flashed my best evil eye instead. "Ah," he continued, "I see you do. It comes from a poem by an American, Emily Dickinson. Number 1263. The first line goes 'Tell all the truth, but tell it slant.'"

"Sounds like an excuse to practice the fine art of bullshit." My vulgar mouth was in fine form, but this time it didn't silence him as it had at our first meeting.

"People have read that line many ways, yet they forget the rest of the poem. Here is how it ends: The Truth must dazzle gradually or every man be blind —"

"Oh well then, thanks for clearing that up," I said.

"You are angry with me, Jane-san, but know this. I do not practice to deceive."

"And I should trust you because you can quote–someone famous? Well, why the hell not? It's sure done wonders for me with Borges." But then I regretted my words, not because I didn't believe them, and not to spare Bashō's feelings, but because I still loved Borges, loved him blindly, without reason. Uttering his name was the worst pain of all, for I knew he had died, and I would never see him again.

The old man sighed. "I must go. Goodbye, Jane-san." When he reached the door, I called out to him with the most spiteful thing I could think to say.

"Walk away, then, whatever your name is, you're always walking away, aren't you?"

He stiffened, but took his time responding to my jibe. Many seconds passed before he answered. "It has been and always will be about the dreams, Jane-san. I fear you will forget much before this one ends and the next one begins." Then he vanished the way a match's flame disappears when you blow it out. It bothered me I couldn't remember who he was, when a moment before I knew his name. Then I stopped thinking and let sleep take me.

BOOK II

CHAPTER 13

The mission church was about an hour's drive south of the city. Established in the 18th century, its pews, claustrophobically close together, had been designed for shorter, thinner people than those in attendance today. Their aroma filled the nave with the scent of well-maintained oaken planks oft polished using expensive oils. Sitting in the first row, I stared at the altar without seeing it. My precious son died ten days ago at age twenty. Whatever purpose my life served died with him.

"That's a Quatrefoil Cross," my ex-brother-in-law David said. A B-list actor, he and I remained friends after his divorce from my husband's youngest sister. I allowed him and no one else to sit with me. He pointed at the altar. "Beautiful work, isn't it?" I nodded and said nothing. A black veil covered my face to hide my tears, though there were none left to be seen. The week the police took to release James' body drained me of all my tears.

Behind me sat my four sisters-in-law, along with their suspicion, jealousy and disdain. Upon his birth, my son inherited my father-in-law's estate eight months after the man I married, their only brother, died on a ledge overhanging those wicked falls in British Columbia during our honeymoon. I survived because a Japanese tourist hiking through the forest found me and carried me on his back to a ranger station. From there a helicopter took me to hospital. I knew far too well how much each of my sisters-in-law wished I also died that day, and my unborn son with me. James Lewis Borgman III, named after his father, for I could not refuse my now dead father-in-law's one request, to preserve the family name after his only son, my newlywed husband, was so cruelly taken from him.

That name, and the line it represented, now ended. My father-in-law died within a month of my son's birth from cardiac arrest–a true broken heart. With the death of my son, I was the only remaining Borgman, not that

I counted as one in the eyes of my sisters-in-law, their spouses and children, except as the unworthy inheritor of my son's trust fund.

Most everyone else in attendance had money, mostly old money. Seated in the front row, I refused to turn around. I didn't want to see their faces, nor them to see mine. They were of a piece, people who have all known each other from childhood, or who might as well have, with only a few overachieving strivers in the mix. Their pedigrees were long established, well maintained and filled with the petty evils of lives lived for no purpose other than their own selfish desires.

I wondered what they thought of the section cordoned off at the back that I reserved for the staff and residents of the homeless shelter James funded when he attained his majority, the same shelter where he volunteered all through high school. Then again, they knew nothing of him, his passion to help others and his resentment toward his family and their social circle, all of whom shunned him since he was a small boy. Was it any surprise that he saw the world in different terms than they ever would? To me, he was remarkable, but to them, he represented the cuckoo in the nest, an outlier of little note. Only after he died did I learn how much they esteemed him so. It must be true, for I saw the many television interviews they gave.

He died a hero, sacrificing himself during a mass shooting at the Great American Concert Hall, using his body to shield a girl of twelve from the rifle fire of the lone gun man. My son took her as a treat to a concert by her favorite rap artist. Now, the same girl my son saved sat in the back of the church with the rest of the shelter's representatives, sobbing. In the row behind me, my ears registered murmurs from my sisters-in-law. Were they upset with her open display of grief, or the fact she received more attention from the media than they did?

Then again, their moment to bask in the media spotlight would not have come about if the concert venue's surveillance cameras had not captured his death in all its futile glory, footage sold to one of the major networks that at last count had over sixty million views worldwide. I considered suing them for violations of my son's and my privacy, but my lawyer talked me out of it. "Why pour gasoline on a bonfire?" he said.

I turned down all requests for interviews. My lawyer released a short statement on my behalf that one of his associates drafted. It said very little, which was more than enough. I refused to feed the beast that devours the misery of others for profit. I left that role to my son's beloved aunts. They would have invited the cable networks to televise his memorial service, had I not insisted on keeping it private. Several of my "nephews and nieces" were particularly upset when they learned I banned all mobile devices and anyone attempting to sneak one past security would be denied entrance. A shame they wouldn't be able to sell their videos to the gossip sites.

Enough, I told myself. *Better not to dwell on such unpleasantness.* My mind drifted backwards in time to the day of my marriage, in a grand old San Francisco church on the last day of July 1989. I hadn't believed it possible to arrange such a large and expensive wedding so fast, but James' mother simply took over.

"My dear Jane," she said. "A shame you have no mother to help you. A tragedy she died so young. But don't worry. We'll take care of everything. And it will be fabulous!" Those weren't her exact words, but close enough. Pushed aside, she left me only the most minor of minor decisions: whether to have gilt lettering on the napkins for the reception, what sort of cake to order—though not the design—and the choice of meat or fish as the main entrée, nothing else. I didn't even choose my dress. My mother-in-law to be and her oldest daughter engaged a fashion designer they patronized to prepare a proper gown, afraid I'd choose something too gaudy if left to my own devices. In the end, they selected a Mermaid design, very restrictive and intended for a bustier woman than I. Wanting something simpler, I complained to James and suggested he have a word with his mother, but he asked to see me in it, instead.

"Isn't that bad luck to see the bride in her gown before the wedding?"

"A superstitious scientist? You can't believe that nonsense."

"No, but I was hoping you would."

He laughed, but regardless, I modeled the dress for him. "See? I don't fill it out up top, and it's way too tight elsewhere. I can barely breathe."

"But you look gorgeous!" And so I lost my chance to wear what I wanted and went with the gown his mother and sister chose. Did they wonder what James, a junior partner in his father's old-line San Francisco brokerage firm, eight years my senior, saw in me? Six months after breaking up with his former girlfriend, James presented me to his family, a ready-made bride fresh off a whirlwind romance. That girl out of some ridiculous modern day fairytale was me. In my more insecure moments, I scarcely believed it happened. How could James have fallen for me, a young woman of twenty-two, a scholarship student and recent graduate from a state university with a degree in biochemistry? Other than sex, what appeal could I have for him?

Worse, I came from a working class family. My father, a welder at GM for twenty years before he took early retirement to avoid a lay-off, raised me by himself after Mom died in a car accident when I was five. James' family told them my story, so perhaps they were willing to make some allowances, though I never got the impression that they felt the least bit of sympathy for what her loss meant to me. My father and I were not their kind of people. And then there was the unspoken issue of my half-Japanese ancestry.

My Nisei mom, a graduate teaching assistant, met my father in a remedial reading class for adults she taught to make extra money. Despite a ten year age gap and differences in educational background and life experience, they started dating. Six months later, she was pregnant with me. I was *hapa*, half Asian, half white. No one in James' West Coast, blue-blood family had ever married anyone who wasn't a WASP of the highest social standing. I often imagined they saw me as a half-breed slut who caught James on the rebound, looking to marry into money. Even their compliments damned me with faint praise. To them, I was no different from a mail-order bride, a stopgap measure until someone more suitable came along. They offered me their pity, but I was never liked, much less loved.

My father arrived the day before the wedding. James put him up at the Fairmont Hotel in downtown San Francisco. The hotel's Grand Ballroom was reserved for our reception. James and I also had rooms at the Fairmont. Our reservations lasted until the day after the wedding, before we flew to Vancouver on our fateful honeymoon.

When Dad first laid eyes on James and his family, his expression was telling. My father wore jeans and an old golf shirt, which revealed the tattoos on his arms from his days in Vietnam. That stood in stark contrast to James and his father, decked out in their expensive Italian suits, having just come from a business meeting. James and his father both shook Dad's hand, but James' mother and sisters did not hide their disgust at his appearance. They nodded at him when introduced, but no one said a word of welcome. James Dad hired two limousines to bring everyone to the Fairmont for the rehearsal dinner, one for Jame's parents and sisters, and one for Dad, James and me. James made small talk. My father said as little as possible.

Dinner started right at seven. I had to convince Dad not to order the cheapest item on the menu, a $20 hamburger. While everyone else drank champagne, he sipped a Bud Lite. His reticence in conversation surprised me. This was my father, a tough guy with a mustache running down the sides of his mouth where it met up with his sideburns to form one continuous rope of bristling hair. The man who shaved his head because he thought it made him look badass when riding his Harley chopper with his biker buddies, though he didn't need to. Two tours in Vietnam as a helicopter pilot, earning two purple hearts, was badass enough. On his last combat mission, his left foot ripped apart from gunfire, the field doctors amputated. Despite the prosthesis paid for by the V.A., he never lost his limp.

Later that evening, he raided the mini-bar in his room, drank Jack Daniels from little bottles with me, and asked if I knew what the hell I was getting myself into. "I watched your boyfriend's family," he said. "Don't like a one of them. They don't come out and say so, but they don't give a rat's ass about you."

"They've always treated me–with respect," I told him. "What's it matter, anyway? I'm marrying James, not his parents."

"The world don't work that way," he shot back. "That boy may be crazy for you now, but what about a few years from now when you two hit a rough patch–trust me, it'll happen–and his folks let him know they'd prefer someone else as their grandkids' mother?"

"I know what I'm doing, Dad. James loves me and I love him. Didn't you always tell me that was the only thing that mattered? You and Mom were pretty different, and you managed."

"Don't bring your mother into this!" he snarled. Acidly, I reminded him Grandpa Takashima hadn't been too keen on the punk dropout biker kid who knocked up his daughter. That's when he slapped me, which ended further discussion. I didn't see him again until next day, when, stuffed into a tux, he held my arm just before our walk down the aisle.

"You still goin' through with it?" he muttered, closemouthed.

"Why? You think you can stop me?"

Looking much older than his years, he sighed. "You always were a stubborn little thing."

"I had a good teacher," I whispered back as Mendelssohn's Wedding March began to play. Together, stiff and slow, we strode down the aisle, smiling for the cameras.

Later, at the reception, he drank far too much. Raw emotions exposed for all to see, he gave a meandering, blubbery toast from the head table, interrupted often by outright weeping. I never remembered seeing him so upset, not even after Mom died. At her burial, he stood like a stoic, holding my hand while I hugged my favorite teddy bear, trying to match his granite-like demeanor. Yet at the reception, he was inconsolable. The inarticulate sadness of his ramble shook me. James' family endured his speech with pinched expressions on their faces. Later, when he stumbled and fell during the traditional father-daughter dance, James' mother flat out declared it would be best if I took him to his room to "recover his faculties." When I said he was fine, the sharp teeth came out.

"Jane–dear–your father is making a spectacle of himself. Is this how you want your wedding remembered? This is an important celebration, not a cheap Irish wake."

"Just leave him be," I said, gritting my teeth. "I'll look after him."

"It's well past that point, dear. You are the bride. You have responsibilities to your other guests. You're an adult now. Act like one."

Furious, I wanted to claw her eyes out, but did my best to ignore her bigotry. "He's my dad. My mom died when he was thirty. He raised me by himself. I'm all he has, and this is *my* wedding day. He stays."

Turning my back on her, I went over to my father. We held hands and talked, not about anything in particular, until he cheered up a bit. Out of the corner of my eye, I saw James talking to his parents. They looked irritated to the nth degree. I never learned what he said, but it must have smoothed things over. After he regained his composure, my father wandered over to the open bar. There he chatted up the bartenders and catering staff. I don't think he spoke to anyone else the rest of the night. I was not so lucky. James shepherded me from table to table, introducing me to assorted family friends, distant relations and business clients. He said not to worry, that he could handle his family, so I pretended I didn't have a care in the world. How little we understood each other. How right my father was to mourn the loss of his daughter.

• • • • •

David tapped my shoulder. "Jane," he whispered, "it's time," pointing at the string quartet. I nodded, and he gave them the sign to play Samuel Barber's "Adagio for Strings," my son's favorite classical work. As the music played, the mob in the pews hushed themselves, all but the girl my son gave his life for, though even she did her best to quiet herself. For one moment, I relented and looked over my shoulder in her direction, but I couldn't pick her out from among so many unfamiliar faces. Instead, my eyes were drawn to a dark-haired man, dressed all in black–coat, pants, shirt, shoes–standing at the rear, his face hidden from me by the broad-brimmed hat he wore. I spun around back to face the altar. The image I glimpsed was too unsettling. It reminded me of another man in black.

Each night since my son's death, my old nightmares returned, the ones I thought two years of therapy with a trauma specialist and antidepressant medications eradicated. Nightmares that began a week after my husband died, and which haunted my dreams for over a decade. None of them followed the same script, but in each one, I confronted a faceless, featureless shape-shifting black figure. The dreams began harmlessly enough, but inevitably, things would go terribly wrong. I experienced fear and dread beyond words, snared by an overwhelming evil. This black figure often raped and assaulted me. My pain and terror was so vivid, I believed it real. The worst were those times he strangled me, and I couldn't breathe. After each one, I awakened just before sunrise, terrified and exhausted, curled around my pillows and blankets, whimpering like a small child.

But the stranger dressed in black at my son's funeral was no dream. The string quartet finished the Adagio. Gathering my courage, I risked another look to the back wall of the sanctuary to see if he was still there, but, like a ghost, he disappeared. I twisted back, my body shaking.

"Are you all right?" said David. "I can give the eulogy if–."

"I'm fine," I replied. "I give the eulogy, no one else. You understand? Man in black or no, I will speak for my son." David appeared confused, but knew better than to argue with me. The priest stepped forward and opened the service with a prayer to which I struggled to listen, still afraid of a nameless terror lurking just out of sight.

CHAPTER 14

Gripping the sides of the pulpit, I gathered myself. Tears ran down my cheeks, but I brushed them away. *Almost over,* I thought. Picking the portable microphone out of its holder, I forced myself to exit the pulpit and down onto the steps leading to the altar.

"I know I've gone on about my son, James, and how wonderful he was, and I wouldn't blame you if you thought, well, what mother wouldn't brag on her son, especially one who died so young, and so tragically. A young man called a hero by many, even some of you here today. I wouldn't blame you for that, for thinking it must be easy to praise him, though it isn't easy at all. Not for this mother. I will always remember him, and miss him, long after the rest of the world has moved on from the atrocity that captured the world's attention."

I signaled David, and he made a motion to the ushers in the back of the church. They opened the closed doors, and in came the CNN cameramen, two of them, picked at large from the pool of reporters to cover James' service. Those in the pews looked shocked as they whispered at this development. TV cameras were not what they expected.

"Forgive me," I continued, drawing their attention back to me, "but I have asked the media to come in for the last part of my eulogy, because I do not want my James forgotten. There is so much more to his story than the fact that he gave his life to save a young homeless woman. And to help me explain what I mean, I ask that young woman, who is here today, to help me. Shemeeka Johnson, please come forward."

As the cameramen focused on her stick thin figure, I took a deep breath. Shemeeka's tears ran freely, but as she made her way to me, I saw pride in her eyes. Setting the mike down, I gave her a big hug. "I'm so proud of you, dear," I whispered. "James would be too. Let's do this, shall we?" She nodded, wiping tears away from her cheeks as I picked the mike up off the step.

"Shemeeka, I'm grateful you came today. Many, many people have asked you over the past week what James meant to you, and I don't want to rehash everything, but I wonder if you can answer a few questions for me."

She nodded again. "Yes'm, Miz Borgman."

"Please, call me Jane, dear," I said, smiling at her. She smiled back with a knowing glance.

"Yes'm, Jane."

"Shemeeka, what did you think about my son James, before–" I choked up and stopped myself before continuing. "Before that day."

"That he wuz my friend."

"But you knew he volunteered at the homeless shelter where you stayed, right?"

"Yes'm, I knew. But James, he wuz different than the others who come round to help."

"How so?"

"He wuz there every day, for one. And he weren't like the others. James didn't try to cheer no one up if they was sad, or talk jes to be talking, jes to cover up their sadness. He listened and if we wuz sad, he let us be sad. He paid attention to us is what I mean. Made me feel that we wuz equals. James didn't talk about himself much, he mostly asked about us, listened to our stories, done all the little stuff other people never thought about. I never known no white man like that before. He made sure he knew the kids that had no mom or pops, cuz as he told me, he didn't have no pops himself. That's how we became friends, him asking about me. He could tell who was the loneliest and would go to them, the ones like me, cuz we had no one. He made it–I'm sorry, but I can't think of the right word–but you know, he–he wuz there for us, for me. He wuz the best friend I ever had."

"Did you have any idea that James was wealthy, Shemeeka? That he funded the shelter where you live?"

"No'm. Least ways, not 'til after, 'til after..." She looked at me and shook her head, unable to continue.

"It's okay, Shemeeka, we know what day you mean. So, what did you know about him?"

"Jes that he wuz kind. He wuz always doing little things for us that the others there, and I don't want to badmouth nobody, but that the others forgot or didn't think to ask. Things like remembering our birthdays, or if we had someone in prison, a brother or mom or pops and needed to see them, that kinda thing, He never forgot us and always did whatever we most needed done to make things a little easier. He made us feel someone cared. Though, I wuz his favorite." She paused. "Course, I guess lotsa kids felt the same way. He had that effect on you. Like, when he wuz with you, you wuz the only one that mattered to him in the whole world."

"Thank you, Shemeeka," I said, squeezing her shoulder, pulling her to me. "Yes, James didn't make a big fuss about himself, did he?" She nodded and we exchanged looks again. "But what he didn't tell you, and what I expect few people know, even many here in this church today, was that he wasn't just a volunteer helping a few kids, and he wasn't just a rich man's son, who spent part of his trust fund as a do-gooder helping kids and families in need. He was much more than that."

"He wuz the world to me, Jane. I'll never forget him."

"Yes, Shemeeka. No one should forget him or the life he led in service to the most vulnerable. That is why today, I'm announcing to the world that, before he died, James created a foundation to help people, like you, Shemeeka, thousands and thousands of people, not only here in the Bay area, but across the country, who have lost their homes or their families, people our society has abandoned. Its name is the 'Do Unto Others Foundation,' or DUO for short, and in the days before his death, he transferred over $20 Million dollars from his trust fund to set it up." A loud, audible gasp came from those sitting in the pews, the loudest from my sisters-in-law who looked aghast at this turn of events.

"Its mission?" I continued when people quieted. "To reach out to every community in America to assist existing shelters for the homeless, for battered women, for runaway or exploited children, and establish new ones. In fact, DUO is already in discussion with the Mayors of San Francisco, Oakland and Berkeley to expand and enhance services for the homeless in the Bay area. I am one of DUO's trustees, and I'm honored to tell everyone that Shemeeka agreed yesterday to serve as DUO's honorary chairperson and be its public face going forward. Thank you so much Shemeeka."

A lone man in the back began to clap, and then a few more. I raised my hands to encourage more, and whether they wanted to or not, more people stood and applauded, until even my sisters-in-law, with their TV smiles, stood and clapped. They knew the cameras were recording them live. As the applause died down, I spoke into the mike again.

"James intended to make DUO his lifework and to endow it with his own funds, but he didn't anticipate his sudden death, or he would have re-written his will. His lawyer advised me a few days ago that, aside from bequests to a select group of family and friends, he left the bulk of his estate to me.

"I knew my son. This would not be what he would have wanted, nor is it what I want. James' father, upon his untimely death, left me more than enough to meet my needs. So yesterday, I signed papers transferring all my interests in my son's estate to the Do Unto Others Foundation. Also, as of today, I'm stepping down from the foundation's board, to avoid any conflict of interest. The world may see James as a hero for the way he died, but he deserves to be remembered for how he lived and for his desire to help others. I urge everyone watching, whether here in this beautiful Mission church, on television or online, to please donate to the Do Unto Others Foundation in memory of my son, James Borgman. Thank you all for coming to honor and celebrate James' life, but also, and this is my most sincere desire, to establish DUO as his legacy going forward."

I squeezed Shemeeka's shoulder one more time and whispered in her ear. "Remember, you'll always have a home with me." David signaled the string quartet to play, before escorting Shemeeka and me to our seats in the front pew, where we clung to one another, waiting for the service to end.

• • • • •

Back home, I sat with feet tucked underneath me on a loveseat, lazily swinging back and forth from hooks attached to my gazebo's canopy. The gazebo served as the centerpiece of an English-style hedge maze constructed on our property, a present for my son's tenth birthday. James fell in love with mazes after we watched the film *Orlando* together. The scene where Tilda Swinton, playing the main character, runs through a garden maze as an eighteenth century lady, only to be transformed halfway through into her nineteenth century self, fascinated him.

The hedge maze became his favorite place, and he often went there whenever he was upset or wanted solitude. I interred his ashes underneath the precise center of the maze alone by myself. The family demanded a formal burial next to his father and grandfather, but I refused, despite all the pressure put on me. It would "comfort you in your time of grief," they said, but I knew better. They would ruin the moment–a mother's last chance to be alone with her only child. I did not care what the press might say or what the family wanted. None of them cared a damn for my son while he lived. Why should they be there at the final moment marking his death?

"You carried it off very well." A strange voice startled me. I jumped off the loveseat and looked wildly about until I spotted him, the man dressed in black from the church, standing where the maze ended by the gazebo. This time I could see his face, his dark hair mixed with traces of gray. Something about him looked familiar.

"Who are you? How did you get in here?"

"You delivered a splendid eulogy," he said without answering my question. "I especially liked when you dragged that poor girl up to the front of the church to stand by your side. A nice touch, too, announcing your son's entire estate will go to his foundation. Makes any attempt to contest his will look petty and mean-spirited." He moved toward me and I fumbled for the large unicorn charm on a chain around my neck.

"Stop!" I shouted in a shrill voice. I held the charm at eye level so he could see it. "This contains a panic button. Come any closer and I push it. A security detail will respond in seconds. I promise they will not treat you well."

"You mean the security detail that allowed me to enter unnoticed?" His mocking tone sent shivers through my spine. "I would not bother calling them if I were you. If I wanted you dead, I would have done it by now."

I pushed the button as he casually approached me. At the gazebo's lower steps, he stopped and cocked his head, as if listening for the sound of the guards, before emitting a sinister laugh. Backing away, I continued pushing the button on the underside of the charm. *Where the hell are they?*

"Perhaps they're on their lunch break," he joked, though I wasn't laughing. Then, seeing my face, he changed his tone. "Ah, my poor Jane. You don't recognize me. I hoped you would, but no such luck."

Now he blocked my only exit. A cedar trellis enclosed the gazebo's deck on all sides except for the short flight of stairs where he stood. The trellis, at three and a half feet tall, rose above my waist. I could climb over it, but the deck was a good two feet above ground, making for a drop of five feet to a Japanese rock garden, which encircled the gazebo's perimeter. Jump and I could easily break a leg or sprain an ankle. Even if I avoided injury, I doubted I could escape him.

"Jane, please don't consider it. A woman of your age, well, your bones are not as strong as they used to be, *n'est-ce pas?* I'd hate to see you hurt yourself."

Is he reading my mind? Then again, it wouldn't be that difficult to recognize my only escape option. "What do you want?"

"I mean you any harm, Jane. Truly."

"Why should I trust you? You said you could kill me if you wanted. And stop calling me Jane!"

"Yes, a poor decision to speak of murder. But we know each other so well. A pity you don't remember me." A hint of sadness crept into his voice, which I found even more disconcerting than his earlier laughter.

"Who are you?" Stalling for time, I tried to imagine any other way I might call for help, but my nearest neighbor lived a good half mile away, and my cell phone rested in my purse, inside the house where I intentionally abandoned it so no one could disturb me as I placed my son's ashes in the ground.

"Who am I? We must begin again with introductions?" He mounted the first row of steps up to the deck. I froze. Before I could move, he was right next to me. When he raised his hand, I closed my eyes, fearing the worst. What happened next was impossible, yet it happened nonetheless. His hand whisked the hair away from my face, and all my forgotten memories returned.

Opening my eyes, I recognized him, as tears clouded his eyes. The man I saw at my son's funeral wasn't the man in black of my dreams at all. He was my Borges. The two of us fell into each other's arms and held one another in a mixture of grief and joy and a thousand other feelings that coursed through our bodies, or at least through mine.

• • • • •

Sitting on a stool with his elbows leaning on my kitchen's island, Borges sipped the tea I made for him. His appearance wasn't that different, but he looked older, with gray hair creeping up his temples. Unlike me, he chose not to dye it. Our left hands touched one another across the cool granite countertop, and stayed that way, the only sound the clink of our teacups on their saucers.

"Thank you, Jane," he said, putting his cup down. "That was perfection." He squeezed my hand, and my chest filled with the warmth that only love provides.

"How did you survive?" It was the question I wanted to ask since my memories of him returned. "When I left you on that ledge with your broken leg, I feared the worst."

"It wasn't me," he replied. "I awoke that morning in the tent to find you gone. Just you, not your gear. I thought you went off to–"

"But I saw your fall. You ordered me to get help. I forded a river for you." I stopped when he shook his head.

"Whatever you remember, it wasn't me you tried to rescue." He glanced down at the floor, pausing as he so often did whenever he needed to collect his thoughts. "I looked everywhere for you. For two days, I searched, but found nothing; no footprints, no trail to follow. Only later did it dawn on me. You went Elsewhere, Jane. It must have happened while you dreamed during our last night together in our tent."

Confused by his story even though it seemed plausible, I shook my head, thinking I should distrust him, that he was hiding something from me, though I lacked any proof that he was lying. "So why are you here? Why are you not in–"

"The world you left behind?"

"Yes."

"That's what's so strange. You left, yet also brought me with you to this– this new world. At the Park Information Center, I bought a *New York Times* in the gift shop. The date on the masthead was September 4th–of 1989. The big story on its front page was about a Russian passenger jet that crashed in Havana, killing nearly 200 people. When I informed the Park Rangers and RCMP you were missing, they said they had no record of anyone with the name listed on your forged passport. Only my name was in their records. That's when I knew for certain."

"But how...?" I couldn't finish, because I didn't know what to ask.

"How did I know you and I were in the same Elsewhere? I didn't, but I believed that was what must have happened because of my mother. You remember I told you she shared your-gift. Once, she used her power to flee from a man. She never told me why she felt the need, yet the same thing happened to her that happened to you. Like me, he tracked her down."

"You've been looking for me for the last twenty years?" Inconceivable was the word that came to mind, yet I couldn't deny my own eyes. Here was my Borges, sitting in my kitchen, after I spent half a lifetime as a wealthy widow, and now the bereaved mother of a dead son.

"Yes," Borges answered. "Three times, I nearly gave up, but always started over. I chose you. Remember?"

I nodded. Yes, I remembered the day we met, when I had a seizure at Loring Park in downtown Minneapolis, and a homeless man named Jorge Luis Borges saved my life. I remembered meeting him again at his antique store, where my boss, the now deceased Marty Schneider, sent me to pick out an anniversary present for his wife. Though, was Marty still dead in this new world that I-created? And was there another younger me and another Borges in this reality? Just imagining the possibilities were dizzying.

"No, there's no other you or me roaming around; no risk we'll run into doppelgangers of ourselves," Borges said, again rattling me with his knowledge of my thoughts. "I put that same question to my mother once. When you go Elsewhere, you do not go to a place where another you already exists. Mother would know. She used her gift multiple times in her life. Do a search for yourself under your previous name. There's no other Jane Takako Wolfsheim here."

"No," I said. "I believe you." Whatever my ability did, it wasn't time travel. Back in my former reality, Barack Obama was President. In this one, President McCain defeated President Kerry the year before, after the economy collapsed. My son and I were lucky. At the advice of our financial advisors, we pulled all our money out of stocks before the great bull market collapsed in 2008. His aunts lost half their investments, another reason they hated us so much.

"We must go back," Borges said, interrupting my train of thought, "to the time and place we first met. Here. Look at this." He gave me his iPhone. It was open to a breaking news story. "Israel Bombs Iran's Nuclear Facilities With U.S. Help," read the headline. The war everyone feared was about to come to pass.

"I never want to see that ledge with you, or whoever it was, on it again," I replied.

"We won't go there, just to the campsite and our tent the night before," he answered me. "But this world is about to tear itself apart. We're in great danger."

"All right. But promise we'll be okay." To that, he nodded. Then a question popped into my head. "What did your mother do after the man she ran from found her?"

"She killed him," Borges answered, "because he murdered her daughter."

CHAPTER 15

Borges looked at me and I looked at him. I couldn't take a breath. All the fear and mistrust of this man that my love suppressed came rushing back.

"The answer is no," Borges said.

After a moment, I regained my composure. "And what is the question?"

"Did I murder your son?" he replied. "No, make that did I murder our son?"

Why would he deny murdering my son? And then I remembered Marty Schneider.

"What do you mean, our son? He is-was mine. What right do you have to claim him?"

"Because he was my son, too, Jane." Borges' eyes shifted to the floor beneath his feet. "Think," he added. "Do you even remember your husband?"

A strange question, I thought. "Of course I do. I mourn him every day." *Every damn day.*

"Tell me about him. What kind of lover was he?"

"I-he was..." I stopped, unable to bring him back to life. He was a-a tender lover. Passionate, but-tender." These were lies, for I recalled nothing about our lovemaking, either before or after our marriage. His face, the color of his eyes, any feature of his, all were vague and mysterious, as if he never existed. *Why can't I remember his touch or his scent, something? My son is always present, even when I wish he wasn't. Why not James? What's wrong?*

"You don't remember much," Borges said. "Yet you remembered leaving me behind on a ledge overlooking Devil's Falls and then crossing a treacherous river on my behalf, in a desperate attempt that almost cost you your life. Am I right?"

"Yes."

"And what do you remember of the day before we parted? Anything specific come to mind."

"Stop! Just stop." I wanted to cry then, but held back my tears. They would do me no good. At last, I said, "We had sex. Are you happy now?"

"Where?" Borges asked, relentless as always. "When?"

I gritted my teeth, but told him what he wanted to hear, that yes, I remembered it very well. Standing me up against that tree, taking me from behind, my shorts draped down around my feet. Every detail was as clear as the day it happened, over twenty years ago. How was that possible when I the man I married remained a blank to me? I glanced at Borges, expecting to see vindication, but a deep sadness played across his features. When his eyes met mine, his sorrow pinned me in place as if it were an arrow and I its target.

"That was the day he was conceived," Borges said in a lifeless tone. "Our son, the one I never knew about until the day he died." Then he cried, turning away to hide the pain, and I did nothing but watch, helpless. In that moment, I believed him. No one could feel such grief over a person he murdered. Not even Borges.

• • • • •

Awakening to moonlight shining through the blinds, I reached out to ensure Borges was still with me, but a soft snore confirmed his presence before my fingers did. Somewhere, distant sirens sounded, drowning out for a time the low hissing noise of the Jerusalem crickets outside. The image of my son's dead body came to me unbidden. Both the one where he lay in his own blood that the cable networks had repeatedly broadcast, and the one of him on the slab at the morgue, body riddled with the exit wounds created by the nine bullets that killed him. I cried in silence. Easing out of bed, I went to the window and stared at the moon in the western sky.

Borges and I had fierce sex all afternoon and into the evening, and each time he climaxed, he clutched me to him as his body heaved with great sobs. The last time, as I lay atop him, his arms around my back gripped me so tight, I couldn't breathe. In all the times we'd made love before, I never saw him so full of desire and sadness and anger. I felt the same. My son still dominated my thoughts, and Borges' grief intensified mine. Our passion was the battlefield on which it played out.

When we were both done, the two of us lay facing each other, side by side. His fingertips traced the outlines of my naked body. When he cupped my left breast in his hand, I grabbed his wrist. "They're not as firm as they used to be, are they?" I said. "I've grown old."

He made no reply as he gently extricated his hand from my grasp and resumed tracing my skin, now lower down over the curves of my hip, pausing at the spot where the bone presented itself. "Bodies tell their own stories," he said. "Ours haven't spoken to one another in a long time." We lay together on the bed as the sun set, and neither of us moved away from the other. He asked me question after question about our son. What had he been like as a toddler, a pre-schooler, a kindergartener? It was hard to endure his incessant questions for he was that parched man who walks out of a desert and cannot stop drinking water, unable to slake a terrible thirst. I did the best I could, telling him stories of my son's life until the day a madman's gun stole him from me, at which point words failed me. Borges wanted more, wanted what I could not give him: the twenty years of our son's life forever lost to him. His sunken eyes were straight out of a painting by Goya. After talking so long, my emotions left me stripped to the bone. I yawned. Heartsick, I needed rest. But Borges panicked each time my eyelids shut.

"Not yet," he begged. "Please, not yet. What if you dream and leave me again?" It was a question for which I had no answer. For the first time, I got a hint of the boy he must have once been, afraid of nightmares, wanting reassurances only a mother could provide. This went on until Borges could no longer keep himself awake. Lying on his back, he slept, motionless, except for the slow rising and lowering of his chest. Only then could I close my own eyes and forget the world existed.

Now, awake again, I looked through the bedroom window at the shimmering lights of the city below. Chilled, I found my silk robe. Putting it on, I tied the sash around my waist after ensuring it covered me up to my neck. I crossed my arms, pushing my breasts together. *Such a day and a night*, I thought.

Borges made a noise. Looking at the bed, I noticed he shifted position, now resting on his side. I gazed on him with pity. His fear that I would go Elsewhere without him, I knew to be groundless. Nothing justified my belief. I simply took it as an article of faith we had a bond neither of us could escape. Our fates would remain entangled for whatever time was left us.

For better or worse. Isn't that the vow? Somewhere along the line, we must have tacitly made one. For when I tried to leave him behind in the mountains of British Columbia, he still followed me to my new reality. Perhaps my unconscious threw him a lifeline. I glanced at the not-quite-full moon, seeing and not seeing its slow movement, traversing the slate blue sky above the city, waiting for dawn.

"You didn't leave."

His voice by my ear, and his hand on my shoulder, startled me. Reeling me into him, he held my head against his chest. The scent of dried sweat, his and mine, was everywhere. "Did you think I would?"

"Yes," he said, his voice quivering.

"But here I am."

"I can't quite believe it."

"Believe." He squeezed my arm hard, a token of his anxiety.

"We must go soon."

"Hush. Let's not talk of it now. Look up there. Isn't the moon beautiful?"

"Yes," he said hoarsely. "It is."

"Our son loved watching the night sky. Many nights he used his telescope to pick out the brightest objects. Planets, stars, comets, meteor showers, but he always returned to the moon."

"Then we must watch this one for him."

We stayed like that until the sky grew lighter and the stars disappeared. I led him back to bed then and we spooned until, in mutual exhaustion, sleep took us again.

• • • • •

"Hypnosis?" I said. "That's your plan? To put me under and make me dream us back to where we first met?" I took a bite of sushi, waiting for his reply.

"Not hypnosis, *per se*, my love. What I propose is more akin to a guided meditation. Have you heard of it?"

I'd more than heard of it, having spent a semester in college learning to lead them. As part of the course, we underwent several directed by our instructor, and acted as practice subjects for our classmates. What Borges proposed seemed far more ambitious. The recreation of an entire world, even one I knew well, seemed a monumental task.

"I understand your concerns," he said, surprising me again with his uncanny ability to know what was on my mind. "But I won't merely guide you step by step into a dream to take us there. You'll be an active participant, not a passive subject."

"But you spoke of an enchantment," I said. "A trance-like state."

"No, no, no!" he said, loud enough for heads at nearby tables to perk up. "It's not like that." In frustration, he grabbed his leather coat and slid out of the booth.

"Where are you going?"

"To smoke a cigarette and give you more time to think it over." In one seamless motion, he shrugged his coat over his shoulder, slipped his arms inside, and then lifted a pack of Camels from his side pocket. "See you in a bit." He walked off, never once looking back though I stared at him all the way to the exit.

"I can clear those plates if you're finished, ma'am."

Our server, a tall blonde girl, her hair pulled back into a high, sweeping ponytail held in place by a red headband, pointed to the leftovers on my plate; two half-eaten California rolls, some slices of pickled ginger and a glob of musabi. I ate four pieces of maguro, and two ebi, before my appetite waned. The food wasn't great, but then what can you expect from a diner that offered King Crab Legs–Borges' order– as their lunch special? *Only in San Francisco*, I thought. "By all means," I said.

"And the gentleman's?" she enquired with that same cheery, yet indifferent tone that everyone who worked at this place seemed to have mastered. "I can bring a box to take home if you like."

"Not yet. He stepped outside for a smoke. I'd rather he make that call." Bending down for my plates, I noticed a necklace hanging from her neck with a strange golden pendant. An ancient thing, dangling on a silver chain, flashing in the sunlight. It reminded me of an animal, but so stylized I couldn't tell which one. "What's that around your neck?" I asked? "I've seen nothing like it before."

"Just an old family heirloom," she said. "It's an amulet. Supposed to be a horse. My Norwegian grandmother gave it to me to protect me." She laughed. "Not sure what it protects me from, but I've been wearing it since I was a little girl."

"It's stunning," I said. "Never would have guessed it was a horse. How old is it, if you don't mind my asking?"

"No idea," she was her blithe reply. She stood, plates balanced precisely on one arm. "Is there anything else I can get you while you wait?"

"No thank-you. Just bring the check any time." She nodded and disappeared like a magician's assistant ducking down into an empty case. I didn't bother figuring out the trick.

"A frog drowses–the sun-warmed pool slowly cooks it into silence."

"Bashô?" From nowhere, he appeared across from me.

"You should lower your voice, Jane-san. The others here..." he waved his arm in a wide arc, "cannot see me, remember?"

"Where have you been all this time?" I asked in a near whisper, covering my mouth with my hand, a habit I picked up from my Japanese mother. "Why did you abandon me?"

"I never left, Jane-san. You simply forgot I was with you. I enjoyed tending your gardens."

"You were my gardener?" I couldn't believe it. *Mr. Kasahara? That old fossil?*

"You saw what your mind allowed you to see, Jane-san, in this your most expansive dream yet."

"So, how are you–how did you get here?"

"We are connected." That was it, nothing more. Enigmatic as always.

"So it seems. Just like Borges and I."

Bashô shook his head. "Not the same. The difference lies in who tied the knot."

"Do you ever speak plainly?" I whispered, irritated.

"I speak as I am capable of speaking," he answered. "Yet what I say is plain enough if you examine my words and to whom I speak them." Then understanding came, like an unanticipated guest. The focal point for everything he said was me. Viewed in that context, my goal was to derive meaning from them.

"So, I'm the frog that drowses. And that makes Borges the sun-warmed pool, I suppose." The barest hint of a smile creased Bashô's face, the only confirmation he gave. But it was enough. Now many things Borges spoke about as we ate our delayed breakfast made sense. The desire to depart this awful place where our son died, I shared. His "escape plan" required the use of my ability to dream us away from here, but why must it occur under his influence? He needed control over me, but I harbored a measure of skepticism, despite my urge to trust him, which clouded my reason whenever he spoke. Bashô intended his words as a warning regarding my Borges. Yet, though every rational bone in my body screamed at me to abandon Borges first chance I got, I hesitated to follow Bashô's advice because of my love for him.

"Does Borges love me back?" I asked.

"Only he can tell you that, and only you can decide whether he is telling the truth."

I bit the underside of my lip. *Thanks for nothing, Captain Obvious.* "Fine," I continued, "then why am I so important to him?"

"He's told you, many times."

"He hasn't told me shit," I muttered.

"There is a French expression that fits here," said Bashô. "I believe it is '*Au contraire, mon ami.*'"

"Au contraire what? Just tell me straight for once."

"As you wish, Jane-san. He told you he chose you the second time you met face-to-face at his shop, did he not? He deliberately tied you to him by saving your life. And later, he said that he had been looking for someone with your... *powers,* let us call them, his entire life, a woman like his mother."

"But why does he need someone like me?"

"Why do you think?"

"No idea."

"You would if you considered everything you've learned about your Borges."

My reaction to that comment was to sit up straight and bang my head on the bronze railing above the padded seat back, which elicited a sharp pain. When did I ever speak the term "my Borges" in Bashô's presence? How much this self-described yōkai knew about me was disconcerting. "Like what?" I said, rubbing my head.

"You are a movie fan, are you not?" This was not the answer I expected, but Bashô was either incapable or unwilling to give me a straight answer. Tell it slant, indeed.

"Yes. What of it?"

"You know the famous film *Gaslight* starring Ingrid Bergman and Charles Boyer?"

"Nope. What's it about?"

"Manipulation." Then he vanished as if he'd never been there, as Borges slid into the now empty seat across from me.

"You look like you've seen a ghost." When I didn't respond, he added, "Sorry to spook you. So, have you given my idea any more thought? We're running out of time." He shoved a copy of *The San Francisco Chronicle* at me, which he must have picked up at a newsstand. The headline blared in 36-point print, *IRAN SINKS AMERICAN CARRIER USS ENTERPRISE—PRESIDENT MCCAIN VOWS RETALIATION*. "It will accelerate now," Borges said, but all I could think about was Bashô's last word, "manipulation," intended as both a clue and a warning. Yet how could Borges manipulate events in this world I created? It made no sense. What could Bashô have meant?

"Let's go to my home," I said. "We'll figure it out there." *I must learn more about this movie, Gaslight.*

"Things are spiraling out of control very quickly, Jane. We have no time for careful deliberations." He got out of the booth and reached for my hand to pull me out, too.

"We haven't paid the bill," I protested. But Borges simply took out his wallet and tossed a $100 bill on the table.

"I'm sure that will cover it," he said with a grim expression.

"I still want to go to my home."

"As you wish."

As we approached my car, I felt a sharp prick in my neck. Spinning my head around, I saw Borges place a syringe in his pocket. The ground shifted beneath my feet and the sky began to spin around my head. "What did you do?" I said, slurring my words. When he didn't answer, I choked out a garbled, "Why...?"

"Sorry, but you left me no choice."

An array of stray colors and shapes swirled round my head, like the afterimages a flashbulb leaves behind, before darkness descended.

CHAPTER 16

The dream disturbed and confused me. Fires and storms appeared, great walls crumbled, and I saw a shattered and broken Daibutsu toppled from its pedestal, lying face down on the dead earth under a tumultuous sky. Sulfurous fumes filled the air, and I tasted copper on my tongue. It was the Book of Revelation come to life, monstrous and sickening.

Orange colors danced before they took the shape of flames. Now awake, on a cot near a small brazier, reality returned. Some smoke drifted near me, but most escaped through a vent hole in the ceiling above. I tried to sit up, but my head exploded, a raw blast of lightning that illuminated the inside of my skull, and brought searing pain. Groaning, my head dropped onto a folded blanket that served as a pillow. Only then did I hear voices. The words were familiar, a Japanese dialect, but one mangled and mixed with foreign words–English, Chinese, some Russian–so I understood about half what was said. Not that I cared. My head kept reminding me just how much agony a human being can endure. A cool hand reached down and covered my eyes. The throbbing aftershocks resounding throughout my head subsided as if a miracle worker touched me. A gentle voice cooed me back to sleep.

The second time I woke to the sound of rain. Dim light suffused the open space around me. A thin, steady stream of water fell from a hole in the ceiling. Large wooden troughs placed under the ceiling vent captured most of it.

"Good morning." An old white woman, with sharp features and skin like porcelain, greeted me. She stood overhead for a short while before kneeling to grab my wrist. It took a moment for me to realize she was taking my pulse. Staring at an old windup wristwatch, her lips soundlessly counted out the beats of my heart. When I tried to say something, she shushed me. "Let me complete my examination, dear," she said, taking a stethoscope around her neck and placing its rubber tips in her ears. "This won't take long. After that, we'll talk, if you feel up to it."

• • • • •

"You've had a rough time," the old woman said, "but you'll recover. You're young, after all. That never hurts." She rose and stood over me, her well-wrinkled face framed by pure white hair. Her stone blue eyes, with a hit of cornflower yellow around the inside of her irises, looked down at me, a poker face that gave nothing away.

"Where...?" I croaked out before my voice failed me.

"I wouldn't try that again if I were you, not until we can get you rehydrated." She snapped her fingers and instantly, a small Japanese girl appeared with a round ceramic flask. The white-haired woman spoke to her in the pidgin Japanese I'd been hearing. I understood enough to know she ordered the girl to lift my head 'yukkuri to shizukani'–gently and slowly–so I could drink. She dribbled a small amount of water into my mouth until I choked. My dry throat made swallowing difficult. Over the next few minutes, the old woman and her young assistant offered me sips of water until I feebly waved my arm at them to stop because I felt nauseated.

"*Kono mizu wa anzendesu ka*?" I said without thinking. Light laughter erupted, bewildering me. What was so funny?

"Ah, you do speak Japanese," the old woman said in English, though she didn't sound surprised. "I told them you would know the old language. To answer your question, yes, the water is quite safe to drink. It's rainwater we collect and then filter through barrels filled with crushed charcoal. Then we boil it just to go the extra mile, though perhaps I should say the extra kiromētoru." Laughing at her own joke, her arm moved in a semicircle. A sea of faces bobbed nearby me, gibbering. So many, that, as they crowded in, the air oscillated like a desert mirage. The old woman shooed them away, and the hallucinatory effect ended.

"Where am I? And who are you? You're not..."

"No, I'm not Japanese. I'm originally from Norway, though that was ages ago. As to where you are, we're in the former Kanagawa Prefecture on the

Miura peninsula in the open city of Uraga, or what's left of it. This building is part of a complex that once housed a TEPCO power station for a research facility before the Great Change."

"TEPCO? Great Change?"

"TEPCO was the corporation responsible for the Fukushima disaster. Do you remember anything about that?"

"Yes," I responded. Who could forget Fukushima? Several cousins of mine evacuated the town of Futaba after the reactor meltdown. One of them, a girl of fourteen, died of radiation sickness.

"As for the Ōkina Henka, or the Great Change, as I translate it, that is a subject best left for another time when you have regained more of your strength. We need to get some solid food in you first, Jane. A pregnant woman eats for two as they say. Then we can talk."

"You know my name?" I said, dumbfounded, followed by, "I'm pregnant?"

"Oh yes," she said, matter of fact. "I detected a fetal heartbeat when you were first brought here two days ago. As for your name, well, you talk in your sleep, dear. I've been expecting you, or someone like you, for a while. But we'll discuss all this later. First, you rest." She exchanged a great number of words in a short time with the young girl. I gathered she was to be my personal caregiver. I wanted to sleep, but there were so many questions buzzing around my head. Did I dream us here under the influence of the drug Borges gave me? How did I get pregnant? Who was this stern white woman acting as if she owned this place? I needed an answer to at least one of them.

"Wait," I said. "Who are you? What's your name?"

"My name," she repeated as if pondering a great mystery. "Call me Ulrikke, if you like. I'm the mother of Jorge Luis Borges. I believe you know him." Then she walked off at a brisk pace. Stunned, I lost my chance to ask how Ulrikke could be my Borges' mother when she was dead. And why say she'd been expecting me? Then I noticed Borges was nowhere in sight. *I can't have lost him again*, I thought, as I slipped into unconsciousness.

• • • • •

Five days passed before Ulrikke came to see me again. By the second day, I was eating a mixture of mashed rice and cucumbers, and drinking as much water as my 'nurse' allowed despite my morning sickness. Desperate for information, I barraged her with questions about everything, but especially the whereabouts of Borges, who I described as my companion. The girl hesitated to say much at first, whether out of fear or extreme wariness, I could not tell. By the third day, though, she began to open up, though it wasn't always easy for the two of us to make ourselves understood. Her name was Yoshi, short for Yoshiko, and she was twelve, a member of the generation that had been born after. That was literally how she described herself and her peers: Ato ni kuru hitobito, the People Who Come After. Now she went on about almost anything–except Borges. She said he was found with me, but not much else. "He is safe," she said, but when pushed for more, she changed the subject. Her body language implied speaking of him was off limits. That she confirmed his existence was a transgression, one I suspected she regretted.

Yoshi was more forthcoming about Ulrikke, or 'Urikei,' the name used by the people who lived here. She was one of the "Erudāzu," a word that translates as elders, but which I soon learned referred to anyone who survived the Ōkina Henka. Yoshi said that no one knew where Ulrikke came from, only that she had taught English in Tokyo for at least a decade before the series of catastrophic events occurred that ignited the Great Change.

Yoshi told the story as they taught it in her school. For twenty years, recurring droughts, fires, floods, famines and other disasters battered the world. Terrible wars were fought over diminishing supplies of food, fresh water and energy resources. These catastrophic events coincided with great migrations, as people did everything they could to escape their fate. Perhaps four billion or more died. At some point, a war fought in space between the Americans and the Chinese destroyed all the remaining telecommunications satellites, effectively ending the information age. Though spared the fate of the two Koreas, which eradicated each other with atomic weapons, Japan suffered from the resulting fallout and radiation sickness.

Nor did it avoid a plague that many believed the Russian military released to forestall Chinese migrants attempting to escape famine caused by desertification. Faced with both plague and famine, and low-level nuclear exchanges between the Chinese and Russian militaries, many Chinese who lived in its eastern provinces took to whatever boats they could find, fleeing to Taipei or the Philippines. An untold number also landed on Japan's shores, bringing the plague with them. Within a few months, the central government in Tokyo collapsed, and with it, all possibility of maintaining social order.

Not many records remained from those times. Most electronic data was erased. Once the ubiquitous computers and servers no longer functioned, whether because of destruction at the hands of angry mobs, or otherwise, any chance to document accurately the history of that period was gone forever. When asked why she thought all this happened, Yoshi gave me her best schoolgirl answer. "They were stupid and greedy people," she said. "They failed to honor their ancestors."

"Yes, they did, Yoshi," said Ulrikke, whose presence I didn't notice until she spoke. "They failed utterly." She dismissed Yoshi, telling her she could return to her other duties. Yoshi gave a short bow to Ulrikke, and a smile for me, then ran off, skipping as she went.

"She's been a good friend," I said. "Will I see her again?"

Ulrikke smiled at that. "I think so. There aren't that many of us living here, after all."

"What did she mean that the people failed to honor their ancestors?"

Ulrikke gave a wan smile. "Yoshi, like many her age, practices Shinto. She burns incense every night at the shrine of her parents, and to the Emperor, of course."

"There's still an Emperor, then?"

"The Emperor lives only in Heaven now, watching over his people."

"You mean he's dead?"

"I meant what I said." My face must have betrayed my shock, because she added, "There are as many rumors about the Emperor as there are stars in the sky. But in all of them, he ends up in Heaven." She gave off a brief sigh. "It seems Japan is destined to always have an Emperor." After that, her eyes hardened, and I dropped into a dark pit of fear whose source was the woman towering above my futon. "Now," she said, "let me examine you before answering any more questions. Your color is much improved, and Yoshi tells me you are strong enough for short walks, but I prefer to trust my own eyes–and ears." She lifted the stethoscope off her chest. "Lie still please, so we can get this over with as soon as possible."

I did as I was told. If I was ever going to get any answers about this place, my Borges and how Ulrikke could be his mother, I'd have to follow orders, just like everyone else. *She holds all the leverage*, I thought. Ulrikke's next words scared the crap out of me. "I do hold all the leverage. Do you know the etymology of the name Ulrikke, by the way? It means 'power.'" She smiled again, but this time, I saw no sympathy in it. "Don't worry, Jane," she added, almost as an afterthought, "I don't consider you my enemy. Not yet anyway."

I shivered as she placed the chest pad of her stethoscope between my two breasts. It felt especially cold. "You appear to have made a strong recovery," Ulrikke said after helping me to my feet to take my standing blood pressure. "I've finished. Now it's time you answer a few of my questions."

I gave her a quizzical look. "I thought you could–"

"Read minds?" she said, interrupting me. "I can and I can't." Her statement surprised and confused me. To be honest, I suspected she was lying.

"Hear me out," she continued as if she knew what I thought of her. "I can sense general feelings and pick up the stray thought here and there, but I'm no mind reader. You, too, will acquire these–skills–if you haven't already." I didn't respond, not knowing what to say. Yet something in her tone of voice rang true. Would I learn to read others' thoughts? Or was she giving me false hope, catering to my selfish side? With so little information available to me, I resolved to remain a skeptic, whatever she might say.

"Let's get started, shall we?" continued Ulrikke. "I don't have many questions, but each one is important, so consider your answers carefully. I'll know if you are lying or hiding the truth, so don't try it."

"All right," I said, but trembled involuntarily.

She looked me in the eyes, like a jeweler with her glass, appraising the quality of a rare gemstone. "What age were you when you first met my son, and what year was it?"

"Twenty-seven," I answered. "It was 2010." She nodded. I soon learned that this was a reflexive habit, indicating when she trusted what she'd been told.

"And when did you first display this power of yours, this ability to go 'Elsewhere,' as my son calls it?"

I hesitated. How *does she know about that?* "I'm not sure."

Her head cocked to one side. "Explain." So I told her about my trip with Borges to Kamakura to visit the Daibutsu. I left nothing out. I described the powerful effect I experienced in the Great Buddha's presence. I even told her of my first dream of the featureless man in black forcing himself on me. Her eyes remained fixed on me, never once blinking.

"What happened next?"

I went over the rest of my story, leaving nothing out beginning with my time in Costa Rica, believing myself a madwoman, to the twenty years I spent in an alternative San Francisco as the wealthy widow of James Borgman, with no memory of my past, until Borges came and restored my memories.

"How did you end up here then?"

"I don't know. The last thing I recall before waking up was him sticking a needle into my neck and drugging me."

"I see," said Ulrikke.

"See what?"

She ignored that question, instead asking another one of her own. "How did you become involved with my son in the first place? Give the real reason, not the maudlin story of your love affair. Use as few sentences as you can, preferably only one. Take your time, but choose your words with care."

Her not-so-subtle threat caused the hairs on my arms and legs to stiffen down to their roots. How did I come to be with Borges? The ground wavered beneath me, creating a vertiginous sensation. Then it came, as if out of a fog. "He chose me," I said.

The stern expression on Ulrikke's face collapsed. I saw her eyes glisten with tears. When next she looked upon me, her gaze was a dark pool of pity and grief.

"You poor thing," she said.

We both said nothing after that, just faced each other, and for the first time, she looked old and frail, not a threat at all. A nearby fan blew her white hair in various directions, exposing bare spots on her scalp. Her eyes were distant and unfocused. They struck me as the eyes of a woman who lived too long and suffered too much. At last, I couldn't stand the silence anymore.

"Why do you say that?"

The expression that appeared on her face then was dominated by sorrow, but also something else I could not discern.

"Because my son is a monster."

I gazed upon her in shock. "But you're his mother."

"Please, let go of me, Jane," she replied, glancing at her arm.

When I followed her gaze, I discovered my left hand clenched tight around her right forearm, turning it ghostly white. I let go immediately, ashamed. It was as if my hand acted alone, directed by some other power.

"You are stronger than you appear," Ulrikke said, in an ironic tone.

"I'm sorry," I said. "I didn't know, I didn't mean to–forgive me." I stumbled over my words like a small and naughty child.

"Shall we sit?" Ulrikke responded, dropping onto my futon. She sat in the traditional Japanese style, resting on her legs, knees forward, back straight. I followed suit, but bent my legs, twisting my feet underneath them in the Sukhasana yoga pose. "Why call my son a monster? Because, like you, Jane, I love him, but I also fear him, knowing what sort of man he's become. For example, I know he means to kill you as soon as your son is born. That's why he is being held as our prisoner, while you are kept safe under my care."

"I don't understand." *Borges would never harm me, would he?* "How do you know this?"

"Because he told me as much, years ago when he was still a child," she said. "He refers to it as his *prophecy*. I didn't know it would be you, simply that he would find a woman possessing the ability to go 'Elsewhere'–as you call it–that he would convince her to fall madly in love with him and she would bear him a son. After that, his plan is to eliminate you."

I felt sick to my stomach. "He said all that?"

"Not in so many words. But the way he spoke made it clear that whoever he chose would die. He would take the boy, and the woman would no longer play any role in his life. I asked what he meant by that, and he shrugged. 'She'll have served her purpose,' was all he said."

"But why does he need a son? What possible reason could he have? You must tell me."

"I don't know," Ulrikke said. "He never told me that part of his prophecy." But something in her manner made me suspicious, and then angry.

"I don't believe you! And I don't believe you're his mother. You invented this bizarre prophecy. My Borges would never kill me. That's not who he is. He loves me." *He must*, I thought. *Why else would he have searched twenty years to find me?*

She laughed in my face. "Your Borges?" She sneered as if I were a fool. "Your Borges," she repeated. "Yet you're having doubts about him right this second, aren't you? Don't deny it."

I gasped, for it was true. Anxiety roiled my brain, for I had doubts, and not just about Borges' love, or whether he posed a threat to my life.

"If I doubt him, that doesn't mean I trust you," I said with all the strength I had.

"Then I must convince you I'm telling the truth. Will you give me the opportunity? Though I warn you, it's a long story, and you will hear much you might regret. For example, did he ever tell you he murdered his sister, my only girl child, because, as he put it, it was part of his *prophecy?*" She spat that word out in a way that made it an obscenity. Her steely blue stare was back, and the fragile old woman I glimpsed only a moment before no longer showed herself.

This isn't happening. I kept repeating that thought in my head as if, like a mantra, it could salvage my situation, but without success. Because, like it or not, I couldn't deny that I was here in this strange and terrible world, sick, weak, alone, and at the mercy of this strange, intense woman, who scared the hell out of me. I had no choice. I needed to hear her out. I needed to know what she knew.

As if reading my thoughts, Ulrikke pounced. "You must listen to me without interruption. That is my one and only condition." I swallowed what little saliva was in my mouth, and then, as if under a compulsion, nodded. Upon receiving my blessing, Ulrikke began the story of her life. If she didn't tell me everything, she said enough, more than I could have ever imagined. Her prediction also proved true, for I did come to regret what I learned.

INTERLUDE: ULRIKKE'S TALE

My first memory is of my father throwing me high into the air, so high that I believed I could fly like the birds I loved. I was perhaps three. It was spring. Most of the snow was gone, and the ground beneath me was flooded with fresh patches of *engsoleie*. You would know them as buttercups. I remember laughing from the sheer thrill of it, and my father laughing with me, as with each new toss, I went further and further upwards before plummeting back down to earth.

He was a giant among men, and very strong, but I was not afraid, even when, as I fell, he snatched me up only inches away from smashing onto the rocky ground. My mother was with us, but she said nothing, nor did anyone else. He was King Haraldr Sigurðarson, known as Harald Hardrada, the greatest king of the Northlands, and no one dared challenge him, for if they did, he would destroy them and all those they loved.

Another memory. No more than nine, I attended a banquet in the great hall at Nidaros, now known as Trondheim. The entertainment that night included a juggler who, after the usual marvels, performed a new act never seen before. He threw ten knives, the same ones he previously juggled, at a slave girl no older than me. She was lashed to one of the tables upended for just that purpose. Each knife he threw at her came closer and closer to her head until her terrified screams pierced even the thunderous roars of the men of my father's *hird*, his private war band that were loyal only to him. At the peak of this spectacle, the girl, madly thrashing about, pissed herself. After the juggler threw his last knife, just missing her neck, the hall erupted in cheers. Then my father raised his hand. In an instant, the hall went dead silent, all except for the pitiful creature held firmly to that table, reduced to nothing more than a mindless animal. My father beckoned the juggler to the head table, not far from where his show was performed. He came quickly, no doubt expecting a large payment of golden coins for having done so well.

"You are quite the master with knives," my father told him. "Have you ever missed and drawn blood?"

"Never, great king," the juggler boasted.

"Is that so?" The juggler nodded in reply, a broad smile on his face. Greed oozed from the pockmarks on his misshapen face.

"Then let us make a wager, you and I."

At this, all color from the juggler's face drained away. "A wager, great king? I am no lord. Surely, I am not worthy of this high honor."

"Are we not men?" my father said, louder this time. "Or do I speak to a worm?"

The juggler's back stiffened at the insult. "If the great king wishes to wager with me, a lowly worm, then the worm accepts." You know the saying from the Bible that pride goeth before a fall? It's a cliché, but only because it is so often true.

My father left his high seat and came down to stand beside the proud worm, a slender figure now dwarfed by the "Great King." My father suddenly slapped him hard on his back and he pitched forward, barely managing to keep his feet.

"A bold man, to speak so in my hall," said my father, his lips pulled back in a menacing grin, "but a brave man." My father surveyed the hall, before speaking again. "Here is my wager, master juggler. It is one thing to throw knives at a helpless slave, for what matter if she dies? Who would mourn her but God? I propose a better test of your skill. You throw your knives as before, but this time, the target shall be a person of my choosing, someone of great value to me. If you succeed, and no blood is spilled, I will increase your reward tenfold. If you fail, you forfeit all. Are we agreed?"

The juggler, forced to bend his neck to meet my father's stare, took a step back. Then he bowed in agreement. "I accept. Choose your man."

"I never said anything about a man, did I? Only someone of value to me."

"Then, Great King, choose whomever you desire. It makes no difference."

"Marie, come down," my father called. That was my given name. Marie, youngest daughter of my father's first wife and Queen Consort, Elisev of Kiev, daughter of Yaroslav the Wise, Grand Prince and ruler of the Kievan

Rus. I was noble born, if families that ruthlessly murder their own kin for the sake of power are noble. When called, I did not hesitate, but ran to his side. Was I frightened? Yes, but I adored my father, and trusted him utterly. I accepted his decision to be the juggler's target. I could tell he counted on the fact that I would not cower or show fear. And the juggler had not missed a single throw ever, as he himself said. In my naiveté, I did not entertain the possibility that his boast might conceal a lie.

"Great King," the juggler said, "I beg you to choose another. It would be cruel to frighten such a young and innocent child." His forehead beaded with sweat.

"Do you accuse my daughter of cowardice?" said my father. He then turned to me. "Are you scared of this man and his tiny blades?" I told him no, I never feared anything he asked of me. I knew my role.

"But, sire, she must hold very still. It would be unseemly to put ropes on a member of your house, especially a princess."

"Then no ropes will be used," my father blithely announced. He pointed at the slave girl, still blubbering. "Marie will stand and hold the same position as that one, and keep as still as you demand." He directed a servant to untie the now unhinged girl and lead her away. Then, together, my father and I walked over to the upended table. After a servant swept away the urine soaked straw and replaced it with fresh rushes, he placed me at the exact spot where the slave had been unwillingly restrained. With Father's help, I lifted my arms away from my body and spread my legs apart in imitation of the pose the ropes imposed on the slave. He then returned to his high seat.

"Master Juggler, begin!" my father shouted.

Visibly shaking, the juggler picked up his first knife. I looked straight past him and made a silent prayer to my Lord and Savior to give me the strength needed not to dishonor my father. The juggler did not move. After a minute elapsed, and he still made no move to throw his knife, I repeated my prayer. Meanwhile, a low, guttural noise began to arise from those present, but the juggler did nothing other than hold his knife above his head. His arm shook ever greater as the noise rose. Finally, my father shouted down at him, "Throw! Now!"

The juggler's first knife missed the table completely, striking the tapestry on the wall behind me. A great clamorous din came from my father's retainers. Their voices contained both mockery and scorn, but my father silenced them and ordered the juggler to throw his next knife. I knew before he released it, he would miss, and he did, this time striking the table's upper left corner, a good four feet from where I stood as motionless as the marble cross on the altar of the chapel I attended each day. My father bellowed again, but this time, the juggler could not control himself. His third knife slipped from his fingers and clattered upon the floor.

 This was too much for my father. Knocking his chair aside, he rushed from the dais. The juggler fell to the ground, begging for his life, kissing my father's boots, but my father kicked him aside as easily as another man might kick away a small dog. "Collect this fool's toys and bring them to me," he ordered. Within seconds, all seven of the remaining knives rested on a sideboard next to him. Then he threw them at me, one after the other in rapid succession.

 I did not have time to prepare myself. My father was no trickster who spent hours practicing knife-throwing. His weapons of choice were his lances, his swords, his mace and his bare hands. Yet each knife he threw struck the table, each closer than the juggler's failed attempts. One even grazed the hair above my ear, slicing a few strands off before striking the wooden planks hard enough to rattle my head. I felt all my senses at once: the sound of the juggler whimpering, the stink of the men and their mead, the odor of roasted meat, and even the cool draft from the open shutters that let in fresh air.

 Time was suspended for me until the last knife struck the table, nicking my little finger, the only injury I suffered, though I did not feel the sting, so slight it was. I looked at my father, as he regained his senses, returning from that mindless state that, during battle, men named *berserkergang*. I waited for him to call for me, rather than run to his side. As I said, I knew my role. He did not make me wait long, once he recovered his wits. He held out his hand and when I gave it to him, he weakly drew me close. When he was strong enough, he lifted me onto his shoulder and paraded me around the hall. His men cheered, though I cannot say whether for their King's skill, my bravery, or both. But it did not matter. All that mattered was that I did not dishonor his glory and name. When we completed one full circuit, he placed me down next to where the juggler lay on the floor, curled into a ball, gibbering incoherently.

"Is not my line the bravest in all Christendom?" he asked. "Even my daughter has more steel in her than many a brave warrior." Then he crouched down to my level. Pointing at the juggler, he asked what we should do with the man.

"You are King, Father," I said. "It is not for me to give you advice."

"You answer rightly, daughter, but a king may also grant a boon to a warrior who displays great courage and aid in battle. Today, you were my warrior, and I leave the decision to you. Should we gut his belly open to let the dogs feast on his entrails, or release him to go wherever he chooses?"

I thought for a while how best to answer. My father was kind when he wished to be kind, but he was called Hardrada, or "hard ruler," for a reason. When it came to those who earned his wrath, he held nothing back. I did not wish the juggler to die on my account, even though I cared little for him. I also knew I must come up with an answer that my father would respect.

"Our Savior and Lord, Jesus Christ, teaches us to show mercy, and so the juggler should not be killed," I said. "But this fool lost the wager. For that, he should forfeit everything he was promised, as you said. And I take everything promised him to mean everything he brought with him here this night. The gold he expected, but also his knives, and all his possessions, including his clothes. Strip him of his sinful pride, for the Bible says a man should be humble before God. You, Father, are God's representative on earth. I say, humble him. Take away all his goods, paint him red, and then send him out naked into the night, banished from all your lands."

My father took a moment to ponder this before smiling broadly. "A wise decision, daughter. You are correct. A king must sometimes show mercy. Do as she commands!" His words were a great relief to me.

In 1066, I turned sixteen and was promised in marriage to my father's chief supporter, Eystein Orre, brother to his second wife and uncle to my half-brothers. That year, my father entered into an alliance with Tostig Godwinson to overthrow his own brother, the newly crowned King of England, Harold Godwinson. Upon their inevitable victory, England would be divided between them. I suspect my father planned to cheat Tostig and claim all the English lands for his own, the very same strategy that worked well for him in the past.

My mother, my sister and I accompanied his fleet to the Isles of Orkney, lands under his control just north of Scotland. Why he wanted us close by, I do not know. Perhaps he feared we might be taken as hostages back in Norway. Whatever the reason, my mother and I, and our attendants, shared quarters together in a castle owned by the Earl of Orkney, who owed fealty to my father. Soon after arriving, he left us, sailing off to England and his doom. I warned him not to go, the only time I dared to give him unsolicited advice, for I dreamed he died fighting as a berserker, near a river. My insolence led him to place me under armed guard at the castle, thus preventing me from saying my goodbyes the day he departed.

One night, in late September, after I retired, I dreamed a far more unusual dream. Alone, overlooking a rocky coastline, I sat on an outcropping of black rock high above the shore. A darkening sky hung over the lifeless sea, full of threatening clouds. The gray waves rolled ceaselessly toward me. A cold north wind swept back my hair, and salt spray from below stung my eyes. The sound of loud wheezing caused me to turn around, only to find an old beggar in dirty rags, leaning on a tree branch, bark still attached, which he used as walking stick, making his slow way up the narrow path to where I perched.

"Stop, stranger," I shouted through the wind. "Name yourself before coming any closer." But he either ignored my warning or did not hear it. A tattered hat, as ratty as the rest of his attire, hid his eyes. A long straggly beard, white, but with darker streaks running through it, covered his chest, which heaved from the strain of the climb. He stopped ten feet from me. Rising to my full height, I looked him over, but did not consider him a threat to my safety.

"Who are you and what do you want of me, beggar?" I said. "Or are you some petty thief come to rob me because I am a woman?"

"I am neither beggar nor thief, Maria Haraldsdotter," he said, and at the sound of my name, I gasped. Witnessing my reaction, he quickly added, "Fear me not, great one, for I seek nothing from you. I come only to offer advice and a small gift, after which I shall take your leave." That speech set off a coughing fit that wracked his entire body. I waited for it to end before answering him.

"Then you came in vain. Leave me, old soothsayer. I have no desire to have my fortune told by you or any trickster, even one who presumes to address me by my Christian name, but refuses to give his own in return." Then I turned my back on him.

I spoke haughtily, as fools often do, but he seemingly took no offense. Neither did he do as I bid him. Instead, as I looked to the sea, he shouted into the wind, "Look upon me again, oh great one, and see if you know me now."

I should have insisted he leave, this time with harsher words, but some instinct compelled me to turn round to face him. His hat no longer covered his head, for he held it in his free hand. A sudden burst of recognition came to me. One eye was missing, its socket an empty cavern.

"*Óðinn*," I whispered. Chief of all the gods my father sought to replace with the one God of Christianity. Ruler of Asgard. Master of ecstasy and fury. Patron of rulers, warriors and outcasts alike. Seeker after wisdom and power. Shaman. Trickster. Cunning and sly beyond all others. The most dangerous of all the gods for he was known for his deceitful and cruel nature, which he displayed often for no other reason than his own amusement. Yet he was also the god who granted the greatest benefits to mortals. On cue, the moment I spoke his name, a raven descended from the sky and settled on his shoulder. It eyed me suspiciously until *Óðinn* whispered to it, after which the bird flew off out of sight.

"Now will you listen?" he said.

"I don't understand," I muttered. "Why speak to me, a Christian, named after the mother of our Lord and Savior, who my father promotes against your interest?"

"I care not if you put your trust in the Prince of Peace or whatever he calls himself. The three that are one god have their realm, and I have mine. You may choose to listen or not. I have other errands this night that concern me far more than this one. Answer now."

"I will," I said, lowering my head in obeisance. It is unwise to refuse the advice of those wiser than ourselves, be they gods or men. Or Buddhas.

"Good," said Óðinn. "You may yet prove to be of value. Now, hear me well. Your father will die in the morning, his war lost, as will the man to whom your father promised your hand in marriage. I myself will escort them into Valhalla. Your half-brother will survive and return to rule your father's kingdom. Your fate will be bleak. I foresee an early death, unless..." Óðinn paused.

"Unless what?" I asked.

"Unless you accept this least of gifts I bring. Few have been deemed worthy of it, and even fewer have used it well, but I have faith that you will prove deserving."

"And how will this boon protect me from the bleak fate you spoke of?"

"Ha!" cackled Óðinn, and he capered about in apparent glee. "You do not trust me, and would delay me from accomplishing my other tasks, especially the one concerning your father. You are a delight, Maria, named for the mother of the one God. Very well, I shall tell. Then you may decide. But do not test me further. Time is not your friend."

"What do you mean?"

"My gift is a simple one," he replied. "If used wisely, it will make you master of your fate. It is the gift of choice, the choice to start your life over whenever and wherever you wish."

"What is required of me in return?"

"The better question is what do you desire?" he said.

"How do I know you are telling me the truth about my father?"

"What concern of that is yours?" he replied. "If I lie, then your father will come to no harm. If I speak truthfully, there is nothing you can do to prevent his doom. I foretell that my gift to you will prove a great blessing. So again, I ask, what do you desire?"

"To go to England." I left unsaid why, for I meant to use his gift to warn my father and prevent his death. He claimed to be a Christian, having spent many years in the East, fighting for the Byzantine Emperor. Yet Father had not foresworn all ties to the old gods of our people before the good news of the Christ, King of Kings, came to our shores. I intended to go to his war camp before the battle, to give my warning.

"Very well. Do you accept my gift?"

"Yes," I said without hesitation.

With that, Óðinn lifted his walking stick and touched its tip to forehead. "Go back," he said.

I awoke suddenly, tossed upward before landing hard on a wooden bench inside a horse-drawn carriage, though I did not yet know that's what it was called. I cried out in alarm, and a strange man, dressed in even stranger clothes full of lace and ruffles, reached out to take my hands in his own. He made odd soothing sounds, attempting to calm me. Sitting beside him was another stranger, in similar attire. Neither carried on their person any sword or dagger, nor wore any tunic the like of which were familiar to me. They spoke briefly to one another in a language I could not understand.

Then the first man spoke to me in the Saxon tongue. "We are here to help you, child. Do you not remember yesterday when we arrived to take you under our protection with the blessing of your parents?"

"You speak Saxon?" I said, not so much a question as a statement. "That is not my first language, but I know enough to follow your words if you speak slowly."

"Yes, so you told me last night," he replied. "Do you not remember?"

"Oh, yes." I lied, sensing danger to my person should I say too much. "Forgive me. I was tired last night and did not recognize you when I awoke."

The answer appeared to satisfy him. I took a moment to look around the inside of the carriage that jolted us as it moved at good speed over uneven ground. Fashioned from dark wood, the inside was cramped. Unknown runes and symbols had been carved into it by a carpenter of great skill. A black fabric covered openings on each side. The fabric swayed back and forth, letting in a little light. I caught glimpses of fields and hedges and many tall trees. The smell of horse was everywhere.

"Please, prod my memory. Where are you taking me?"

"We travel to Norwich, to the home of Sir Thomas Browne, the most celebrated physician in all England." He gestured to indicate the older man seated with him was Thomas Browne himself. "Dr. Browne is a preeminent scholar with especial knowledge of the ways and practices of witches."

His words provoked panic in me. For the first time, I began to understand the nature of Óðinn's gift. My wish had been granted, but not in the way I hoped. I did go to England, but not to the England I knew. This England was much different. I could not save my father, as Óðinn said. And now, I faced great peril, for any accusation of practicing witchcraft always ended in the accused person's death.

"I am no witch, but a good and pious Christian woman!"

"No, no, you misunderstand," the Saxon speaker said. "Doctor Browne's assistance has been requested because your father feared you have been bewitched. Not but a fortnight ago, you lost all recollection of your native tongue, speaking only in dead languages from centuries past. Dr. Browne was asked to investigate your condition to discover the truth of the matter and how best to lift the curse laid upon you."

"Why would such a puissant man, as you said, do that for me?"

At this, he turned and spoke to Dr. Browne, and again I understood nothing of what they said to one another. "Your father is the Ambassador from the Court of Frederick III, King of Denmark and Norway. As a courtesy, and at the request of King Charles II of England, Dr. Browne agreed to see you. After his examination yesterday, your father and Sir Thomas agreed that you should be given into his care for a time. I tried to explain this to you last night, but perhaps my failure to speak clearly is cause for your confusion."

"I see," I said. "And how is it that you speak Saxon if it is, as you said, a dead language?"

"I am a lecturer at Merton College in Oxford," he replied, "and my name is Jonathan Chandler. I teach the Latin and Greek classics, but also study other ancient manuscripts, and in particular, the Saxon Chronicle from the time of King Alfred the Great. I belong to a society of scholars dedicated to keeping knowledge of that language alive."

"Thank you, Sir Jonathan, for your kindness in answering my questions. Since this curse was placed upon me, I have suffered a great bewilderment."

"You are most welcome, dear lady. But I should correct you on one matter. Address me as Master Chandler, not Sir Chandler, for I have not been granted any title by the Crown."

"As you wish, Master Chandler," I said. "I trust under the guidance of Sir Thomas and yourself, I will soon recover my memories, and the curse be lifted from me. May I ask one further question of you?"

"Anything, my lady."

"In my confusion, I have forgotten many things, but one in particular troubles me greatly. Can you inform me of the present year?"

"Of course," Master Chandler replied. "Today is the Twenty-fifth day of September in the Year of Our Lord, Sixteen Hundred and Seventy-four."

My eyes grew wide. What he said was impossible. If true, my gift transported me six hundred years in the future. I pinched my arm, and the pain assured me this was no dream, but harsh reality. Óðinn said his gift would make me master of my own fate, but it seems he kept the full truth from me.

"Thank you, Master Chandler. Please convey to Sir Thomas my deepest gratitude. And now I should rest, if possible." I closed my eyes and feigned sleep, meditating on all that I knew, and all I did not. The latter far outweighed the former.

CHAPTER 17

"I'm going for tea," said Ulrikke, rising to her feet. "Would you like some?"

I shook my head, inspecting a small tear in my futon from which a tuft of cotton poked out. I could have sworn it wasn't there the day before. How fast things change when we're not paying attention. Then Ulrikke's hand lingered on my shoulder, its interlaced web of veins and fine wrinkles, oddly beautiful.

"Are you all right, Jane?"

"I'm fine," I said.

"I'll bring enough for two in case you change your mind. And some onigiri, should you feel hungry. I know I do."

As she walked away, I wondered how all this happened. Too weary to cry, too sad to laugh, I thought about Ulrikke's story and what it meant for me, my Borges, and my unborn child.

• • • • •

How many times did Ulrikke start her life over? Even she didn't know. "It took me countless attempts to master my gift," she said. "Even now, I still make mistakes, if I am not careful. It is easy to lose one's way, to go somewhere I didn't intend." Her first efforts were utter failures. She kept trying to return to her father's time, to spare him the disaster of the Battle of Stamford Bridge, only to learn her gift required exquisite precision. Far too often, she missed the mark, and found herself in places where the languages spoken were not ones she knew. There, people considered her mad, or, as with Sir Thomas Browne, bewitched.

By trial and error, she learned not to travel too far into the future, or too far into the past. In time, she gained mastery over her ability, but never took it for granted. "Each new choice I make is a leap into the unknown," she said, "no matter how well I prepare." The only constant was that, in each new life, she was a sixteen-year old girl, the same age as when she dreamed of Óðinn's visit to her in 1066. She also remembered her past lives each time, which differed from my experience, a fact I found troubling.

She kept to Northern Europe, mostly: England, Scandinavia, the German principalities, where she either understood the language or could pass herself off as a foreigner until she learned enough to speak as a native. A born linguist, she acquired new languages with ease. "The hard part was reading and writing," she told me. Browne taught her to write the English of a 17th century scholar, but styles change. She struggled in other times and countries for she couldn't explain why she could speak and write English so well, but not the native tongue.

After many new lives, she felt confident enough to try once more to save her father. "I still thought as a child thinks. Because I could change my destiny, I believed I could change the destinies of others. I was mistaken."

She arrived right after her father captured York. Upon evading troops commanded by his English allies who sought to rape her, one of her father's retainers recognized her and took her to him. But their reunion did not go well. He suspected she was a spy sent by the English king, for she looked like a young Saxon peasant. To prove her identity, she spoke of things only the two of them could know. It almost worked, but then his paranoia kicked in. Proclaiming her a witch, he ordered his men to burn her at the stake.

"It was a close thing. I could not accept my failure until the smoke rising from the pyre began to choke me. I barely escaped by transporting myself to mid-century Victorian England." There, she assumed the identity of a servant to a prominent politician, Lord John Russell, the British Foreign Secretary.

This was during the time of America's Civil War. Ulrikke waited upon many Americans, from both the Union and the Confederacy, in private dinners held at his Lordship's estate. Their manner and customs intrigued her. The rigid class structure so prevalent in England appeared more malleable in America, at least in the North. "I heard of a women's rights movement, something new and astonishing." Intrigued, she next chose a life in Albany, New York, as a wealthy merchant's daughter. Eventually, America became her favorite destination. "I never forsook my attachment to my home country, nor my adopted one in Britain," she said. "But I gave up my dream of saving my father. I accepted that I would forever be an exile from the world of my birth."

And so she spent countless lives, so many, she could no longer remember them all, moving from one time and place to another. Sometimes she chose them at random, but other times, out of necessity. "For we are not immortal, Jane," she said, "despite our abilities. We can extend our lives indefinitely, but the risk of death still exists. I nearly died several times because of chance events. I became wary and cautious by nature, choosing to live in eras that avoided risk. You know the Japanese saying, 'Deru kugi wa utareru?' I did not want to be the nail that stuck out from the others. I never gave my complete trust to anyone again, as I had with my father. I no longer knew my role. Instead, I invented new ones as needed. As they say, I adapted. I preferred living in late twentieth century America, as it was the safest society, even during times of war, for people like me, a white, Northern European woman."

After making the rash decision to live in Norway during the Nazi invasion, where she was mistaken for a resistance leader, escaping execution at the last moment, she next chose a more comfortable life as an immigrant in Austin, Texas in 1955. It was there in 1961, during her senior year at the University of Texas, that she met the writer, Jose Luis Borges, father to my Borges. Ulrikke's story of their relationship fascinated me.

Jorge Luis Borges' international fame occurred late in life. 1961 was the turning point. That's when he became known to the world, as an *éminence grise* of world literature, the first major South American writer recognized as a great writer. He shared the Prix International de Littérature prize with Samuel Beckett, which led to the University of Texas granting him an appointment as visiting professor in the Department of Romance Languages. Ulrikke, an honor student majoring in liberal arts with an emphasis in Spanish literature, received a cherished spot in his class on Argentinean Poetry. It forever changed her life. "That was when destiny caught up with me, after so many years of managing to evade it."

Ulrikke's austere demeanor and Scandinavian accent charmed the older man, who began to call on her often in class. That he singled her out for special attention surprised her. But that was not the only effort he made to know her better. His blindness required him to seek help navigating the campus and the city. Although his mother accompanied him to Austin, she was elderly and often ill, and did not find its climate 'agreeable.' The university assigned student guides for him, and when asked if there was anyone in particular he wanted, his first choice was Ulrikke.

"Why did I accept?" she said. "There were many reasons. He was a wonderful conversationalist, and the aura of his burgeoning fame, of course, made the job attractive. And the university assured me that time spent as his guide would not affect my coursework or my class rank. Indeed, the Dean of my college said my work for Borges would be treated as eight credits of independent study, for which I would receive the highest marks. Also, two upper-level courses, required for my major, were deemed satisfied, a great benefit. But frankly, Jane, in the end, like you, I did what I did because he chose me. I, who had always controlled my fate, now let another decide it." My heart skipped a beat when she said that.

Soon, Ulrikke became the principal companion to the "great man," a term Borges used to mock himself. She escorted him around campus, often to the library, where he would simply stand and breathe in the air. "I always feel most at home in a library," he told her. "The odor of print and paper and dust is so familiar to me. I am reminded of my home in Buenos Aires." She also shepherded him to formal dinners and other affairs where university and city officials could show off their prized possession to Austin's rich and powerful, including the Governor and other political figures. That Borges, a famous literary dignitary, chose the University of Texas, and not other prominent colleges, for his initial foray into the world of American academia was a point of pride for Austin's political and business elites.

Borges soon fell in love with Austin. Ulrikke said that he often commented on the city's beauty and that it came as a revelation to him. She asked him how that could be, considering his poor vision. He smiled and simply told her that, "Some of the best dreams of my life have come to me since my arrival in Austin."

"Though he gloried in his newfound fame," Ulrikke said, "he never fully trusted it would last. Anxious, he once remarked that life was just a dream, an illusion, and thus his fame might vanish at any time. A romantic, he wanted to believe that the sudden acceptance of his greatness by so many would last. But he spent forty years in the literary backwaters of Argentina, where he struggled to receive his due as a great writer. Longstanding insecurities made him view the people of Austin, who accepted him so easily, as fabulous creatures, morally and culturally superior to his countrymen. Borges' ego desperately needed Austin."

He told her of the bad years when he was younger. After his family's fortune collapsed in the thirties, he lowered himself, taking any job he could find. He wrote stories for local newspapers, movie and book reviews, and articles for women's magazines. He translated business documents for companies that dealt with foreign firms, and even wrote ad copy for products like yogurt. As the strain of being the family's only breadwinner intensified, he took a full-time position at a library in a suburb of Buenos Aires. "Nine of the worst years in my life," he said, and the misery of them never left him.

Ulrikke understood far better than Borges the true nature of Austin's elites who fawned over him. Underneath their new openness to 'culture' and refinement, bitterness, hatred, self-loathing and fear governed their thoughts, and above all, fear of the civil rights movement, and hatred for America's President, John F. Kennedy, who they felt, as did most Southerners, was far too sympathetic to the Negro cause. White Texans, even Austin's upper crust, seethed with anger at the glamorous and youthful Yankee President who gave speeches that supported an end to segregation. "I rarely heard people refer to JFK by name," she told me. "He was always 'That Papist in the White House,' or the 'Niggers' President,'" slurs not limited to lower class whites. Ulrikke heard the same epithets from her closest friends and most professors. "It confounded me," Ulrikke said, "that they could adopt this previously unknown South American writer, a man they would have considered their inferior a year earlier, while openly despising Mexicans and blacks, treating them like my father treated his slaves, as less than human." However, they hid their ugly side from Borges. No one cared that he came from a country of which most of them knew nothing other than it was a haven for former Nazis. He was the newest international literary celebrity, and that was all that mattered.

As for Ulrikke, Borges' relentless affability charmed her. She found herself, despite their many differences, falling for him. "Was it love?" she said. "Who knows? But he was the most interesting man I ever met." She tried to flirt with him in her stiff-backed, stoic way. To her surprise, he recognized her efforts for what they were and flirted back, employing his dry wit and self-deprecation to great effect. As they grew closer, she came to understand that his modest manner was a thin veneer that covered over his anxiety regarding affairs of the heart. He once said he succeeded wildly in his romance with literature, but not so well in his dealings with real women.

"I make it a habit to fall in love once a year with a woman who would never consider me a suitable lover," he said one night when she dropped him off after another dinner, one where he drank more than usual. She asked him why, and, after a moment's consideration, he replied, "Because, my dear, like the troubadours of old, I believe in the salvation that only a love that is never consummated can provide."

"I knew then that he wanted me," Ulrikke said, "but would never take that first, vulnerable step. I suspect he thought the difference in our ages, and his ravaged figure, excluded any chance I might accept. Ironic, isn't it, that I, who lived so many lives, was too young for him?" Instead, Ulrikke assumed the role of Borges' confidant, the only person with whom he revealed his vulnerabilities. The initial crush she felt for him, and which she suspected he reciprocated, grew into a powerful bond. Listening to her, I thought I understood why. Both of them were strangers in a new world, outsiders. It only made sense to me they would end up as lovers. Ulrikke didn't see it coming until that fateful day it did.

"It was October 30th, and that year Texas' Indian summer lasted longer than normal. Borges was passing through a crush of students who wanted to speak to him after one of his open lectures. 'Take me somewhere far away from all these–people,' he said. 'Some place peaceful, and quiet with flowers and sun and trees, where the two of us can be alone and enjoy ourselves.' I reminded him of his appointment with the University Chancellor that afternoon, and he frowned before a sudden, mischievous smile creased his face. 'Call and cancel. Say I have been fighting a great fatigue and need my rest. He'll understand. And, in good faith, it's not a lie, is it?' He had a point. I made the call."

She drove him to Onion Creek Falls in a Buick Skylark provided for his use. Onion Creek Falls was a local attraction below high bluffs north of Austin. They were on land once owned by one of the original American colonists who migrated to Texas at the invitation of the Mexican government in the 1830s. His widow sold the land to the James Smith family, whose great-grandson, J.E. "Pete" Smith still owned it. "Luckily," Ulrikke continued, "one of Mr. Pete's youngest daughters, Alison, belonged to my sorority. I called her mother from a gas station phone booth. She was happy to let me show 'our distinguished guest' around the ranch.

"Onion Creek Falls have an eerie, almost haunted beauty. Its bedrock eroded over time, creating winding channels that sculpted the rocky landscape until they resembled a playground for a race of giants. Water flowed over ten-foot high shelves of limestone, carving it into fantastical shapes. 'It's wonderful,' I told him. 'You'll love it.'" Once through the ranch's west gate, Ulrikke drove down a dirt road until it dead-ended. Then she led Borges along an old cattle trail, protecting him from obstacles along the way. The competing scents of numerous wildflowers overwhelmed Borges. She rattled off the names: Black-eyed Susans, Bluebonnets, Mexican Hats, Pink Evening Primrose and many others.

"Songbirds chattered in cypress trees that shaded us from the sun, while honeybees and fireflies buzzed near our heads. Borges didn't say a word, displaying an easy, enigmatic smile, as if he were somewhere far away." Within a half hour, they arrived at the falls, to their mutual delight.

"It sounds like the waves crashing upon the beaches of Partido de La Costa outside Buenos Aires," he told her. "Not too loud, just a steady sound that soothes away all distress." They stopped along the southern bank of the creek at a small eddy below the falls proper where, after removing shoes and rolling up his pants, he dangled his feet in the tepid water. "Remarkable," Borges said. "Thank you, my dear, for this treat."

Laughing, he kicked the water like a small boy, splashing them both. "We sat together for long stretches, not speaking," Ulrikke told me. "We listened to the rushing water, the birds, breathed in the humid air, and let the sun warm us. I became drowsy, and told him I needed to rest awhile. He did not object. I snuggled down upon a bed of crushed flowers and wild grass under the nearest tree, no more than a few feet from where he continued to kick at the water. I awoke to a red sun in the west with Borges' hands caressing my shoulder. He stopped at once and blushed a deep red."

I broke my promise to keep silent and interrupted her. "What did you do?" I asked. I couldn't help thinking about my Borges, and the first time we made love. Ulrikke's story about her Borges made me yearn all the more to see mine.

"What did I do?" Ulrikke reflected my question back at me. "I took his hand in mine. 'You may have me,' I said to him, 'but not here.' He started to speak, but then wisely stopped himself. I brushed my lips against his and then led him back to the car. I checked us into a hotel, one many professors used for their affairs with female students."

Upon entering their room, Ulrikke told Borges she needed to freshen up. She took a quick shower to wash off the sweat and dirt from an afternoon spent sleeping on the ground. After drying herself with a rough towel, she told Borges to turn off all the lights and then sit on the bed. "'Are you ready?' I asked after the lights dimmed. He made a faint reply, but by the sound of his movements, I knew he complied. Letting the towel drop away, I went to him. Sunset over, only the city's lights coming through the window exposed my naked body, though his blind eyes could not see it. When he did not reach for me, I took his hands and placed them on my breasts. He groaned and we began."

"Was he a good lover?" I asked, before I could stop myself. My cheeks flushed in shame, I tried to take it back. "I'm sorry. I have no right to ask–"

But Ulrikke showed no anger with me. "Don't trouble yourself, Jane," she said. "It was a lifetime ago. Many lifetimes, so I don't mind answering. Was he a good lover?" She paused. "Yes and no. He was long out of practice, but he was tender and followed my lead. I undressed him, showed him where to kiss me, and then I straddled him, cowgirl style, as they say in Texas. I took him in my hand and I slipped him inside. He groaned again, a sound indistinguishable from either pain or pleasure. As I rocked back and forth, he placed his hands on my hips. It was then I had a premonition, the first and last one of my life."

"A premonition?"

"Yes. I saw myself giving birth to a boy, and I knew with absolute certainty that it would be his. Knowing I would bear the son of Jorge Luis Borges excited me. I moved faster, grinding myself against him, taking him deep within me, tightening my grip on him with every thrust. I could feel my orgasm building for a full minute before it hit me, filling me with an ecstasy that I believe equaled the promises in the scriptures, which speak of the joy the faithful will experience in the blessed presence of Christ. As my pleasure dissipated, Borges, with his hands gripping my thighs, grunted twice, his body shuddered, and I felt the heat of him filling me. When we finished, I collapsed on his chest and let his hands wander all over my skin and through my hair. When he tried to talk to me, I placed my fingers on his lips. 'No more words must pass between us,' I said. An hour later, both of us dressed. I drove to the house he shared with his mother, led him to the front door and kissed him once on the cheek, before walking away.

"The next day, I left Austin forever, and never saw or spoke to him again. Our son, your Borges, was born nine months later, July 1962, in New York, where I stayed with my parents. They pestered me to name the father, but I refused. 'It doesn't matter,' I told them. 'Only your grandson matters.' Eventually, they stopped asking. I completed my degree at NYU and landed a job with a major publishing house. A few years later, I became pregnant with my daughter. But you already know what happened to her."

CHAPTER 18

I reflected upon Ulrikke's years raising my Borges, watching him grow from a small child to the man he became, a man she said showed a propensity for violence at an early age when he killed her daughter, his sister. Obsessing over the prophecy Ulrikke alleged threatened my life, her return, carrying a red and black tray, took me unawares. The tray held a small kyūsu, steam wafting out of its spout, two rustic-styled, brown ceramic teacups without handles, and four triangle-shaped onigiri on two small plates. "As promised, there's enough in case you've changed your mind." Placing the tray on the futon between the two of us, she proceeded to pour green tea into her cup. Head tilted, she then raised one eyebrow, an unspoken question directed at me.

"Domo arigato," I said. "Please, I would like some tea, if it is not too much trouble." Even as the words came out of my mouth, I wondered why I spoke with such formality to her. Ulrikke had not stood on ceremony in any of our previous conversations. Quite the contrary. She was informal to a fault. Yet as I recalled her stories regarding my Borges, her son, and the horrible things she claimed he'd done before I came into his life, I understood my caution. Should I believe her? I feared the answer.

"No trouble at all, Jane," she replied, interrupting my uncomfortable musings, as she filled a second cup for me. Breathing in the delicate fragrance of the macha, we sipped our tea in peace. She put hers down first and picked up one of the rice balls. When she took a bite, my stomach growled. I picked up one of the three remaining onigiri in what now struck me as a ritual meal. It tasted delicious with the sweet flavor of rice wine vinegar. After another bite, I set it down on one of the small, lacquered plates.

"Sumimasen," I said. "This is all so, so-perfect. To what do I owe this great honor?"

"You know why, Jane."

"Perhaps, but I don't know if I am capable of doing it."

"It's been my experience that anyone is capable of killing another human being under the right circumstances. He will destroy you if you don't. The moment after you give birth, you will become superfluous to him."

"You don't know that for certain," I said, raising my voice.

"Jane, I told you of his prophecy and what that means. He said he would find a girl with the same gift as mine, and now he has. Once he has his son, your fate is sealed."

"I only have your word on that," I said. "If he's so dangerous, why don't you do it now and spare me?"

"I'm his mother! I will not go to my grave with his death on my head!"

Her intensity frightened me, and I raised my arms as if to ward off a blow. Then I saw tears streaming from her eyes.

"I'm sorry," I said. "I didn't mean to upset you."

Ulrikke sighed. "It doesn't matter, Jane, so don't worry about that. I'm not strong enough in any case. I'm dying. Didn't Yoshi tell you? I have breast cancer. Stage four." My eyes opened wide at this news.

"I see," she continued. "Well, perhaps she didn't want to burden you. The best guess of our doctors here is that I have six months, maybe a year if I'm lucky." She gave off a short laugh. "Would you like to feel the lymph nodes under my arms?" She slipped her arm out from under the oversized t-shirt she wore and covered her breast with her opposite hand. Just below her armpit, I saw several large growths, one the size of a robin's egg.

"I-I believe you."

"You're sure? These could be an elaborate ruse. Thomas, the doubting apostle, insisted on touching Jesus' wounds. Perhaps you have similar doubts."

"Please," I begged her, "put your shirt back on. I said I believed you."

"Arigato." She let her shirt fall down and then slipped her arm through its sleeve, wincing as she did.

"I'm sorry, Ulrikke." When she said nothing in response, I risked another outburst. "You don't have to die. You could begin again somewhere else. Perhaps I could, too."

"He would find you," Ulkrikke responded, locking her eyes onto mine. "You know this." Then she looked away. "As for me, I explained why I no longer wish to use my gift.

"I've lost the will to live. You, having just begun his journey, cannot understand what it's like. All the years, the love affairs, the despair of losing so many dear to me, it eats away your soul. And there's the tragedy of my son. I thought he would be my one joy. Instead, all he brought me was fear, anguish and self-loathing. Giving birth to him was the great curse of my life." I found it hard to accept what she said about my Borges. She sounded sincere, but I still loved him, and wasn't prepared to accept her story. Not without more proof.

"Let me see him," I said. "You know I must, right? How else can I judge between what you've told me and what he has to say? Today is the first I've heard of his prophecy. The first I've heard he murdered your daughter. All the horrific things you claim he did during the years he's been seeking me, it's–it's a lot to take in."

"He killed that lawyer right in front of you," she bluntly responded. "I would think that would be more than enough to convince you he is a great danger."

"He had good reasons for killing Marty!" I protested. "He was protecting me from the monster who murdered my parents."

"Yes," she said, "but then he always has good reasons for his crimes, doesn't he?" The look on her face struck me like a punch to the gut. In an instant, I couldn't breathe. My vision devolved into a blizzard of patchy snow. I struggled not to faint.

"You're asking a lot," I gasped when I could breathe again. "I cannot kill the man I love based solely on your word that he may murder me if I don't strike first." Ulrikke hard bright eyes were daunting, but I continued. "I won't make that choice until I hear what he has to say. You owe me that!"

Ulrikke poured herself more tea, before answering me. "Do you want to know why I go by the name Ulrikke?" she asked, the last thing I expected, but I nodded.

"In 1977," she said, "working at a publishing house in New York, I received word from a friend that his firm was publishing a book of newly translated stories by Jorge Luis Borges. Knowing my interest in his work, though not the reason for it, he asked if I would like an advance copy. I said yes. The next day, it arrived all boxed up with a little bow, like a present. Inside was a small book with his name in big white letters over the title 'The Book of Sand.' I flipped to the table of contents. The second story listed was "Ulrikke," a woman's name in Norway. I knew then he wrote it about our affair."

"Was it faithful to what happened?"

"Yes and no. It's the story of a middle-aged, rather meek South American academic, who meets a young Norwegian woman at a conference in Yorkshire, near where my father lost his life in battle. The fictional Ulrikke is quite a mystery, more a symbol of womanhood than a real person. Yet in her character, I recognized myself. His description of the woman's appearance matched mine, and he patterned her dialogue after the way I spoke to him the night we made love. The male protagonist even mentions a failed romance with a slim blonde in Texas from years before, a woman he describes as looking just like Ulrikke. Like me.

"It's his only story in which sexual attraction is a major theme, though told from the man's point of view. It ends when Ulrikke leaves after they have sex, both knowing they will never meet again. So, there are kernels of truth embedded within the artifice he titled 'Ulrikke.'"

"I see."

"I hope you do," she responded. "Because, if I allow you to see my son, you should know that, in all the most important aspects of his personality, he takes after his father far more than he takes after me. Both tell lies to manipulate others."

"When will I see him?" I asked, ignoring her last remark.

"Not today." She stood. With a quick gesture, she beckoned a young woman standing against the far wall near the exit. It was Yoshi. With my attention on Ulrikke, I hadn't noticed her before now.

"Yoshi," Ulrikke said, "Jane-san is well enough to go outside. The fresh air will do her good. She needs exercise. Take her for a short walk. The greenhouse perhaps."

"Hai," Yoshi responded with a quick nod.

"The snap peas there are blooming and almost ready for harvesting," Ulrikke said in an aside to me. "The flowers are pretty, though small. And quite *oishii*."

When I threw her a look of surprise, Ulrikke laughed. "We waste nothing here. The blossoms are edible. They have a sweet taste."

She then whispered something to Yoshi that I could not hear. From Yoshi's reaction, I could tell she did not like what Ulrikke said. Yet Yoshi bowed to her and murmured, "Hai, *Urikei-chōrō*." Her use of the honorific, *chōrō*, struck me because it was so unusual. It was the first time I heard Yoshi use a word referring to Ulrikke as her superior.

Ulrikke touched my shoulder. "Goodbye, Jane. I leave you in Yoshi's good hands. Please follow her directions to the letter. I don't want you to overextend yourself, not when you are in such a fragile state." The friendly, chatty, even vulnerable Ulrike was no longer there. Instead, the woman with all the leverage spoke, her blue eyes staring right through me. I found it difficult to respond, but somehow marshaled the strength.

"When will I see my Borges?"

"When the time is right."

"And when will that be?"

Ulrikke shrugged, as if it was a matter of little concern, before striding off.

"You can't keep me from him forever," I called after her. "If I'm strong enough to talk to you, hear everything you had to say, true or not, I'm strong enough to see him." Ulrikke stopped walking, though she kept her back to me. Yoshi tugged at my arm, but I pulled out of her grasp.

"As your doctor, I make that decision," Ulrikke said after a short delay.

"And when will that be?" I said, louder this time. Yoshi was distressed at this most inappropriate of interactions, but despite a tinge of guilt, I carried on. "Tomorrow? The next day? Never?"

"After I learn what you are capable of withstanding," Ulrikke said, in a reply that could mean anything, and so told me nothing. An answer that enraged me, though the thought flashed through my head that was her goal.

"And when will that be?"

"*Watashitachi ga futatabi au toki*," she said. *When we meet again.*

"I don't believe you. I don't believe my Borges is your son, either," I shouted at her.

She turned around. "But I am his mother, Jane," she replied with dead eyes. "Your belief changes nothing."

Her reply put me in my place, a warning that my fate was subject to her will alone. What could I say? She acted as she did to anger and humiliate me. Why let her know she succeeded? I thought of my Borges, Ulrikke's prisoner. Earlier, Ulrikke implied, when describing her gift, that the choice to go Elsewhere was always open to me. Yet where would I go? And now wasn't the time. Not while I was pregnant with Borges' child. I understood so little. Why did I still felt so in love with him? Was it simply because he "chose me," as he said? I had to know. And as long as Ulrikke held him captive, I was a prisoner, too, for I lacked full knowledge about my ability, and how to control it, which was a great frustration to me after hearing what Ulrikke accomplished. Yoshi pulled at my sleeve, a reminder she was still with me. Her face quivered; a sign of fear.

"It's all right, Yoshi," I said. "I'll go with you now. I've never eaten flowers before. Not that I can remember, anyway." That made her smile, my one good deed of the day. I followed her to the exit. Though I felt a moment of nausea, it soon passed. The act of walking felt enervating. My strength was returning faster than expected.

Outside, under a sky drained of color by a blanket of clouds, Yoshi led me by the hand over a muddy, straw-laden path toward a low-lying structure that resembled an ancient longhouse. Its pale green color reminded me of a watercolor painting.

"Yoshi, may I ask you a question?"

"Hai, Jane-san."

"Why did you refer to Ulrikke as *Urikei-chōrō* a little while ago? I've never heard her called that before."

Yoshi's face tightened. "Everyone calls her that," she said. "*Urikei-san* has knowledge that benefits all. She is an honored person among us, as are many others. I was showing her respect, that is all."

"She's your leader?"

"We have many leaders, Jane-san."

Yoshi was not being as forthcoming as I hoped. The honorific *chōrō* in Japanese is an archaic word. Originally, it referred to senior abbots of Zen temples, and during Japan's medieval era to great Daimyos, feudal lords, and army commanders. In brief, it was how subordinates addressed prominent spiritual and secular rulers. Yoshi's refused to discuss where Ulrikke stood in the community's hierarchy, but whatever her position, it didn't seem honorary. Yoshi slipped up by calling her *Urikei-chōrō* in my presence. On a hunch, I said, "Urikei asked something of you, didn't she? You've been told not to talk about her to me, haven't you?"

"I cannot answer you, Jane-san," Yoshi said, her voice breaking. "*Sumimasen*, but do not ask about her again. You will learn much about our ways soon enough. Please, let us just enjoy this day. The snap pea flowers are so beautiful. You will see."

"All right," I said. "We'll leave tomorrow's concerns for tomorrow."

"Hai, Jane-san. That is the proper attitude, as the Buddha teaches us. Tomorrow will come in its own time. Today, we are happy, are we not?"

"Yes, Yoshi," I said. Then my foot struck a rock buried under the soft ground and I stumbled. Yoshi caught me just in time, her agility saving me from a bad fall.

"*Arigato gozaimasu*," I said after I recovered my balance. "I must have missed that stone. *Sumimasen*, Yoshiko. Forgive me for being so inattentive."

"You must be more careful, Jane-san," she said. "Now is not a good time to act with haste." Then, taking my hand, she led the way to the greenhouse and its promise of edible flowers.

CHAPTER 19

The next morning, I awoke to someone shaking me. My eyes opened, I expected to see Yoshi, but this was a different girl. I jumped, and she instantly removed her hand. "Who are you? Where's Yoshi?"

The girl shrunk back, raising both hands to cover her face, trembling in terror. Using gentle pressure, I tried to pull her hands down, but that only made things worse. It took several minutes to calm her down, using very few words, only the occasional "It's all right" and "I won't hurt you" mixed with lots of cooing and shushing. Eventually, she stated her name was Junko. Junko Asahi.

Junko was my new *Sābanto*, my servant. When I enquired why she awakened me, and not Yoshi, Junko said only that Ulrikke instructed her to see to my needs. "I do not know why *Urikei-sama* chose me to be your *Sābanto*, Jane-san," Junko said, "only that you are important to her. I humbly apologize for my unworthiness, and promise to do my best to serve you." Then she knelt, laying her forehead on the cement floor in a posture of submission. Many minutes passed before I could coax her to sit up.

Junko, with her long blue-black hair, was a great beauty, if you ignored the tumorous growths that ran along the right side of her face, ending under her chin. She wore her hair loose and let it fall across her face to hide them, but to no avail. I made the mistake of asking if they were cancerous. She blushed and pulled her hair over her face to hide it.

"Iíé," she said, shaking her head, "I was born with them." Them. A telling reply. I heard both shame and despair in her voice, and asked no more about her condition.

Junko moved my futon into a small room off the larger hall, which she said was hers, and now, by Ulrikke's order, also mine. With a cotton sheet for a door, it afforded me a modicum of privacy, and included a toilet and sink, for which I was thankful. Using the communal lavatory made me uncomfortable because of the sideways looks people gave me and the silence that occurred whenever I entered. Now, I wouldn't have to worry about that.

As I got to know Junko, I came to believe she suffered from *taijin kyōfushō*, a fear of relating to other people, because of her facial deformity. Whenever I asked her a question she blushed, and I noticed that, when called on to introduce me to the people we met on our walks, she trembled with anxiety. She spoke in a slow and halting manner, never saying more than necessary. Conversations were painful for both of us.

To help her, I took to introducing myself to whoever we encountered on our daily walks. When Junko protested, I explained I needed to practice my language skills. Whether or not she believed me, she looked grateful this duty was no longer hers to perform. I also made it a point to praise her for the least little thing she did. Perhaps I overdid it, but over the next two weeks, and after much effort by me to restrain my bad *gaijin* manners, I could sense her warming up to me. When she first laughed at one of my silly, self-deprecating jokes, I felt the wall between us begin to crack.

One night, after about a month, she volunteered why she spoke in such a deliberate fashion. The tumors extended inside her mouth, making it difficult to enunciate her words. "Few know this," she said, lowering her eyes. I took her hand in mine and thanked her for showing me such trust. Then I told her she had a beautiful soul that more than matched her outer beauty, and though she blushed, she did not hide her face or turn away. Instead, her finger touched my collarbone, her first display of physical affection. With a tremulous voice, she said that it was I who was an *Idaina tamashī*, a great soul. I accepted her compliment, but only after denying it three times, the minimum required to preserve the spirit of *wa* between us. Yet inside, I seethed with anger.

What a cruel thing Ulrikke has done, I thought. I could guess why Ulrikke replaced Yoshi with Junko, for no two girls could be such polar opposites. Yoshi, an extrovert, was more than my *sābanto,* she was a budding friend who might have succumbed to the temptation to take me to Borges. Junko's condition eliminated any chance of that happening. Junko knew nothing about my Borges' captivity, for almost everyone avoided or ignored her on sight. By assigning Junko to me, Ulrikke revealed herself a sadist. As my *sābanto,* Junko had to interact with the very people who daily rejected her. Those exchanges were painful to watch. It made me more determined to defy Ulrikke and find Borges, regardless of the risk. Yet I lacked any knowledge about where Ukrikke kept him. Frustrated and upset, it took a long time to fall asleep that night.

• • • • •

Darkness enveloped me. Dressed in a loose gown made of paper, I felt a chill each time the breeze picked up, and hugged my arms around my chest. In the gloom, I strained to see. Then a dim white light appeared. On bare feet, I walked toward it, though it never grew brighter, remaining weak and scattered as if by a dense fog. To keep my anxiety at bay, I counted my steps, but lost track after passing one thousand. At some point, the soft earth under my feet turned to stone tiles.

When I stumbled upon a series of steps, I recoiled in shocked recognition. These were the same steps I once climbed to reach the temple square in Kamakura where the Daibutsu, the Great Buddha, imposed an air of awe and serenity. Now, only a remnant of his former dominion remained. Signs of irreversible damage appeared the closer I approached. Much of his left side was ripped away, exposing the hollow expanse beneath the outer bronze shell. The Daibutsu's head remained intact, though it leaned forward at a dangerous angle. Cracks, large and small, ran throughout his lower body and the stone pedestal on which he perched. A series of symmetrical holes near the right shoulder looked as if they were made by a large industrial drill.

Except for the hand resting in his lap, his left arm was missing. Palm up, its fingers continued to touch those of his still intact right hand. Scrambling up the steps, I approached with tears blurring my vision. Then I heard a frail voice, at first a thin whisper, calling me.

"Takako. Jane. Takako."

I froze. Hearing the Daibutsu's voice, I forgot my discomfort. Light shone from the slits that formed his eyes like water bubbling from a spring.

"Who did this?" I said. "How did it happen?"

"You have forgotten my teachings, child," he replied. "The world is shadows and fog, filled with suffering and despair. Death rules all. Your attachment to it is leading you down a path to destruction. Let go of all your ties. Leave..."

His last words trailed off. Only the light from his eyes remained, though now it dimmed. I stood alone by the ruin of the Daibutsu, no more a Great Buddha. Then, out of the darkness, a black hand struck my shoulder, heavy and cold. I screamed, and...

Awake, I got up from my futon and drew aside the sheet that served as a door. Dawn's light filtered throughout the large hall. I went over to a small brazier to warm myself. A man wrapped in tattered robes squatted there. When his head lifted, I recognized the face.

"A bird stirs itself; a rising sun's crimson light colors winter trees."

"Bashō?"

"*Ohayō gozaimasu*, Jane-san." His rheumy eyes and wispy beard gave him the look of an ancient prophet. "You have awakened into a new dream."

"Yes," I said. "Worse than my dream of San Francisco."

"You spoke with the Daibutsu." He was not asking for confirmation.

"While I slept."

"He told you to flee, did he not? But then, he would, for you created him."

"I–what did you say?" *I created him?*

"You still do not understand yourself, Jane-san. You are like a *kami* that, having wandered far from home, has lost all connection to its place in the universe."

"You're right, I don't understand."

"The Daibutsu is a symbol." Bashō replied. "He has no life-force except what you, sensing the Buddha's presence, project onto him. Like a mirror, he reflects it back to you."

"But he gave me my power," I said in rebuttal.

"Did you not say you awoke from one dream into another, Jane-san?"

"That's different. I've seen the Daibutsu outside my dreams."

"The white-eye sings, defying the sparrow hawk; a shadow falls."

Another hokku, I thought. *Always another hokku*. "Stop," I said. "Just one time, I wish you would give me a straight answer."

"Is time straight?" Bashō responded. "Or curved? Does it run toward the unimaginable future? Or is it an endless loop doomed to repeat over and over for all eternity?"

"I need answers, not more riddles."

Bashō smiled. "True, Jane-san, but my riddles point to answers you already possess in your no-self."

"Please, cut the Zen bullshit."

"Tell me," he continued, ignoring my impertinence, "you have had other dreams in which the Daibitsu spoke. What did he say to you then?"

"You mean Costa Rica?"

"If that is one you remember, then yes," Bashō said.

I wracked my brain. Costa Rica was so long ago, a memory from a previous life. Fleeting images emerged; a vision of the Daibutsu emanating rays of many colors, his voice speaking with the force of a god.

"He said Borges was a dream. That Borges had always been a dream. Would always be a dream. And something else: That he had no power. He could only teach his dharma. It made no sense."

"*Sō desu ka?*" said Bashō, implying I missed something, that my memory was incomplete. So, I struggled again to recall what the Daibutsu said.

"I pleaded with him after he said that, something like, 'Please find my Borges and return him to me.' And he said back, 'As you wish, so shall it be.' When I awoke, Borges was there."

"*Sō desu ka,*" said Bashō, with the same expression. There was more I couldn't quite recall about the limits of the Daibutsu's power, but I said nothing, assuming Bashō knew my memories were incomplete or even false.

"And now you found your Borges, again."

"It would be more correct to say Borges found me."

"As you wish," said Bashō, and my face turned red.

"Don't mock me! That's–*futekisetsu na*!" His use of that phrase was a deliberate insult.

"*Gomen nasai,*" Bashō said, bowing low to me. "Forgive me, Jane-san. I am ashamed and regret angering you."

I reached over and tugged at his cloak until he sat back up. "Never mind," I said. "You're forgiven. But it's not like I chose to come here. Borges tricked me."

"And yet, here you remain, close to your Borges, do you not?"

"I suppose," I said, unprepared for this quick transition. "Can I go Elsewhere? Maybe. But it's complicated. Borges is here. I'm pregnant with his child. His mother, Ulrikke, is keeping me from him. If I left, Ulrikke said he'd just find me again, like the last time in San Francisco." *And I don't really know how to control my power, either.*

"Ah, Urikei. I know her well."

"What?" I said, but then my ears picked up the familiar clicking sound of Junko's wooden geta sandals. I turned round just as she kneeled, holding my breakfast tray.

"*Ohayo*, Jane-san," said Junko. "It's good to see you awake. Are you hungry?"

"*Ohayo*." A perfunctory response. "*Sumimasen*, Junko, but could you give me a moment? I need to finish talking to my friend." But when I turned back to Bashō, no one was there.

"Old Koike-san?" she said. "He can be like that, coming and going without a thought for anyone else. Please excuse him."

Koike-san? But that was Bashō, I was sure of it. How could Junko confuse him for someone else? "How old is Koike-san?" I asked.

"I do not know, but people have been calling him that since I was little. He became *fuzai* this last year. I hope he didn't upset you."

"No, not at all," I said. "*Fuzai?* I'm not sure what that means."

"More and more, he forgets where he is, and what he says. But he's harmless. Not like the other *Furui mono*."

"I see." Her words were polite in the extreme, but they implied he was senile. Whoever 'Old Koike-san' was, he couldn't have been Bashō. So why did she confuse them? Then, a memory bubbled up from my unconscious. After Borges reentered my life, and I regained the memories I lost for 20 years, Bashō spoke to me in a San Francisco diner. I asked why he abandoned me, and his answer rang as clear as a church bell through my head:

"I never left, Jane-san. You simply forgot I was with you. I must say, it was good practice for me, tending your gardens."

It appeared Bashō could cloud the minds of those who knew him, if he chose to. But why did Junko see him in the first place, much less as this Koike-san person? Was he obligated to help her? If so, perhaps he didn't want Junko to know I, too, knew him, and for a similar reason. But I feared to ask Junko about him. And now, I doubted whether Bashō would be honest with me if I asked him about her.

"Would you like some tea?" Junko said, as she poured *macha* for me, then offered it in the traditional manner, one hand holding the bottom of the cup, the other one wrapped around the side, using a small cloth as a buffer against the heat.

"*Domo.*" I took a quick sip. But my mind was still on Bashō and my dream of the Daibutsu. We ate breakfast in silence.

When finished, we headed south on another of our treks, as I called them. I asked Junko where we were going, even though the chance I might see something new seemed unlikely, having already been to so many places: barns, pastures, gardens, a forest where logging occurred, the giant compost heap (not a fond memory), the school, and buildings where scientists and technicians worked to repair solar panels, storage batteries and other old tech. We even visited a windmill under construction. *What more could there be?*

"It's a surprise," Junko said as she walked ahead, and I swore I could detect a hint of playfulness in her voice.

"What kind of surprise?" This was not like her. She always answered me with no attempt at evasion.

"You'll see," she said giggling, as if she were just another Japanese schoolgirl and not the shy, serious person I'd come to know. *Well,* I thought, *a surprise might be nice.* Junko set a fast pace, much faster than that first day when Yoshi took me to the greenhouse. The walks must have strengthened me. Plus they distracted me from my morning sickness.

Junko soon left the path and walked into a field overgrown with wild grasses and the skeletal stalks of weeds. The ground was uneven, filled with ruts and holes, and I slowed, wary of twisting an ankle, but Junko never hesitated. To her, this was familiar territory. While staring at the ground to avoid a fall, I lost track of her, until I heard her call, "*Ojii-chan!*"

Looking up, I saw her leap into the arms of an elderly, but well-built man wearing a peasant hat. Junko smothered him in kisses. I stopped, stunned. I never imagined her capable of such joy. And then I remembered. *Ojii-chan.* This was her grandfather, and her evident joy a sign of how much she must love him. Tall for a Japanese man, he exuded physical strength. In his arms, Junko was a tiny ballerina. Putting her down, he called to me.

"Ohayō, Jane-san. It is an honor to meet you at last. I am Tanaka Asahi and Junko is my granddaughter. My only granddaughter."

"Ohayō gozaimasu, Tanaka-san," I replied. *So this is your big surprise, Junko,* I thought. *Damn, you got me good.* Junko, hair whipping about in the wind, beckoned. Walking to them, I experienced a vertiginous sense of the sky and earth spinning around me, but it passed. Halfway there, Junko grabbed my arm, pulling me to them with great urgency. Up close, Tanaka Asahi towered over me. Besides the hat, he wore a light-blue work shirt and an old pair of faded jeans. Large and well-worn leather boots completed the picture. His hand reached out, and I took it. The grip was firm, but I suspected he was going easy on me.

"Jane-san," he said again, "it truly is an honor. And please, no more Tanaka-san. Call me Ray." He spoke English with a pitch-perfect SoCal accent. *Who is this guy?* I wondered. *And where did he come from?*

"I'm pleased to meet you, Tanaka–I mean, Ray," I responded. "Your English is excellent."

"Thanks," he said, "it should be. I spent twenty-five years in the States, teaching at major universities and working as a project manager for DARPA. Ray was my chosen American name. Much easier for people to pronounce."

"DARPA?" I said. "The military's secret R&D department? The one that developed drones and stealth bombers and…?"

"Oh, we worked on much more than that. Yep, that DARPA."

"What did you do, if you don't mind my asking?"

"I was, or still am, a materials scientist. Received my Ph.D. in Material Physics from Cal Tech. Did my post-doctoral work in chemistry and electromagnetism as it relates to phase change materials." My deer in the headlights look elicited laughter. "Forgive me. Old men love to brag about their accomplishments and no one more than an old academic."

"That's all right," I said. "Sounds like you worked on some important stuff."

"We thought so at the time," Ray said. "Now?" He shrugged. "Now it doesn't seem so important."

"So why did you–"

"Return to Japan?"

"Yes."

"I received a warning from some friends to leave as soon as possible. I wasn't American, after all."

"They deported you?"

"No. My colleagues at Los Alamos got wind the FBI was investigating me as a foreign agent working for the Japanese government. Relations between our two countries had soured. I got out just before they issued my arrest warrant. My wife, adult son and daughter-in-law followed. It was especially hard on my boy, who was born in America, but I feared the US government might imprison him or worse because of me. I couldn't risk it."

"Were you a spy?" I asked, thinking too late how rude that must sound.

"No, but I'd stopped working for the U.S. military two years earlier and returned to teaching." He sighed. "The times were–it's difficult to describe just how paranoid everyone was. The world had gone to shit, and when that happens, governments find scapegoats to distract people from the truth."

"What truth?"

"That they were helpless. Events were spiraling out of control and there was nothing they could do. Not just in America, mind you. So many governments told so many lies for so many years, made so many promises they couldn't keep, fought so many unnecessary wars, allowed so many to die, and now the butcher's bill was coming due."

"And you ended up here."

"Yes. The Japanese Defense Ministry asked me to be the director of a basic research facility as it transitioned to research for military applications. The prior director died under mysterious circumstances, and they needed a replacement. They were well aware of my work for the Americans. I didn't have much choice. Not if I wanted to bring my family here. Who knew that within two years, there wouldn't be a Japanese government? That's how fast things fell apart.

"Excuse me a moment." He turned to his granddaughter. "Junko, why don't you pick mushrooms while Jane-san and I talk? You know the ones I mean."

"Hai, *Sofu-san*. Goodbye, Jane-san." With a wave of her hand, she ran off down the hill. I soon lost sight of her.

"She speaks English?" I said.

"Of course. I taught her myself. I've had no better pupil." His face shone with pride in a very un-Japanese way. Then, again, he was like no one else I met here. *If he's telling the truth*, I reminded myself.

"She does well in school?"

"Junko has never attended the community school," he said. "When she came of age, the parents of the other children wouldn't allow it, fearing her condition was contagious. Not unexpected, but I hoped for better from them."

"That's ridiculous! Didn't your son and daughter-in-law–"

"They died of a variant of the Spanish Flu released by one of the great powers when Junko was three. I'm her only family now. And this is Japan, Jane, not America. To fight for her to attend school would not have beenproductive. When she was younger, the children accepted her, but as they grew older... Well, you know how malicious kids can be. As for their parents..."

"I'm so sorry," I said. Then a nasty thought came into my head, but one I couldn't ignore. "Excuse me, Ray, this may be out of line, but Junko never mentioned you before."

"And you find that suspicious. I can't say I blame you, Jane. Junko, as I'm sure you've discovered, is different. Shy. Afraid of people. And she is not wrong to feel that way. Because of her appearance, she's treated as an outcast. She was terrified of you."

"I know." Hearing Ray's concern for his granddaughter, I became angry all over again at Ulrikke. "Any idea why she was assigned to me in the first place?"

"Because I asked her to."

CHAPTER 20

What the hell? I thought. "Asked who? Ulrikke?"

"Her, too. But first, I asked Junko."

"Why would you do such a thing?"

"I needed to meet you alone without Urirkei's knowledge."

"What do we have to talk about that's so important it requires a private conversation, out here in the-"

"Middle of nowhere?" Ray finished my question for me.

"Exactly."

"Let's get to that," he said. "I am the head, the Chiifu, if you will, of our defense committee. We have a great deal to discuss, including the matter of your friend, Mr. Borges."

"You know where my Borges is? Can you take me to him? Please, you must help me." This was the break I hoped for.

Ray Tanaka didn't react to my outburst. He just became harder to read. "If I can help you, I will," he said, "but first, you and I must discuss Urikei, whose behavior of late troubles me a great deal. That's why I sent Junko away. I don't want her to know anything, for her own protection."

"You're starting to scare me, Ray."

"Good. That was my intention." He laughed, not unkindly. "Come. I have quite the show and tell prepared." He motioned with his hand, and, after a split second, I followed.

"I suppose if you've gone to all this trouble…"

Ray Tanaka smiled, but his eyes stayed serious. "Don't worry, we have transportation. I hope you don't mind a golf cart without a windshield. With luck it won't take long, and I'll get you back long before the storm rolls in later this afternoon."

How apropos, I thought. *A storm.* The irony was not lost on me.

• • • • •

Ray and I made our way up a steep hill through waves of susuki grass. We left the golf cart, now about 100 feet below, at the end of a dirt road, which Ray said no one used except him. The ride had been rough, with many twists and turns through a thick, wooded area of rugged hills. I asked Ray where we were. "Near Sagami Bay," was all he said.

About ten yards from the hill's crest, Ray motioned to stop. "From here on, we crawl," he whispered.

"You're joking, right?" Five months into my pregnancy, that was the last thing I wanted.

"Sorry, but what you're about to see is off limits to everyone but those who work there. If we're spotted, the consequences would be–"

"What?"

"Better you not know. Please, do as I say."

His edgy tone convinced me. "Okay, I guess we crawl." Looking relieved, he helped lower me to the ground. Pushing through the dense grass on the hillside was not pleasant. When we reached the top, Ray pushed aside the tall grass, and a valley came into view. A peaceful stream meandered across it from east to west. On the other side, was a large ramshackle building, perhaps an abandoned lumber mill. Bleached by sun and rain, its aging wooden exterior was driftwood gray. Lifting my head to get a better look, a brown and white bunny darted past, startling me. Ray chuckled softly while pushing my head back down.

"That *nousagi* is a good reminder to keep out of sight," he said. "Did you not see it there, only a few feet from your hands?"

"No," I sputtered," I'm a city mouse, not a country one." Ray laughed again before turning serious.

"You would do well to adopt the nousagi's attitude. We're too far from the motion detectors to have picked us up, but there are guards down there, even if you can't see them, and they constantly scan the area for intruders."

"Motion detectors?"

"Yes," said Ray Tanaka. "About halfway down the slope, hidden among saplings and thorn bushes. Their range is limited, but we also use other surveillance measures. CCTV cameras cover this entire area and someone constantly monitors the feed. This time of day we should be in a blind spot, but camera angles change often."

When I stared at him, bemused, he added, "Even the Chiifu of the Defense Committee delegates. The woman in charge of this facility handles security. We can't risk outsiders learning the truth of what we hide down there."

My mind reeled, though Ray had mentioned an extensive network of security systems protected "Fāmā-mura," literally "Farmer Village," a name that also served a security purpose as *maskirova*, the art of deception. Who would expect to find research scientists living as simple farmers? Surrounded by brutal warlords and gangs of roving bandits, the goal was to appear poor and harmless. I looked again at the innocuous building, which contained four small nuclear reactors somewhere inside.

"So that's where they are?"

"Yes," replied Ray. "We dismantled an abandoned warehouse and reconstructed it here to camouflage the facility that once conducted particle physic experiments. Most of it's underground. Our 'gadgets' are on the lowest level, fifty meters below the surface."

"Gadgets?"

"Sorry. An inside joke from my days at Sandia Labs. When Oppenheimer conducted the Trinity test of the first plutonium bomb at Alamogordo, they nicknamed it the 'Gadget.'"

Charming euphemism. I wondered if the men involved in the first A-bomb test understood how soulless its name sounded. To be fair, it wasn't any worse than "Little Boy" and "Fat Man," the nuclear bombs dropped on Hiroshima and Nagasaki, 'gadgets' that killed hundreds of thousands of people. It felt eerie knowing that devices I assumed could be reconfigured as nukes were down there. It also brought to mind Ray's story of the day Fāmā-mura acquired them, from, of all people, Ulrikke.

It happened in the year Japan's government collapsed amid a sea of riots and uprisings over food shortages. Fāmā-mura was a remnant of the research complex that existed when Ray took over. Inside, a few hundred scientists, technicians and their families, plus a small security detail, fought to survive Japan's collapse into chaos. "Many people died during that time." That was all Ray would say.

One rain-soaked day in July, six months after the government fell, a large semi-tractor trailer drove up to the main gate. Behind the wheel was a slender, old white-haired woman of European descent. After she spoke to them, the guards waved her through with no inspection of her vehicle, a serious violation of security protocols. She must have known Ray was in charge, because she asked for him by name.

"Tanaka-sama," she said, bowing low, "my name is Ulrikke Maria Borges, and I have something that might interest you." Unable to resist, he followed her to the rear of the trailer. "It seemed the most natural thing in the world," he said. He wasn't alone. No one in the crowd that assembled and surrounded the truck objected to this strange gaijin woman's presence. "It was like we already knew her," Ray said. "There is an aura about Urikei that people find soothing, even attractive. I'd call her 'charismatic,' but that doesn't do her justice. I knew she was special, but not that she would be our salvation. Without her, we'd all be dead by now."

Ulrikke opened the trailer and Ray couldn't believe his eyes. Inside were four fully operational mini-reactors designed for Japan's Defense Force, each capable of generating ninety megawatts of power. When combined, they provided more than enough electricity for the community's needs, including defensive needs. In subsequent trips, Ulrikke brought them several rail guns, including a large artillery-like piece that Ray claimed could throw a twenty kilogram metal projectile over 100 kilometers at hypersonic speeds. "Faster than a bullet," Ray said. "We named it 'Bigukyonon.' Not that original, but accurate."

"Bigukyonon?"

"Sorry," Ray replied. "Big Cannon."

The one and only time they used their "Big Cannon" occurred when the most powerful local warlord, the Yamamoto Shogun, announced his intent to annex Fāmā-mura. The Shogun, who claimed he was the reincarnated spirit of Admiral Yamamoto, was a former major in the Defense Force who commanded a large arsenal near Tokyo. When the government fell, plunging the country into economic and social collapse, he used those weapons to take advantage of the situation.

Many former military units rallied to him because the arsenal included artillery and several tanks. That firepower allowed him to establish control over much of the central coast of eastern Honshu. Almost a year after

Ulrikke's arrival, over one thousand armed men appeared at Fāmā-mura's eastern border. Among their vehicles was a tank. Four uniformed men carrying a white flag of truce met Ulrikke and Ray in the middle of a deserted field. They demanded Fāmā-mura summarily submit to the Shogun or face annihilation.

"They didn't expect any resistance," Ray said. "Not from a bunch of farmers. I still recall Ulrikke's response. She remarked, offhandedly, that, if they valued their lives, the Shogun's forces should retreat and never return. They laughed in her face.

"None of them knew we possessed operational rail guns. Ulrikke asked where their Shogun stood, since he had not deigned to come and present his request in person. Furious, one man in a tattered Air Force uniform, pointed at the tank atop the ridge. He told us we had five minutes before it opened fire.

"Ulrikke then raised her arm and pointed at the hill. Within seconds, we obliterated the tank, and a good section of the ridge on which it sat, with one round from the Bigukyonon, killing the first Yamamoto Shogun and hundreds of his elite shock troops. The remaining Yamamoto forces scattered as fast as they had appeared. We are now on excellent terms with their successor, the Cowboy Bebop Clan.

"You know," he continued, "she never told me where she found those rail guns, or the reactors. And I've never asked. Even today, whenever we're face to face, I cannot bring myself to raise the subject."

A shiver ran down my spine when he said that, as I had a pretty good idea how she obtained them. Not the exact details, but it was clear she used her gift and go to past timelines of this Elsewhere, doing whatever was necessary to assure she could provide what her community needed to survive. How did she endure reliving countless lives over and over to do that? The answer, when it came to me, was obvious. She could manipulate her age when using her ability. She lied about always starting each new life as a girl of sixteen, the age when Óðinn gave her his gift in the 11th century. Her powers went far beyond what she told me.

What other lies did she tell? Was she dying or could she manipulate her body, making it appear she had cancer to gain sympathy, further reinforcing her hold over those who lived in Fāmā-mura? For Ulrikke was a feudal lord in all but name. Fāmā-mura's people were her subjects, even if most didn't grasp that. Her control over them reminded me of Borges' hold over me. Yet Ulrikke's efforts to compel me to do her bidding me failed. That I, unable to resist Borges, could resist his mother was a paradox.

• • • • •

Ray nudged my arm, bringing me back to reality. He handed over a pair of lightweight binoculars. "Take a closer look," he said.

"I don't see steam. Don't reactors generate steam?"

"These aren't water-cooled. They're cooled by both air convection and liquid helium. The helium coolant changes to a gas as it passes through the reactor core, then spins a turbine to generate electricity. It's then re-converted to its liquid state using high efficiency air compression, and the process repeated. That's why they're so much smaller and lighter." He paused, and his eyes glazed. "So, it's true what Junko said about you. You are a traveler."

I did a double take. "What's a traveler?"

"A traveler can imagine a different world, whether in the past, present or future, and then travel there by willing it into existence. The power to manipulate space-time through will alone makes no sense from a scientific standpoint, but based on what I know of Urikei, I believe she can do it. Perhaps your friend Borges possesses the same ability. And I now believe you can travel, as well."

I said nothing at first, amazed that Ray could deduce so much of the truth about me with so few clues. "How did you know?" I said in a small voice.

"So, it's true then? I've been right all these years about Urikei!" I was furious. He tricked me.

"It's not like that, what you said." I blurted out. "There are limits to what I can do–to what she can... It's more complicated than you think."

"Oh, no doubt, no doubt," Ray said. "But I have the gist of it, don't I?"

I nodded, but then changed my mind and shook my head. "I'm not like them!" I said, meaning Borges and Ulrikke. "You say Ulrikke can convince people, *persuade* them, to do whatever she wants, right? You called her charismatic. That's mind control. I'm can't do that. I can't even make people like me."

Ray eyed me skeptically. "I think you underestimate yourself. Yoshi fell under your spell within a day. She would die for you. I overhead her say that to Urikei."

"Yoshi's a young, impressionable girl." The wind picked up then and strong gusts flattened the grass hiding us from the prying eyes below. Ray said something I didn't understand. I pointed to my ears and shouted that I couldn't hear, so he leaned in close to my ear.

"Junko loves you," he said. "More, she trusts you. Do you know how rare that is? I am the only person in the village who receives any affection from her, and, until now, the only person she trusted to talk about her feelings. Now she thinks of you as a big sister. You accomplished that in only a few weeks' time. To me, that's nothing short of a miracle." Just then, the sky lit up with huge bolts of lightning and a loud crack of thunder blasted my ears. Raindrops struck my arms and face.

"The storm's arrived early!" Ray shouted. "We need to get off this hill!"

The two of us slid down the slope until Ray felt it safe to stand. Then we took off running downhill helter-skelter, arms and legs flying in all directions. Out of sheer dumb luck, I didn't fall. We made it to the golf cart just as the floodgates opened. Like rats, we scurried under a canvas tarp Ray dragged out of a storage compartment under the seat. He crouched over me with his arms and legs wrapped around its four corners to anchor it. I grabbed two of its sides. We did our best to hold on as the wind and rain pummeled us. An abrupt drop in temperature accompanied the storm. Lying underneath the tarp on rain-slicked ground chilled me to the bone. Then I panicked.

"We have to find Junko!" I screamed. "She's in danger!" I struggled to wriggle out from under Ray, but he forced his body down on mine, freezing me in place.

"Junko's fine," he shouted. "We built storm shelters all over our territory. I sent her to find mushrooms, remember? Mushrooms near one of the shelters. She knew a storm was coming, and what to do when it hit. She's safer than we are."

My fear for her subsided. But then I thought of something worse. "What about Ulrikke? Won't she send out a search party? What happens when she doesn't find Junko and me together?"

"I didn't tell Urikei about the storm. She's much too busy right now to bother about you. She'll assume Junko took you to a shelter, as would anyone else. Once this is over, we'll find Junko, and you'll return together. The storm will explain any delay. Please, Jane. Relax."

"All right," I said. But I couldn't. In one short hour, everything changed because of what I learned from Ray. How many others suspected that, like Ulrikke, I was different? What did Ray want from me? Why did Borges bring us to where his mother ruled a small corner of a dying world? I didn't trust either him or Ulrikke, but I couldn't find it in myself to abandon him. The storm lasted a half-hour before it passed eastward toward the ocean, but it felt so much longer, as I huddled beneath the tarp, thinking about many things, most of them regarding Borges.

When the wind subsided, Ray shoved the tarp off us. The sun's rays to our west shone through the clouds in that familiar pattern that suggests God is looking down on his creation. To my disappointment, no rainbow appeared. As a child, rainbows always comforted me after a storm, and I badly needed a little comfort.

"So much for our meteorologist's forecast," Ray said. Then he added, "That's a joke, Jane. We don't have a meteorologist, just a few physics students who do their best with the limited radar array we have. And this is the monsoon season."

"I didn't know Japan had a monsoon season," I said.

"A lot has changed over the last fifty years. The tropics are uninhabitable during the warmest months. Weather patterns shifted further north. Extreme storms are common this time of year. Without access to satellite data, predicting the weather is much harder. Everything is more difficult, but we're lucky. Most people live lives as bad as the peasants did during the Sengoku jidai." He referred to the Warring States period of Japan's medieval era.

"That bad?"

"Worse. Based on the stories from the few refugees we take in, wars, famines and plagues are the new normal. Millions died in Japan alone. Fāmā-mura is an oasis amidst a sea of chaos."

"Thanks to Ulrikke?"

He nodded. "We're a well-educated people: scientists, doctors, even the techs and lab assistants. But we're not natural warriors, except for the few families descended from our original security detail. Without the resources she provided, and continues to provide, our enemies would have slaughtered or enslaved us a long time ago.

"That is only a small measure of her true worth. Do you know the name our neighbors have for her? Himiko, the Great Witch Queen. They say she cannot be killed except by an army of demons. The awe and fear her name generates among them is our greatest defense. No ruler would last long if he proposed an attack on us. His own warriors would kill him and a new ruler would take his place, one less reckless. I've heard rumors that suggest this has already happened."

"So, what do you believe? You say we're 'travelers' who can alter the laws that govern time and space, and implied we can control people's minds to make them do what we want. How do you square that with your background and training as a physicist?"

"I'm not wedded to any grand scheme regarding what constitutes reality," Ray answered. "I trust only data, whether from experiments I've run myself or personal observations. And I've been observing Ulrikke over ten years."

"Just anecdotal evidence," I protested. "You can't rely upon that."

"Not true," he replied. "I cannot control for all variables, but that goes to the weight one assigns to specific data points, the confidence factor, to use stochastic terms. My observations of Ulrikke are not unlike data from experiments run to test the theory of quantum mechanics. You know you cannot be certain about what will happen, but there's a probability function applicable to every observation."

"Hold on. Probability function?"

He laughed. "Let me put it to you like this. Suppose a hermit living in the mountains wrote down his observations as he went about his daily routine. A list of the birds he saw each day, for example, or other animals. And what if he kept a record of the weather, whether it was sunny or cloudy, wet or dry, cold or warm? Over enough time, he would accumulate a lot of valuable information, even in this simple way I've described. A scientist could take that and use it, find connections between animal sightings, say, and seasonal variations. Evidence of how the local climate changed over time. Make sense?"

"Go on."

"The same principles apply to observations about people, including data regarding how individuals affect the dynamics of social systems. That is what I have done with Urikei-sama."

"You're kidding me," I said. "Memory is fallible. Even I know that."

"Only old memories. I started a journal a few months after she joined us. Each night, I write down everything that occurred between the two of us that day. And anything other people tell me, too. Like my hypothetical hermit's observations, it's a record of interactions people have had with Urikei."

"Why did you do it?"

"That's a long story, Jane, and our time grows short. You and Junko need to get back to the main compound. We don't want to draw people's attention to your absence. We'll speak further about this tomorrow, or the day after."

"Just give me the bullet points then."

"As you wish," he replied, and it was odd hearing the same phrase Bashō and Borges so often used coming from Ray Tanaka. On our way to Junko, he shot those bullet points at me fast and furious. For one, he said, not only did everyone grant Ulrikke membership in the Fāmā-mura community, despite her status as a gaijin, but also no one questioned or complained when, in short order, she assumed the role as their most prominent leader. Second, she possessed a prodigious knowledge of medicine, chemistry, biology, agriculture and even a smattering of physics.

"It was if she lived a thousand different lives," Ray said, "and remembered everything from each one."

Whatever she proposed invariably was done the way she wanted it done with no fuss or hard feelings. Trade negotiations with neighboring warlords always ended with deals struck on her terms. If the community lacked something vital, she always obtained the needed items, from antibiotics when an anthrax epidemic broke out to more powerful storage batteries when existing ones failed. She filled many roles for the community: fixer, judge, medical doctor, trade negotiator and Commander-in-Chief.

"Yet people are blind to the power she exercises unless I point it out to them," said Ray. "Even then, they say she's only acting according to the will of the community. She can do no wrong. That in itself defies belief. Have you ever heard of a leader immune from criticism?"

I had no answer to that, but I did have one question. "Why do you see this when no one else does?

"I don't know. I'm not impervious to her. When she's asks something of me, I do it without fail. But I've always recognized how different she is from the rest of us. Perhaps that's because I am different myself, having lived so long in North America. I abhor the practice of consensus common in Japanese society, preferring to draw my own conclusions. That's why I kept a record, because whatever she is, and whatever you may be, it varies so far from the norm for human beings, I cannot quantify it."

"You don't know me," I said. "I'm not like her."

"Ah, Jane, there you are wrong. Put aside your ignorance about the current state of affairs in Japan, or the history of the past half-century. From the moment security personnel discovered you and your friend lying half-dead inside our borders, Urikei-sama kept you isolated. She advised us to avoid contact with you, ostensibly because of your health. Until you regained your strength, no one other than herself and Yoshi were permitted to talk to you. Don't you find that strange? Then, when Yoshi showed signs of becoming too familiar, Ukrikke replaced her with my Junko, the last person Urikei expected would develop a close relationship with you.

"This is not standard operating procedure when we admit a *Sutorenjā*, a refugee, to join our ranks. Normally, we assist them in finding a place in our community. You're healthy enough now, aren't you? Yet Ulrikke's informal ban on interacting with you remains. That tells me Urikei fears you. And she hasn't let you see your friend, Borges, has she?"

"No," I confessed. "But she promised me I'll see him soon."

"Did she define soon?"

I lowered my eyes.

"I see you have your own suspicions regarding her motives. Let me provide you more reasons. The day after we found both of you, Urikei announced to everyone that the Council of Elders determined your friend Borges was banished as a spy for the Crazy Eight clan." He sighed. "Easy enough to believe, for the Crazy Eights, led by their avaricious leader, present the greatest threat to our territory. Though they've made no direct moves against us, we've captured several of their spies over the past year. Yet she convinced the Elders to allow you to stay."

"Borges isn't here? He's no spy!"

"Don't worry. Urikei convinced the Council to spread that lie about him. She interrogated him by herself with no one else present. When finished, she insisted we keep him as a prisoner because, though dangerous, he might later prove useful to us. But she never said how he could help. At the same meeting, she ordered us to keep the two of you apart, because, even though she said you posed no threat, your emotional ties to him might prove problematic."

"That's crazy. Borges and I... We were lovers once, okay? I may have feelings for him, but it's not like she said." Worried Ray might reject a request for his help, I omitted telling him the extent to which I still loved Borges. "But you know where he is, yes? And you've spoken to him?"

"I do," Ray said after a long pause. "And I've spoken to him. His story was quite–"

"Fantastic."

"Thank you. That's the perfect word."

"Did he say he's Ulrikke's son? And that she was the daughter of an ancient Viking King who died trying to conquer England?"

Ray's eyes widened. "How did you know? He said you knew nothing about Urikei."

"Because Ulrikke told me. And yes, we aren't like you. Both of us can-travel, as you said. Go wherever and whenever we wish. But we have limits, or at least I do. And something else: Ulrikke hates and fears my Borges, even if he's her son."

"I see." Ray sounded noncommittal.

"Take me to him, Ray. I'm pregnant and I'm certain he's the father. Second, we came here because he drugged me. I awoke in Fāmā-mura with no idea how I got here. And forgive me for saying this, but it's not a place I would have chosen. Look, somehow he got me to bring us here. There's a reason he did that. I need to discover what it is. I bet you do, too."

Ray stopped the cart at the top of a hill close to where Junko left to gather mushrooms. From where we stood, I could see Sagami Bay in the distance, whitecaps dotting its blue waters as the west wind drove off the last storm clouds. But Ray's eyes didn't focus on the view. With a sudden turn of his head, he stared at me. *He's made up his mind*, I thought, *but which way?* Then, Junko arrived, put down her bucket, threw her arms around me and pulled me into a fierce embrace of sheer infectious joy.

CHAPTER 21

Six days later, thirty minutes after lights out, Junko and I snuck out of my room. Silent as ghosts, we made our way to the pre-arranged spot by the greenhouse. From there, Ray would take me to Borges. I gave Junko a quick hug goodbye. "Arigato, little one," I whispered in her ear. Then she vanished into the night.

Those six days had been an eternity for me. I only saw Ray once, in an abandoned shed rotting away in a dark wood near Fāmā-mura's western border. Junko brought me there and then left for an hour. Ray's eyes were red, and every few seconds he looked over his shoulders, fearful of being discovered. At his insistence, we whispered, though I saw no sign anyone had been there in years.

"I'll take you," he said. "But it won't be easy. He's imprisoned in a hermetically sealed room designed for experimental research but no longer in use. No one can speak to him on Urikei's orders. A deaf technician delivers all his meals as a precaution. Despite that, I defied her and spoke to him."

"How?"

"I put myself on the guard rotation one night, and we had a little chat. He told me many things that don't match your story."

"Like what?" I asked.

Borges told Ray he could also "travel" and that I came with him to Fāmā-mura of my own free will. Borges' lie about not drugging me was bad enough, but his claim he could travel Elsewhere stunned me. If true, why hide it? Ulrikke said he didn't have our *gift*, though he possessed other abilities. For a moment, I doubted everything I knew about him. Then, I thought, *Why bother drugging me, if he could do what I do?* He must have lied to Ray. Still, it troubled me that each time I traveled it happened a different way. I never recall choosing my destination. Until I learned how to control my power, I was trapped in Fāmā-mura, as much a prisoner as Borges.

Just as troubling was what Borges didn't reveal. Why persist in keeping me in his life? And, after searching for twenty years to find me in that alternate San Francisco, why place our fate in the hands of his mother, a woman who wanted me to kill him? Was it his damn prophecy Ulrikke spoke of, but which Borges never once mentioned? Was I just a pawn in his game, which he would remove from the board whenever it suited him? I needed answers, but for that, I needed to speak to him. And according to Ray, that was problematic.

"He's at the same place where we keep our reactors. Guards cover each entrance and patrol all six underground levels."

"But you managed it before. There must be a way."

"Only if you can persuade others to obey you as well as Urikei can."

"I don't know if that's possible," I admitted. "I've never tried before."

"Then you will never see him again. I believe in you, Jane, but you must trust yourself. Can you?"

"I have no choice," I said. On that melancholy note, we parted. And now I waited alone in the dark for him to come and take me to Borges.

• • • • •

I felt Ray's touch on my arm, before I saw him.

"It's time, Jane. Stay close. It would be easy for you to get lost if we become separated." I nodded, and we set off. After a long, circuitous route, we arrived at a secret entrance to the underground facility hidden in a grove of beech trees fifty yards from the wooden structure that masked its existence. Ray cleared away some brush, exposing a rusted manhole cover. He pressed a small button, and it popped open. A ladder led to a tunnel below. "After you," he motioned. We climbed down, my heart beating like a drum.

A guard's eyes lit up when he saw me. Raising a handgun, he demanded Ray explain what we were doing. Ray gestured to me. Now came my moment of truth. I bowed low to the guard, as one would to a superior, and then looked him straight in the eyes.

"Setsumei sasete kudasai," I said, asking him to permit me to explain why we were there. Then I handed him a small piece of rice paper with Ulrikke's mark on it. Ray never told me how he obtained her personal hanko, and I didn't ask. The guard examined the paper. I concentrated on appearing as convincing as possible. "Watashi no hōmon o shōnin shitekureta no wa Urikei-Chōrō desu. Tōshite kudasai." That meant Ulrikke authorized our visit. He hesitated, and I thought I failed until he handed the paper back and waved us through with a short, "Hai."

"You did it," Ray whispered in my ear. From then on, my confidence soared. There was no further trouble with the guards. Before long, we arrived at a metal door, which Ray opened. At the far end of an expansive room, I saw Borges behind a thick glass wall, in a chair by a small desk, reading a book, his legs and arms in shackles. Behind him, on the floor, lay a futon. Pushing his chair back from the desk, he put his book down and stared right at me through the glass, as if this was all perfectly normal. *Well, what else is new*, I thought.

I had to speak to Borges face to face, so Ray unlocked a circular door that opened into an airlock. Stepping through, I stepped over to a second door, a few feet inside the airlock. "See that wheel there?" Ray said. "Turn it counter-clockwise to access the inner chamber." Then he locked me inside the airlock. I placed both hands on the wheel and pulled on it until I heard a hiss. Then I pushed against the inner door until it opened. And there he was, my Borges.

"Jane," he said, rising from his chair. I rushed to his side before he could get out another word and kissed him hard on the lips. I can't lie. It felt good. Then, holding him at arms' length, I gave him the once-over. Just as he began to smile, I slapped him as hard as I could across his cheek, enough to make my hand sting.

"No more lies. Why in the hell did you bring me here?"

"Good to see you're still alive and well," Borges said. He didn't answer my question, a fact not lost on me.

"That's funny, because your mother, you know, the woman who runs this place, wants you dead and asked me to kill you. I wonder why. Oh, and I'm pregnant. I don't recall being pregnant before I woke up in this hellhole. But let's put that aside for now. Again, why did you drug me and bring me here?"

Borges' eyes shifted downward. "You chose to come," he said. "I remember your exact words. 'I want to go to Japan.'" Not the response I was looking for.

"I don't remember a thing from the time you stuck that needle in my neck." His lies were so obvious that I couldn't keep the anger out of my voice. "How does someone like me lose four months of her life?"

"You got me, but I drugged you because the world you created was about to annihilate itself. You remember Iran sinking an American aircraft carrier, don't you? McCain was about to retaliate with nukes. You forced my hand."

"It's all my fault?" I said in disbelief. "Seriously, you want to go with that? Because I have a million and one reasons not to trust a single thing you say."

"Believe, disbelieve, it makes no matter," Borges replied, "but it's the truth. You chose this." His red-rimmed eyes went hard with anger. If it was an act, it was a good one.

"Fine," I said. "Tell your tale, lies and all. Entertain me."

"You're an ignorant woman, Jane Takako Wolfsheim," Borges responded, "and that ignorance will get you killed if you're not careful. You say you spoke with my mother, and now you don't trust me, but I say you shouldn't believe anything she said, about me, about herself, about anything."

"She isn't relevant to–our discussion."

"And yet, you brought her up."

"You're stalling," I replied. "Answer me. How could I, unconscious, chose to go anywhere?"

"I used Midazolam, a common hypnotic agent. You might know it by its trade name: Versed."

"Versed?" The name sounded familiar. "That's a sedative, isn't it?

"Yes, but it also has hypnotic effects. I gave you enough to put you in a trance-like state, then suggested you take us to this Japan. You did the rest. I'm sorry, but it was necessary."

"I see," I said. "You injected me with this Versed stuff, said let's go to where your mom lives, I agreed and–voila–here we are, in the worst possible future I can imagine. I'm sure you can see the problem I have with that." Borges shook his head, his face a mask of confusion.

"Let me make myself plain then. Not only does your story lack critical details regarding how we arrived in this specific place, but Ray Tanaka, your mother's head of security, let slip that you're calling yourself a 'traveler,' like me. So, pardon my skepticism about that story. Let me offer an alternative one. You used your own ability or power or whatever it is to bring us here. Who knows why, but I'm betting it has something to do with your mother, who wants to make me your murderer."

"I don't doubt she asked you to kill me," Borges said. "I'll bet she told you why you must do it and not her. But even she would agree I do not have her gift, one that offers her and you virtual immortality. I've never had that power, much as I have sought after it, though I have other things–"

"Like making me love you, for starters?" I said. "The Jedi mind tricks you employ so ably? Why else would Ray Tanaka do your bidding and bring me to see you against your mother's explicit instructions to keep us apart?"

"She fears you." Borges replied. "But you still found a way, didn't you?"

"Yes, I did. But now that I see you, I'm not buying what you're selling." I turned away from him, so he wouldn't see my eyes tearing up. Damn you, Borges! I thought. Why do I still love you?

"If you still love me, Jane," Borges said, "It's not my doing."

"Stay the fuck out of my head and shut up!" I lost it and made a mess of myself, a bravura performance. When the tears ran out, he spoke again.

"May I continue?" He stood there in chains, and deservedly so, but I said nothing, which he must have taken as my tacit consent. "You've grown far beyond any ability of mine to control you, Jane. I see that now. It's one more confirmation of the prophecy. You're the one."

"What?" My knees buckled. I assumed Ulrikke invented the story about Borges' prophecy. Yet here he was, admitting to it. That familiar sensation of vertigo returned.

"So," he said, "Mother kept a few secrets from you. How like her."

Before I could react, Ray broke in on the intercom. "Urikei's coming! Someone triggered the alarm. You must leave. Now!" Moments later, he rushed in and, with a set of keys in hand, unlocked the shackles on Borges' wrists and ankles.

"Hey, I don't get a say about this?"

"Afraid not, Jane-san," Ray said.

"A jail break was never part of the plan, Ray." Pointing at Borges, rubbing his wrists where the metal shackles left them raw, I added, "Bringing me to him was the agreement."

"The guards you convinced to let us through tonight, do you think they won't tell Urikei I came with you? Do you have the slightest idea what she'll do to me once she learns I disobeyed her? Or to Junko? If you care about her, we must make it appear that you forced me to do this."

"How do we pull that off? And where can we go that Ulrikke won't find us?"

"He knows," said Ray, looking at Borges.

"Tanaka-san set up a hide-out for the two of us," Borges piped up, "on the off chance things went sideways." Ray avoided my gaze.

"Why didn't you mention this before, Ray?"

"You never asked."

"You mean he told you not to tell me." I turned to Borges. "You used me, again!"

"All right, I asked Ray to keep you in the dark. Don't blame him. It was my hope to convince you myself, but I couldn't be sure we'd have enough time before Mother showed up."

"Ray's been your puppet all along. That's just great. That's just peachy." My head swam in circles as I considered my options. Should go I with him, or just leave and let him deal with mommie dearest himself. But Ray Tanaka was right about one thing. He and Junko were in grave danger.

"Let's say I sign off on your getaway scheme," I said to Borges. "What's to stop Ray from telling Ulrikke everything once she shows up?" My question was aimed at Borges, but Ray answered it.

"Order me to lie to her. You're as strong as Urikei. You know this. She couldn't convince you to kill her son. If you do as I ask, I can't reveal your hiding place. I'll say you forced me to bring you here. Do that and we have a chance."

"You're taking an awful risk if you're wrong."

"I have no choice," Ray replied, shooting a glance at Borges. Of course, I thought. Ray never had a choice once Borges got to him.

"So this was all your idea?" I said to Borges, my voice dripping with acid.

"We're running out of time," he replied, as if that was sufficient.

"Please, Jane-san," Ray pleaded. "You must do this, if not for me, then for Junko."

I cringed. But what other option did I have? Staring into his eyes, I ordered him to tell Ulrikke I persuaded him to bring me to Borges.

"Now what?" I said.

Ray gave me his pistol and sat down in Borges' desk chair. "Cuff me arms behind me. Use those." He indicated the handcuffs he removed from my Borges' wrists. After Borges cuffed him, Ray looked at me. "Jane, I must ask one more thing. You have to knock me out with the butt of my gun."

Looking at the handgun I held, my hand shook. "No way in hell." I tried to give Borges the gun, but he backed away from me.

"This won't work unless you do it," Borges said. "Mother will run the interrogation. She'll know I planned everything if he can't tell her. Now knock him out. It must look like you're in charge."

Borges had me boxed in. I wanted to blow his damn head off right then, but what else could I do? Nothing, if I wanted to protect Junko and Ray. I closed my eyes and swung the butt of the pistol as hard as I dared at his head. When it connected, there was a sickening, crackling sound. I opened my eyes. Ray slumped over, blood pouring from his scalp. The gun fell from my hand. Borges pulled me away from the man I just brutalized.

"Run!" he said. So, I did.

• • • • •

Wet, cold, naked, and scared, I shivered underneath a musty wool blanket. Its white patch with a red dot in the center indicated it was surplus from the now defunct Japanese Self Defense Force. Borges said we would warm up sooner if we removed our wet clothes. We stripped, and he hung them over the backs of two metal folding chairs to dry.

In our rush to escape Ulrikke, we ran into a typhoon with gale-force winds that uprooted trees all around us. Funnel-shaped tornadoes spiraled down south of us. For two hours, we battled through it. Often, Borges half-dragged, half-carried me, because I lacked the strength to make it by myself. Without his help, I might have died. My reliance on him galled me.

Now, teeth chattering, I huddled on a tatami mat in an abandoned bunker dug into a hillside. According to Borges, JDF soldiers guarding the perimeter of the former research installations at Fāmā-mura once used it. I barely listened, however. I kept thinking about Ray, his silver-gray hair doused in blood gushing from a large gash to the side of his head. For all I knew, I fractured his skull.

"Don't worry about Ray," Borges said, once again reading my mind. "He'll be fine."

"How would you know? If he dies, it would be my fault! No, it would be yours!"

"Because I've seen men killed by pistol whipping," Borges said with no emotion in his voice, which only made me more frightened. "At worst, you gave him a nasty concussion. Scalps bleed a lot. They just do. It looked worse than it was. Besides, we had to delay my mother. Any time she wastes on him works to our benefit. Don't forget that." *What a cold and calculating thing to say.* I shivered, but this time not from the cold. I asked no more questions about Ray.

Ray picked the bunker as our safe house because no one from Fāmāmura came here anymore, Borges said. In recent years, the Defense Committee deployed an advanced array of surveillance devices along its borders, from CCTV units covering the visual and infrared spectrums, to sound and motion sensors. The project had been Ulrikke's biggest priority. Once her advanced warning network went online, the bunker, a forward command center, became superfluous.

Stripped of lighting fixtures and communications equipment, it was a dingy hidey-hole. Other than the folding chairs, it had bunks for six people, sans mattresses, in a separate room. Another room had a small sink. Water miraculously still flowed from the faucet. Borges produced a cup of tea for me, heating the water with a propane-fueled field stove. It left a metallic aftertaste in my mouth, but at least I wouldn't die from thirst.

Besides the field stove, Ray stocked the bunker with futons, blankets, a week's worth of ready to eat military rations and a small oil lantern that Borges lit after closing the steel door that was the only entrance or exit. Light shone through a narrow window. Borges said it was blast resistant, constructed from glass fibers and layers of polyvinyl butaryl pressed together with military grade adhesives. When I asked how he knew so much, he just answered, "Ray."

"Don't worry," he assured me as I listened to the muffled sounds of howling winds. "We're safe."

"Even from rail guns?"

"How do you know about those?"

"Ray," I replied.

"Mother won't use them against us," he said after a brief pause. "That would be wasteful, and if there's one thing she's not, it's that."

For once, I thought he might be telling the truth. Ulrikke wanted her son dead, but she hadn't *persuaded* any of *her people* to do it, nor drive him from her territory out into the barbaric lands beyond its borders. Instead, she exerted all her efforts on convincing me to kill him. *Why?* Perhaps she believed I was the only one who could. Otherwise why keep us in Fāmāmura in the first place? Borges must know the answer to that question, plus a great deal more he wasn't telling me. Information I needed.

"Why not use them?" I said, referring to the rail guns. "She more or less begged me to–what's that word your goons used, the ones who disposed of Marty? Oh, right, to *clean* you. But why me? Your mother's more than capable of doing her own dirty work, like you." I was pushing him hard, but I needed him to believe I just might do what she asked.

"An educated guess," he said. "But does it matter? We're together again. We can leave now and be free of her forever. You can do that for us, Jane."

"Oh, my dear Borges," I said, "that's straight from *The Maltese Falcon*."

"I have no idea what you mean."

"Don't you? Ever since you *chose* me, my life's been one bad thing after another. My illness that began the day we met. Costa Rica, when you did your best to drive me insane. My parents' murders. Knifing Marty in front of me. My son's death. Maybe you're not responsible for all that's happened, but there's isn't very much on the other side of the ledger to suggest a better future awaits me if I do what you want. Just that maybe I love you and maybe you love me." I couldn't resist paraphrasing Bogie's lines as Sam Spade.

"You know you love me." His eyes flickered in the faint glow of the lantern, and I came close to wavering. But I didn't.

"That's not how Brigid delivered the line in the movie," I said.

"What are you talking about?"

"I'll make myself clear, then. You've counted on my love since the day I came to your store. And I've gone along with you, despite the consequences. That ends now." His familiar stare reappeared in all its intensity, but I refused to look away. If I did, he'd see it was all a bluff. I couldn't let that happen. Not this time. Not again. I held my breath, not knowing what he'd do. As always, it wasn't what I expected.

"You want to know why Mother wants to kill me and why she can't."

"I want to know a lot of things," I said, "but that'll do for starters."

"You won't believe me."

"Probably not, but try anyhow."

"It's simple," he said. "She killed me many times. It just never took."

CHAPTER 22

"You honestly think you're possessed by your father's sprit? That it drove you to do the terrible things you've done? I don't believe that. And I don't believe your mother tried to kill you, but this demonic spirit brought you back to life."

"I said you wouldn't," Borges replied with great weariness.

Yes, you did, I thought. *I should have listened.* That the soul of the great writer, Jorge Luis Borges still existed, controlling my Borges' actions, I found ludicrous. The outrageous fairy tale he spun for me, it must be another lie.

"I know how it sounds," Borges remarked, unsettling me again with his ability to read my thoughts. "But is it any more absurd than you talking to your dead poet friend, Bashō? Or your ability to go Elsewhere by dreaming up a new world? Or that you can bend other people to your will? Think. What would you have said a year ago if someone told you any one of those was possible?

"I'd have called bullshit. But this story that you're both you and your father is nuts."

"Only because I'm saying it, Jane," Borges sighed. "And for the record, I never said I was two people. What I said was that my father's consciousness, a slice of his soul, if you will, split off and at the moment of my conception, latched onto my soul, and ever since my life has not been my own."

He spoke with such despair in his voice that I almost felt pity for him. Then I remembered the many lies and half-truths he told when I was at my most vulnerable, how he manipulated me to doubt my sanity, and my heart hardened. "So, find an exorcist." My words tasted bitter in my mouth, but I needed them to be bitter. Otherwise I might slip back under his spell. I cursed the day he chose me.

"It's not that simple," Borges replied, ignoring my sarcasm. "It's not as if I commune with my father. I just know things, things I shouldn't. There are times I forget who I am and lose hours, sometimes days. I feel like a man with a will of my own, but it's an illusion.

"I don't understand," I replied. "You can't sense his presence?"

"Yes and no. He doesn't speak to me, but there are times I perceive someone or something resides within me, and whenever I exercise any of my powers, such as the time I chose you, that perception is at its strongest. For years, I've been aware that another entity determines my actions, and controls my decisions. I can't explain it any better. I just know this thing inside me is connected to my father. And he's only present in me because my mother brought him into her life. A shame she never told you about what that did to me, even her version of the story. But then she is cleverer than I. Once she couldn't force you to do her bidding, she changed tactics. She's good at improvising. When her first plan failed, she contrived it so you would seek me out, and learn the truth from the one person you both love and hate in equal measure."

"If I hate you, that's on you. You're to blame, not me."

"That's harsh," Borges winced, "but I can't deny it. I am a monster, as my mother said. But not by choice. You can't imagine what my childhood was like, knowing things I shouldn't know, living with a mother who feared me more and more each day. I didn't ask for this, Jane, but I couldn't help it, I couldn't ...." He broke down then, shedding tears.

Crocodile tears, I thought. I steeled myself against the compassion welling up inside me. Yet I couldn't help wanting to believe him. I loved him, but hated myself for letting him manipulate me. I was like that slave girl tied to a table a millennium ago, terrified by the knives thrown at her to entertain Ulrikke's father and his men. But I couldn't leave him, Ulrikke or Fāmā-mura, because I didn't how to control my ability to go Elsewhere. I, also, was trapped. All I could do was lash out at the man who brought this upon us.

"Everyone's childhood's shitty, but not everyone becomes a monster. So what was so different about yours? Feel free to share."

"You mock me," he said. "But as you wish. We're stuck here for a while, anyway." He grabbed another folding chair from the stack along the wall and slid into it like snow shifting on a roof. His tears had long since dried, but his watery, red-rimmed eyes gleamed like light off a pond.

"My first memories were of strange, blurry lights, and the sounds of human voices, so many of them. I recall people laughing one moment, arguing the next. Voices of people marching in unknown streets, chanting slogans, repeating the same name over and over. *Evita!* My mother claims my first word was Evita. It offended her.

"And then there were my dreams, dreams normal children do not have. Naked bodies of grown men and women bouncing on beds, screaming and crying out in pain, or so I thought. They frightened me. Yet nothing was as bad as the nightmares that plagued me, of a dark man who would–"

"Stop!" I shouted. This couldn't be possible. "What dark man? Could you see eyes, a face, anything about him?"

"No," Borges said with a note of dread. "Only an infinite blackness, but set in a body that stalked me. When caught, his hands would grab my throat and squeeze until I couldn't breathe. I'd wake up gasping for breath. The worst of it was that I never knew when he would appear. I tried not falling asleep, because even the liquor and barbiturates I stole from Mother couldn't stop those dreams. Whenever he appeared in one I knew something terrible would happen."

The blanket draped over me slipped a bit, leaving my shoulders bare. I got up off the tatami mat. *This is the same man in black as mine.* "Do you still dream of him?"

"No. Not anymore."

"And when did they–he stop?"

"Why, when I met you, Jane. When I met you."

Mouth open, I stared as one stares at a mass grave, unable to turn away from the dead bodies, unable to believe the horror.

• • • • •

We shared a *paku-meshi*, one of the ready-to-eat JDF meals Tanaka provided, rice and pork curry. Borges found a bottle of saké, which we drank cold. I decided not to say anything about the man in black from my dreams. Perhaps Borges already knew, but I hoped not. He was in a talkative mood, so I just let him ramble on about his life, his mother–anything at all–and so many stories tumbled out. I paid close attention to every detail, no matter how bizarre or incredible. The strangest by far were about his mother's attempts to kill him. He related anecdote after anecdote of the myriad ways his mother tried to "exterminate" him with a detached air that I found disconcerting, if captivating.

"The first time, she smothered me with a pillow while I slept. I was five or six. No, six. I'm certain because my birthday party was the weekend before. The morning after she did it, I walked into our kitchen and asked for Lucky Charms for breakfast. She shrieked so loud, the neighbors in the apartment upstairs started pounding on their floor to get her to stop." Borges chuckled as if filicide was an amusing incident that might happen to any little boy.

But that was just the beginning. She pushed him out the window of a twenty-story building, injected him with an overdose of heroin, tied him down with weights and dropped him overboard into the Hudson river, and 'blew my head off' with a shotgun at close range on a camping trip to the Blue Ridge mountains. "She went to the trouble of burying what was left of me in a grove of pine trees," Borges said in a bemused tone, "as if that would make any difference." But in each instance, Borges would re-appear the next day, showing no sign of injury.

"Why'd she do it?"

"Knowing my father lived in me terrified her."

That Ulrikke could not kill Borges I found incredible. Part of me wanted to believe him, but that was my heart talking, not my head. My head said these were just more lies to gain my sympathy, which he would then exploit for his own purposes. Regardless, I asked why Ulrikke hadn't succeeded.

"My father doesn't want me to die," Borges said, referring to the spirit he claimed inhabited him. "Not yet, anyway. He has plans for me. Didn't my mother tell you about my prophecy?"

"Not much other than you received a revelation regarding your future. The gist was that you needed to find a woman who shared her gift. That finding me was a means to achieving immortality. She also said that I was the woman you'd long searched for and, after I give birth to our son, you'll take him from me. Then I'll die, either in childbirth or through murder."

"Ah," was his only reaction.

Shocked, I said, "Is that all you have to say? There's must be more you can tell me, because I don't want to believe her. I don't want to believe everything you've put me through was done to steal my son and make me your sacrificial lamb. Talk."

"Some things you can't know yet," he answered, defiantly crossing his arms in front of him.

"What the hell?" I took several backward steps until stopped by the cement wall behind me. Scared, I took a defensive pose, sliding my right leg forward to narrow my profile, while raising my arms, left hand slightly forward of my right.

"I won't hurt you, Jane," he said. He winced as if looking at me caused him pain. "Please, sit." He sounded tired and worn down.

"Not on your life." I trembled as I spoke. Like a chameleon, he could change in an instant to threaten me. I couldn't take the risk. I kept my guard up.

"You don't trust me."

"Nope."

"All right, then let me ask you something. Have you ever considered where your fantastic abilities came from, and I mean fantastic in its original sense, beyond ordinary reality?"

"Are you joking?" Sweat rolled off me like water.

"No, I'm serious. I've spent most of my life, wondering about such things. Take my mother, for example. As a boy, I believed her story a Norse god gifted her with the ability to go anywhere, anytime, anyplace she could imagine. But as time passed, and I saw how she treated me, how she reacted to my visions, I began to have doubts. We—you, my mother, myself—are not comic book characters with super powers. If you cut us, do we not bleed?" He loved quoting Shakespeare. "In your case, if I inject you with the right drug, I can make you go places you could never imagine.

"We're human, but we're not normal. You converse with a dead poet. You and my mother can stave off growing older. And I cannot be killed, at least not so far, though I do grow older." Borges paused, waiting for a response, but I stayed mute, out of fear, but also hope. *Keep talking*, I thought. *Just keep talking*. The less I said, the better the odds he might reveal something useful, something I could use to break his power over me and escape both him and Ulrikke.

"Very well," he said, as if reading my thoughts. "Perhaps you haven't had time to ponder our peculiar natures. Let me suggest something. What if the *gifts* we possess are a new thing in the universe? Have you ever heard of the concept of emergence? No, I suppose not."

"You're stalling."

"If I am, why not leave? You can go anywhere you want. Yet you stay. Why is that, Jane?"

I didn't answer. I'd leave if I knew how, but I also wasn't ready to try, and, what's more, something inside me resisted the idea of leaving Fāmāmura. It was a puzzle.

"Emergence," he continued, "is a simple concept. The world is governed by fundamental laws. Science has uncovered the basic principles that underlie our universe. There's chaos and unpredictability, but also complex organization. Life's the best example. Out of a few elements, chemicals formed, interacted with one another, and then, after billions of years, sentient life emerged."

As he spoke, my fear of him ramped up at an ever faster rate. I felt poised on the edge of an abyss, a dangerous nexus in time and space that could destroy me or prove my salvation. Soon, events over which I had no control would decide my fate. It was only my intuition talking, but I was convinced he held the key to my survival, even if he also posed the greatest threat to my life. Hoping Borges might, by mistake, provide the answers I needed to break his hold over me so I could leave him and this awful place forever, I let him babble on.

"Think of what we do as magic," Borges said, and my body went rigid. "Who believes in magic? Yet people believe all sorts of imaginary things. Like a God who sacrificed his only begotten son out of love for all mankind, a son who was just a different manifestation of this very same God. When the son came back to life, he announced that whoever believed in him would receive eternal life. And every day, people put their faith in this God, one they have never seen, who never speaks to them, who doesn't even answer their prayers for help. The treat him as a magical being, who controls the fate of the world.

"Not that we are magical beings. We're just the next advance in human evolution. And suppose what we are and what we can do came from the mind of a single man, one with an intense preoccupation for viewing reality through the lens of his imagination? A man like my father."

Who's saying this? My Borges or his father's spirit? But then I recovered my wits. The whole possession narrative couldn't be true. I opted to provoke him, instead. Get him angry enough and he might slip up and give me what I needed.

"You sound like the founder of a cult. You want to be the next L. Ron Hubbard? That's a tall order, but you've got the skill set for it. You tell the best lies."

His cheeks flared red, and I thought he might explode, but then he chuckled softly to himself. He was about to reply when the locked door burst open. There stood Ulrikke, dripping wet, the lantern's light silhouetting her against the storm raging outside.

CHAPTER 23

"Excuse me. Am I early? I hope not. I've been looking forward to this all day." Ulrikke strode through the doorway, tall and erect. In the lantern's pallid light, her eyes glowed like two half moons. She looked thirty years younger. I edged closer to Borges, an unconscious reaction to her sudden appearance.

"Don't worry, children." Her hands raised, palms open. "I'm not armed, and no one's waiting outside." She closed the door, then went to the chair on which our wet clothes hung. Knocking them to the floor, she sat down with a sigh of relief. "Some tea would be nice. Black, please. I'm tired of the green stuff."

"What do you want, Mother?" Borges' razor sharp tone couldn't hide the fear I sensed in him.

"Just to chat." Ulrikke used a gloved hand to swipe her wet hair to one side. "You owe me that much."

"Owe? Owe!" Flecks of spittle flew from his mouth. *He's unhinged*, I thought. Ulrikke ignored his aggressive posturing, however. Her gaze rested on me.

"Dear Jane, I fear my son has momentarily misplaced his manners. Would you be so kind as to make the tea? It's here somewhere. I gave Ray Tanaka very specific instructions, and he's ever so diligent."

Dazed, I nodded and sidled past Borges. Ulrikke knew everything. Tanaka was her tool, not his. Whether that was a good thing or a bad thing, I didn't know.

Placing a pan of water atop the field stove, I waited. Once it boiled, I dipped in a full tea ball. Soon, the aroma of bergamot, fruity with hints of oranges, drifted through the room. With slow, deliberate movements, I filled two porcelain cups. No one spoke, as if I were performing *Chanoyu*, the tea ceremony. First, I offered one to Ulrikke, who smiled as she took it from me in one swift, yet subtle movement. The other cup I presented to Borges, but his eyes told me not to bother, so I kept it to warm my hands.

"Please, sit," said Ulrikke. Without much forethought, I grabbed a chair, placed it equidistant between mother and son, and sat down. To calm myself, I took a long deep breath, and then let it out to relieve the tension in my muscles. Borges refused a seat, and stood, trying to dominate the room. Fatigue fogged my brain's ability to function, but after sipping tea from my cup, I felt rejuvenated, if wary.

"Say what you came to say," Borges said.

"Well, mostly I have questions for your paramour, dear," she replied, blowing on her tea. "So, Jane, did he prattle about my many attempts to kill him when he was a boy? I know how he loves those stories. It's so entertaining to hear the new ones he's concocted."

"I can't recall," I said, playing for time, uncertain who was my ally and who my enemy. But Ulrikke saw through my ruse.

"Oh, he did tell you! How delightful. I wasn't sure he would."

Borges snorted. "I only told the truth, Mother."

"And when did I say you hadn't? But truth is so malleable. And whose truth is the question, yours or mine? Or even poor Jane's. But, forgive me for getting ahead of myself. Jane, I won't lie to you. I tried to kill him, but only once. And you can trust me on this, it was justified." She stared hard at me, a questioning look in her eyes, then shook her head. "I see he omitted a few details. Let me fill you in.

"He probably told you I did it when he was five, but he was nearly twelve. That's when covering for his eccentric behavior became impossible. It's easy to laugh off the odd and irritating things young children say, but when a boy enters puberty and he doesn't stop, well ...

"My son was quite the fortune teller, but he never foretold good outcomes, only bad ones. Still, I did all I could, despite complaints from neighbors, his classmates, their parents, even strangers he met on the street. Did he mention the school district required a psychiatric evaluation–twice! I suppose people wouldn't have cared if his predictions didn't have such a noxious habit of coming true. But I put up with it until the day he informed me the daughter I carried in my womb was destined to die."

Blood drained from my face. "How did he know–"

"About my pregnancy?" Ulrikke said, finishing my question. "Not from me. Her conception was an accident, the result of an affair with a poet. Not a famous one, but such a sweet man..." Her lips parted, and her cheeks glowed. "I may have even loved him. I daydreamed about starting over in a happy marriage with a happy family, and that included my son. Oh, Jane. I was so tempted.

"But I knew better than to tell him," she added, pointing at Borges. "He was an incredibly jealous boy, being an only child." Borges gave off a sound somewhere between a growl and that awful cry one hears from wild animals caught in a steel trap. "He would need time to adjust to the idea of sharing me with a half-sister, not to mention a step-father. Yet twelve weeks in, he demanded to know why I'd kept my pregnancy a secret. Trying to laugh it off, I said he was imagining things, but he got that look that–I'm sure you've seen it. Cold. Cruel even. The harder I tried to fend him off, the more his arms straightened and his hands clenched tight. The quality of that look, the pure hatred that emanates from his body, has this strange, yet beautiful quality to it. Don't you agree? Eventually, I confessed, promising him things would be better for him in the new life I planned for us. But he didn't want to hear that.

"'She'll never be born, the prophecy forbids it,' he kept repeating until I sent him to bed without supper. I was furious and, even though I don't like to admit this, a little scared. His predictions always came true, but I thought it would be that way with m. Óðinn himself gave me my gift. Surely, that counted for something. But the scriptures are right, Jane. Pride truly does goeth before destruction, and a haughty spirit before a fall.

"I ate dinner, then settled in to watch television. From the couch in my living room, I had a perfect view of his room. I didn't want him sneaking into the kitchen and defying me. Yet every time I checked, his door was shut. Around eleven-thirty, I drifted off. I vaguely remember Johnny Carson's opening monologue began with a joke about President Ford.

"Two weeks later, I woke up in Mount Sinai's ICU, the victim of a knife wound to my belly. I remembered nothing. The nurses said I was mugged in Central Park on my way home from work. I recall thinking that was odd, because I never took that route. They also said I nearly died from losing so much blood, after the assailant broke my skull. My brain swelled, and they put me in an induced coma. I was lucky to be alive.

"When questioned about my daughter, they looked away. We're sorry, they said. My attacker plunged a knife directly into my uterus, killing her. Too numb to cry, I stared at the glass window that separated me from the nurse's station. And saw my son standing behind it. When he noticed me, he smiled. That's when I knew. He murdered her.

"'How long have I been in here?' I asked, and they said six days. But I couldn't remember anything from the time I drifted off to Johnny Carson two weeks earlier. Fourteen days gone, as if they never existed. How was that possible? Such memory loss was uncommon, but not outside reports in the medical literature, according to my doctors, but I knew better. My son erased my memory. He caused the attack, the knife going in at just the right angle–everything. He hid it well, but I sensed how pleased he was at my daughter's death. Then and there, I vowed he would pay for what he did."

"You lie, Mother," Borges hissed. "I had nothing to do with what happened to you." My heart stopped upon hearing him protest his innocence. But then I recalled the weeks trapped in Costa Rica when Borges kept telling me we'd never been to Japan to see the Daibutsu, insinuating my grief over my parents' deaths drove me mad. Lies were his stock in trade, and I found myself believing Ulrikke. My Borges did murder his sister. Then I wondered if he had stolen my memories, too.

"You did it then?" I said.

"Yes," Ukrikke answered, her voice somber. "Following my release from hospital, I let him enjoy his victory. Pretending not to care about my life, I drank heavily and cried like a weakling. I even let him comfort me. He needed to see I'd lost all hope. Meanwhile, I hid my *hefndarþorsta*–sorry, my desire for vengeance–from him.

"And succeeded. One evening, I shammed passing out on my bed. Later that evening, after I heard him snoring, I crept past his bedroom to the kitchen, and removed a boning knife from a drawer. Then I slipped into his room, my steps barely audible. His spare pillow lay on the floor, and with deliberate care, I bent down to pick it up. Then, in a rush, I jumped on the bed, straddled him, and pushed the pillow down hard onto his face. With my free hand, I drove the knife repeatedly into his chest. In seconds, it was over. My fingers sticky with blood, its smell sickened me. But I wiped the knife clean and showered, ridding myself of his stink. I didn't bother to clean his room. There was no need. The next day, I would be off to a better place. Exhausted, I fell onto my bed and into a dreamless sleep.

"In the early light of dawn, someone yanked on my arm. It was him, no sign of any stab wounds, demanding breakfast. I stiffened, terrified, but then went to the kitchen, placed a bowl of his favorite cereal in front of him and poured in the milk, which he ate greedily. I watched, unable to believe my eyes. When finished, he asked for more. He informed me very matter of fact not to try it again. 'It won't work,' he said. 'Father won't allow it.'"

"You're delusional, Mother," Borges said. "I had nothing to do with your miscarriage." Anger darted from his eyes.

"She believes me," Ulrikke said. "Don't you, Jane?"

I said nothing. To me, they were two of a kind, both dangerous.

"Jane, there was no mugging, no assault. Only a miscarriage. It damaged her uterus. The doctors told her she could never again have children. She couldn't accept the truth, so she invented this fantasy to blame me. That's why she imprisoned me, kept us apart, asked you to kill me. She lives in a world gone to shit, queen of her own little shithole, ruling it like her father. She'd kill me if she could, but she can't. It's why she worked so hard to turn you against me, to turn you into an assassin. But that's not who you are."

True, I thought. *But what am I?* The spiteful banter between mother and son left me more confused. Why was it so damned important I believe one over the other? What did I mean to them?

"Did she explain to you why she lives in this horrible place?" Borges went on, intruding on my thoughts. "Go ahead. Ask her why she chose this and not someplace nicer."

Bemused, I looked to Ulrikke, who shrugged. "What is there to tell? There are no nice worlds. Never have been, never will be. Not where humans live." She stared back at me as if at the entirety of the known universe. "You think this is the worst place I could go?" She laughed in a way that unnerved me.

"There are better worlds than this. Why Fāmā-mura?"

"You know nothing, Jane. This is a paradise, compared to many. And it's just as doomed as all the rest."

Borges face revealed his disdain for that response, but I wanted to hear more. "What do you mean? Doomed how?"

"Doomed as doomed gets. It's a simple enough word."

"Not to me."

"Fine," Ulrikke said. "I'll spell it out. Humanity has no future. All worlds end in some version of Ragnarok, in death and destruction. Whenever I look for one where our species survives, I fail. This world is better only in that humanity dies off more slowly here than in others. And it's the fault of that thing inside him."

"I warned you she was mad," said Borges, but I ignored him. There was more that Ulrikke was not telling me.

"If you believe that, why fight so hard to save these people? Yoshi, Junko, Ray–they would have died long ago without your help. If it's hopeless, why bother?"

"Perhaps I have a weakness for lost causes."

"I don't believe a word of that. That's not who you are."

"You know nothing about me, Jane," she said with scorn. "How could you?"

"I know you pleaded with me to murder your son. There must be a reason for that. Tell it to me or I'll leave you here alone with each other." A sad bluff, but the only option left to me.

"Yes!" Borges cried out. "She separated us when we arrived, and not because she cares about you, Jane. If you kill me, she'll be free to steal our child and raise him as her own."

Ulrikke's eyes flashed with anger, but within seconds, she started laughing. At first, snickering, then giggles. It wasn't long before she lost complete control, and her cackling echoed off the walls. "Yes," she said, after several minutes in a hoarse voice, bent at the waist, gasping for air, "that's it. Who wouldn't want to mother another child like you, son, especially after the first went so well?"

"You can't control Jane, Mother," Borges shot back. "She sees you for what you are, a spiteful wreck that's fallen back on the only thing she knows how to do well: Play the tyrant!"

"That's rich. Satan should surrender his title as the Father of Lies, though I can't decide which of the two of you, father or son, most deserves his crown." She laughed again, but her words stopped me dead. Did she believe Borges' story, that the soul of the shy timid writer she once seduced was the evil spirit Borges claimed possessed him?

"Jane, don't listen to her. Our one hope is to leave now, together." He reached out his hand to me, but Ulrikke stepped forward to swat it away.

"Don't play the fool for him again, Jane. Think. When has he ever told you the truth when it mattered?" The two of them continued arguing, their voices a clamorous, senseless wall of noise.

"Stop!" I yelled, unable stomach their relentless bickering. "I don't want to see either of you ever again, or anyone else for that matter!" And then, as if I dreamed it, they and the bunker vanished from sight.

CHAPTER 24

I sprawled on hard ground. Raising my head, I recognized the Daibutsu, sunlight reflecting off his tarnished bronze shell. I rose, walked across the plaza, and sat atop the stone base on which he rested, gazing up at his enigmatic eyes. He showed no sign of damage. *How did I get here?* I thought, bewildered.

A cool breeze blew, scattering dead leaves fallen from the surrounding trees. Dressed in thin cotton clothes, I wrapped my arms around my body to warm myself. Inside me, the baby kicked, as if he felt the cold, too. Hungry, I looked about, but saw nothing to eat. How could I keep myself and my baby alive in this place? A dirty brown cloak suddenly draped itself over my shoulders, and I shrieked. Spinning around in terror, I discovered Bashō leaning on his cane.

"*Odorokasete sumimasen deshita*, Jane-san," he said, bowing to me. "Forgive me for startling you, but you are cold, and I cannot feel the chill. Thus, the humble offer of my cloak."

"*Arigato*." Its warmth surprised me, considering its owner. "Next time let me know you're there. You scared the crap out of me."

"*Sō desu ne*," he said, bowing again. "You are most correct, Jane-san. I was hasty. It will not happen again."

Rising to my feet, I surveyed the scene. I saw no one else besides Bashō and the Daibutsu. No insects chirping, no birds in the clear sky. Even the wind seemed hushed. *It's winter*, I thought. "Where are we?"

"I would think that is obvious, Jane-san."

I felt my cheeks redden. "You know what I meant," I said. "If this is Kamakura, where is everyone?"

"Praying to Buddha, the monk sought solitude. Snow fell, hiding him."

Shocker, another damn hokku. "So you're saying I did this?"

"You told Urikei and your Borges you wanted to be alone."

"That's not what I said," I replied, irritated. "I said I didn't want to be with anyone."

"And so you went to a place where no one is."

"Then why are you here? Or, for that matter, the Daibutsu?"

"I am not alive, so I cannot be anyone, can I?" he replied. "As for the Daibutsu, do you sense anything other than metal and stone in his presence?"

I turned and focused on the Great Buddha, but felt no awe-inspiring presence, no higher power, no life-force, nothing. "This isn't possible."

Bashō gave off a sigh of frustration. "Jane-san, you still do not understand. You can imagine yourself anywhere, anytime, yet refuse to appreciate all that means. Wanting to be alone, you went to a place where no one exists."

Is that all there is to it? "But I didn't mean this place," I said. "I have limits. Everyone says so."

"Everyone being your Borges and Urikei, you mean?"

"Well.... I didn't know what to say." Then, something came to me. "When I go Elsewhere, my age returns to when I first acquired my abilities. And Ulrikke spoke of others. She couldn't change the fate of her father, despite trying many times. She can't change the fate of anyone. She told me that."

"And you trust everything she says?"

"Well, no," I admitted. "Not anymore. But why would she lie about that?"

"Why indeed?" said Bashō. "Yet right before you came here, she said you know nothing about her. Is that not so?"

"Yes, but –"

"But," he interrupted, "you have taken her and Borges at their word many times, only to learn they lied or misled you. Am I wrong? And look at you. You are still pregnant. I know you felt your baby kick a short while ago. How could you come here, change back to your younger self, yet remain with child?"

He was right. Traveling to this abandoned Kamakura didn't eliminate my pregnancy. The limits Ulrikke spoke about to me, perhaps they were all fictions. How strange to hear this blunt assessment from Bashō, who preferred to speak in riddles. Now he was being far more direct. I wasn't sure I liked the change.

"Why didn't you tell me this before? It would have saved me a hell of a lot of trouble."

"You were not ready for the truth,"

"Ready? Are you serious? Who are you to know if I'm ready or not?"

Bashō looked at me with pity in his eyes. Neither of us said a word. Like little children, we engaged in a stare-down contest, a battle between my anger and his–melancholy? My anger lost. I blinked first.

"You should have told me." A petulant complaint, and a shameful one, but stubborn as ever, I could not let go of it. *He should have told me!*

Bashō eased himself onto the base of the Daibutsu and beckoned me with his finger. "Please sit, Jane-san." Still upset with him, I sat on the tiles of the plaza, but faced away from him. Staring off at the wooded hills, I waited. For what, I didn't know. Perhaps a lecture regarding all my many mistakes. What I didn't expect was a Buddhist parable.

• • • • •

Shigara was a warrior monk of the Negoro-gumi. As a young man, he was blinded while fighting the forces of Toyotomi Hideyoshi during the Siege of Negoro-ji. For the rest of his life, he traveled the land, reduced to begging for food and shelter. However, his cheerful countenance and the equanimity he displayed toward his fate won him renown among both commoners and samurai alike.

One day in mid-summer, on his way from Osaka to the Tōdai-ji temple in Nara, a landslide washed out the road. The samurai for the local daimyō ordered all travelers to turn back and take a detour far to the south that would add an extra week to their journey. Shigara, impatient to get to the temple in time for a festival, asked the samurai if there wasn't a shortcut. They refused to help, mocking him. However, a peasant passing by heard Shigara's request. Struck by his dignified and respectful demeanor, he pulled him aside.

"I know a path through the forest used by woodsmen, which I take every day to get to the rice fields of my village. I can guide you only that far, but you should be able reach Nara if you walk along the border between the forest and the fields until you reach a gully cut into the hillside that leads

back down to this road. It will take you an extra day, but if you agree, we can leave now."

Shigara accepted the peasant's offer and together, they reached the rice fields by mid-afternoon. The peasant turned Shigara so that he faced west, assuring him that as long as he kept a straight path he would come across the gully the next day. "The sun this time of year is always to your left," he said. "If you wander too far into our fields and lose your way, walk in the direction where you feel the sun on your left, and you will still find it." Shigara thanked the peasant and they parted. At sunset, Shigara lay down to sleep under the light of stars he could not see.

The next morning, he awoke, only to find himself lost. Somehow, before sleeping, he drifted far from the forest. Remembering the peasant's advice, he strode off in the direction that kept the warmth of the sun to his left. Around mid-day, he stopped to eat lunch. Just then, the air temperature dropped dramatically. Shigara no longer felt the sun's heat on his face. There must be storm clouds rolling in, he thought, though the absence of any breeze seemed odd, nor could he smell the coming rain. Perhaps he had offended the local kami. To appease them, he kneeled down and lit two sticks of incense, which he pushed into the soft ground. Then Shigara prayed to the kami, asking them to allow the sun to shine again, and promising that, upon his arrival at Tōdai-ji temple, he would leave an offering to the Amida Buddha to bless them.

Upon finishing his prayers, Shigara felt the sun return. Once more, he struck out across the fields, keeping the sun to his left until he stumbled upon the gully. The next day, he arrived at the temple and told his tale to everyone who would listen. The Abbot of Tōdai-ji, hearing of Shigara's miraculous deliverance, invited him to dinner. It just so happened that an Imperial astrologer was also in residence at the temple. That night, after Shigara recited the tale to the Abbot's dinner companions, the astrologer spoke.

"With respect for Shigara-san's reputation as an honest and faithful adherent of the Buddha, I must inform everyone that I too experienced the same event, and I know it was not his prayers that saved him.

"Shigara described a total eclipse of the sun, whereby the moon traverses the heavens, crossing the sun's face for a brief time. Eclipses are rare, and can be observed in only a few places, but if one appears, one can see only a *narrow band of light surrounding a dark center. Down through the centuries, astrologers have kept records of each eclipse, noting the times and places where they occurred. Thus, we can predict them with great accuracy."*

"But," Shigara protested, "what about the cold I felt? You spoke only of the sun's light, not its heat."

"We do not understand everything about the heavens," replied the astrologer, "but whenever the moon eclipses the sun, not only does the dark of night return, but also the air grows cool. Amaterasu-ōmikami, the Goddess of the Shining Heavens governs the sun. The moon is the domain of her brother, Tsukiyomi no Mikoto. Minor kami cannot affect sun or moon, nor do their movements concern the Buddha. Like you, Shigara-san, I too felt the cold, but I saw the moon appear and cover up the sun. The darkness it created caused the cold. If you were not blind, you would have seen the truth, as I did."

• • • • •

I couldn't decide whether to laugh or cry. This was worse than his stupid hokku. "So now I'm a blind monk," I said. "Wonderful."

"You mistake my meaning," Bashō's calm, composed response annoyed me.

"Do tell," I said, rolling my eyes. "Please, elucidate me."

"That is not my responsibility, Jane-san."

"It sure seemed like your responsibility a few moments ago. Or is this another one of those truths I'm not ready for?"

"I have limits, Jane-san, unlike you. What I said earlier tested them. I cannot say more, nor provide all the answers you seek. Those you must discover yourself."

"How convenient. I guess I'm just too stupid to understand stuff, even with all your esteemed guidance. Or maybe all the times Borges erased my memories damaged my brain. Not that you give a damn about that."

"Your anger is misguided, Jane-san," Bashō responded, "and your conclusions flawed. Your Borges is many things, some bad and some good, but he cannot erase memories. If he did, why would he need drugs to make you do what he wants?"

"I don't know, maybe he's just lazy sometimes." As per usual, my conversation with Bashō was going nowhere.

"Your Borges is a master manipulator. He can confuse and make you doubt your mind and whether your memories are true, but that is all."

"That's funny, because I wasn't confused when I went Elsewhere and bore a son, I just forgot everything about my past life. Instead, I was a widow and mother of the heir to a fortune. I lived there for twenty years and never once thought about Borges, or you, or anyone else from my past, until the day when he appeared at my son's funeral and restored my memories. How do you explain that? C'mon, sensei, enlighten me. Or is that also against the rules?"

"Do you remember our conversation in the hospital after you almost drowned trying to save your Borges when he fell at Devil's Falls?" *How typical*, I thought, *always answering a question with another question.* That's the problem with poets. They speak things slant, and I hate slant.

"Not at all. What conversation."

"We discussed Emily Dickinson, among other things. I repeated this famous quotation: 'I do not practice to deceive.' And we spoke about your dreams. Does that help?"

"Not in the least." *This is getting tiresome.*

"I see. Maybe you will remember this. Your last words to me were, 'Walk away–whatever your name is–but you're always walking away, aren't you?'"

"That's like the line from Lawrence of Arabia!" I said, astonished. "How did you...?" And then I remembered seeing him at the foot of my bed in that Vancouver hospital room. Bashō woke me from an awful dream about the man in black. I feared I'd lost Borges forever. Everything we said came back to me. How did that happen? There was only one answer that made sense.

"It was you! You erased my memories!" I trusted Bashō, believed him my friend! Yet he erased my past and trapped me for twenty years in another life. Who else could have done it? Not Borges, who acknowledged he needed drugs to control me when he could no longer persuade me to do as he wished. Only Bashō could have done it. He was the last person I saw before my memories disappeared. What had he said to me as I lay in that hospital bed in Vancouver? 'It has been and always will be about the dreams, Jane-san. I fear you will forget much before this one ends and the next one begins.' And then, as he predicted, I forgot. My eyes filled with hot tears at his betrayal. "Why? And don't say because I wasn't ready. Tell me the truth, and tell it plain for once, goddamn you!"

Bashō leaned on his cane, motionless. Was that sadness in the downward droop of his mustaches and closed mouth, or just some trick of the light? Regardless, my anger shriveled to nothingness in my throat when, at last, he spoke.

"I told you when we first met I owed a duty to you, and I have done my duty as best I could. Yes, I altered your memories. For that, I do not apologize, Jane. It was necessary to protect you from going mad, as you almost did when your Borges held you hostage in Costa Rica. Now, I have nothing more to offer. The choices you must now make going forward are yours and yours alone. The answers you seek, the knowledge you require, you carry inside yourself. It is there you must look."

Confused, my mind bordered on despair. Perhaps Bashō understood, for he closed his eyes and recited one last hokku. "Her cheery trees bloom; awake, her dream disappears. Nothing has changed."

I sensed he was leaving. "Wait," I said, "don't go."

But it was too late. I sat and cried alone with only the Daibutsu to share the pale sunlight of a winter's day in Kamakura.

CHAPTER 25

The next few hours passed in a blur. I went over and over the parable of the blind monk, and Bashō's last hokku and what he meant when he said I already knew everything I needed, but to no avail. The one new thing I learned, that Bashō erased my memories when I traveled Elsewhere still stung. I wondered if he erased them again after Borges drugged me, because I awoke in Fāmā-mura sick and four months pregnant with no recollection of what happened to me in all that time. My mind wandered along a labyrinthine path, passing from anger to sorrow to bemusement to disbelief to fear and worse. I chose to leave Borges and Ulrikke, and now Bashō abandoned me. A terrible loneliness consumed me, realizing there was no one in my life I could trust.

My beloved Borges—and why was I still in love with him? Because he chose me?—ensnared me early on with his lies. But, as Bashō pointed out, Ulrikke also lied to me, including her claim that my power to go Elsewhere had limits.

Regardless, Bashō's betrayal hurt most. Key moments in my life were a blank. Maybe he also erased Ulrikke's memories after the violent attack that killed her unborn daughter, instead of my Borges. He learned of Bashō from his mother, which means she had met him, at least once in her life. How could that be unless Bashō owed a duty to help her? And what else might Bashō have done for me without my knowledge? I never got the chance to ask. Now I was stranded in this lifeless Kamakura. What a joke.

"A joke usually has a punch line," said a voice so unexpected, I fell down from the shock of hearing it.

Staggering to my feet, I looked around me. "Bashō, is that you?"

"No ghosts here."

"This isn't funny, Bashō. Show yourself!"

"You look, yet do not see," said the voice, which sounded familiar, though I couldn't place it. Then it said, "Perhaps you are just like the blind monk, Shigara-san." That shook me. If this wasn't Bashō, who was it? Anxious, I worried that perhaps Ulrikke or Borges followed me to Kamakura, impossible as that might seem.

"Stop it! Whoever you are, show yourself!" My eyes swept the temple plaza, but saw only the Daibutsu, as dead as ever.

"Even dead men may speak if need arises."

"Daibutsu?" I said in a quivering tongue. "Is that you?"

"Yes and no," came the response. "I am the one you call the Daibutsu with whom you've spoken in your dreams. But Bashō was right to tell you I am nothing more than a hollow shell of metal."

"That can't be. If you're speaking, then you're the Great Buddha who gave me my powers. You freed me from my nightmare in Costa Rica."

"Did I?" said the Daibutsu. "Think, Jane Takako Wolfsheim. When have we ever conversed outside the confines of your mind?"

True, I couldn't remember him speaking to me outside my dreams. Yet I refused to accept the Daibutsu was just an ancient bronze statue. "When I first visited Kamakura," I said, "a life force greater than any I ever experienced flowed out of you. Don't deny that."

"I deny nothing. Ask yourself this, though, Jane. Was it real?"

Real? I thought. *Of course it was real.* Nothing made any sense if the Daibutsu's spirit was just a hallucination.

"It's a shame your nature remains a mystery to you," the Daibutsu said, echoing Bashō. "You can travel anywhere you choose, create any life for yourself you wish, and yet you ignore the basis for the powers you wield."

I shook my head out of bewilderment. "I don't know what you're talking about." The lidless eyes of the Daibutsu appraised me, or I imagined they did. *Perhaps I'm crazy*, I thought, just like Marty Schneider said to me before Borges' killed him.

"You're not crazy," the Daibutsu responded. "You know a great many things. But they're locked inside a black box buried deep inside your soul, hidden away. All you need do is find the key and let them out."

What box? I thought, slumping to the ground. My situation was absurd. But in that moment, a remarkable idea came to me. Not so much an idea, but an epiphany, as if all the puzzle pieces that so bedeviled me might at last fit into place. "I've been such an idiot," I said.

"Ah, Macbeth," said the Daibutsu. "'Life's but a walking shadow, a poor player that struts and frets his hour upon the stage–'"

"Shut up, you. I'm thinking."

In the ensuing silence, I thought hard about what my intuition was telling me. One thing was clear. My power required the exercise of imagination. Every time I went Elsewhere, I was dreaming, drugged and under Borges' spell, or in a heightened emotional state. Harness my imagination and I could control my ability. Failure would leave me at the mercy of dreams, emotions and visions, like that time I imagined a green paradise outside the motel room. I must learn to focus and trust myself. Only then, could I go where I wanted to go, and be who I wanted to be. Ulrikke learned to master her powers. If she could do it, so could I.

But that wasn't all. My love for Borges, and our unborn child, still bound us together. Assuming the prophecy was valid, I couldn't break that bond, even if it would lead to a preordained death. But I didn't want to die, nor lose my child, nor lose Borges. And where did Ulrikke fit into the grand scheme of things? What did I know about the two of them, and the prophecy, that was true? To discover answers to my questions required comparing their stories and seeing where they agreed.

One, I knew that both possessed the power to persuade others to do whatever they wanted. As did I.

Second, both agreed that an affair between Ulrikke and the writer, Jorge Luis Borges, led to the birth of the Borges I knew and loved.

Third, they agreed on another central point, one I first thought impossible, but now must take seriously: that Borges was possessed. Borges claimed a slice of his father's spirit attached itself to him at conception. Ulrikke also acknowledged this. Both agreed that he could predict other people's fortunes, and foresee his own, the so-called prophecy.

Fourth, as a child, my Borges told Ulrikke her daughter would never be born because the prophecy wouldn't allow it, and her daughter then died in utero. Ulrikke blamed him for that loss, and, out of a desire for vengeance, tried to kill him. This was consistent with what he said of her attempts to kill him, even if the details of their stories differed, and by a lot.

Fifth, both accepted that the prophecy was real.

Now I examined the points where their stories diverged. Ulrikke insisted the prophecy would cause my death and argued I should kill Borges to save myself and my unborn child. Borges didn't provide any details about the prophecy or its effect on me when I asked, which lent some credence to Ulrikke's claim. Yet, if Ulrikke was right, why did Borges drug me and then use my ability to bring us to Fāmā-mura? He must have known she hated him, opposed his goals, and viewed him as a threat. And she imprisoned him once her people found us.

Ray Tanaka further complicated matters. First, he confided his doubts about Ulrikke, his mistrust of her powers and her use of them to become the de facto ruler of Fāmā-mura. Then he helped bring me to Borges. But once there, I learned Borges *persuaded* Ray to do that, and to assist his escape. Yet, when we reached the hideout that Ray prepared, who should show up but Ulrikke, claiming Tanaka was her puppet. The more I thought about it, the more I suspected one, or both of them, used Ray to distract me from discovering an important truth. But what were they hiding?

Perhaps Borges' prophecy didn't require my death, for if it did, bringing me to Ulrikke was the last thing he should have done. Borges would have to be an idiot to bring the three of us together, since he admitted he knew she would try to persuade me to kill him. So what did the prophecy require? Borges often remarked he spent his lifetime searching for a woman with the same powers as his mother, and that woman would prove his salvation. According to both Ulrikke and him, that woman was me, but only if I bore him a male child. Under the prophecy, somehow the child would grant Borges immortality. But, I asked myself, immortality for which Borges? My insight suggested the prophecy's true purpose wasn't to grant immortality to the man I loved, but to the spirit inhabiting him, the parasitic soul of his father. If that was true, the prophecy posed no threat to my life. On the contrary, it required my Borges to die.

If the soul of his father affixed itself to my Borges' at conception, then I feared a piece of that same evil now inhabited my unborn child. A guess? Yes, but it fit the facts I knew. Ulrikke feared her son because the soul of his father, Jorge Luis Borges, controlled his every move, leading him to do horrific things. And Borges said Ulrikke could not kill him because of his father's plans for him. I presumed fulfilling the damn prophecy was what he desired above all else. My Borges confessed he was a monster. He did many terrible things, not just to me, but to others, including his mother. I counted his involvement in Marty's plan to murder my parents as a black mark against him. And I would never forget Borges' knifing Marty, then letting him bleed out before my eyes.

Mulling these thoughts over, I couldn't help thinking the prophecy didn't foretell the future, but was a scheme intended to preserve the soul of Borges' father, the first Jorge Luis Borges. Eventually, my Borges would die of old age, for he lacked the power to go Elsewhere and reset his age. Where would his father's spirit go then? It would need a new host to sustain itself. I couldn't help thinking my son was the most likely candidate.

But first, my Borges must die before his father's spirit could transfer to my son. And what better way to accomplish that than bringing me to Fāmāmura, where Ulrikke might persuade me to kill him, or failing that, manipulate me into leading him to his death. But I didn't want him to die. Despite everything, I still cared for him, and trusted that he never wanted to become a monster. The evil spirit made him one, ruining his life. I must not let that happen to my son.

However, much of this was speculation. I needed to be certain, and for that, I must get more information to confirm my theory about the prophecy. Intuition told me the man in black from my dreams was how the soul of Borges' father chose to manifest itself to me. If they were the same person, then to learn the truth, and get the information I needed, I must face the man in black. Luckily, I knew where to find him.

Peering up at the now silent Daibutsu, I said, "Domo arigato." It may have been silly to thank a hollow bronze statue, but it seemed fitting.

"What" the Daibutsu asked, though now I understood he was just a voice in my head. "What are you doing?"

"Me? I plan to take a nap." Then I curled up next to his stone base, pulled Bashō's cloak around me and went to sleep.

• • • • •

I dreamed I was back in the villa in Costa Rica, a most vivid dream, but with one big difference. This time, I controlled the dream environment.

The air, still warm and humid, swirled around me, caused by from the fan above my bed. But unlike before, it did not give me chills. I propped myself up with my elbows. And there he was, as expected. The featureless man in black stood against the far wall. The figure I first met when he raped me while I dreamed in my room at the Tokyo Sheraton the evening after I first saw the Daibutsu. The same creature who plagued my nightmares for twenty years in San Francisco, the Elsewhere in which I lived for twenty years. The demon who tormented my Borges throughout his life, and I suspected caused all the harm I suffered after Borges "choose me." And he didn't disappoint. The man in black loomed large over the bed, but I was ready for him.

"Don't bother," I said. "Your tricks don't work on me anymore, old man. I'm not afraid of you. You control your son. Maybe you think you can control my unborn son, your grandson, but you have no power over me. So be a good boy and sit in that chair over there in the corner next to the vanity. We have a few things to discuss, you and I." When he didn't move, I shouted, "Do it!" But he continued to fill the room.

"You think you can bully me?" I said, irritated. "I can end you anytime I want. All I need to do is this." I drew my hand across my throat in a slashing motion. "And don't think I won't. I know who you are. You appear as a faceless evil, but you're only a small portion of the soul of Jorge Luis Borges, the greedy bit of him that's left. If I die, so will you, or at least destroy whatever part of you is growing in my unborn child. Anger me further and I might just do it out of spite." The dark figure wavered and then shrunk to the size of a toddler. His body shook the way a small child shakes the first time he realizes death is real. I had been right all along. The man in black was the soul of the dead Jorge Luis Borges. Whether or not his actions were feigned, I knew his intentions, for his mind was open to me for inspection. He craved eternal life and thought he could obtain it like the mythical Phoenix. But now he feared I might disrupt his grand plan.

I represented both his greatest problem and his only hope. Jorge Luis Borges may not have known when he slept with Ulrikke that part of his soul would pass into the unborn child they conceived, but it happened. And that spirit, which I knew as the "man in black," extended the life of my Borges, and protected him from harm until now. But he couldn't keep him alive forever. Eventually, my Borges would die and the man in black would fall into the abyss with him. He needed another host, a direct descendant of Borges he could inhabit. As the mother of the next host, I comprehended that the prophecy never required my death. No, for it to succeed, my Borges must die.

"You need my son," I said to the dark figure, "but not his father. You mean to kill my Borges right before our son is born. It's clear to me that you can't afford to have more than one Borges running around alive, for the death of one while the other lived would ruin you." The man in black said nothing, but I read his thoughts and saw panic in them. To him, I was unpredictable, a wild card that might cause the prophecy to fail, and that would be catastrophic for him. I knew this because I relived his memories from the day the first Jorge Luis Borges died. His death tore his soul apart. Half was lost forever, but the other half inside my Borges, survived, diminished, if still powerful. The man in black decided he would do anything to avert such an event from ever occurring again. He designed the prophecy as a fail-safe mechanism to ensure he could transfer all of himself into my unborn child without the risk of ever being torn apart again.

And I perceived the man in black's hatred for me. I went Elsewhere while on the camping trip in British Columbia before my Borges' could impregnate me, and then I had another man's son. That was a missed opportunity. My Borges might have died before finding me again. No wonder the man in black tormented me all those years in my dreams. He needed me to bear a Borges' son, for he could only live on in a true descendant of the original Jorge Luis Borges. Once I became pregnant, the man in black, just as happened with Ulrikke, split a part of himself off and that part affixed itself to my unborn child. My worst fears proved true.

My Borges received some of Ulrikke's powers, but not the most important one, the ability to *travel*, to go *Elsewhere*. That made him a failure, for when he died, so would his father's spirit. The man in black hoped my son would succeed where Ulrikke's did not, by inheriting my power. Then the soul of the first Borges could live forever.

Bashō said he failed Jorge Luis Borges because he would not let go of his dream of immortality. When he died, that dream lived on in the part of his soul residing within my Borges. A powerful yet malignant dream that would have ended, but for the continued existence of the half of Jorge Luis Borges's soul that lived on within my Borges.

At present, the remainder of that soul was split between my Borges and our unborn child. But this period of dual possession was a dangerous time for the man in black. He risked much. All of us must stay alive during my pregnancy to lessen the risk of further harm to the man in black. Right before my son's birth, Borges must die, which would allow the man in black to transfer all of himself to his new host without fear of losing the ability to maintain his existence.

But how was the prophecy supposed to accomplish this? What rites or rituals were necessary? Those details the creature kept hidden from me. Frustrating, but this dark sliver of a thing would not give up all its secrets. *No matter*, I thought. *I have the leverage now.* Picking up the shrunken figure, I pulled his head to my chest and held him tight. The warmth of his body surprised me. My nightgown soon dampened from unseen tears. "There, there," I shushed him. "If you do what Mommy wants, you have nothing to fear. But you must promise me. Understand? Nod if you do."

Feeling his head nod on my shoulder, I whispered, "Don't worry, everything will be fine. You'll see." Rocking him in my arms until he stopped whimpering, I then tucked the small black figure into bed. "I have to go now, but we'll see each other soon. I promise." And with that, I awoke back in the Fāmā-mura bunker seated between Borges and Ulrikke, just as I left them.

CHAPTER 26

"You went Elsewhere," said Borges, pale and gaunt.

"But I returned. I hope that's not a problem for anyone."

"But you went Elsewhere!" Borges blurted again. His hands shook so much, I wondered if he thought me a ghost. "Where did you go?"

"Does it matter? I'm here now."

"No," Ulrikke said drily. "It doesn't matter at all. You have always been free to come or go whenever you wish."

"Yet you looked surprised to see me."

"More curious than surprised," Ulrikke said, feigning disinterest. "I thought you finally broke free from my son, I suppose."

"But didn't he choose me?" I said, gesturing at Borges." Am I not critical to the prophecy?"

Ulrikke shrugged. "So I've been told, but who knows? That's a question for him." *She's deflecting*, I thought. This didn't fit what she'd said to me before. An underlying disquiet played out beneath her placid surface. As for Borges, he said nothing, though his body language revealed a number of contradictory emotions: relief, fear, confusion. His gaze shifted back and forth between his mother and me. *He doesn't know what to think.* It was odd to see him like that. Ulrikke must have thought the same. "You're awfully quiet, son, for someone who's generally so talkative."

"At least my absence accomplished one thing," I interjected. "You're not fighting anymore. Or am I wrong?"

"No," replied Ulrikke. "After you left, what was the point? It's not like we haven't said the same things to one another a thousand times before." She rose from her chair. "Now, if you don't mind, I think it's time for Fāmāmura's security team to return my son to his cell. You, Jane, are free to stay with us or go wherever you wish. But it's much too dangerous to leave him wandering about on his own. I'm sure you agree."

Ulrikke pivoted toward the bunker's only door, but I stopped her before she could get away. "Don't be that way, Urikei-chōrō," I said, using the same honorific for her that Yoshi uttered on her last day as my Sābanto. "*Ikutsu ka no shitsumon ni kotaete kudasai.* Can't you can spare me some time to answer a few questions?"

Ulrikke hesitated. She grimaced, as if fighting with herself. Then, all traces of conflict vanished, and she graced me with a smile. "Of course, Jane. I am happy to honor your request. A few questions, you said?"

"Arigatō gozaimasu, Urikei-sama," I said, though I knew she could not refuse. Not anymore. On that point, Borges proved correct. I was the stronger one now. "I just want to clarify a few things." She eased back into her chair, and crossed her legs, arms folded firmly across her breasts. She leaned as far away from me as her chair allowed, a defensive posture. I smiled, leaning forward to shorten the distance between us.

"Let's start then. Is Ray Tanaka alive?"

Ulrikke snorted. "Of course. I wouldn't have allowed such a useful individual to me to come to harm because of you."

I sighed with relief now that I knew Ray lived. "Thank you for clearing up my confusion, Urekei-sama, but I have more questions, of greater importance. First, does Borges' prophecy no longer matter?"

"Not in the least." She dipped her head to the side as she spoke.

"And yet," I pressed her, "only a short while ago, you told me it was a great danger to me. That Borges would take my child and dispose of me unless I assassinated him."

"I don't believe I ever used the word, 'assassinate,'" Ulrikke said, defensive as ever.

"Pardon me. But you asked me to kill him. Do you deny it?"

"No. At the time–at the time, I thought it necessary for your protection, and to prevent a great evil."

"But no longer? What changed your mind?"

"You did," she replied. "When you left us, you demonstrated my son no longer has any hold over you. You're free of him. Free of the prophecy. Free from its threat. Free from fear. Congratulations."

She's lying. I pressed harder. "But what made you believe, when you thought he controlled me, that I would consent to kill him? Where did that idea come from?" When she didn't answer right away, I turned to Borges. "Ever tell your mother I was capable of murder?"

"Never." He said this with a hint of his old confidence.

"I see. Ulrikke, both you and your son agree you tried to murder him and failed. What made you think I could do what you couldn't?"

"It was... it was a hunch. I fled to Fāmā-mura to escape him and his mad vision. I prayed that he would fail and never find anyone like me. But then the two of you arrived here, the one place I believed safe. That was my worst nightmare, him showing up with you, a woman who shared my gift. I convinced myself that if anyone could stop him..." She hesitated. "It was always a long shot. I admit that now, but I believed if you understood the danger he posed–"

"I saw him kill a man with a knife, Ulrikke. The day we shared tea, you reminded me of that yourself." I laughed without mirth. "But, okay. I don't need to worry about him because I broke his hold over me. The prophecy has nothing to do with me anymore. I'm free to do whatever I want. Borges can't stop me. You can't stop me. Have I got that right?"

"Yes," she said. "Though I hope you will stay in Fāmā-mura. You are certainly welcome, and with your talents–"

"You want me here? With you?" The idea was palpably ridiculous. Ulrikke did not share power. No, there must be some other reason. Did she want my baby? I couldn't read her, but I doubted her proposition was benign.

"I am not young anymore. The endless cycle of new lives eats at you, Jane. After so many of them... but I don't want to abandon these people. You could take my place. You can protect them, perhaps better than I." A great wave of empathy for the Fāmā-mura community swept over me as she made her plea. Empathy produced by Ulrikke.

"And why would I want to do that?" I intoned.

"You care about the people here. Some, you love. Yoshi. Junko. Ray." I couldn't help but think of them then, and my eyes watered. But I would not play her game. Ulrikke was ruthless, but the emotions she used as weapons could not bend me to her will.

"This is a doomed world," I answered. "In fact, you said the human race was doomed regardless of what we or any other 'gifted' person might do. Stay or go, what's the point?"

"Maybe I'm wrong." Her muted confession barely exceeded a whisper. "Maybe you will find a way where I cannot. You are young and strong, stronger than I am, perhaps than I ever was." She did her best, but her note of humility rang false. This was not the Ulrikke I knew, only a disguise to confuse me.

"So my options are to leave, or stay and inherit your–what should we call it?–fiefdom? And I would succeed you as its unspoken queen?"

"You're wrong, Jane. You'd be Fāmā-mura's defender, its servant. I could teach you everything necessary to carry on my work."

"What a great honor."

"Then you'll consider it? Believe me, it would be the best thing for you and for Fāmā-mura." It was painful to watch her trying so hard. Trying and failing.

"And what would happen to him?" I said, pointing to Borges. "Is he also free to go?"

"No. He must remain a prisoner until he dies."

"Why? He poses no threat. You said so."

"His prophecy no longer binds you, Jane, but he might find someone else, and it would start again. I can't risk that." *Liar!* I thought. She didn't know that I knew, from my interaction with the man in black, that the prophecy was far from done with me.

"And it's not a risk to keep him here?" I asked. "What if the very person you fear, another girl with all the gifts, is living right under your nose?"

"I'd know. That's why he can never leave. As long as he's my prisoner, we're safe."

"I see." *She's trying to brazen it out. Doing anything to keep me here.* "I have one last question then," I said. "Why did you stop going by your name, Maria? That's who you are, Maria Haraldsdotter. It's your birth name. The name you went by for so many lives. Why change it?"

"Do you know the story of Moses in the Book of Exodus?" she asked in return, a non sequitur. I hesitated before answering.

"Why don't you tell it to me the way you know it?"

"Moses, a member of the royal family, fled Egypt after killing one of Pharaoh's taskmasters for whipping a Hebrew slave. He escaped to the land of Midian. There, he married Zipporah, one of seven daughters of a priest after he fought off sheepherders seeking to steal water from their well. The scriptures say, '… she bare *him* a son, and he called his name Gershom: for he said, I have been a stranger in a strange land.'

"Gershom means 'exile.' After my son was born, I realized my gift forever changed me. I could never again be that simple, trusting girl who loved her father, though he was as cruel and heartless as any man I ever met. The powers *Óðinn bestowed made me an outcast.* I could rely on no one, but myself. No family or people to call my own. So why continue to be Maria? As to why I chose Ulrikke, you know the answer."

"Yes," I said, "I understand. Thank you." It was a clever answer, and a last attempt to manipulate me. *We're both exiles, Jane, no friends, no family. Both of us are women exploited by a Borges. Why not stay with me?* That was her implied message. I wondered if she prepared it in advance or improvised on the spot. Not that it changed anything.

"Now, if you have no other questions," Ulrikke proclaimed, "I must go. I pray you choose to stay in Fāmā-mura, but I must make arrangements regarding my son." She pulled a small com device out of a pocket of her jacket.

"I wouldn't do that if I were you," I said, and she froze. Her body tried to overrule my command, but in vain. It was as Ray Tanaka said. I only needed confidence.

"Borges, my love," I said, "where would you like to go?"

I will never forget the amazement in his eyes. At long last, I was a step ahead of him, instead of the reverse.

"I have a vial of Midazolam and a syringe," he said, pointing to the room with the cots." I'll be right back to give you an injection and then–"

"Don't bother," I cut him off. "You won't need them."

"You have that much control?" His eyes expressed disbelief.

I understood his concern, so I pointed to his mother standing erect, unable to move. "I wouldn't worry. Just think of where you want to go. We'll get there."

"But–" he said.

"Shhhh." My hand lightly brushed the stubble on his cheek. "We'll have plenty of time for that later. Just close your eyes and concentrate."

The place and the date came through clear enough: Ciudad Juarez in the Mexican state of Chihuahua during the last week of July 1979. Taking his hand and placing it in mine, I swiveled back to Ulrikke.

"Goodbye, Maria." Her eyes were full of anger, but there was something else in them, some emotion I wasn't sure about. Then I went Elsewhere, taking my Borges with me.

CHAPTER 27

Borges stood over my bed in our hotel suite. *He thinks I'm asleep*, I thought, but I wasn't. I didn't allow myself to doze when he was up, as he was so often these last several months. Each morning in the hours before dawn, I would sense his presence, but I did nothing to give myself away, and he gave no sign he knew of my ruse. Each night was a repeat of the prior one. Stiff and soulless as a clay golem, he made no sound, not even a murmurous breath. I knew when he was there, but could not sense his mind. Zombie Borges, I named him.

It upset Borges when we arrived, not in Juarez in July, but in Durango, Colorado in early April 1979, but I explained Ulrikke might have read his mind and come after us. We also needed time to obtain money and make plans for our son's birth. I didn't let on that I knew he expected to die in Mexico. After I promised we would still make our way there in July–thus, meeting the conditions of his prophecy–he acquiesced. He even seemed relieved, or part of him did.

For it was clear to me that his self split into three unequal and quite different personalities after leaving Fāmā-mura, though I wasn't sure if the one hovering over me as I feigned sleep was human. When I looked for the mind of Zombie Borges, it wasn't there. But the other two appeared to be real personas, as far as I could tell. The one I liked best was unlike any other version of Borges I knew.

I called him the five-year old, for he interacted with me as a child would, with wonder and curiosity and the naiveté of a young boy. He enjoyed being my companion and friend. When the five-year old was present, we played. Every day was an adventure. Even mundane tasks, such as shopping for groceries, we treated as games. He delighted in frivolity.

To earn money, I bet on baseball games at the Vegas' sports books–sure bets, thanks to short excursions into the future where I read box scores in the local papers. To place the bets, we used tourists as proxies. I persuaded them to do my bidding, which limited the chance of the Casinos tracing the winnings back to me. Over the last two months, we amassed over $200,000. Yesterday, after collecting our haul, the five-year old Borges insisted we visit Circus Circus, because, as he said, "They have a bunch of things to see, Jane. Real lions and tigers, and elephants! It'll be great. Please, can we go?" I felt like a young mother being cajoled by her adorable, if annoying little boy.

"Okay, but not for long. My back hurts. And my feet. I'm eight months pregnant, you know." I doubted he heard a word I uttered after 'Okay.' I tipped the doorman at the casino a hundred dollars to call us an air-conditioned limousine. Borges couldn't stop bouncing on the balls of his feet until it arrived.

Circus Circus resembled a giant circus tent. Inside, among the usual casino games and slot machines, was an area devoted to entertainment for 'Kids of All Ages.' It contained a traditional penny arcade and carnival attractions in one section, while, in another, various circus acts performed. Hordes of youngsters and their parents crowded together. Many small children sat atop the shoulders of their poor beleaguered fathers. Borges' eyes lit up when he saw the big cats leaping through rings of fire; and then, after I pointed them out, the scantily clad female trapeze artists flipping and twisting through the air high above our heads. We spent time at 'The Dart Game' where Borges broke balloon after balloon without missing until he won their biggest prize: a giant panda bear, which he carried on his back, beaming with pride. After two hours, I let him know I couldn't take another step. Alarmed, he gave the bear away to a father of two twin girls, and–God knows where–found me a wheelchair. He rolled me to the main entrance and hailed a cab. On the ride to our hotel, he talked non-stop. Despite my fatigue, I smiled. His exuberance eased my aches and pains.

But once back at the hotel, the second persona, which I named the Commander, appeared. The Commander treated me as a child. Though he ordered me about in a polite and respectful manner, he expected me to obey him without question. In the past, my Borges was sometimes overbearing, but that attitude was always mediated by a dash of humor. The Commander, however, reminded me of a stock player in a repertory company, one with a limited emotional range. Unlike the five-year old, he never exhibited an ounce of spontaneity or joy. He planned our every move like a military campaign, from choosing my clothes, deciding where, when and what to eat, to our evening activities, if any. His mind was difficult to penetrate, but when I did, I found myself confronted by a thick wall. Powerful emotions churned beyond that barrier, but I could not read them. The Commander was more a caricature of a human being than a real one, but I complied with his commands, because it made things easier. Besides, none involved matters I considered important.

Last, there was Zombie Borges, the one standing over me now, mindless and cold. He was the oddest of them all, but I knew why he watched me in the early hours of the morning. A sentinel to protect me, he might be, but also a spy waiting for the right moment to strike and I knew that time was coming soon. I could feel it. The date was July 23rd. Sunrise was approaching. *It's today*, I thought, and in that instant, he proved me right. My mind registered him coming to life, and I threw off my sheets at once.

"Drop the syringe."

"I can't," he gasped. "Don't make me. Please, I beg you."

"Do it."

Borges groaned as if someone slid a knife into his ribs, but the syringe fell to the carpet. I kicked it away. A cry of despair escaped his lips. "The prophecy!" he said in a hoarse voice. Borges' mind, a chaotic frenzy of emotions, stood at the edge of madness.

"Your prophecy says you will take me to Mexico, correct?"

"Yes. To Sonora."

"Then we will go to your desert," I said, "but no more drugs. Those days are over. Understand?"

He nodded. He stopped fighting and his body collapsed on the bed. Relief shone through his face, which I found odd. "I'll take my shower and then get dressed. I assume you have transportation arranged."

"Yes, a 1976 Fleetwood Eldorado Coupe."

"Just so long as it has comfortable seats and air conditioning."

"They are," he said, "and it does." The baby kicked then, stepping on my bladder. *The joys of pregnancy*, I thought as I wobbled to the bathroom, and, for a while, stopped thinking about Borges' prophecy, and my plan to counter it.

• • • • •

Naked and alone, I stood in a vast white space with no boundaries. Stretched thin, my distended belly had a translucent quality to it like opaque glass. Every so often, I felt the baby moving within me. Peering down, I could just see a tiny black blob twisting and turning.

"The moon shines brightly; restless clouds pass overhead. Dawn will come quickly."

"Bashō?"

"Yes, Jane-san, it is I."

"What are you doing here?" I asked. Then, "No, don't answer that. Where am I?"

"In a dream. Your dream." His eyes, half-open, exposed the black holes of his pupils. "So much white. Death approaches, but you know that, do you not?"

"Yes. You were right when you said I knew everything I needed to know to choose my path. Borges means to die. I mean to stop him. What I don't know is how things will go, not exactly. But I will save him." I spoke with confidence, even though I didn't know when my Borges, or, in reality, the creature possessing him, would make his move. Regardless, I was determined not to let the man in black succeed. I kept my plans vague and undefined, in part because I didn't know what to expect, but also because I thought it best to hide my intentions. I didn't want the man in black to view me as an obstacle to the prophecy when the time came.

Bashō chuckled. "One day, you must learn the difference between wisdom and faith, Jane-san."

"I think it's a little late for that."

"Snow blankets the earth; the chrysanthemums vanquished. Song birds pray for spring." Bashō sighed. "I can teach you nothing more, Jane-san."

"No 'help' for an old friend?" I said, but then the baby kicked. A great weight pressed upon me. My eyes opened to the blinding light of day. The black leather seat of the Cadillac burned my bare shoulders. Sweat plastered my bangs to my forehead. Borges shaded me from the sun until I could see again.

"Why'd we stop?"

"You cried out," he said, the worry lines over his brows creased.

"It's just the baby kicking," I said, but his concern remained.

It was the third day of our trip south. After checking out of our hotel in Vegas, the Commander tried to assume charge, but I told Borges I never, ever wanted to see that personality again, and 'poof,' he vanished. In his place, the Borges I knew from before Fāmā-mura returned, or some semblance of him. Gone was the trickster. Gone, too, his usual arrogance. I saw a humbled Borges, and one more vulnerable. Or maybe for the first time, I could see his true self, a man with anxieties and flaws like any other. Though I didn't trust him, I still loved him. His all too human weaknesses on display, I began to pity him.

The first day we made it as far as Tucson, the last time we would enjoy the luxury of a fine hotel. The second day, we crossed the border at Nogales around noon. Twice, we were pulled over and questioned. First, by Mexican border guards who asked to see our passports. I casually told them they didn't need to bother with us, that we were free to go, and that was that. The other time, several Jeeps filled with Federales created a roadblock that stopped us just north of Ímuris, our evening's destination. The men, dressed in green combat fatigues, carried U.S. Army carbines. Ignoring me, their leader, a Captain Martinez, spoke to Borges in broken English. He wanted to search the car because of "drug smuggling," but it soon became clear he wanted a cash bribe. I pulled $10,000 out of my bag, and leaning over Borges, I waved it in the captain's face.

"This enough, Jefe?" The captain grabbed the bills out of my hand, stuffed them into his shirt, then shouted orders to his men, who moved their Jeeps and let us pass. Upon reaching Ímuris, we checked into the only motel in town, a squat adobe structure, with a brick façade. Borges spoke passable Spanish, and, when asked where we could get dinner, the desk clerk suggested a family restaurant within walking distance. The townspeople we met along the way gave us skeptical looks. Two gringos, one of them a pregnant woman, wandering their streets in July, was justifiably strange, but I smiled at everyone, cocooning us within an aura of warmth, and their suspicions disappeared. At the restaurant, the service was good and the food delicious, as promised. Back in our room, satiated and tired, I slept well. When I awoke the next morning, Borges was sitting in a chair by an open window, smoking a cigarette, his hands shaking noticeably. *Today must be the day*, I thought, before yawning loud enough to give him time to compose himself.

• • • • •

Borges gently placed his hand on my abdomen.

"Just checking to see everyone's all right." On cue, the baby gave a little kick and Borges smiled, perhaps for the first time since we started south. Earlier, he exited the main highway, turning onto a narrow dirt road with deep ruts. At some point, I drifted asleep. Now that we stopped, both of us got out of the car. Borges went to stretch his legs and grab a smoke, while I wandered over to an Ironwood tree not far from the road and did my business there. The beauty of the Sonoran desert helped me ignore the heat. A variety of strange trees mingled among the ubiquitous cacti; some of the most unusual vegetation on earth, spread out between mountain ridges that rose thousands of feet from the valleys below.

Upon my return, Borges stared at the sky. Dark clouds tumbled over the western mountains. A fractured bolt of lightning flashed. Several seconds later came the roar of thunder. "We must get going," he said, "if we don't want that to catch us." I climbed in and closed the car door, but the storm headed right for us. Avoiding it looked impossible, but Borges gunned the engine and off we went. The faster he drove, the more the Caddy caromed back and forth on the road, often brushing against the branches of Joshua trees, protruding yucca shrubs, and other strange plants.

Going over bumps, the Caddy would leap into the air before crashing back to earth. Borges' face alternated between scowls and brief expressions of exuberance. He drove like a wild man, tempting fate for some purpose all his own. I searched the mind of my unborn child, concerned about the baby, but everything was fine. "Don't worry," Borges announced, as my body swung back and forth, tossed about like a Raggedy Ann doll despite the seatbelt strapped low and tight over my thighs, "We'll outrun it!" We didn't.

The rains hit five minutes later, accompanied by strong, battering winds. Day imitated night, except for intervals of pale blue lightning that imbued the clouds above us with an eerie glow. The hardpan road flooded, and Borges, possessed by a frantic energy, did not slow down. The road's course followed a creek, which now overflowed its banks. The Caddy became a speedboat bouncing over choppy waves. The spray, kicked up by its rough passage, obscured our view, making wipers useless. Somehow, Borges managed not to careen off into the underbrush or slam into the Palo Verde and Ironwood trees. I should've been scared witless, but I assumed Borges' prophecy wouldn't end in anything as banal as a car crash. *He's testing his faith in the prophecy,* I thought. Secure in my belief that events would turn out in my favor, I remained calm. As the song goes, "We all want to rule the world." And so, like two drunken teenagers, we screamed to drown out the roar of wind, rain and thunder, and the outraged noise erupting from the Caddy's engine. Distinctly present, each moment obliterated eternity, until I closed my eyes. *This world's an illusion,* was my last thought before losing consciousness.

CHAPTER 28

I awoke alone. Dazed, I checked to make sure the baby was all right, and was reassured to feel movement. I struggled to sit upright, because I was lying almost sideways, but otherwise I felt as well as one could expect. But where did Borges go? I searched for clues as to his whereabouts.

Looking out the windshield, I observed a low, flat-roofed brick building with no windows. A naked bulb flickered on and off over a parched wooden door perhaps six feet high, the only visible entrance. Beneath the light, a metal sign, with the word *Taberna* embossed on it, hung from a rod. It creaked, waving in the wind. *That's where he'll be.* Then the baby stepped on my bladder. *God, I hope there's a toilet in there.* Opening the passenger door, I stepped into a puddle, which covered my canvas shoes, soaking me up to my ankles.

An unpaved gravel and dirt road ran past the front of the Taberna. A chewed-up morass of mud and standing water, it twisted through a narrow valley between two opposing sharp ridges. Both rose to steep heights I could only guess at. The setting sun cast shades of red and orange light that rimmed the jagged crest of the eastern ridge. The western mountains lay in shadow. As the sun set, I struggled to see the town that the road bisected in a snakelike manner, where squashed adobe buildings shimmered as dusk descended. The town existed out of time, ageless, fashioned from something magical. Stars appeared through breaks in the clouds. A pockmarked full moon rose in the east, salmon colored. For a while, I lost myself in the austere beauty around me. Then I remembered Borges must have stopped here for a reason. Many old trucks and cars parked in a haphazard fashion alongside the Caddy. Doing my best to avoid them, I stepped gingerly around mud puddles toward the door with the noisy sign. A small bell rang out when it opened.

The Taberna comprised a single narrow room lit by candlelight. A long rough hewn, unpainted wooden bar with a slab of slate maybe twenty feet long that served as its countertop faced me as I pushed into the main room. The bar roughly divided the Taberna into thirds. To my right, a shabby curtain blocked my view. To my left, I saw a few empty tables. Men clustered around the bar, sitting on stools or leaning on the counter with their elbows. They looked up when I entered, but soon resumed drinking as if an unfamiliar pregnant woman was not worthy of their attention. The man behind the bar wore a sleeveless shirt and light cotton pants held up by a piece of cord tied around his waist. Unlike the others, he kept eying me as he polished a glass with a rag. His sharp angled features suggested a mestizo heritage. With careful deliberation, he poked someone in the shoulder. It was Borges.

"Es tu esposa?" he said, jerking his head at me.

"Si, senor," Borges answered. "Esa es ella." I gathered Borges identified me as his wife. At that, the man put down the glass, swung the rag over his shoulder, and walked out from behind the bar. He was a little taller than me, with a sharply defined chest and arms with taut, sinewy muscles. Gently, but firmly, he placed a hand on my arm. "Por favor, Señora," he said, directing me to a round table in the corner of the room furthest from the bar. Borges followed. The table's chairs looked about to collapse. After seating us, he left to get Borges' drink, some milky substance that triggered nausea the moment I detected its strong odor. The barman laughed at my reaction.

"A ella no le gusta el pulque," he said to Borges.

"No," Borges replied. Then he pointed to my swollen belly. "Embarazo."

"Si, si." The bartender laughed again. "Mejor ella que yo."

Tired of being made a figure of fun, I tugged at Borges' arm. "I really need to pee. Ask him if they have a restroom I can use."

The bartender and Borges engaged in a brief conversation. When they finished, Borges said, "The men just go outside and relieve themselves against the rear wall. But he says you can use his family's outhouse, which is not far. He'll take you." The bartender reached for my hand, saying again, "Por favor, Señora." I turned back to ask Borges to come with me, but he was busy downing his disgusting drink. Frustrated, I tapped the bartender on the shoulder.

"What's your name?" I said, but he looked confused. I repeated myself several times, but he shook his head.

"No habla ingles."

I took my hand and placed it on my collarbone, then said, "Jane." Then I pointed at him. "You?"

"Ah, entiendo ahora. Mi nombre es Jose." He smiled, and I smiled back, both of us pleased with our cleverness. I let him lead me out the door down a short path between some weeds to a small broken-down shack about fifty paces, give or take, from the Taberna. "Este es mi baño, Señora Jane."

"Gracias, Jose." Despite the stench and the flies, I entered and shut the door, then gagged. Resisting the urge to puke, I pulled up my skirt and sat down. When finished, I left as fast as I could, only to find Jose waiting for me. Seeing my astonishment, he shrugged and then said something in Spanish. I thanked him, which restored his good humor. Soon, I was back at the table with Borges.

"What the hell happened?" I asked. "Why did we stop here, of all places?"

"You fell asleep in the middle of that thunderstorm," Borges answered in a wary tone of voice. "I stopped because the gas tank's almost empty. I thought they might have some gasoline here."

"And where is here, exactly?"

"Tuape," Borges said.

"Tuape?"

He looked askance, then said, "A small town, south of Nogales."

"It doesn't look like much of anything to me."

"It's not, but the owner there," he said, pointing to Jose, "says he knows a local rancher who will sell us gas in the morning. Overpriced, but..." He shrugged. "In the meantime, his wife is cooking us dinner. It'll be here soon. Amazing what a twenty-dollar bill will get you." He gave me a sardonic grin.

"Okay. You know, actually, that's great. I'm starved. And thirsty. My throat's as dry as toast."

Borges stood up. "They have a water jug at the bar," he said. "I'll get you some." He started to leave, but I grabbed him before he could get too far.

"All things considered, I don't think drinking the local water's a good idea. They have any soda? I'd die for a Coke about now."

"I'll check." Then he left, and I didn't bother to follow him with my eyes. Tired beyond words, I wanted to sleep, if only to stop my stomach churning, but I could not allow myself that luxury. I guessed Tuape wasn't just some random place Borges happened upon. We were supposed to be traveling from Nogales to Juarez on a highway parallel to the border, heading east. Moving south was never the plan before now.

When Borges came back, he handed me a warm bottle of Grape Nehi. Not my favorite, but I didn't care. I downed the whole bottle.

"More?" I asked.

"How many do you want," Borges grumbled. "He's charging us five dollars each."

"So what? Buy his whole supply. It's not like we can't afford it."

"Maybe when the food comes," he said, exasperated. When I gave him a hard look, he gave me one back. "Look, Jane. This isn't the nicest town in the world, if you hadn't noticed. I can't keep flashing our money in front of everybody."

"Are you saying we aren't safe here?" I said. "Because if not, I have an easy fix for that problem." I snapped my fingers, half-joking, half-serious.

"No, no, there's no need for anything drastic," he replied. "It's just, let's keep a low profile." *Low profile?* How could people looking like us keep a low profile in a godforsaken off the map place like this? Yet I sensed panic the moment I implied that we could go Elsewhere whenever I felt like it. His body language screamed he needed us to stay. The emotions cascading through his head were as strong as those I remembered the night he tried to drug me in Vegas. I pretended nothing we'd done over the last few days was out of the ordinary, but why were we here? What drove him to bring us to this not so nice town? It must be the prophecy. I thought things would come to a head when we reached Juarez, but if a shithole bar in Tuape was his choice, so be it. I decided to let things play out, certain I could handle whatever was coming.

"Fine. Just make sure I get another Nehi when the food gets here." I pushed the empty bottle toward his side of the table.

"You will," he said. "When the food comes." With that, he laid his head on the table and fell asleep. He snored, but no one in the place gave us as much as a glance.

• • • • •

"Wake up, sleepyhead. It's dinner time."

Borges shook his head to rouse himself. As he did so, a waif of a girl, with long black hair, and a blank face, like so many women I saw south of the border, put plates of tamales and beans in front of us. Jose helped her, handing us forks, some paper napkins, a second Grape Nehi for me, and another glass of pulque for Borges. Jose's smile beamed, one arm around the girl's shoulder, while his other arm surreptitiously slid close to Borges, his hand extended, palm up. He appeared to be trying to hide his movements from the men at the bar.

"Esta es mi espousa, Francisca," Jose announced.

"Ella es bella," replied Borges as he slipped Jose two twenties. "Eres muy afortunado." Francisca, if that was her name, showed no reaction of any kind to their exchange. Perhaps she'd heard it all before.

"Si, Senor Borges." Jose kept smiling, but he didn't move away from our table. Borges gave him three more bills, which proved satisfactory. Jose nodded his appreciation and then looked at his wife. "Vamonos," he said, slapping her backside. They left, and we settled in to eat. I peeled the corn husks off the tamales, and eagerly dug my fork into a mixture of tender pork, ground corn and green chilies in a creamy sauce that reminded me of goat cheese. The tamales were milder than I expected. It amazed me that Francisca could find the ingredients to make such a delicacy. No wonder Jose wanted so much for them. I only drank half the Grape Nehi, but Borges wasted no time downing his pulque and, each time he finished, Jose appeared out of nowhere to refill his glass, an old mason jar. Borges ignored his food. This was out of character for him, drinking so. *Liquid courage,* I thought, and then felt ashamed.

Jose came again and stood just behind my left shoulder, close to the wall. After a short nod to me, he asked Borges a question, and Borges said something back. They both spoke so fast. I kept wishing I'd taken Spanish in high school rather than Latin, which was my father's choice. To Borges, I said, "What's he want?"

"He wants to know if you're done eating, so he can clear everything away. Are you?"

I looked over the remains of my meal and then considered my stomach. Food no longer appealed to me. Jose bent at the waist, awaiting my reply. "Yes," I said. "I mean, si, Jose." I waved my hand over the plate. "Por favor."

He displayed a toothy grin and bowed. "En seguida, Señora." He reached around me to pick up the heavy clay plate, being careful not to touch me. As he lifted it off the table, Borges raised his empty glass in the air. "Pulque," he demanded.

"Haven't you had enough?" I said, leaning toward Borges. As he looked at me in anger, something hard struck the side of my head. My vision blurred. The last thing I heard was the sound of the plate shattering before I blacked out.

• • • • •

I came to with a throbbing pain in the back of my head. I was on the floor. Upon opening my eyes, the room began to swirl around and around. It was difficult to get my bearings, and the cacophony of voices ringing in my ears didn't make things any easier. I tried to sit up, but that just made the dizziness worse. I recognized Borges' legs nearby, though they kept swaying from side to side. Turning my head, I thought I saw him holding one of the table chairs in front of him like a lion tamer. *Strange*, I thought. *Why's he doing that?*

Then another man came into view. A large fat man, but well-muscled, eyes narrowed. He wore a loose Hawaiian shirt. In his right hand, he held a knife, which he waved back and forth. The crowd from the bar gathered behind him. They did the yelling, most of it in Spanish, but every once in a while, I heard bits of English mixed in, like "Motherfucker!" Borges said nothing, just stood there, thrusting the chair at them when they came too close. Jose was nowhere to be seen.

"Not good," I said to myself. I needed to get us out of here, but in my concussed state, I couldn't concentrate. I thought myself prepared for every contingency, but not one where someone knocked me unconscious. Jose must have done it. I should have sensed his thoughts and stopped him, but I didn't. And that was the most disturbing thing of all. Thinking back, I realized I never got a read on anyone in the bar. That should have set off alarm bells, but it hadn't. From the moment I walked into the Taberna, all the men were ciphers to me, their minds as unreadable as the Zombie Borges who spent so many nights standing beside my bed in Vegas. Somehow, I let myself be blindsided. I spent all my time worried about Borges' state of mind. I forgot about everyone else.

"Offer them all our money," I shouted.

"They aren't here for that," Borges hissed back. "They want you."

"Me?" That made no sense. Not that I was capable of figuring out why. My head was pounding, and it was taking everything I had not to vomit.

"I won't let them," Borges added. "They'll have to kill me first."

Shit! I thought. *This is what he wanted. This is the main event! I've been set up!* The room still spun, accelerating my sense of doom.

Unexpectedly, the crowd quieted. I watched as the men made way for a tall, cloaked figure that pushed through them to stand beside the man holding the knife. I couldn't make out the face, but glowing eyes peeked out from underneath the hood, two circles that reflected the light from the flickering candles. Everyone was silent. Time stilled. Then, with surprising quickness, the hooded figure pulled out a second knife and threw it at Borges' feet, where it stuck a good half inch into one the floor's ancient planks. Then he (or was it a she?) pushed their way back through the crowd. I heard the door open, the bell ring and then the sharp click as it closed.

The fat man stared at the knife at Borges' feet. A few seconds later, he threw his own knife down at his feet, until it also stuck upright, embedded in the floor. He motioned at Borges, who understood without words what was up. Borges flung the chair against the back wall with enough force to smash it into pieces good only for kindling. The corners of his mouth curled upward into a ghost of a smile. The fat man's face, like a death mask, revealed nothing.

"Don't do this," I begged. "I can get us out of here. Just play for time until I feel better."

"Hombre!" It was the fat man. "Cállate la puta!"

Borges shot me a look, his eyes red. "Don't say another word."

I couldn't believe this was happening. The sickening thought came to me that, once more, he deceived me.

"Thick summer grass; last remnant of the Great Lord's dreams and ambitions." I didn't need to look to know it was Bashō. I didn't respond. I didn't have the time or the energy. Not that my silence silenced him. "Roads are dangerous. Many die while traveling, even the wisest."

I wanted to scream something unmentionable about stuffing his destiny crap up his phantom ass, but before I could speak, a voice shouted from among the faceless mass of men, "Uno!" Time was about to run out.

"Dos!" rang out another anonymous voice. Borges and the fat man crouched low with their arms spread wide, knees bent, ready to pounce.

"Tres!"

Then both men lunged for their knives, and the fight for Borges' life, and mine, was on.

CHAPTER 29

The fat man was far more agile than I anticipated. He fought Borges to a standstill and cut him twice. The first slashed Borges' cheek under the left eye, a superficial wound that bled very little. Far worse was the second, a deep gash, near his right elbow, that just missed the large veins. Several times, I feared the fight would go against him, as the fat man used his bulk to smash Borges against the rear wall more than once attempting to knock Borges down or cause him to drop his knife. Borges always wriggled out of the larger man's grasp, but the blows drained him. During much of the fight, I couldn't watch as the constant movement made me sick. In the end, Borges got lucky. The fat man made a feint to Borges' left side while trying to switch the knife to his other hand. Borges must have seen through the ploy, for he batted his adversary's knife away while it was in mid-air. Dizzy, I missed what happened next, but the crowd, which had been yelling throughout, went silent. I turned in time to see the fat man sliding to the floor, grasping at his bloody throat. He collapsed a foot away from me. Blood poured out of him in great spurts until, eyes open in disbelief, he died.

Borges gasped for air, knife held loose in his left hand. With difficulty, I pushed myself into the corner behind him. The pool of blood from the fat man slithered along the wooden planks and its sick, heavy scent got to me. I bent over and emptied my stomach in great heaves. White light flashed before my eyes, triggering an explosion of pain throughout my head. Two hands took hold of my shoulders and set me back up against the wall in a sitting position. It was Borges. He stained my shirt with the fat man's blood.

"Hombre!"

I jerked my head up, and through a cloud of agony, saw another man standing out in front of the others. Short and thin, with wiry ropes for arms, he wore a sleeveless red t-shirt and ragged jeans, a knife clenched in his left hand. His eyes were small and dark and reminded me of a lizard. I did my best to see into his mind, but couldn't. Not that it mattered. If it wasn't clear before, it was now. Each of these men would take their turn, and no one would stop until Borges was dead, or they all were. I groaned, not only out of pain, but also despair. That caught Red-shirt's attention, and he spoke to me directly.

"We fuck you, puta," he said, pointing his knife at me and then brought it back to point at Borges. He laughed, and behind him, the crowd joined in. Laughter that grew louder like the voices of a demonic choir until it seemed I could see the sound waves bouncing off the walls of the Taberna, pummeling me like the ocean crashing against a rocky shore. Then, Borges' new opponent leapt forward, slashing at Borges' face to begin the second fight.

It didn't go well. Borges looked exhausted. He parried each thrust by his new enemy, but made none of his own. The red-shirted man seemed to know this instinctively. He forced the action, slashing and stabbing at Borges, never giving him a moment's respite. Most were off the mark, but striking a single fatal blow was not his intent. He fought to wear Borges' down. It was a war of attrition that Borges was unlikely to win. And even if he got in a lucky blow and killed Red-Shirt, there would be another to take his place.

"You are right to feel helpless. The old man has thirsted for this moment for many years. The son will die as the father intended." *Bashō?*

"What do you know of it?" I lashed out even though it cost me, as the painful throbbing in my temple increased.

"You are badly hurt, Jane-san." He spoke as if no rebuttal was possible. And he spoke the truth. I couldn't focus. I couldn't read the crowd, and doubted I could say anything that would stop them from doing what they were here to do. It was hopeless. But from some place inside me, a great anger started to build. How many times had I been used? Lied to? Cheated? How many times had my needs, my desires, been ignored and subverted, as if my life lacked any significance? Not to Borges or Ulrikke. Now Bashō, too, implied my life held little value.

Rage is a powerful emotion. I staggered to my feet, seething, pushing my torment aside. Red-shirt noticed me standing there and then Borges, too. For a split second, the fight stopped. I couldn't tell what was going through the mind of either of them, but I know what they did next. Borges stumbled backwards. Fear covered his face like a shroud. Red-shirt, that skinny little bastard, now closer to me than to Borges, let out a triumphant howl. His knife held high in a reverse grip, the blade's tip pointed at me, he leaped into the air.

I lost sight of everyone and everything. There was no time for a coherent thought. A red mist encircled my eyes, narrowing my focus. At its center, I saw every one of those men and the bloodlust engrained in each of their souls. In my mind, a red flame took shape as a blade, and I watched as it cleaved all their heads right down the center. I may have screamed as this happened. But in that singular moment, the world of the Taberna vanished. I was alone in darkness. How long, I do not know, but Borges calling my name brought me back. "Jane?" His voice sounded weak, but full of concern. He was lying on his back, his face turned toward mine. Our eyes locked, and we smiled simultaneously at each other, smiles of relief.

"You got them all," he said. "You saved our son."

Confused, I lifted myself up on my elbows and looked. Bodies lay piled all over the place, many of them atop one another, each with a small hole in the center of their foreheads. No one moved. One lay nearby, the knife in his hand reaching just short of where I fell to the floor. Like all the rest, he was dead. I killed them. I was responsible for this slaughter.

"Don't cry," said Borges in a rasping voice. "You had no choice. You're alive, and our son is alive, because of what you did." He was right, for I felt the baby moving, but Borges' words didn't diminish the fact that I was now a murderer. Yet the sound of his voice allowed me to focus on the living. I couldn't undo the past, but I could still help Borges. Crawling awkwardly, I dragged my swollen body to his side. Only upon reaching him, did I see Red-shirt's fist holding the knife meant for me, stuck in Borges' chest. Borges must have thrown himself in front of me, taking the full force of the blow from the dead man's hand.

"No!" I grabbed for the knife to pull it out, but my hand slipped, and struck Borges near the middle of his ribcage. He let out a spasmodic whistling noise that ended in a feeble cough. I could feel his thoughts, a mishmash of contradiction; joy, fear, pain, and fierce determination, but, above all else, a desire not to move. Once more I reached for the knife, but his right hand swatted at me.

"Don't," he said between clenched teeth. "Don't even think about removing it."

"We have to get you out of here. To a hospital."

"No. I'm dying, Jane. You cannot stop it."

"Don't talk," I said. "I can save you, I know I can."

"It's in my heart. Nothing can be done. The prophecy..." His chest rose and his back arched. I screamed, but then heard loud coughing. Borges lifted his head, struggling to breathe. In a panic, I swung back to him as he choked out his last breaths. His hand grabbed the collar of the old loose shirt of his I wore. "I. Want. This." Then his head fell back down, eyes closed. I feared the worst, but after another round of coughing, his eyes opened, and his hand, which never loosened its grasp, weakly pulled me closer. In his mind, I could see he had something to tell me. I bent my head close to his lips and waited.

"Son," he said.

"The baby? Do you mean the baby?"

He nodded with great effort. "Keep away."

"From who?" He made no answer, but his eyes pierced mine with an unnatural glow, and in that instant, I saw an image in his mind of darkness ringed by fire, and at its center, Ulrikke. A last warning. Then his eyes lost their shine. His chest sunk, emitting a last, slow hiss of air. My Borges was no more. I screamed my grief out into the world.

I was still wailing when the door opened and, on light feet, in strode Ulrikke. Not the old, white-haired woman I knew from Fāmā-mura, but a young woman with golden hair, the same color as the girl who waited on Borges and I at the diner in San Francisco. For the first time, I saw Ulrikke as she must have appeared on the day she received her powers from Óðinn. She looked nothing like her older self, except for the bone structure of her face, but I knew her. Gazing down at Borges, a single slow tear slid down her young face.

"You! You killed him!" Spit flew as I shouted at her.

She turned to me. "Borges wanted this."

"Which Borges?" The question was rhetorical.

"Both of them." She did not sound defiant, she sounded defeated. "Don't you remember what I told you, Jane, before we became enemies? The day I met Jorge Luis Borges was when destiny caught up to me. I could not evade my doom. Neither can you."

"You lie," I said. "None of this would have happened without you. You chose to help him. You made the prophecy come true. Or maybe it was your prophecy all along."

Ulrikke snorted. "Don't be ridiculous. Look around. These men died because of you, and still, you couldn't stop the blade that pierced the heart of my son. We both played our roles to perfection." Then she wept.

I clutched at her son, my love, as the last of his body's warmth slipped away. Distracted by grief, pain, and the horror of the deaths I caused, I did not notice Ulrikke standing above me until I felt her shadow overhead, and the chill air it brought with it. "Leave me alone, you murderous bitch."

"I did not kill my son, or these poor men, Jane," she said with no sign of remorse in her voice. "You did. It was your failure he died."

Whipped around like a dog whose chain was given a vicious yank, I struggled off the floor to face her. "But you planned it. You made them your slaves, filled them with a bloodlust to kill him, and then, like the coward you are, slunk out the door. It was you." I spat again, pleased to see some of my spittle land on her sandals.

"You're wrong," she replied. "My son's fate was never in my hands. His doom was sealed whether I helped or not. Often he said no one could save him. The prophecy required his death. And he desperately wanted his life to end."

"Did the prophecy require you be his executioner?"

"The prophecy, as told to me, said he must die in a knife fight defending the woman he loved. And so he did, defending you."

That struck me hard. The room circled again, like a carousel whirling too fast, but I used all my powers to stop it. *She lies*, I reminded myself. *She wants to throw me off balance.*

"So, why come at all then?"

She laughed, and the sound of it rang bitter in my ears. "I did not agree to help my son just to see him die. No, Jane, I came to kill you."

"Kill me? That's preposterous! I'm carrying your grandchild. You'd never risk losing him."

"Risk it? Don't you understand what you carry in your womb? But of course you do. We both know what it is and what it will become once it's born. I would risk anything to stop the birth of another Borges."

"You'd kill me and my child?" I said, unwilling to believe Ulrikke capable of such a thing. Then, the intensity of the light in the room flared to a level impossible for candles. *Did she do that?*

"Borges is evil!" Ulrikke shouted, her words echoing off the walls. "To know a Borges is a curse. To be a Borges is a curse. And the greatest curse of all is to be a mother to a Borges!" Then she dropped to her knees, spent, tears gushing from her eyes. "If you don't know that by now, then you are truly lost."

"Stop with the act!" Furious, I spoke without thinking. "I'm right here. You want kill me? Do it!" In my mind, I already saw her lying on the floor with all the men from Tuape she used and discarded, a dark hole burned though her head, like theirs. I expected her to rise up so I could strike her down, but she did nothing of the kind. She stopped her tears and began to laugh.

"Oh, Jane, you are precious," she said at last. "Kill you? I couldn't kill my own son when that damn thing possessed him. Where do you think it is now? Inside your baby. After you released all that energy, and killed those men without a scratch to your name, the demon, the one you call the man in black, moved all of itself into your son not yet born while my son died. It protected you then and it will protect you now. Just as I could not kill my son before, I cannot kill you. Not while you carry your baby."

"Then why didn't you kill me earlier, after Jose cracked my skull?"

"Think. That foul thing would have just slunk back into my son, and I would have gained nothing. That is why, Jane. And the search for another one like you would have started all over." She sighed. "My son was not immortal. He aged, even if that thing made him appear younger than he was, and kept him from harm. But at some point, he would have died of old age. The soul of Borges can only survive in another Borges." Then she paused. "Why am I telling you what you already know?

"I had one chance to destroy it, at its most vulnerable, before it could finish moving all of itself from my son to yours. I needed both you and my son to die together, mortally wounded in the same moment. To accomplish that, I did my best to keep you and that demon focused on whoever fought my son, distracted and unaware of my real purpose."

"It was you who threw down the knife at my Borges' feet. It was you behind the cloak."

"Who else?"

"And then you ran away, like the coward you are, hoping these men would do your dirty work."

"Coward?" Ulrikke laughed again, brief and bitter. "Jane, how little you understand the powers you wield, and the power that, through your unborn child, the devil soul of Borges wields. Had I stayed, one of you would have seen through me. I would be as dead as all these men here, and the only goal that mattered to me would have died with me. My one chance was to absent myself during the fight and hope my real purpose went undetected.

"My son merely wanted was to die to satisfy his damn prophecy. Only in death could he be free of that demon. I assured him I would help. But I lied. I couldn't let that evil discover my real plan to destroy it. If both my son and you received fatal wounds instantaneously, then that thing, trapped inside the last two Borges descendants, could not have saved itself. When you died along with my son and your child, it would have been destroyed.

"You see that dead man over there, nearest to you? He was supposed to kill you. At the moment my son threw himself in front of the knife of the man he fought, taking a death blow to save you, that one aimed his knife at your heart. You never noticed him because you only concerned yourself about saving my son."

She was right. I never saw the threat to my child and me. Thinking I was strong enough to defeat the prophecy, drunk on my own power, consumed by the desire to rescue my Borges from death, I allowed this travesty to happen. My arrogance blinded me and killed the man I loved. And along with him, all these other men.

"But you failed, too," I said. "You missed your chance. I killed your assassin before he could kill me. The man in black lives on, and now I am must deal with him." My baby kicked then, as if in agreement.

"Yes, I failed," said Ulrikke in a wounded voice. "I first learned of you, the woman he needed for the prophecy, when he sent me a vision from that strange San Francisco you created. He told me he accepted his doom and asked for my help. The pain he suffered, the burdens that demon soul of

Borges placed upon him, he could no longer bear them all. For him, the prophecy was his only way out. I agreed to help, but only because I knew this endless cycle would continue unless I could kill both of you. I laid the best trap I could. And you fell for it, Jane. But it didn't work, whether by luck or because this evil, this man in black you speak of, discovered my plot. Perhaps, I was as big a fool as you, and it never had a chance. Regardless, the evil I sought to destroy survived. It lives inside your baby, soon to be born, where it will continue to dwell for the rest of time."

"Why should I believe any of this from you, of all people?"

"Believe what you want," she said.

"If Borges was cursed, why did you sleep with him in the first place? The man you gave yourself to, he sounded nothing like the Borges you speak of now, this monster that wants only to live forever, no matter the cost."

"I can't explain it. The man I loved, he was nothing like the demon that stole my son's life. The Borges I knew was kind, shy, a man incapable of violence. But that was his great flaw.

"Have you read his work? All the stories he wrote about torture, murder, violent death? The code of the gauchos, which he mythologized. For all his knowledge of literature, religion, philosophy, for all his genius, he was a naïve romantic. He never experienced war. Even when Peron rose to power, he suffered only a blow to his pride.

"He knew nothing of the world that lived and breathed outside the realm of his imagination. He was drawn, repeatedly, to write stories in which the protagonists were outlaws, whose knife fights he glorified, or cowards who could not live with their shame after failing to show courage. To him, the real world was an illusion. Only the fantasies he created in his stories meant anything to him. The gods or fate moved his characters like chess pieces on a board. Time, identity, reality were all suspect, all open to question. He believed the world was a dream. And now, all of us must live with the dreams his spirit released. Why do you think I cannot find any world where mankind does not go extinct? It is because they are all contaminated by the Borges curse. It will be the same for you. No world you travel to will be spared.

"All of us carry the burden of our sins. All of us have a dark side that longs to live forever, beyond good and evil. It was my destiny to meet the one man whose dark side became so powerful, so greedy, that one life was not enough, and so it broke God's law, and sowed its darkness within the soul of my son, spreading its pestilence everywhere. This demon's dark designs are leading humanity to its doom. And now that monster you call the man in black will continue to live on in my grandson. It would have been better if you had died with my son rather than relive my fate. But then, we were both deceived. You could not save my son, because you loved him, and I could not stop the evil that chose him as its host from perpetuating itself."

Her conclusion shook me, but then, as once before, an impossible idea bubbled up from my unconscious. *What if...?* I thought, but shook my head, unable to follow the idea to its logical conclusion. Yet it would not leave and grew inside my mind until a dizzying panic overwhelmed me. Exhausted, confused, distraught, is it any wonder that's when my child chose to be born?

"Your water broke!" exclaimed Ulrikke, as the first contraction hit and I slumped to the ground. "We must get you to Fāmā-mura," she said, reaching her hand out. "There, I can help you."

That was the exact wrong thing for her to say. "Back off! Don't come any closer!" I meant to kill her, should she try anything.

"Jane now is not the time to let your emotions overrule good judgment. Hate me if you must, but I can help. Fāmā-mura has modern facilities for birthing. Anesthesia. Obstetricians. Whatever you need, we have it. And your friends are there–Ray, Junko, Yoshiko."

"Help? From you?" I laughed, but then another contraction came, and the pain of it drained me. When I could breathe again, I said, "Fāmā-mura is the last place I would go. You'd kill me and imprison my child."

"You're wrong, Jane. Think. I have no reason to kill you now. I never wanted to kill you. I just saw no other way to stop that monster. And I have lived this life before, forced to rear a boy cursed by the twisted soul of Jorge Luis Borges. Don't make the mistake I made of thinking you can raise him yourself."

"If not going with you to Fāmā-mura is a mistake, at least it will be one I choose for myself. You'll never see your grandson, Ulrikke. That's my prophecy. There is a better world elsewhere."

Then I went to it.

CHAPTER 30

It was early spring in Kamakura. The songbirds were singing, unafraid of the hawk circling overhead. Soft cumulous clouds drifted by riding a slow breeze. One looked like a hare; another, a winged horse. The scent of cherry tree blossoms filled the air, mixed with flowering hydrangeas from a garden nearby. A single squirrel dashed about the stone tiles, looking for god knows what, and it made me laugh as I sat in the lotus position on the granite base beneath the Daibutsu. He was talking about time.

"Time is granular," he said, "not continuous."

"I thought time was a river, or was that a flat circle? I can never remember."

"You are confusing Heraclitus with Nietzsche, both of whom were idiots."

"That's mean," I said, "considering you're a figment of my imagination."

"Even a figment is allowed his own opinion." The Daibutsu's annoyance with me made me laugh again. I enjoyed him so much more, now that I knew I created him in my own image. "You think the Buddha never felt angry?" he said. I assumed he overheard my thoughts, which, when you come to think about it, he must have.

"Not the Amida Buddha. That's who you represent, right?"

"You yourself are proof that time is discontinuous," he replied, ignoring my taunts. "Time and space are two sides of the same coin, both of them ephemeral and illusory." He reminded me of my Borges when he lectured.

"Don't be cross with me on such a lovely day," I said.

"I'm trying to focus your mind."

And that's when Bashō interrupted us. He entered the square and strode briskly over to me. "It's time," he said.

I awoke from my nap on the couch in my apartment in Geneva. Bashō stood over me. "That was a terrible pun," I told him.

"Urikei arrives soon," he said. "Are you ready? Seeing her again is not wise. So much time has passed, and Urikei is unpredictable. You could have evaded her. There was no reason yesterday to alert her to your presence here."

"Why do you care, Bashō? Is coming here bad for her, or for me? Did you advise her not to come, just as you advised me not to visit Fāmā-mura? I know I provided a trail for her to follow."

"I cannot speak of such things, Jane. Those I serve can never know the others to whom I owe obligations. You know this." To the extent he could sound peeved, Bashō did.

I let out a sigh of frustration, but didn't pursue the matter. Let him keep his secrets. Instead, I said, "She would have found me, eventually. Better a time of my own choosing, than one of hers."

"Is it?" Bashō said. "You were much stronger than her when you faced each other that night in Tuape, when your Borges died, because you were carrying his child, and received the help of Old Borges' spirit. That may not be the case anymore."

"You've told me that theory of yours before," I reminded him. "It doesn't matter. Ulrikke's biggest weakness is she can't escape her past. Her imagination is limited."

"And yours isn't, because…?" He left his question dangling, perhaps to irk me.

"No, it's not. If you can't see that after all this time, I don't know how I can convince you now."

"I'm not the one you must convince, Jane-san. You believe many things based on speculation. You convinced yourself that your choice to come to this Elsewhere prevents Borges' spirit from exerting power over you and your child. You think your decision to come here will, in some fashion, allow you to alter the fate of humankind. Perhaps you are right, but how can you be sure? You don't know if the son you lost in San Francisco was not Borges' son, even though that's what you now believe based on your dream where you read the mind of this spirit you call the man in black. He could have been lying."

"But I know that's true! I read the man in black's thoughts. He couldn't hide his anger at me for bearing another man's son. Besides, his worst fear was that another Borges, in which a piece of him existed, might die. He'd have been injured or destroyed if the father of my son in San Francisco was a Borges."

"And yet, you have never given me a satisfactory explanation how you became pregnant when you traveled to that Elsewhere."

"Because it wasn't Borges who fell, but James Borgeson, a different man. I traveled Elsewhere during a dream of mine the night before. Borges himself said he awoke alone in our tent on the same day that I thought he fell to his death."

"So, when did James Borgeson father your son?"

"Just stop," I said. "I don't have time for this right now. I need to prepare for Ulrikke's arrival."

"As you wish," was all he said, something I wished he would stop saying. To regain my composure, I looked out the window at the street, bathed in the late afternoon sun. *Such a peaceful scene*, I thought. Hard to believe that a few hundred miles away, thousands of young men from France, Germany and Britain were dying in great numbers on the first day of the Battle of the Somme. Why so many people slaughter one another over something as ridiculous as an appeal to patriotism has always eluded me.

The bell rang, interrupting my contemplation of the evils of war. I opened the window and looked down at the sidewalk. There stood Ulrikke, in the guise of a middle-aged woman, but still her. I walked down the short flight of stairs to the main entrance. After I opened it to let her inside, we eyed one another across the divide. A cool breeze blew in from the lake, sweeping her hair away from her face.

"Come in, please," I said. "Our apartment is this way." I turned my back on her, knowing she would follow. I sensed her conflicting emotions. Excitement, yes, and even a note of triumph, but also anxiety about what she did not know. And pride. With Ulrikke, there was never any absence of that.

"Please," I said once we were inside, "sit on the divan over there while I go get tea." She said nothing, but seated herself as requested. I returned with a tray of various sweets, some scones and a traditional English tea service, complete with porcelain cups and saucers, silver spoons, a bowl of sugar and a small, fluted pitcher of fresh cream.

"You have no servants?" It was more a statement than a question.

"The apartment is small, and we have no need. A maid comes in once a day to clean, but she left hours ago."

"You surprise me," she said, changing the conversation.

"How so?"

"I would never have thought you would have your son, my grandchild, relive the life of his grandfather, Jorge Luis Borges. It took me decades of searching before I sensed you here and realized you chose to raise your son as the scion of Buenos Aires, the famous writer to be. By the way, are we alone?"

"Yes. My husband is escorting his mother on a trip to a nearby spa for treatment and rest. She hasn't been feeling well."

"But surely your son is here. Show him to me."

"I told you, Ulrikke, you would never see your grandson, or did you forget?"

"No, I did not. And yet here I am." She glanced around the apartment as if I might have hidden him somewhere.

"Would you like a tour," I said "to put your mind at ease, if nothing else?"

"That won't be necessary. He will come home eventually. I'll wait."

"As you wish." I poured more tea for the both of us, and we ate in silence. A comfortable silence for me, as I nibbled on an almond scone between sips of tea, but not for her. Her thoughts exposed a growing turmoil in her mind. She did not like uncertainty. "I hope you have not neglected the good people of Fāmā-mura while off searching for your grandson," I said, putting my scone down. That drew a scowl as her neck stiffened and her nose tilted a few degrees upward.

"My travels will never cause me to forego my responsibilities to my people. I always return to Fāmā-mura at the exact moment I left. Years may pass for me, but not for a second have they ever lacked my protection."

"How foolish of me then to suggest such a thing." I removed the tray and placed it on a sideboard. "And how are they, the people of Fāmā-mura? How is Ray Tanaka? And Junko? Yoshi? Are they well?"

"Ray passed away several years ago," she said in a monotonous tone that offered no comfort, nor expressed any grief. "Stomach cancer."

"How awful! How is poor Junko doing?"

"Better than you would imagine, Jane," she said, using my name for the first time. "She married a young engineer, and they have two children, a boy and a girl. Ray knew both of his grandchildren before his death. Junko mourned him, but not more than usual. She is too busy raising her children and teaching at the village school to wallow in grief over an old man who lived well into his eighties. The community accepts her now. She has never been happier.

"As for Yoshiko, she also married. Unfortunately, she did not make a good match. Her husband drinks too much and neglects her, but she is making the best of it. As my new Director of Fāmā-mura's Defense Committee, she has poured herself into her work, which is just as well. There are still so many dangers we face. Dangers we could have avoided, had you chosen the wiser path and returned with me when I gave you the chance."

"Now don't go and spoil our reunion, Ulrikke. It's unbecoming of royalty."

Her eyes flashed with anger, but then she tamped the fire down. "Forgive me, Señora Borges," she said, "for any offense I may have given. None was intended."

"None taken," I replied. Neither of us pretended to be sincere.

"So, do you still call yourself Jane, or did you take the name of Borges' mother as well when you came to this place?"

"To a few friends who I trust, I am Jane, but yes, my husband and the rest of this world know me as Leonor Acevedo Suárez Borges."

"Do you really believe you can pull off this mad scheme of yours?" Ulrikke said, moving back on the attack. "To re-make the original Jorge Luis Borges into your image of him? That isn't mere foolishness, but reckless. You risk more than you know. The evil spirit of Borges will fight you, defeat you utterly, and then take control of your son. What do you possibly hope to accomplish?"

"Who can say?" I said, deflecting her question with one of my own. "No one can see all possible futures, all the many forks in the path a person's life may take."

"You know nothing," she responded. "It will not end well for you or for him."

"And what is it you think I'm doing?"

"Trying to change the course of humanity's future from what I can see. I warn you, it's impossible. You will only bring misery and sorrow on yourself."

"Please," I said, "go on. My curiosity is piqued. What led you to this conclusion?"

Another scowl. "Don't play coy, Jane. You knew my son, what he became, and what he passed to my grandson. I told you that the fate of humanity is extinction by its own hand. And you think you can change that?" She laughed, but with no hint of humor. "Borges, the writer, was a man trapped in a world of his own imagination. An imagination made even more vivid and powerful because of his isolation and his intense introspection. An imagination that became more powerful than the vessel that contained it. You know of what I speak: the man in black that terrorized you in your dreams."

"You never used that name before. You always say the spirit of Borges, or call him a demon. Did he appear to you in that form, as the man in black?" I asked.

"Yes," she said with disgust. "A foul creature, as you know. I dealt with him during the months before my son was born. I bear many scars from those encounters."

"For the sake of argument," I responded, "let us agree that I accept what you say is true. What of it?"

"What of it? Are you mad? This life we lead is an illusion,. Worse, we can see it for the illusion it is, and yet know there is nothing we can do to change it. The dreams of Borges permeate everything we know. We are nothing but puppets dangling on his strings. And the harder we pull against them, the tighter their grip."

"If that's true, why did you try to convince me to go to Fāmā-mura to have my child there after you failed to kill all of us in Tuape? If every world is doomed because of the madness of Jorge Luis Borges, why bother?"

"I was desperate," Ulrikke replied.

"You still believe there's a way out of this trap, in other words," I responded, "but you want to be the one in charge of fixing the mess. Tell me I'm wrong." Before she could answer, I heard footsteps on the stairs.

"Ha," she said. "My grandson returns. It seems you were wrong."

I shrugged. The door opened and in walked my daughter. Ulrikke's eyes widened.

"Hola, Mama," my daughter said, but she stopped the moment she saw Ulrikke sitting across from me. "Excusez-moi, maman, je ne savais pas que vous aviez un invité."

"It's all right, Georgie," I said. "I forgot to tell you this morning I was expecting a visit from an old friend, Ulrikke Haraldsdotter. And there's no need for your limited French. My guest understands English quite well. Ulrikke, this is my oldest, Jorgina Luisa Borges, though we call her Georgie. Her grandmother, my husband's mother, is English, thus the nickname."

"Pleased to meet you, Madame," my daughter said. She walked over to a dumbstruck Ulrikke, bent down and kissed her on each cheek in the French fashion.

"The pleasure is all mine," Ulrikke blurted out after a short pause. "Your mother did not mention she had a daughter."

"I'm sorry," Georgie replied. "Mama is so fond of her little surprises."

"Yes, she is," Ulrikke said in a bemused tone. "I am beginning to understand that about her."

Georgie's laughter at this remark rippled through the room. "She's always torturing my poor Papa and me with her little pranks. You're such a horror, Mama, you know that." I smiled.

"So," Ulrikke continued, addressing Georgie, "you are your mother's eldest child?"

"Yes, for better or worse, as Mama often tells me." Georgie's laughter rang like a flute in my ears.

Ulrikke frowned. I could see she was not pleased, that, as predicted, she would never see her grandson, for I produced a granddaughter instead. But she did not take long to cover up her dismay at discovering that I altered the gender of my child. I could tell she viewed it as a blasphemous and dangerous act, but I cared little for what she thought. There was nothing she could do to change anything, anyway.

"Forgive me for asking," said Ulrikke, "but isn't Jorgina a rather unusual name for a girl?"

Georgie answered her before I could. "I suppose it is. But my father's name is Jorge, as was his father's, my grandfather. He wanted a son, to pass it on to, but when Mother gave birth to me, he settled for Jorgina. I rather like it, having a name that no one else shares. And as George Eliot is my newest favorite author, I now appreciate my nickname. Have you read her? I'm reading Middlemarch now. It's absolutely divine."

"No, I'm afraid not."

"But you should. Her prose is that good."

"What other surprises have you kept from me?" Ulrikke directed this to me with just the right edge of irritation. "Do you have a son?"

"No," Georgie answered for me. "Mama tried to give me a little brother, but instead I have a younger sister, Norah. At least that's what I call her. Her given name is Leonor Fanny Borges, but we all call her Norah now. I'm surprised she's not with you, Mama."

"Norah went to the lakeshore to continue her sketches of the harbor before my friend arrived," I said. "She should be home soon."

"My sister is a very good artist. Papa enrolled her in the École des Beaux-Arts, one of the best art schools on the continent. Someday, she will be famous, I'm sure of it."

"And what of you?" Ulrikke said. "What talents do you possess?"

"That is a good question. I love to read. I could spend all day reading the books in my father's library and be satisfied with my life. But for now, I am a student at the Collège de Genève."

"Is that so?" said Ulrikke. "I was not aware they accepted women."

"They didn't, but they made an exception in my case. At first, they denied my application. But then Mama and Papa spoke to the governing board of the college, and after that meeting, the board permitted me to sit for their examination. I was very surprised, but happy to do so. And I did well enough that the entire board voted unanimously to allow me to enroll. I'm fortunate to be their first female student."

"Yes, that's quite the achievement," Ulrikke muttered. "Congratulations, my dear. Your parents must be so proud." Ulrikke rose from her seat on our couch. "Well, I must get going," she said in a voice louder than necessary. "I've taken up too much of your mother's time as it is."

"Please don't go on my account," pleaded my daughter. "Mama, tell her she can stay. I will go to my room and do some reading. I promise to be as quiet as a mouse."

"No, dear," Ulrikke replied, "I really must go. Your mother and I have finished our tea and our reminiscing about old times. But I'm certain you and I will meet again. I have a feeling for these things. Perhaps someday, you can come visit me in Japan."

"You live in Japan?" Georgie exclaimed. "Mama visited Japan before she married Papa. The stories she tells of her trip are fantastical. Are you close to Kamakura, where the statue of the Great Buddha sits? The one they call the Daibutsu? Mama has talked about it so much, I almost feel as if I've seen it myself."

"I live not far from Kamakura," Ulrikke replied. "You have an open invitation to visit me anytime. That is, if your mother approves."

"Perhaps someday," I said to Ulrikke. "One can never predict the future, can one?"

Ulrikke gave me a cutting look, but then smiled for Georgie. It certainly wasn't intended for me. "Well, goodbye for now, Jorgina. And you also, Jane." Ulrikke opened the door to leave. "Jane, I hope to see you again. Seventeen years is too long an absence for friends such as we used to be to one another. I wish you well raising your daughters."

"Au revoir," my daughter called from the doorway as Ulrikke made her way down the stairs. I heard her push open the door on the ground level and then heard it swing shut. At the window, I tried to catch a last glimpse of Ulrikke, but she was already gone.

"Your friend seemed very nice," said my daughter, "but why did she call you Jane? And is it true that you haven't seen one another in seventeen years?"

"My dear child," I said, "allow me to keep a few secrets. I promise to tell you someday all about Ulrikke. But today is not that day."

"You really are an old horror, Mama. But I forgive you." She laughed again, as only the young do, effortlessly.

"As well you should, my dear. Now what are those books you are carrying? Did you add to our bill at the Librairie Jullien again?"

"No, Mama. The owner said I could borrow this edition of Schopenhauer's collected works, after he saw me flipping through the pages in the aisle at the store. It's in German, but I won't have any trouble getting through it."

It was my turn to laugh. "That wouldn't have been the case last year."

"My German is much better now, Mama," she replied in a hurt voice.

"Oh, my dear, I was just teasing. And what are the other ones in your hands? Hmmm."

"A book of essays on Taoism, Buddhism and other eastern philosophies. Simon recommended to me. And one about physics that Maurice gave me."

"Your Jewish boy friend?" I said, with an emphasis on the last two words. "I think he thinks he's more than just a friend."

"Mama, stop. It's nothing like that. Maurice, to me, is the brother I never had. Our friendship is platonic, if you must know."

"To you, perhaps," I said. "Trust me, young men don't waste time with girls they view as sisters."

"So you say."

"I do say so. Grant me the benefit of a little more knowledge on this subject than you, if only because of my advancing years." But my daughter was no longer interested in our verbal jousting. She placed her books down on the side table and sank into the cushions of the divan abandoned by Ulrikke.

"Did you know, Mama," she said in a desultory tone, "that the light we see is not instantaneous? Its speed is a known quantity and is far slower than we imagine. The very stars we look at in the night sky are not real, not in the sense that we can say we are observing them as they exist now. What we see is light that has traveled a great distance and taken many, many years to reach us. We are looking at the star's past. For some stars, the light they emitted is many millions of years in the past. Think of that. We never see the present. And this is true of our own sun. It takes almost ten minutes for sunlight to travel to us."

"Is that so?" I said. "How remarkable."

Georgie sighed the sigh all young women produce when something is troubling them. "It's not remarkable at all! It's horrible. I can never look at the night sky again without realizing I am looking at what may no longer exist. I can never see the present, never know that what I'm looking at is real, or the remnant of something long dead.

"And it gets worse. There is a man–his name is Einstein–who wrote several theoretical papers challenging fundamental aspects of Newton's laws. He's claimed that the closer anyone comes to traveling at light speed, the more time slows down for the one traveling so fast. Years could pass for us here, while hardly any time at all would pass for the speeding traveler. He also makes other strange predictions. Time and space are one thing, not two, and gravity effects them both. Or it. The larger the gravitational force, the greater the effect. It sounds insane, but if his theories are right, the gravity from stars and planets can even bend light. And Maurice believes this Einstein is right! Can you imagine that? Nothing we thought we understood about the world would be true. Time would be an illusion. I wish I never learned about Mr. Einstein and his ideas."

This outburst was not unusual, except for the subject. Georgie could be very emotional and become agitated when something disturbed her, although she rarely showed that side of her personality to anyone but me. But I sensed her grievance with Herr Einstein was not the underlying cause of her current distress. "What's really bothering you, Georgie?" I said. "It can't be the strange ideas of some little-known thinker that you find so upsetting. You look as if the world is ending."

"Did you hear the news?" she asked. "There's another awful battle in France. Near the Somme river. Thousands more dead, they say. And so soon after Verdun."

"Yes, I heard."

"Why is the world filled with such evil?"

"I see we are into considering the profound question of theodicy today." I smiled, but did not receive one in return.

"Leibniz called this the best of all possible worlds," she replied, "but how can that be? What God would allow such cruelty and horror?"

"The gods have never offered mankind much hope in that regard," I said. "You know what your father would say."

"Yes. He would tell me that each of us is alone in this world, cut off from one another, unable to understand or feel what others feel. That in such a world, war, and the sorrows it brings, are inevitable. He frightens me sometimes with his pessimism."

"And yet you plan to read Schopenhauer."

"I need to understand why Papa feels the way he does. Why he cannot imagine a better world." She picked the book off the table, as if to read it then and there, but after a moment, put it down. "The Japanese say the world is an illusion. Isn't that right?"

"Some practicing Buddhists say that, yes, so I suppose some Japanese do, too."

"Then why is our illusion such a nightmare?"

"Maybe people need better illusions," I said. "Ones not provided by religion or by those in charge of our civilization today."

"By which you mean men." Georgie could always see right through me. Not that deciphering my ambiguous remarks ever proved that difficult for her.

"Yes, men–but some women, too; everyone who doesn't see the beauty all around us because they are lost in a world of their own selfish desires. They lack the imagination to believe in something else, a world governed by what's best in people, not the worst."

"None of the old stories admit of such a place," my daughter replied, "other than sacred scriptures that promise mythical paradises."

"You are a deep thinker, dear. A creative spirit. I've always seen this gift in you. Why be bound by the past? Write your own stories."

"It's you and Papa who want me to be a writer."

"You have the talent for it. And you've often said it's what you want most in life."

She looked at me, and fierceness shone from her eyes. "But men do not take women seriously except under rare circumstances. Not as writers or rulers or anything other than the producers of sons needed for the battlefields of wars to come."

"Perhaps you could change that," I said. "Or be part of those who change it."

"Where do you find this faith in me, Mama, when I can't find it myself? Every day, my mind is full of doubts. It seems, unlike Socrates, my Daimon does not believe in me."

"Don't worry, child," I said. "You will. I promise. You're so young yet."

A dark shadow fell across the room for an instant, blinding me. But I knew from where it derived. I knew also it could not sustain itself for long. When it lifted, I sat down next to my daughter and held her, my arms wrapped around her shoulders. She placed her head against me and went limp as her body leaned into mine. I felt her let go of the dark. Light once again shone throughout the room. Ulrikke was wrong. The man in black would never control my daughter's destiny.

"The sun sets and yet it also rises."

"What did you say, Mama?"

"Nothing important, dearest. I would tell you not to worry, but most young people your age worry, even those who pretend otherwise. Let me worry for you for a while, instead, eh?"

"If you wish, Mama," my beloved daughter said. She yawned then. "I'm so tired. Maybe I will nap and dream of a better world. Or at least one where the stars in the sky are real and not phantoms from a past that haunts us." With that, her eyes closed. Soon she was breathing, asleep in my arms.

"Dream well," I said.

THE END

ACKNOWLEDGEMENTS

No author, no matter how talented, is solely responsible for the book he or she manages to complete, much less publish. That is certainly the case with my first novel, "My Travels With Dead Man." It began in 2015 as a short story that morphed into a novella, and then expanded to become the book you have before you now. During the many long hours I labored to fashion from the slimmest of conceits the characters and plot of this novel, I received the assistance and help of many people, all of whom I can never fully repay.

First, I am very grateful to my classmates at Allwriters Workplace & Workshop, LLC, who along with our instructor, Michael Giorgio, read and reviewed my initial draft and subsequent revisions, among them Pam Pfenniger, Cindy Griffing, Peter Wolkoff, Frank Richards, Pauline Goza and Tracy Stewart. Their critiques were a great help to me during the writing of my first draft, and the early stages of the revision process.

In addition, I would be remiss if I did not mention two of the earliest readers of my nascent manuscript, Lisa Gordon and her husband Yves Jalbert. They provided valuable advice and constructive criticism that helped me find the voice for Jane Takako Wolfshiem, the novel's protagonist and narrator.

Furthermore, I cannot say enough about the guidance and editorial assistance I received from Kathie Giorgio, my writing coach, mentor and friend. Kathie worked with me for months to hone and polish earlier drafts, eliminating the rough edges and helping me to reduce many errors, grammatical and otherwise. She pointed out what was redundant and could be discarded, as well what the story lacked and needed to be included in order to create a cohesive plot with believable, well-rounded characters. Her efforts proved invaluable. Without her help, this book simply would never have seen the light of day. Kathie, I owe you more than you will ever know.

Speaking of publication, I am very grateful for assistance provided to me by the good people at Black Rose Writing, my publisher. Special thanks go to its founder, Reagan Rothe, who took a chance on an unknown writer lacking a graduate degree in either creative writing or literature, who had never previously published a work of fiction of any length, much less a novel that presumed to include as a principal character one of the most famous authors in the world.

I also want to thank my family. Without their love and emotional support this book would not have come to fruition. In particular, I owe a great debt to my Aunt Shari, who spent her working career as an editor at a major publishing company. She saw something in my earliest attempts at fiction to encourage me to continue my passion for telling stories of all kinds. Without her inspiration, guidance and editing chops, my dream that someday I'd be able to call myself a published author would not have come to pass. I am forever in her debt.

Lastly, I'm deeply grateful to Jorge Luis Borges, whose stories and essays, and the themes that he explored in them, captivated me from the very first time I read his work in translation. Without him, I never would have imagined the fabulous characters who, with great persistence, insisted I tell their story.

ABOUT THE AUTHOR

Steve Searls retired from the practice of law in 2002 due to a chronic autoimmune disorder. Raised in Colorado, he now lives with his adult son in Western, NY. *My Travels With a Dead Man* is his debut novel.

NOTE FROM THE AUTHOR

Word-of-mouth is crucial for any author to succeed. If you enjoyed *My Travels with A Dead Man*, please leave a review online—anywhere you are able. Even if it's just a sentence or two. It would make all the difference and would be very much appreciated.

    Thanks!
    Steve

Thank you so much for reading one of our **Fantasy** novels.
If you enjoyed the experience, please check out our recommended title for your next great read!

Shadow City by Anna Mocikat

"*Shadow City* reads as the perfect combination of a dystopian future, cyberpunk and fantasy creatures." *-Excentrieke Dame*

"This exciting mashup of horror and action-adventure tropes is sure to have readers tuning in for the next installment." *-Publishers Weekly*

"*Shadow City* is full of adventure, thrills, and twists and turns."
-IndieReader

View other Black Rose Writing titles at www.blackrosewriting.com/books and use promo code **PRINT** to receive a **20% discount** when purchasing.

Lightning Source UK Ltd.
Milton Keynes UK
UKHW011003290820
369029UK00001B/25